THE CITY
ABOVE
AND BELOW

MATTHEW E. NESHEIM

For my wife, Kate.
We did this together.

PAR

12.11.2387 – Planet Vellus, just outside Alba Calea

There he was and wished he wasn't.

The voice of a young boy echoed in his head like the conscience he had long forgotten. It was the middle of the night on Alba Calea, right around 23:50 intergalactic standard time, and Par Riordan was trying to open the back door of a mansion. The knob jiggled but would not turn. Locked.

Here you are, and here I am, too. It's a lovely night, don't you think? At least I think it is. Where are we again? And why are we trying at locked doors?

Par got down on his haunches and brought his eyes level with the keyhole. It was simple enough. Keyway, deadbolt, cotter pin, tumblers… He closed his eyes and pictured the mechanism as he spoke to it like a man spoke to a well-trained animal, and soon everything turned and with a *click* the door swung slowly open. He let himself in.

Such a strange manner that you visit your friend. I never visited my friends this way. It's almost like the two of you are playing some kind of game, isn't it? If it is a game, I want to play, but I suppose you'll have to tell me the rules first. No one can play a game properly until they know all the rules. Rules are an important part of life. You taught me that, remember?

Standing in the foyer, Par closed his eyes again to tune out the voice in his head and listen instead to the stillness of the house around him. It was a cloudless night, and there was little sound except for the breeze as it whistled though the apple trees outside. He released his Shade. A cloud of gray metal flecks blew out of his body as thousands of tiny nano-machines launched themselves from his pores and flitted about the mansion like mechanical gnats. Searching, they found the children asleep in their beds and the mother asleep in the master bedroom. They saw the night watchman still outside, meandering through a path in the orchard. They found the dog, and a few of the bots crawled up against the creature's skin and injected it with a sedative. Everything and everyone was where they should be, including the man he planned to meet.

Par took off his shoes and closed the door behind him. There was no need to be impolite. He was arriving unannounced, after all.

It really is a game. All of it. It's all a game that you've been playing all of your life, and not just with your friend the senator—you play it with everyone. I never really thought of it that way before. I suppose I have to play now…

Par found Senator Nerus Petronus right where he knew he would: In his study, reading a book. The Senator was a native Illyari in every sense. Pure human. Fifty-two years of age with silver hair and eyes as sharp as his mind. Nerus looked up as Par quietly shut the door behind him.

Par pulled out his revolver and, sitting down in the chair, he set the gun in his lap and folded his hands over top of it.

Nerus let out a curt laugh and pointed at the gun. "Is that for me?"

Par stared evenly at the other man and pointed at the table between them. "Don't be silly. You have a message from Rufus."

Lying on the table was Nerus's communicator, its yellow light blinking with a new message. Nerus picked it up and scanned his messages. Par watched as the senator's face slowly turned white. Nerus tossed the communicator back onto the table where it clattered against the polished glass. Then the senator turned in his seat to stare out the open window. A minute passed in silence.

"I'm sorry it has to be like this," Par said as he stared at the carpet. Leaning forward in his chair, Par's hands cradled his pistol like a cup of coffee. "If we could have done it differently, I suppose we would have."

Nerus glanced at him. "Is she …?"

Par nodded solemnly.

"How did they get to her?" the senator asked. Par could hear the emotion that Nerus was trying to hide.

"We're not sure. It's likely they discovered the affair and then simply coerced her." Par shrugged. "Or perhaps she went to them."

"She would never…" The Senator's voice was defensive now. Nerus stood and faced him. "Who sent *you?*"

Par let out a reluctant breath. "Critus. His orders. Though Rufus knows as well. I don't think anyone else within the Alliance knows yet."

"Yet. But they will by tomorrow." Nerus looked back out the open window where the wind was once again rustling through the apple trees. "I have done this to myself, I suppose." The Senator sighed. "Will my family be looked after?"

"Of course." Par pointed at the communicator. "Didn't Rufus…?"

"He did, but I needed to hear it from you." The gray-haired man craned his head toward the glass as if he were looking for something, but Par could see that his eyes were distant and far away.

Par sat back and nodded solemnly. "Of course. I'll look into it myself once this is over."

"Thank you," Nerus said.

A quiet moment passed as the Senator stared out the window, and Par stared at everything that wasn't the Senator. Finally, Par's friend nodded to himself. "I suppose we don't have a terrible amount of time, do we?"

Par shook his head.

Nerus glanced at him. "And I suppose you're not here to give me a ticket off planet. Are you."

It wasn't a question, but Par shook his head anyway.

Nerus sat back down in his recliner. "Alright. What do you have?"

Par pulled a vial out from his coat and set it on the coffee table between them. The clear liquid wobbled against the glass. "Tasteless. Takes about five minutes. It's like going to sleep."

Nerus picked up the vial and held it to the light of his reading lamp. "I suppose that's about as much as anyone in my position can ask for." Then his eyes shot toward Par. "They'll know, of course."

Par shook his head. "They can suspect whatever they want. It's my own invention. Leaves no trace. Looks like a stroke."

Nerus unfastened the cap, took one last look at the ceiling as if imagining a last wordless prayer, and then downed the vial. Licking his lips, he returned both vial and cap to the table, then picked his book back up and continued reading.

It's important to always play by the rules, and if you don't know the rules, you have to ask. That's what Mom told me, and so that's what I do whenever I don't know the rules of a game. That way I don't get in trouble and no one can get angry at me. It's never fun when someone is angry.

Par let out the breath he had been holding and watched Nerus read, waiting for some kind of reaction, but the other man never looked up. A few minutes later, as Par had promised, the Senator's eyelids began to drift slowly closed until they stayed shut. Then his breathing became deeper and deeper until he began to snore lightly. Par kept an eye on the wall clock. Around 0:14, Nerus's body shuddered twice, and then was still.

I don't like it when people get angry. Especially if they're my friends.

Par rose from the sofa to check Nerus for a pulse. Nothing. He closed the Senator's eyes and asked his Shade to check the house once more. Then he asked it to move into the orchard, the front yard, the driveway. Then he called it back to him, and when it returned to the study it crawled back inside him like an old, dead friend. Everyone was where they should be. The children and the wife were asleep in their beds. The dog was asleep by the front door. The watchman was now circling around the front drive, lazily dragging his feet over the graveled road.

Par left the way he had come.

DELEA

4.27.2388 - Planet Arc, Refugee Camp

The whisper was as desperate as it was annoying.

"Hey! Wake up!"

Delea Etain opened one eye to see her little sister shaking her arm.

"Fel, what do you want?" she mumbled quietly.

"Heya, I need your help. I gotta pee."

Delea shook the cobwebs from her skull as she sat up to see her little sister dancing in front of her.

"C'mon man," Fel whined. "I waited until it was light out and I can't wait any more."

Delea looked around her sister to see the faint gray light leaking through the tent's front flap. Then she looked back to Fel, who was hopping from foot to foot with a pained and anxious look on her face. Delea let out a long, drawn out sigh. She wanted to let Fel know how annoying this was even as she came to terms with the prospect of getting up from her cot.

Neither sister was permitted to go anywhere in the camp alone. It was a rule their mother, the Queen, had strictly enforced with the help of their assigned bodyguards. This was almost certainly the sole reason her little sister came to her on mornings like this. The three guards on duty tonight were Dakko, Marental, and Kress, and while Fel could just as easily have found one of them to escort her to an outhouse, in the two months that they had been at camp, Fel had decided her older sister was her chosen outhouse escort.

"Hey, you weren't even asleep, were you?" Fel said. "I can tell, you know."

Delea sighed again as she rubbed her eyes. "Fine, but this is the last time. If you come get me again when I'm asleep, I'll smother you to death with my pillow."

Fel hissed between her teeth and stuck out her tongue. "Will not."

Delea sat up on her cot and slipped on her boots. "Just try me, Youka."

Watching Fel hopping frantically ahead of her, Delea was reminded of why their father, King Teum Etain, had given his youngest daughter the nickname in the first place. Youkas were fairy spirits said to live in hidden places like walls or floorboards or gutters, where they would sleep during the day and come out at night to steal or make trouble. Only the youka did not steal normal things like normal thieves. No, a youka stole a piece of your hair, or it stole your keys, or it unlocked your door, or turned on your stove when you weren't home. Their father had taken to calling Fel a youka when she was a toddler full of mischief. While no one else had dared called the King's daughter anything other than 'Princess' or 'Your Highness,' the nickname had stuck within the family.

The morning carried with it the cool warmth of late spring. A breeze ran a friendly shiver up Delea's spine as she followed her little sister across the top of the hill to where a pair of outhouses had been dug deep into the ground. Sisters of sixteen and twelve, Delea and Fel Etain looked as different as two Duathic girls possibly could. Where Delea was tall and shapely, Fel was short and thin like a boy; where Delea had light blue skin with straight jet-black hair that ran past her waist, Fel had a gray skin tone with black freckles and her hair was a curly blue mop.

"Hurry up, okay?" Delea hissed.

"Psshhh, this isn't a social call, Del,"

"I have to piss like a horse, alright?"

Delea stretched her arms and yawned. Months of sleeping in tents had forced her to become a morning person, but today she still felt drowsy and irritable. Above her, the twin moons of Arc were fading into the western sky while the morning redness was rising in the east. Waiting on the hilltop, the waking camp rose to greet her. A pair of dogs were barking to each other while an owner shouted for quiet. The friendly smoke of the morning cookfires tickled her nose and her stomach. Across the hilltop, a pair of washerwomen were chuckling over gossip and the morning laundry.

Their mother, the Queen Anyse Etain, had built her refugee camp on the opposite side of the valley from their capital city of Sindorum. Here, on a hill overlooking the Bay of Sardis, stood the ruins of an ancient palace built centuries ago by the legendary Empress Aelia. The Queen and her daughters had set up the camp's medical station, as well as their own tents, amongst the ruins.

"Fel! Aren't you done yet?" Delea asked in a harsh whisper.

"Hey, c'mon!" Fel whispered back. "I been holding it for a really long time, so shuttup okay?"

Delea sighed and yawned and looked back at the row of tents. A small crowd of night-shift nurses had gathered beneath a nearby gazebo for cigarettes, coffee, and gossip. Someone was telling a funny story and everyone was boiling over with laughter. From what Delea could hear, it was a bit of graveyard humor about a cripple and a corpse. Curious, she tried to listen closer, but then the door of the outhouse finally clattered open and Fel emerged, stepping gingerly across the dew-covered grass.

"Why didn't you put your shoes on?" Delea chided.

Fel hissed back at her. "I dunno. I like to walk in bare feet, okay? Get off me."

Delea laughed as only an older sister could. "You're going to track dirt into your sleep sack and then you're going to have dirt all over your legs and your feet and you won't be able to get back to sleep."

"No, I won't, because I wipe me feet off on my towel every time."

"Well then you're going to have a dirty towel, stupid."

"My towel is already dirty, stupid, and I don't care."

"You're such a filthy little cretin sometimes, you know that?"

"Psshhh…" Fel stuck out her tongue. "Quit being such a scab, Del. I'm gone to play poggers with Vanin and Ryce and them, when I'm done with chores, so I'll clean up when I get back! Sheesh!"

Delea was about to lecture her little sister about why she needed to keep herself clean in a refugee camp, but then the sound of thunder rolled across the valley. They both stopped and looked east as a great white flash broke across the far mountainside. Another orbital strike had just struck Sindorum.

Fel looked forlornly toward the city. "Are we ever going to go see Dad?"

Delea shook her head. "No, of course not. Don't be silly, Youka, they're bombing the city."

"*You're* a Youka…" Fel said as she kicked a rock down the hill.

Another explosion rocked the far city and the burst lit up the entire valley like daylight. Sindorum, their capital, sat on the eastern side of the valley where it wrapped itself around base of Mount Gedron. Delea could see the faint outline of the second shell's trail, straight as a ruler, as it had fallen from the sky. Somewhere high overhead trolled *Unifier*, the great and terrible flagship of their enemies: the Coalition.

"Mom said that when we came here we would go see him after we set up the camp," Fel whined.

Delea hated it when her little sister whined.

"That was before they started bombing the city. We've been here for two months, Fel, you should know better by now."

Seconds later, she heard her little sister follow, jogging across the wet grass as she caught up. "Is he ever going to come see us?" Fel whispered.

"I don't know. I don't think he wants to leave his soldiers." Delea remembered having this same conversation with Fel yesterday, and she was tired of it already. *He's too busy losing the war to bother himself with the likes of his children and his wife. We'll probably never see him again.* But Delea knew better than to say that to her younger sister. Fel still saw their father through the eyes of a twelve-year-old, a father who was great and wise, not proud and foolish and maybe—after years of war—even a little mad with hate.

Fel sighed. "He doesn't have to say he's leaving. He can just sneak over."

Delea laughed. "What? Do you think they're going to pause the whole war just for you?"

At that, Fel only scowled and kicked another rock.

When the war started, both sisters had been too young to under-stand *why*. All Delea remembered was that it was something about trade routes and who owned what rights to what star gate. Even today she heard people debating over who was to blame about an Illyari Republican diplomatic shuttle that, years ago, had been shot apart in one of the contested zones. Everyone agreed that had been the final straw. Despite the Duathic people's protests and pleas, the Illyari Republic had said enough was enough. King Teum and his silly little kingdom had to go. In an emergency session, the Illyari Senate had declared war. Three years of bitter stalemate had followed before the Republic had convinced their allies within the Imperium of Umbrea to join them. The Duathe had not won a battle since. Now all that was left was their capital city, Sindorum, where their father was preparing to make his final stand.

Delea was more and more thankful every day that she wasn't there.

They stopped at their tents where Fel ducked inside and re-emerged a second later with her shoes in hand. Fel grunted through her nose as she put on her shoes. "Heya Del, you hungry? You want to find Dakko and them and drag them down to breakfast with us?"

Delea scratched at her scalp. She had not bathed in over a day, and though she smelled much worse than a princess should, her stomach had been grumbling since she first smelled the cookfires. She could bathe after she was done with her morning chores.

"Sure. Why not?" She shrugged. "But we need someone to go with us."

As if on cue, the shadows of two giant women walked out from between the other tents. Kress and Marental each stood nearly seven feet tall and weighed over three hundred pounds, with arms as thick as a man's head and legs like tree trunks. The two women were nearly identical replicants, and the only non-Duathe in their entire bodyguard. Only their hair color told them apart: Kress with her long, red braid that ran nearly to her waist, Marental with her thick, golden blonde hair that fell over her shoulders.

The two women had been given as a gift by the Umbrean Imperium. Bred under special orders from the Teth Gideon himself, Kress and Marental were the only female replicants ever produced from the elite Kodayene strain.

Fel giggled as she saw the two giant women step out from the shadows. "Aye Mary, you big basher, you givin' me a ride down the hill, or what?"

Marental smiled and dutifully got down on one knee as Fel climbed up on her back.

Marental looked to Delea as she stood. "Were you planning on going to breakfast, your Highness?"

Delea yawned again. "I suppose."

Fel let out a war whoop from atop her bodyguard's back as they all set off to find breakfast. Cresting the rise, Delea saw a dozen cookfires burning at the bottom of the hill. Here, the camp's cooks had dug pits between the ancient broken walls of the ruined palace. As they were every morning, an army of cooks were there tending the fires, preparing the food, and serving the people of the camp. The line of people spotted the two princesses coming down the hill and cleared a path to the front of the line, but Delea gestured for Kress to lead them to the back.

"We're in no rush this morning," Delea said quietly. She looked back at her sister. "We don't need to step in front of anyone today, Youka."

"Pshhh…" Fel said with the scowl of a twelve-year-old. "You're the youka and you're gonna make me late. I got chores to do and I don't have all morning. C'mon, Mary. We be quick!"

Delea heard Marental's muted chuckle as she carried Fel to the front of the line. Delea frowned at her little sister's impatience as she watched Fel hop off her bodyguard's back. Grabbing a bowl from the nearest cook, Fel scurried off into the camp with Marental close on her heels. Delea saw the burly replicant woman look back and give them a playful salute before she disappeared into the city of tents.

Nearly every ethnicity of the Duathic people were in line with her: red-skinned islanders, green-skinned Duathe from the tropics, and the pale blue northerners who had fled the destruction of Arc's northern arctic regions. However, most of the Duathe of their camp were blue or dark blue, like Delea and Fel. That was the skin color of mid-land Duathe, those who originated from continents that ringed Arc's equator.

With Kress's tall shadow beside her and with the royal pendant on her shoulder, Delea received a few bows and curtsies and "Good morning, your Highness" as she waited in line. However, most of the people here were used to seeing the Queen and her daughters among them in the morning, so the line moved quickly and with little fanfare. The cooks were pouring the porridge into bowls in big heaping scoops and cutting slabs of freshly cooked ham and throwing them on top. By the time she and Kress reached the front of the line, the cooks had everything ready.

Two large boxes sat waiting for them on the table next to the head cook.

"Thank you, Feleg," Delea said.

The mustachioed cook bowed humbly as he handed the first box to her and the second to Kress. Delea thanked him, as she always did, then led their way back up the hill. Each box was stacked with a dozen breakfasts made ready for the patients of the camp's critical care tent. Two nurses met them there and helped them hand out the meals. There were just over a dozen patients this morning and so Delea and Kress helped themselves to a pair of left over plates before cleaning up.

After throwing out the trash, they spotted Roake standing outside a pavilion-sized tent. The leader of the Royal Guard was an older Duathic man with dark blue skin, greying hair, and the faded tattoo of a knife on the back of his neck. He gave Delea a sharp salute as she pushed through the flap. Inside, she found her mother kneeling next to a cot and bandaging a young boy's arm.

While at court, the Queen Anyse had never been seen in public wearing anything less than high fashion, but here, among the refugee camp, she wore a plain gray shirt, tan khakis, and a pair of work boots. Her long, black hair was tied up, and she wore no make-up or jewelry except for the royal pendant on her shoulder that marked her royal station.

"Good, you're up," Queen Anyse Etain said as she wrapped the gauze around the boy's forearm. "Have you eaten this morning?"

"Just did," Delea replied.

The Queen glanced out the tent flap. "Where did your sister run off to this morning?"

Delea permitted herself a small sigh. "She said she was doing the chores you had given her."

The Queen didn't respond to that but finished tying off the bandage on the boy's arm. "There. Now tell your friends to stay away from the cliffs. That place is too dangerous for children to be playing there."

"Yes, your Highness. I will your Highness." The boy said with a big smile as he jumped off the cot. Then he bowed as quickly as Delea had ever seen anyone bow before he ran out of the tent like a shot.

The Queen turned back toward her eldest daughter. "Who did your sister have with her?"

"Marental," Delea answered.

"Good," her mother nodded as she began straightening the linen on a cot. "Did you get to those things I asked you for last night?"

Delea listed off the chores she had completed the night before: sweeping the nurses' tent, folding the laundry, cleaning the spare cook pots, and so on. She was eager to work this morning but Delea could not help but feel the hollow weight of someone awaiting their parent to assign them work.

When her mother made no reply, Delea glanced over to see her frowning to herself while straightening the linen on a cot.

"Is there more that you'd like for me to do this morning, mother?" Delea asked.

"There always is..." The Queen sighed as she finished refolding the sheets against the cot.

Delea watched her mother walk over to the tent flap to look out at the rest of the camp. When the Queen finally looked back at Delea, her face looked worn and tired. As the echo of another bomb rolled across the valley, her mother rubbed her eyes and sighed again.

"Our time in these camps has done you and your sister well, Delea. Whatever comes, these lessons will serve you. I take great comfort in that."

"What will happen to us when it's all over?" Delea asked, "Where *are* we going to go?"

"That I don't know yet, but I am hoping that soon I will." Her mother smiled weakly at her daughter before her neck stiffened and the royalty returned to her face. She gestured toward the rest of the tent.

"Now, as for the rest of your morning, I need you to straighten all of the empty beds in here and to change out any dirty linens you find. Then bring them down to the bottom of the hill to be washed. I also need you to take out these last few bedpans over there and clean them out. I don't care which you do first, but there are only a few bedpans left. Nurse Phane and Nurse Elya had started them, but they had to run out. Something about someone having a seizure down along the southern block. Keep Kress with you at all times. There are so many more people here now, and some of them are more dangerous than you girls know. Oh, and if the washers have any clean linens, take those out to be dried as well. And when you're done with that, come back here."

Delea bowed dutifully and gave her a "Yes, mother" before getting to work. She started with the bedpans. Kress helped her carry them to the nearest outhouse where they pulled a hose inside and Delea sprayed the contents of each pan down the plastic hole. Her mother rarely wasted any time setting her eldest daughter to work in the morning. There was simply too much to do. The refugee camp they had built around the Summer Palace had grown to nearly fifty thousand souls, more than the Queen had anticipated.

All of this had meant that, years ago, Delea Etain was demoted from princess to field nurse. She now looked the part too, with the sleeves of her shirt rolled up, and her pants and her boots muddy from days spent cleaning medical tents and helping her mother care for the refugees. She had not worn a dress in months, but such was the way of things now that the war had reached their home world of Arc.

The elder of the King's daughters, she had received a year of customary military training as a part of her royal upbringing. She had opted to specialize as a combat medic. While she had never formally joined the war effort, her training had proven invaluable once she started helping her mother's humanitarian projects. However, because there was so much to do, Delea's days often began with such mundane tasks as these.

Returning to the tent, Delea travelled from cot to cot, replacing the bed pans beneath each of the beds that did not have one. Over half the tents were filled with the sick or the dying, and so Delea stripped the other half and Kress helped her carry the dirty linens down the hill. Together they exchanged the dirty for the freshly cleaned and then marched back up the hill.

The clothes line she used was strung between two scrawny trees that stood just outside Delea's own tent. An angry wind was coming in off the sea, accompanied by a misting rain. She looked out at the Bay of Sardis to see whitecaps rolling over the sea.

"Do you still wish to hang up the clothes your highness?" Kress asked beside her.

She shook her head. "We'll just take down what's there and head back."

The hilltop narrowed here as it came to meet the stony shore. The foamy waves of a morning squall were crashing against the rocks below as Delea and Kress began pulling the laundry down off the line. Even with the morning rain, Delea was reminded of how much she liked it here. The backside of the hill was secluded from the rest of the camp, and over the last two months she had often come here alone to read in peace.

She was taking down a pair of Fel's socks when Kress grabbed her by the arm.

"Your highness, can you hear that? It sounds like someone crying out."

Delea held still and listened. At first all she could hear was the wind of the morning squall and the sea as it crashed against the rocks, but then there it was: Someone, a boy or a young man, was yelling from somewhere below the cliff. She threw the socks into the laundry basket and ran to the edge of the hill.

A girl with a pregnant-looking silhouette was setting herself down on a sandy spot beneath a tree. Below her, a young woman and a boy around Delea's age were helping an elderly woman navigate the jagged shore. A wooden rowboat sat in the water, lolling between two rocks. Suddenly, the pregnant girl let out a cry and reached down to grab at her leg. Delea could see something small, black, and shiny writhing against the sand.

Delea spun around to her bodyguard. "Kress, go get help! Find Nurse Phane or Nurse Elya and bring them here right now!" Then she turned and sprinted back toward her own tent, which was only a row in from the laundry line. She ducked her head in the front flap, grabbed her aid bag, and then sprinted back toward the cliff.

Kress had disappeared by the time returned to the cliff. The rain was coming down in sheets now as she raced down a narrow path that led toward the tree. Her aid bag on her shoulder, Delea followed the path through a pair of jagged rocks. Once through, she spotted the dead body of a snake lying on a rock. The boy had leaned over the pregnant girl's ankle and was sucking at the wound.

Still running at a full sprint, Delea threw down her aid bag and fell to her knees as she came to a sliding stop next to the pregnant girl. "Get off her!" She yelled as she pulled the boy away. When the boy gave De-lea a confused look, she gritted her teeth. "You'll only poison yourself, you fool!" Then she pointed at him and the rock behind him. "Bring me that snake right now!"

Then Delea pressed her hand against the girl's belly and was rewarded when she felt the baby kick. "Breath slowly and deeply and try to calm yourself so you can slow your heart rate, miss. I may have an antidote if I can find one."

The pregnant girl nodded and pursed her lips together as she forced herself to take long, frightened breaths. Then the boy carefully set the dead snake down on the gravel behind Delea's bag, and she needed only a glance to know what it was. *A Black Aspyrus. They could both be dead before the anti-venom kicks in.* Opening the side pouch on her bag, she pulled out her anti-venom kit and flipped it open.

The pregnant girl was lying with her back against the tree, and she looked at Delea with fear in her eyes. Delea filled a syringe with the clear, yellow fluid and then grabbed the pregnant girl's forearm.

"Is she going to be okay?" the boy asked from behind her.

"I'm giving her the anti-venom now," Delea said as she pressed the needle against the girl's vein. Her needle struck the girl's vein on the first try and Delea injected the yellow anti-venom into the girl's arm.

"Here. Hold this against her arm," Delea said as she handed a piece of bandage to the boy. He pressed it against the girl's vein. Delea saw the other girl and the old woman come up behind them as she pulled out her stethoscope. She asked loudly if anyone else was bit.

"No," the boy said, shaking his head and Delea saw him fight off a dizzy spell. Sitting on the sand, he swooned. Delea ripped open another pocket on her aid bag and pulled out her stethoscope.

"That's good," Delea replied, "but it looks like you swallowed a good bit, didn't you?"

The pregnant girl cried out in pain. "I can't! She's… I *can't!*"

The girl's water had just broken.

"By the Weaver," the old woman whispered.

Delea pressed her stethoscope down on the pregnant girl's stomach. A heartbeat like the wings of a hummingbird thrummed in her ears, paused, fluttered, and then stopped.

FEL

4.27.2388 - Planet Arc, Refugee Camp

Fel crept quietly through the tall wheatgrass that lined the outer edge of the camp. Parting the leaves with her hands, she settled in among the towering stalks. She knew it was here somewhere. She could hear the *buzz, buzz, buzzing* the pogger made as it hovered around, trying to stay hidden. Hiding at the edge of the tall grass, she waited for her quarry to come into view.

The children of the camp were playing Run the Pogger, a game where everyone divided into two teams and two territories. Then two poggers, fist-sized metal balls that hovered about with robotic guile, were let loose on each side of the border.

Fel was a dasher, chosen by her team to cross over into the other team's territory to steal their pogger and bring it back across the border. The team that did this would win. She would have to evade the hooks and the bashers of the enemy team to do this, all while their own hooks and bashers defended their side. Most of the kids in this particular game of Run the Pogger were two or three years older than Fel, but she was sneaky and she was fast.

The bright sun of late afternoon was hanging over the Sinvoresse Valley as Fel left her hiding spot and crept along the edge of the tall wheatgrass. Crouched and walking slowly, she picked her way through the heavy stalks. She had to be cautious, because if a basher caught her here they could tag her, and she would be out until the next game. She spotted a wall, waist-high and made of rough-hewn rock, standing less than a stone's throw away from her. That was the edge of the refugee camp. Fel could see people lighting torches and cook fires as the sun descended in the west. What Fel could not see, however, was the enemy team's pogger, nor the three hooks assigned to guard it. The game had grown late and she was one of the few dashers left on her team, so she stayed still and quiet and hidden amongst the tall grass. Minutes passed in tense silence and as the sun slowly lilted toward the horizon, and Fel's mind began to wander. It was nearly evening and she could feel a hole growing in the pit of her stomach.

Then the grass shivered and parted as a glowing golden ball floated out of the grass and along the wall. She had found the pogger. Hopping along behind it were the twins Yanor and Solde, boys who were only a year older than she was. Fel was also fairly certain she could outrun both boys. They had been bashers the last game and had caught no one. Fel was readying herself to spring before a third figure emerged from the grass and gave her pause. Vanin, a tall and dark-blue-skinned girl, had been the first person picked when teams were chosen that morning. Lithe and athletic, Vanin wasn't just one of the fastest children in the game—she was one of the fastest people in the entire camp. Two of the last three games had ended with Vanin running a pogger across the border and Fel's entire team had breathed a sigh of relief when Vanin had promised not to be a dasher the next game.

Still as a statue, Fel's eyes tracked the three hooks and the robotic pogger as they wandered along the edge of the wall. She had been a dasher enough times to understand the patterns that the poggers took, and she had guessed, correctly, that the pogger in this game would follow the outer wall of the garden at some point. Now, after nearly half and hour of hiding in the wheatgrass, she was within thirty yards of her target. Now all she had to do was figure out how to steal it away back to her side.

The pogger came to a bend in the wall where it turned, and Fel finally had to get up and follow, carefully picking her way through the grass so as not to tip off Vanin and the twins.

Then a blur of a boy leapt out from behind a corner and someone shouted "Hey!" as he jumped up and snatched the pogger right out of the air. Fel saw that it was Ryce, one of the other dashers on her team, with the pogger in his hand as he dived into the grass. Vanin, Yanor, and

Solde were hot on his heels, and soon there were four furrows running through the stalks.

Fel leapt up and raced after them.

"I got it! I got it!" Ryce called out as he sprinted through the grass, waving the metal ball above his head like a prize.

"Get him!" Solde cried out as he stumbled and fought his way through the grass.

"Help me! Help me!" Ryce cried out as he ran.

Fel's teammate was short and quick, but he had to know he had no chance of outrunning Vanin in a straightaway sprint. If Fel could catch his eye, he might throw her the pogger before the older girl caught him. Once Fel had it, she knew she could run it through the goal for the score.

Fel sprinted through the grass, cutting at an angle across the field, hoping to come up next to Ryce before Vanin could catch him. Looking ahead, Fel could see the tops of trees coming closer and closer, and she knew the tall grass would end soon as it gave way to the woods. When the stalks parted before her, Fel stopped to wait as a plan came to her mind.

"Ack!" Ryce hollered as he burst forth into the open, dodging and diving to his right and away from the outstretched arms of Vanin. Fel waited for a half second as the two of them ran out in front of her, and then she jumped out and crisscrossed behind them.

"Ryce! Over here!" she shouted, waving her arms in the air as she ran.

Vanin was almost on top of Ryce then, but when the tall, dark skinned girl leapt forward to tackle him, Ryce dove and spun and tossed the pogger toward Fel. Then Ryce and Vanin collided together with the ground in a tangle of arms and legs and curses as the pogger soared through the air. Fel tracked the fist-sized metal ball as it flew toward her, and she saw the pogger light up and slow its ascent as it shifted back into hover mode. Still running, Fel slowed to a crow-hop as she snatched the pogger out of the air—and as her hand closed around it, its lights turned off again. Fel hit the ground running.

"Oh no you don't!" Yanor shouted as he jumped out from behind a tree, cutting her off.

Fel's shoes skidded in the dirt as she spun around and ran back into the grass, clutching the pogger in her hand. The stalks of wheatgrass whisked by her as she ran to the south.

"Get her, Solde!" Yanor called out from behind her.

Fel could hear the two boys grunting as they plowed through the grass behind her. Still sprinting at full speed, she heard one of them trip over something in the grass as he fell forward with a thud. Glancing back, Fel saw the grass shaking where Yanor was helping Solde pick himself up off the ground. She turned and took aim for the boundary.

The towering stalks of grass parted again to reveal the wall, not far from where she had first spotted the pogger. Not breaking stride, Fel jumped up atop the wall and ran along its crude stone spine. She chanced another look behind her to see both of the twins—first Solde and then Yanor—run out from the grass, looking winded. She had no doubt this was not their first chase today. Fel, on the other hand, had fresh legs from hiding and waiting for the pogger to come to her. And now it had. She was almost there. Putting on another burst of speed, Fel saw the red and yellow lights of the boundary goal winking ahead of her. The wall turned sharply and Fel hopped off the stone, then landed on the ground with a skip and a bounce. She could see the apple trees where the goal lights were hanging. Another fifty yards and she would be there.

Then a blur of blue and brown burst out of grass and struck Fel like a hammer, driving her to the ground.

"Got you, you little rabbit!" Vanin shouted as she picked herself up off the ground. "I'll have that pogger back now, your Highness."

Fel sighed in defeat as she rolled onto her back. Sitting in the grass, she took a moment to catch her breath before she opened her hand. Grinning, Vanin snatched up the pogger from Fel's palm and tossed it back into the air. Fel watched the shiny metal ball light up again like a globe of gold as it hovered in the air above her. The golden ball was just starting to float back to the north when a cry went out from the other side of the apple trees. Fel sat up and looked toward the goal line. The other team had scored.

"Better luck next time, Princess," Vanin smiled as she helped Fel to her feet. "You're a lot quicker than you look."

Fel thanked the older girl for the hand up, and then gave one more longing look at the boy who had scored. He would get to be a captain for the next game and pick his own team. She could hear the pogger— the pogger which had almost been hers—humming away behind her. If only she had been a little faster.

"Your Highness?"

The voice was deep and feminine, and Fel turned around to see Marental, her bodyguard, standing on the other side of the wall. For Fel, the wall was just over waist high, but for the Kodayene woman the wall barely rose above her knee.

"What it got, Mary?" Fel asked as she glanced back toward the crowd.

"Your mother, the Queen, has ordered our return for the mid-day meal." The burly woman checked her watch. "If we leave now, we may yet avoid being tardy."

"I guess," Fel shrugged as she turned and hopped over the wall.

Glancing back again, Fel saw that a loud and raucous group had gathered around the winning dasher, and the twelve-year-old girl within her longed to join them, even though she knew she could not.

She followed Marental across the grassy field to an empty path. Once they were well out of earshot, her bodyguard's giant fist nudged her gently on the shoulder.

"You nearly scored, your Highness!" Marental's husky voice was filled with pride. "I saw you running. If that older girl hadn't been so fast, you would have beaten them."

"Yeah, I know. Vanin is the fastest girl in the camp." Fel brightened a bit and stole a last glance over her shoulder. Vanin had joined the crowd and several of the kids from the winning team were congratulating her. Fel thought she saw the older girl glance back toward her, but she couldn't be sure.

Marental nodded knowingly. "In any case, I radioed Roake to give him an excuse in case we are late."

Fel shoved her fists into her pockets as they walked. "What did you tell them?"

"That a boy had sprained his ankle and that you were helping them tape him up."

Fel furrowed her brow. The excuse sounded familiar. "Did he believe you?"

Marental's deep voice chuckled. "I cannot say, but I also think Roake will not mind either way."

They followed the path down into the trees. The sandy path would lead them back to camp but in a roundabout way, winding down toward the beach where it crossed the river before curving back inland. These were the Gardens of Eire that Empress Aelia had built around the Summer Palace after she had abdicated the throne and descended into retirement. Fel loved the ruins of the Summer Palace and its gardens. They were so much better than the palace back in Sindorum, where they had spent practically half their time in the basements and bomb shelters as the Coalition shelled the city outside. The Gardens of Eire were a wonderful place to be a young girl, and Fel loved everything about them. She loved the trees and the grass and the flowers and all of the games she could play with the other children. And she loved all the secrets, too.

There were a *lot* of secrets.

Fel knew where the deer came at night to feed. She knew every beaver dam along the river, even the one that was hidden where the stream was narrow and the trees hung low over the water. She knew where a family of rabbits kept their hovel, and she knew where the hawk that hunted them kept her nest. There was even one night when she had sneaked out of her tent without anyone knowing, and she went down to the beach and watched as a whole nest of sea turtles hatched and scurried out into the water. That night was one of her favorite memories from her time here, and it was an important secret that she had never told anyone, but that was not the most important secret. No, the most important secrets were the Places, and Fel knew for a fact that she was the only one who knew what a Place was.

Fel and Marental followed the sandy path as it wound its way through the trees and over the rolling earth until it crossed a bridge and a stream. Fel stopped at the middle of the bridge to listen to the rushing water. She could feel the bridge shuddering beneath her feet as the white-capped water rushed beneath it. It was late spring, almost summer now, but it had been a heavy winter and the deep snows were still melting off the faces of the Blackfriar Mountains. Looking over the side, she could see the shining black shadows of fish flying by in the water below. A month ago, the waters had been so high and the fish so thick that they would leap over the bridge like shining black missiles.

However, none of that was why she stopped. This bridge was not just any bridge, but it was a Place, and whenever Fel found a Place she knew that if she listened she could hear whispers from the world that sat on the other side of this one. Whispers that only she could hear. Whispers from the Otherworld.

She heard Marental calling to her from the other side of the bridge, but Fel pretended not to hear her and instead walked to the bridge's railing, where she pretended to look down at the water. Then she closed her eyes and listened intently.

Yesterday she had heard it. She'd heard a rattle and a hum, a song like a drumbeat mixed with a murmured chorus. The words were unintelligible, but she had heard its melody clearly. Today, leaning against the railing, she had hoped to hear another whispered song, but all she heard was silence and the rushing of the water. She heard a fish leap out of the water as its tail flapped in the air. She could hear Marental's heavy footsteps thumping across the bridge. Then, like the long, hollow moaning of a tree, a ghostly sound came into her head. It was a thrumming beat. She did not hear it so much as feel it—a drifting moment of melancholy, a twinge of sorrow that arrived and quickly fled, like the moment you wake from a sad dream that fades even as you try to remember it, and then is gone.

Strong fingers grasped her arm. "Your Highness, is everything alright?"

Fel shivered as she opened her eyes. "Aye Mary, I'm sorry. I was just listening to the waters here."

"Of course, your Highness, but we have to go. Your mother is waiting." The towering woman said with the half-smile of a worried adult. People were always looking at Fel in that way and she had learned to just ignore it.

"Yeah, I'm sure she is." They followed the sandy graveled path as it wound down toward the bay, and for a few minutes Fel could hear the waves lapping against the shore as they walked. Then the path curved again, leading them back up through the trees and into the camp. The smell of the green and the trees and the grass receded, giving way to the cookfires and the stench of thousands of people camped too closely together.

They followed the path as it travelled a meandering route along the camp's outer edges, winding in and out of the tents like a snake. It was not the fastest route back, but Fel knew it was the one that Marental preferred because the crowds were sparse here and the tents more spread out, which allowed a single bodyguard to watch over one princess more easily than if they were in a crowd where danger could come from any angle.

Marental walked so closely next to her now that Fel's shoulder often rubbed her bodyguard's hip. Her bodyguards always stayed close in the camps, but Fel refused to hold anyone's hand. She was not a little girl and she was not stupid, not like her sister Delea thought she was. She knew how to stay safe.

The tents passed by like a rainbow. They were one of Fel's favorite parts about the camp. Many of the tents had started out all white, because her mother had taken every leftover military tent she could find when the army returned to Sindorum. However, as soon the people got hold of them, they harvested a multitude of dyes from the flowers and the trees that surrounded the Summer Palace, and so a kaleidoscope of colors had sprung up, seemingly at random, as every person and every family dyed their tent in their own color.

Then the path curved again, turning away from the tents, along the beach and up the backside of the flat-topped hill where Fel's tent was. They passed a rowboat, bouncing between two rocks in the water. The shore was rocky here and they followed a path as it wound through the crags that ran all the way up the hill. Rising from the hilltop stood a tree with a wide, beautiful canopy of leaves whose shade fell nearly halfway down the hillside. Picking her way through the crags, Fel was near the top when she heard a woman scream. It was a scream filled with agony, pain and fear. Both Fel and Marental instinctively broke into a run. Then, as they crested the hill they met the base of the tree where they were greeted by a pair of women, one young and the other old, huddled together in prayer. Beyond them was a dramatic spectacle.

Fel recognized Doctor Sharin, Nurse Phane, and her sister Delea among the small crowd gathered around the base of the tree. At the center of it all, lying flat on her back between the tree's knotted roots, was a pregnant young woman with sweat rolling down her face, and her legs were splayed. Fel saw the girl's left hand gripping a tree root so tightly that the knuckles were white. The pregnant girl let out another long, pain-filled moan as her eyes rolled back in her head.

Fel stood dumbfounded as she watched Doctor Sharin unfold his medical case. He filled a syringe with clear liquid and handed it to Delea.

"We need to give the anti-toxin time to set in," the doctor said. "This should calm her down a little." Fel watched as Delea took the syringe and injected it into the girl's arm. Then Fel felt Marental's hand on her shoulder.

"Your Highness, we should…"

Fel took a step back but moved no further, as she could not take her eyes from the scene. She watched the pregnant woman spasm as Delea pulled out the syringe. Then a breeze hit the tree's canopy in a rush of rustling leaves, and the pregnant woman let out another agonizing cry. For a moment Fel could not see the woman as Delea and Nurse Phane shifted positions, but when she did, she saw blood flowing from the woman's nose as her eyes rolled back in her head and her body shook with convulsions.

Beside her, Fel heard the two other women reciting their prayer. "Blessed are those who wash their robes, that they may have the right to the tree of life and may go through the gates and into the hidden city…" It was, Fel realized, a prayer for mourning and deliverance. "…we pray for grace and peace and mercy from the Weaver above and may his servant, the Silver Lady, be with her in truth and love…"

Then Fel saw Delea place a brace between the pregnant girl's teeth as she spasmed again, and Fel saw Doctor Sharin check the girl's pulse.

"I'm afraid that…" the doctor began to say, but then the spasms stopped and the girl's body fell still. Her eyes were frozen open, staring blankly up at the sky. Doctor Sharin checked the girl's pulse again and then shook his head. Beside her, Fel heard one of the praying women sob.

"Hold her torso!" the doctor said as he reached for his bag.

Delea and Nurse Phane affixed their grips tightly against the girl's hips and her shoulders as the doctor produced a circular saw as long as his forearm and with a blade half as wide as his hand.

Fel looked away as Doctor Sharin lowered the saw, but she could hear the spinning blade as it cut through flesh and bone. Then, when the doctor turned off the saw, he reached back into his bag for another pair of tools, and Fel heard the sound of scissors working as the doctor reached inside the girl's torso and removed a small, bloody thing of pink flesh. The baby's eyes were closed, but Fel could see it shivering. Then the leaves of the tree rustled overhead as everyone around her gasped in disbelief when the child let out a cry.

PAR

12.12.2387 – Planet Vellus, just outside Alba Calea

He could see lights coming down the drive as he mounted his jumper. *Just in time,* he thought as the jumper's ignition fired and the air bike leapt off the ground. Keeping his lights off, he steered the jumper toward one of the many strings of traffic that perpetually hung over the great city of Alba Calea. Below him the city sprawl blossomed in a pallet of lights big and small. He swung in behind a bus and flipped on the jumper's lights.

He was a Taker, a human who had been mechanically augmented and cybernetically bonded with an artificial intelligence. Often referred to as a "Shade," Par's A.I. was composed of a thousand of tiny nano-bots, robots smaller than the eye could see. They inhabited and enhanced his body, his senses, and his mind. Linked to both his conscious and unconscious mind, he could communicate with his Shade without saying a word. And it was his Shade who spoke to him now as he followed the traffic over the city.

Last week, I was playing a game with my friend Andrew at his house. It was all made up, with made up names and made up places and made up rules that we came up with as we went along. After a while, we decided that I would just be the game piece and Andrew would be the player, because we couldn't both keep track of all the rules and play against each other at the same time. So, I just did what Andrew told me and we played together against the Gamemaster—who wasn't really real, we just made him up—and it was really fun because we lost when I stepped on the wrong square and we both laughed until our eyes watered.

Then you showed up and took me home.

Alba Calea was the capitol city of the Illyari Republic and the largest population center on the planet of Vellus. Flying overhead at two hundred feet, Par watched Alba Calea Proper—the city's center—roll by beneath his feet. He could see the white shadow of the Senate building in the distance. Mansions and villas owned by the Republic's governing noble families passed by below him. Wide, well-lit streets. Gardens. Parks. Then he flew over the city's inner wall, and just like that he was flying over the Low 28, Alba Calea's outer districts. The city's inner districts were nearly all from upper classes—pure bred humans, Meaudean and Illyari mostly. Out here in the outer districts, Alba Calea was a melting pot: Illyari mixed with Meduan and the dark-skinned Ribari, or the pale-faced Umbreans or even the multi-colored Duathe. Rumors had it that there were even a few runaway replicants from the Imperium.

The jumper's navigator buzzed and Par turned out of the traffic line and sent the air bike into a gentle dive toward his apartment building. He set his jumper down on the roof and locked it to a chain bolted to the concrete. Then he punched in the security code and made his way down to third level. Rufus was waiting for him in his living room when he opened the door.

Rufus Galbinus was a middle-aged man who moved and looked like someone much older. Bald with a bushy black beard and a comfortable paunch, Rufus stood with a hunch to his back and walked with a prominent limp that were both products of a now decades-old war the Republic had fought with the Ribari. A war in which he and Par had met, and Par had been recruited to their cause. Par heard Rufus lock the door behind them, and as soon as the two men were seated, Par sent out his Shade to watch and listen. The two men shared a trust and a friendship that Par knew with few others, but tonight was not a night for carelessness and idle conversation.

"An unfortunate thing, what happened tonight," Rufus said as he shut the door behind Par. "I expect that was hard? Taking Nerus like that? All over some carelessness with a woman no less."

Par shrugged as he sat down in the nearest chair. "Little different from any other. He was good about it. He understood."

Rufus nodded as he walked to the kitchen and poured himself a glass of brandy. "Would you like a glass, Mr. Riordan?"

Rufus was one of the few men who knew Par's family name, and whenever Par heard it he was reminded that it was a name that had nearly disappeared from the universe.

Nearly, but not yet.

"No, I'm fine thank you," Par replied after a pause, waving the glass away.

Rufus set the empty glass back on the shelf. "I figured as much, especially after tonight, but if you change your mind, just let me know." The gray-haired man gave him a serious look as he dropped a pair of ice cubes into his glass and walked back into the living room.

"I certainly will, Rufus." Par smiled. He rarely drank, especially when there was business involved.

Rufus sat down on the sofa across from him and took a long sip of his brandy. Par folded his hands in his lap and waited while Rufus swirled the gold-colored liquor around in his glass. Par knew Rufus well, and something told him that this was more than just a recounting of the day's events.

"There are rumors, you know." Par raised an eyebrow when Rufus said this. "The Praetors are suspicious. Which means we may have to contend with Ataline Cato and her followers again soon. As you well know, Cato would act on even the slightest suspicion. To make matters more complicated, they say she is already mining for candidates among the women in Consul Marius' upper echelons. If she were to find the right one, it could be a formidable challenge for us."

Par nodded. This was an effort many decades in the making, and several of their plans were nearing fruition. Par knew that he was just a cog in the machine, a role he was more than happy to play, while Rufus had to watch the entre picture.

"There are people hunting us now," Rufus continued. "If they've found Nerus, and they have, they can likely find others. The other principals have grown nervous. They wish to act. This is why I need you now, more than ever." Rufus took another sip of his brandy as Par sat up in his seat.

"You know you have only to ask, old friend, and it is done."

Rufus nodded solemnly. He held his thumb to his mouth for a moment, his eyes shut, and Par could almost feel the other man thinking. Finally, Rufus opened his eyes and let out a long breath that he had been holding. "You are the most skilled Taker that we employ, Par. Perhaps the most skilled Taker in the Republic…"

"There are many others who can do what I do."

"But not with your tact and your discipline." Rufus leaned forward. "I want you to know that we do not spend your talents lightly. Today, for example. This job. Nerus's carelessness put us in a corner. We had no other way out." The Senator raised his hands in the air. "This morning nearly all was lost, and now here we are, no more than a whisper again. And all thanks to you."

Par folded his hands in his lap and leaned back in his chair, staring at the ground. "I feel you are going to ask me for another difficult thing."

"I am," Rufus stated, shifting in his seat. His voice was suddenly cross now, and Par could see the anger plain on his friend's face. The change had been swift, like Par's question had opened a box of emotion that Rufus had been sitting on all day.

"I did not want to ask you what I am about to," the senator continued. "You may not want it either after you hear it, but nonetheless, here we are. I was outvoted. I preach patience. Others preach action. For years, my voice was louder. Now with Nerus compromised, the vote has swung against me."

Par opened his mouth but then thought better of it, unsure if Rufus's temper was more from wounded pride or the decision that had been reached. Perhaps both. Par watched as the Senator took another sip of his brandy and then set his glass on the table with a clank.

"We need to get you to Arc before this war is over. There is some business we need you to attend to there." Rufus raised his eyes to meet Par's, and Par saw in the other man a look of profound regret, even sorrow. "Specifically, we need you to infiltrate the capital city of Sindorum, locate any surviving members of King Teum's royal family, and either kidnap or kill each and every one of them."

DELEA

4.27.2388 - Planet Arc, Refugee Camp

Sitting on her knees and holding a wad of bloody bandages, Delea stared at the corpse of the dead woman lying against the tree. Behind her, the aunt and the cousin of the deceased were wailing and holding the newborn baby

Her name was Noemi, and she had died beneath an Ulvus tree in the middle of the morning. She was twenty-two. It was the snake bite that had pushed her into labor, her body reacting to the poison, but Noemi had died before giving birth. By the time Doctor Sharin had arrived, it had already been too late—the young pregnant woman was gasping and nearly catatonic. The poison had seized her lungs and not let go, he said. He pumped her full of more anti-venom anyway and then went about performing an emergency C-section there beneath the tree. Noemi had breathed her last breath before he cut her stomach open, but miraculously the baby had been rescued. Doctor Sharin said that somehow the mother's system had protected the child from the poison. The baby was a boy, and when Noemi's aunt held him, she named him Micah. That was the name Noemi had picked out for a baby boy, she said.

The aunt held the crying baby while she spoke of how they had travelled all the way from Arvod, across the entire western continent and across the Harrid Sea. Beside her, Noemi's sister sat and wept.

Delea had listened until she remembered to check over the fool boy who had tried to suck the poison out of the pregnant woman's leg. She found him lying on the grass, semi-conscious and dizzy. Using the smelling salts in her aid bag, Delea brought him around. He said his name was Elias, and Delea asked him to help her carry the dead girl to the makeshift morgue they had set up on the back side of the hill, away from everything and everyone else in the camp.

There was only one other corpse in the morgue tent, and it was lying on a cot in the back with a green blanket lying over top of it. Delea knew from Nurse Phane that it was an old man who had died of pneumonia the day before. An old man dying of an old man's illness. She and Elias set Noemi's corpse on a cot near the front of the tent and left.

They would be back to bury her once they were ready, Elias said, though he did not know how long that would be.

Delea spent the rest of the day hauling laundry up from the river and handing out medicine. Once, her mother found her crying behind a tent. Delea felt a pair of arms wrap around her as her mother whispered, "I know, I know, I know…"

After the night shift had taken over, she found her mother's nightly cookfire where the Queen and Nurse Elya were cooking up kebabs. The Queen had built her fire pit in the shadow of an ancient bell tower where Empress Aelia had kept her garden and entertained her guests a thousand years ago. The broken stone walls loomed like shadowy sentinels around the fire. As Delea sat down between her mother and her sister, she could see the shadows of bats flying in and out of the bell tower above, soaring to and fro on their nightly hunts.

"Aye, Del, what's the long face, and d'you want a spot of the apple or no?" Fel said as she held out an overlarge canteen.

"I would love some, thank you." Delea sipped on the juice between bites of lamb. "And do you *have* to talk like that?"

Fel shot her a look. "Talk like what, mate?"

Delea sighed. "I'm not your *mate*, I'm your sister and we're royals so we don't talk like we barely know how to read."

"Aye, there it is." Fel rolled her eyes. "My friends know how to read just fine, thankyoumuch."

Delea sighed again as she swallowed a bite of lamb. "I'm sure they do, but you don't have to talk like them all the same. You have an *education*, Fel. You're *smart*. And besides, you sound so *fake* when you talk like that."

Fel snorted. "Maybe you thinking that, big sis, but not my friends. And maybe I might want to be sounding a little less royal around my friends right now, huh? You think about that? You might be royal and you can just go keepin' on being royal, but I'm about to become Fel Etain and that's it."

Delea rolled her eyes and said nothing, allowing the subject to drop. Her little sister had never understood and probably never would. Fel had never lived at court in the way Delea had. In fact, this camp was the closest they had been to the capital city in years. Fel had been all of six years old the last time they had slept in the palace, and it was likely she barely remembered living there. However, what bothered Delea most was that her little sister was at least partly right about one thing. Barring a miracle, their father would soon no longer be king, and that made them … well … Delea wasn't sure what that made them. Delea had ignored this fact for so long that when it finally hit her, she sat staring at the fire for a moment. She was still staring at the flames when the old woman sat down.

"Aye, Demetria," Fel said with a mischievous grin. "Can I trade you for a story, ma'am?"

Blinking hard, Delea turned to look at the old woman. Demetria had only recently arrived at the camp with nothing more than the clothing on her back and a pet rat that she had trained to live in her pocket. No one knew exactly where Demetria had come from, because every time she was asked, she seemed to give a different answer. The one thing that was certain was that she was a skilled doctor, and so their mother had immediately put her to work. After some debate with the doctors, the old woman had settled on the night shift, which she said was to better keep up with her rat, lest he be running about unsupervised while she slept.

Delea watched as the old woman slipped a piece of kebab into her shirt pocket and then looked sideways at Fel, like she was inspecting the girl for something. When she spoke, it was with a voice filled with rust and age. "And what do you want to hear a story for, your Highness?"

Fel shrugged, grinning from ear to ear. "I dunno."

Demetria let out a grunt of annoyance. "You think this old woman is just made out of stories?"

Fel shrugged again, grinning even wider. "I guess."

"Hrmmmm…" Concealing a smile, Demetria took a sip of her tea as she hummed to herself. "Well if you did, you'd be right, child. If he would forgive my blasphemy, I believe I have more stories than the Weaver himself. So, I suppose I'm bound to tell them lest they go to waste." The old woman set her tea cup down on a stump and looked sideways again at Fel. "And what kind of story is it that you want to hear, your Highness?"

Fel shrugged. "I dunno. A good one, I guess."

"A *good* one?" Demetria chuckled as she handed another piece of kebab to the rat in her coat pocket. "I only have good stories your Highness, but not all good stories are happy stories, your Highness, but I suppose if I am telling stories to a princess on an evening such as this, then I had best stick to telling a happy story…"

Demetria glanced sideways again at Fel, and the girl squeaked in excitement.

"Dem! You know I don't care nothing about happy or sad!"

"Hrmmmm…" the old woman hummed. "I suppose I could tell the one about Nimroh the Hunter."

"You told that one already," Fel said, "two nights ago, it was."

"Bagh!" The old woman waved her hand at nothing. "Then I suppose I can't get by on the story about the boy and the spider."

"No! You've done told that one twice!" Fel cried. "Last night you said you were gonna tell the story about the secret, and so you know that's the one I want to hear!"

Then the old woman smiled as the rat's face emerged from her pocket to look out at the fire. Demetria nodded to herself as the rat chewed. "Very well, your Highness… If that is the story that you want, then I will tell it to you. And in order to tell it, I must begin with the Weaver, for the Weaver is the source of all, the creator and the father of the universe, and this story tells a tale that begins on the day after his creation of our Universe, for that is when the Weaver looked down on all that he had made and he said that this was good. The Weaver said this because he had made many universes before, many realities, and those that he saw that were good, he kept, and those that he saw that were not, he unmade. He would take the leftover thread from those that he had unmade and use them to make new universes." Then the old woman seemed to catch herself. "Ah, but I digress ..."

Demetria reached down to give a kernel of corn to her rat and as she did this, she scratched her chin and looked up at the sky. "And so, the Weaver was looking over that which he had made and he decided that he must create something to watch over creation, for he knew there would be those who sought to destroy it."

Then Fel piped up. "And that's why we have the Silver Lady? As a spirit to watch over us?"

Demetria shook her head. "No. The Silver Lady came later as a messenger, so that we may know the truth and be one with God. No, the beings I speak of now live in the universe with us, even if they are distant and withdrawn. No, the beings I speak of now are the Volda, or as we know them from the Scripts, the Watchers."

Fel interrupted again. "But I thought the Watchers were angels. At least that is how they are always in the stories."

Delea had been listening intently to the old woman's story, but her little sister was completely entranced. She saw now that Fel was sitting almost on the edge of her seat and her feet were balanced on her toes, as though she were ready to spring from her seat at any moment.

Demetria shook her head again. "No, child. Far from it. The Watchers are neither good nor evil. Neither kind nor cruel. For they were placed here to watch, to guard, and to defend this universe from those who would steal its secret."

"What's the secret?" Fel whispered.

"*Bah!*" The old woman scoffed as she threw her hands up in the air. "No one knows child! That's why it's a secret!" Demetria let out a self-satisfied huff as she scratched her chin again. "But even if I tell you I don't know, for I truly don't, I can tell you who *does*."

"Who?" Fel breathed.

"The Mother and her Children," the old woman whispered.

As the fire crackled and the light from the flames danced against their faces, the old woman seemed to revel in that moment as she fed another kernel to her rat. Then, with her rodent gnawing at the corn, the old woman began her story.

"You see, the Weaver tasked the Watchers with keeping the secret, but even as he did this, he did not tell them what it was. And so, among the Watchers there once came a woman who decided she needed to know what the secret was. She was so determined to find it out that she lived her whole life for it. She travelled the Universe, in ways that only Watchers can, and she found the smartest, the strongest, the fastest and the wisest of all the people she could find, and she lived with each of them and loved them each in turn for their whole lives until they died. And then she moved on to the next, and so on. With each man, she bore a single child.

"Now, this was early on in the Universe, so early in fact that it was when the first of each race were just beginning on their home worlds. Now, no Watcher had ever done this before, mixed herself with the lesser races, and so these children became new beings—immortals like the Watchers, but beings bound to mortal bodies, and each with the extraordinary gifts of their mortal fathers. In all, there were seven: there was a Hunter, and there was a Killer, and then a Gardner. Next there was a Tinker, a Lover, and then a Dreamer, and last of all came the Thief. And so, by the time the Mother was with the Thief, she had already lived the lives of all six of her other husbands and given birth to a child from each, and so when she gave birth to the Thief's child, she knew that she had given birth to the last of her children. And she was glad, for she knew then what she had to do to uncover the secret of this Universe.

"However, all was not well for the Mother, for the other Watchers had gotten wind of her plan. Because they had sworn to the Weaver that they would protect the secret of the Universe, the Watchers knew they could not let even one of their own come to know the secret. So they hunted the Mother across the stars. They tracked her from world to world, all of the places she had lived, all of the men she had loved. Until one day, when the Mother woke up from her chores, she looked up at the sky to see the Watchers standing over the heavens. She knew then that she was trapped. Knowing that she could not escape, the Mother hid her children among the people of that world and helped them all get away before the Watchers came.

"Now, when the Watchers captured the Mother, they immediately found that she had given birth to many children. But try as they might, the mother never told the Watchers what became of her children …

"And so, the Children have wandered the universe ever since. Some search for their mother. Others search for clues to the great secret that their Mother sought. Others seek out each other. But they are out there, they are out there now, and their Mother, whom the Watchers could not destroy, she sits in her cell and calls out to them. Waiting. Calling. Hoping that one day one of them may hear her so that she can escape and seek out the truth that has so long been hidden."

Then Demetria closed her eyes and hummed to herself once more, and then all was quiet as the fire crackled and burned. When a long moment of silence had passed, and it was clear that Demetria was done with her story, Fel let out a long sigh.

"What happened to the children then?" the young princess asked.

"Ah… hrmmm… " Demetria closed her eyes and hummed to herself again as the white rat climbed out of her shirt pocket and crawled across her shoulders. It came to perch next to its owner's head as Demetria smiled at Fel. "It is a story for another night. Perhaps I will remember it tomorrow, but now I think we should pray, for it is a night for praying together, I think."

Fel bowed her head along with the old woman, and Delea stole a glance back toward her mother—who was packing up the extra food—before bowing her own head.

"Blessed are those who believe, for they will rest beneath the Tree. For his messenger has visited them and given them his word. And when the Spirit says follow, they will follow, and enter the city by the gates and all will be judged by what they have done. And so it will be."

"And so it will be," Fel repeated.

"And so it will be," Delea said.

When Delea raised her head and opened her eyes, she saw Demetria looking straight at her.

"But will it?" the old woman asked Delea.

"Will it what?" Delea replied just as her sister looked up at her.

Demetria did not answer her, but stood and bowed instead. "I must be on my way. My shift begins, or, more accurately, it has already begun, and I am late."

And with another short bow, Demetria left. Delea could see the white rat staring at her over the old woman's shoulder as she walked away. *It was a beautiful story, but nothing more,* Delea thought as she watched the old woman leave. *A folk-tale, something imagined or exaggerated. They're all folk tales, really. Pretty stories that help people rationalize the madness that is life.*

"Delea. Fel. Can you girls help me with this extra food?"

It was their mother, who had one cooler in her arms and another pair of coolers sitting at her feet. The sisters replied in unison with a "Yes mother" and hopped up off their seats. Marental and Motya, the other guardsman for the night, rose as well, ready to follow. The sisters each picked a cooler up and followed their mother into the dark.

Their mother led them along the back side of the tent row, where there were no lamps to light the way. Reaching the last tent, Queen Anyse led them off into the trees that lined the north side of the hill. Once they were out of earshot from the nearest tent, Delea began to wonder where their mother was leading them. Then her mother stopped and set her cooler on the ground.

"Stop and sit, girls. We need to talk." Motya and Marental wordlessly turned around to keep watch behind them as Delea and Fel sat down on their coolers. Delea opened her mouth to speak but then her mother held up her hand. "I wanted to talk to the two of you alone," their mother whispered. "So, listen, because there is not a lot of time. This war is likely to end tomorrow, and if not tomorrow, then the day after, and when it does we will no longer be the ruling family of this, or any, planet."

"We understand," Delea said.

The Queen set her jaw as she frowned. "I know you do. I spoke with your father and tried again to persuade him to surrender, but he has insisted on fighting, as he has always done." The Queen's eyes travelled from one daughter to the other. "He has a plan, he says, as if that will change anything that has happened or will happen. I asked him, if his last plan did not turn them back, then how will this one? He does not listen."

There was no sadness in her voice as she said this, only the flat tones of a woman stating the facts, but Delea could see her mother's eyes grow distant. So often these days their mother was the Queen only and nothing else, but for that moment Delea saw a glimpse of someone else. The wife of a king. A wife whose husband was gone. Then Delea's mother blinked twice, and the Queen returned.

"But it is no matter to us now, as your father will not be with us, and if he makes it through to the end, I fear we still will not see him. And so, I have been speaking to the leaders of the Coalition, this Consul Marius, and he has been most agreeable on many things, but for the fate of your father he will not bend. Unless King Teum surrenders, he says, he must face judgment before the Republic."

"What's this, Mom?" Fel's fear was written plainly on her face. "We done know this by now. Dad's gone and we here with the rest of us. We can't go to him because you won't let us, and so I know Dad's gonna be goners. We know, Mom. We know."

"I know, darling. I know you know." Queen Anyse reached out and touched her youngest daughter's face, but Fel pulled away. "I asked you here to tell you that *you* are leaving. I have arranged for the two of you to take refuge on Linneaum with the Duchess of Tue. She is your great aunt and an old friend of mine and your father's."

"But how?" Delea asked. "Don't they have ships in orbit? Like, their entire fleet? Haven't they blocked the gate, too?"

"They can try to block the gate, but they cannot keep it from opening. Not yet, anyhow. Not until they take the palace, and that is why I must get the two of you out now, because if I wait any longer our chance will be gone."

Fel's voice was frightened as she spoke up. "But what about you, Mom? You're coming with us, aren't you?"

The Queen shook her head. "No. Not right away."

Something about her mother's plan still did not add up to Delea, and so she pressed further. "But if the Consul is allowing us to leave, why do we have to leave now? Why can't we stay with you? Here at the camp?"

"Because Marius would not negotiate your freedom," the Queen answered as her chin rose defiantly and her voice trembled. "He said to me that King Teum's daughters will become prisoners beside him…

and that is why I will not let him have you. This is also why I must stay, to see that the Consul honors his agreement with me to take care of our people after the war."

"But what about the blockade? How will we get past their ships?" Delea pleaded.

"Your father and I have had a plan for that since the beginning of the war. Although he may have forgotten, or chose to forget, I have not."

Delea's mind was swimming. This was it. They were finally becoming exiles. "But if you're sneaking us away," she asked, "won't the Consul be angry that you're going back on him? Won't he go back on you too?"

"Your mother knows more tricks than either your father or the Consul know." Queen Anyse then grasped them both and hugged them. "Now, we have talked as much as we can, for if we are away any longer, people will notice and suspect we are up to something." Then their mother held them and looked each of her daughters in the eye. "I want you both to pack your things tonight, but only what you can carry, for you must travel light and you must travel fast. Now, come, let us return."

FEL

Fel sat staring at the flames for a long while after. Her sister had returned to her own tent, taking Marental with her, and the Queen had gone to visit with the night shift, leaving Fel alone by the fire. Only Kress remained, her towering bodyguard stood silent, watching the fire.

Then Fel caught a glint of firelight shining against her chest. It was her royal pendant, a crown set against a circle of crimson and gold. Removing the pin, Fel turned it over in her hands before tossing it gently into the fire. She didn't want to be a princess any more.

Her stomach grumbled, hunger gnawing at her belly. Briefly, Fel considered sneaking off down the hill to see if Feleg and the cooks had anything left, but then she spotted a plate of kebabs sitting on a log. It had likely been left out for the night shift, Fel knew, but her hunger got the best of her and she claimed a stick of grilled meat and vegetables. Sitting back down, Fel listened to Nurse Phane telling a story to Motya about the old man she was treating for pneumonia and who spent all day telling dirty stories to the nurses. Motya laughed and smiled as he listened.

When Fel finished the kebab, she threw the stick into the fire. As she took another swig from her canteen, her mother pulled up a chair next to her.

"Are you up for a game, Fel?" her mother said as she pulled out a deck of cards from her pocket.

"Yes, ma'am, of course."

Her mother dealt and they played wickets while Fel slowly finished another kebab. Fel won the first hand, her mother won the second.

"Did you have a good time playing with your friends today?" her mother asked as she shuffled the cards.

"Yeah. It was fun," Fel said as she looked at the fire.

Queen Anyse began to deal, and Fel saw her mother's eyes flicker toward her chest, right where the pendant used to be. Her mother had never chastised her for not wearing it, and she didn't start now.

"What game did you play?"

"Poggers, like usual."

They picked up their hands.

"What position did you play?" her mother asked.

"They let me be a dash today. I almost scored! But Vanin caught me at the last second before I could cross the border goal and they won."

"Vanin must be pretty fast to catch a Youka like you," her mother said as she took the first trick.

"She's the fastest." The adrenaline-fueled chase replayed itself in Fel's head now and she could hardly look at her cards. "If Vanin hadn't caught me, I was goners clean and free!"

Fel related the story of the final Run the Pogger game then, recounting for her mother how she had hidden in the tall grass for nearly an hour, waiting in ambush for the pogger to come by. When she was done and Vanin had caught her again, the third game had gone to her mother, who picked up the cards and began shuffling the deck again.

"Are you meeting again tomorrow?" her mother asked as she shuffled.

"We were, but..." Then Fel caught her mother's eyes and she remembered. "Aye, they're all meeting again after everyone's dinner."

"That's good. You have my permission to join them, so long as your chores are done and you take someone with you."

The rest of the night shift nurses and doctors were now trickling in. Few stopped to eat at the fire, but took their food with them, bowing to the Queen in thanks as they passed. Fel's mother greeted many of them by name and wished them a good night as they walked by.

They continued their game, mother and daughter flipping cards on the stump between them as the firelight flickered against their faces. Fel took the fourth hand, and her mother the fifth, and that was the game.

"You've gotten better," her mother said as she put the deck back in its case.

"I've learned a lot," Fel said.

Her mother handed the case of cards to her daughter. "You should keep them until we can play again. I have to go now. Roake and I have things to look after before tomorrow's business."

Her mother kissed Fel on the forehead and placed the deck in her daughter's hands before she walked away into the dark. Somewhere out in the camp a preacher was yelling loudly, and Fel could hear a woman's commanding voice echoing against the hillside and the ancient ruins.

"Oh faithful, pray listen, and watch our sighs and mumbled moans. Half muffled by this piteous patch of wretched memorial stones! We rest and lament here on our unfounded fears, for we know we're bound to the great hereafter. Come, gather together for the great supper of God, so that you may eat the flesh of kings, generals, and mighty men, of horses and their riders, and the flesh of all people, small and great."

Fel remembered walking past a preacher on her way out to meet her friends for Run the Pogger, and she wondered now if it was the same woman. She had been a gaunt and grim woman of dark blue skin, with a head of thick black hair streaked with white. The woman Fel heard now sounded the same, but it was hard to tell at this distance. As she sat, watching the fire burn, Fel continued to listen as the preacher went on about the world ending, and how people could seek salvation and shelter from the coming storm.

Then something brushed past Fel's leg, jolting her mind back to where she was. Looking down, Fel saw a small, round, fuzzy thing with black and gold fur. She watched as the fuzzy thing meandered, waddling around her left foot and then behind her right. The fuzzy thing tottered and wiggled as it walked away from her, and Fel watched it hop its way along the edges of the firelight until it reached the shoes of Nurse Phane. Fel could see it clearer now that it was on the other side of the fire. It looked like nothing more than a puff of black and gold fur, so fuzzy that Fel could hardly see its feet, but it was not until the animal jumped up on Nurse Phane's lap that Fel could tell that it was a Kotling.

A Kotling from the Otherworld.

Nurse Phane, for her part, had no idea the creature was there, for she could neither see it or feel it any more than she could see or touch a ghost. However, a Kotling was not a ghost, it was a visitor from the Otherworld, a world that was parallel to this one. Kotlings were among the most frequent of the Otherworld's visitors, for they came here seeking people's dreams—a commodity that, Fel was told, the Kotlings could only find here. And Kotlings loved dreams, for dreams to a Kotling were a special treat, as were hopes and wishes and many of the other wonderful thoughts people had about things they wanted.

Fel knew that this Kotling was drinking from a very real and happy dream, because she could see the Kotling close its eyes and hum to itself as it sat there with Nurse Phane. She was a thin woman, with a thin face and a receding hairline that she hid beneath a scarf she kept wrapped around her head. She was pretty in her own way, although not as pretty as Nurse Felya. All of the men seemed to crowd around Felya even when she was working. However, tonight Nurse Phane looked prettier than usual and she was talking to one of the royal guardsmen named Motya, who was telling her a story from when he was a soldier, and Nurse Phane was laughing and giggling like a little girl, which Fel though was silly because the story was not that funny.

Looking around the fire, Fel could see there were nearly a dozen Kotlings now, crawling around the campfire, listening to people's dreams and humming along to themselves. Fel knew she was the only one who could see them. She had been able to see them since always, and for the longest time everyone had assumed that she was making them up, like imaginary friends. Whenever Fel had insisted that they were real, people had laughed at her and called her "imaginative" or "creative" or "a funny little girl," and so Fel had stopped. She had stopped and listened and watched. Just like she was watching now.

A Kotling was crawling up her leg. Light as air, the Kotling's tiny claws pricked her leg as it made its way up her shin and over her kneecap. She bent forward as it rounded her hip and crawled up her back before it settled on her shoulder. Fel held very still as the Kotling made itself comfortable.

The last time a Kotling had visited her was last winter when her mother had them helping at a camp near New Kote. The Kotling had crawled up inside her sleeping bag in the night, and when she woke it had whispered a secret in her ear about her mother that she did not understand. This was because Kotlings carried the secrets they came across while drinking people's dreams. Because sometimes people have secret dreams that they hide deep inside themselves, and when a Kotling comes across such a dream, it carries that dream inside itself until the Kotling finds the best person they can give it to. And of course, most people don't hear them, but they *know* what the Kotling says anyway. And that is how people accidentally come to know things they shouldn't, because the Kotling's secret takes them to the truth. So, when the Kotling crawled on her shoulder, Fel held very still and she listened very hard.

However, when the Kotling finally did begin to whisper, it was not a secret from this world that Fel heard, but a secret from the Otherworld. The world that sat on the other side of this one. The Kotling whispered that they needed her help with a task. It was something only she could do, for it had to do with her father. And what was more: she would have to start tonight. She would be visited by music, it said, a song that would wake her and she would have to follow. It would be a song that only she could hear.

Fel waited until the Kotling on her shoulder was done whispering, because she wanted to ask if she would have time for all this before she had to leave with her mother. However, as soon as Fel turned her head to ask, she saw the Kotling was gone. In fact, when she looked around the fire, she saw that all of the Kotlings had disappeared.

Well, there's only one thing to do then, Fel thought as she watched the dying fire. *Get ready and go to bed.*

Fel got up from her seat and walked back to her tent. Kress followed and stood guard as she packed her things and got ready for bed. The last thing she did was to pack her backpack for the morning. Tomorrow, they would be leaving for good. One by one, she packed her things. Her clothes. Her multi-tool. A small first-aid kit. Her translator. And finally, her copy of the Duathic Scripts. It was an older copy of the holy text, one that her father had found for her in the Imperial library. She ran her fingers over the sign of the Weaver engraved on the cover. A circle with five curved lines that arced from its center.

Leaving the top of her pack open, she read the Book of the Seeker until her eyelids grew heavy and she drifted off to sleep.

Hours later, Fel woke. She could feel a strange energy buzzing within her as she lay in her sleeping bag, staring at the tent ceiling. She was not sleepy or groggy and she did not have to pee. No, she was simply awake. Outside she could hear the insects chirping and the murmur of conversation, but behind it all was something else, the something that had woken her. Music.

She had awoken to the music, just as the Kotling said she would, and she could hear it now as she climbed off her cot. It was a stringed solo, like a violin or a fiddle but much more unsettling, where the notes were drawn together and mismatched as the strings rubbed together in some schizophrenic harmony.

Fel pulled on her boots and coat and slipped quietly out of her tent. It was that dark and cool hour when everything was waiting for the dawn to arrive. She could hear Kress and Motya talking softly together at the gazebo, so she snuck around back, putting the tents between her and her bodyguards. Silently she walked, heel to toe, heel to toe, just as she had learned in her many games of Run the Pogger. Up ahead, she could hear the strings singing their song on the breeze.

She found an ancient stone walkway with weeds growing out the cracks, and she followed it across the hilltop. A bat flew overhead as she passed beneath the ancient bell tower where Demetria had told her story and where the Kotling had whispered in her ear. The camp was full of stillness as the cracked pathway led her toward the back side of the hill. The only other people that were moving about were the night watchmen and them she saw only at a distance.

Reaching the edge of the hillside, she paused. An unease had come upon her, a nervous energy, as though some great change were about to happen, a catalyst that would affect not only her but everyone she knew. She knew that if she turned back now, if she returned to her tent and closed her eyes, then none of it would happen, and everything would go on just as it should. Fel considered this. The song she heard was certainly not a comforting song. No, the music itself was a warning to her, for the song she heard was like a warning. Like something that played while the villain stalked his next victim. If she were watching herself right now, she would be screaming to turn around. However, Fel did not like the way things were going. She did not want to leave her home world of Arc, she did not want to leave her friends, and she especially did not want to leave her father, wherever he was, no matter what her mother and her sister said about him.

She could hear, just over the hillside, the ocean waves crashing against the rocks. And behind that, the song. And so, after a moment of standing and thinking in the dark, Fel followed the music and ignored the wary twist at the pit of her stomach.

Walking beneath a broken arch, Fel followed the ancient walkway over the hillside. Cracked stone gave way to gravel and sand. Green grass gave way to rock and cliff. And the music grew louder. The shivering strings were holding the same note now, like a predator waiting to strike. A mist from the sea spray hung over everything like a fog, dimming the stars and both of Arc's moons above. Then the path turned toward the water and the music fell away.

Fel stopped, listening. She could barely hear it now, a single note shivering on the breeze. Cautiously, she took another step forward. The music stayed. She took another step and then another and then two more before music died. Looking around, she could see she was halfway down the cliff. A wave crashed against the rocks below as the spray sprinkled her face. Was the music behind her, or ahead?

Am I in the right spot? she thought as she looked up and down the shore. *Or did I lose track of it as I crossed over the hillside?*

She decided she would descend first, climbing down the sandy path as another wave struck the rocks. The curls of her hair were soon soaking wet as the waves crashed in front of her, but still the music did not return. *Up now,* she thought. Still listening closely, she climbed back up the path. This time the music returned, the strings still singing the single, trembling chord. When Fel looked up, she saw she was standing beneath an Ulvus tree.

When she spotted the dead snake lying against the rocks, Fel realized she was standing beneath the same tree where the baby had been born just as its mother died. Again, a shiver of terror ran up her spine. *Perhaps I should go back. Perhaps that would be best. What could I do anyway? My father is on the other side of the valley, somewhere in the city. King's daughter or not, what could I do to help him? I'm just a girl…* Then her thoughts were interrupted when she saw a shadow take shape in the mist.

As the black form rose before her, Fel could tell right away that it was an Onier by way its wings curled around it like scythes. Like the Kotlings before, the Onier was a visitor from the Otherworld, and while the Kotlings were the most common Otherbeings to visit, an Onier was among the rarest. Fel was one of the few who could see an Onier straight on, as most people could only see them by *not* looking—any time you thought you saw something out of the corner of your eye, only to turn and see nothing there, that was when you have just seen an Onier, for an Onier can travel only in darkness, jumping from shadow to shadow during the day, until night when it can move freely.

The Onier swooped down from the mist and perched atop a rock. Then it folded its dark, feathered wings around itself like a cloak as it loomed over her, leaning down with its long, black-beaked face. When the Onier spoke it sounded like the sigh of an ancient tree. "Welcome, Little Sister. Greetings from the Land of the Others."

Fel was speechless for a moment, her mouth hanging open as she gaped at the strange being hanging above her. It looked like a vulture crossed with a dragon, all made of swirling black smoke.

Finally, she cleared her throat and asked, "Why have you brought me here?"

The Onier cocked its head like a bird. "A task. A favor only you can accomplish. I have gone to … great effort to reach you, to travel from where I am to the Here, to speak with you now."

Her heart was racing in her chest, but she forced her outer self to remain calm. "What do you mean, the Here?"

"The Here?" The Onier seemed to look surprised. "The Here is this world, where all of everything happens. The Otherworld, the place where I am from, is merely a shadow of this one, and that is why here is the Here and there is the Other."

"I would very much like to visit your world one day," she said.

The Onier narrowed its smoke-filled eyes. "Our world would seem very strange to you, as yours is very strange to me."

"That is why I would like to visit," Fel replied.

"Perhaps strange is not the right word… Threaten? Swim?" The Onier scratched itself beneath its beak. "It matters not, for you may get your wish sooner that not, as someone, or many someones, are now trying to cross over from your world to ours."

Fel looked to the west. "Now? Are they close by?"

"Close? This is a strange word, let me think… Yes and no, but they *are* near. They are near to you and not the others we can reach within the Here, and that is why we commune now, you and I, even though you are new. No … young? Yes. Yes, you are young to be troubled with such things."

"The Kotlings mentioned my father."

"Yes, our wayward king. He flirts with powers he does not understand. We need your help with him, lest he stumble."

Fel's heart trembled in her chest. "And how do I help him?"

"You must … catch? … no … ride? … no … carry? No. Follow … yes … that is the word. For you are too far behind in time and in space, and he will reach the gate and it will close. Yes. That is why."

"Why what?" She had done tasks and favors for Others before, but always it had been something minor. Like leaving a piece of glass near a tree. Or taking a rock from a path and setting it on the shore. Never anything that sounded this important. Never something that had to do with a *person*.

However, instead of answering her, the Onier extended a long, bony claw, and pointed. "Behind you."

Turning around, Fel saw the Onier was pointing at the tree. Only the tree had now grown to the size of a castle tower, its roots spilling over the rocky shore like giant tentacles and with a canopy so large it covered the stars in the sky. As Fel stood there staring at it, the tree creaked and moaned as a crack opened up in its knotted base.

"What is this?" Fel replied, breathless.

"It is a Place," the Onier answered. "You are familiar with Places, no?"

Fel nodded.

"Yes." The Onier's voice groaned like a sinking ship. "Places are things in the Here that are connected to the Other. This Place is a pocket of my world that was left here a long, long time ago. It is a memory, or many memories, kept hidden for many reasons that are beyond you and I. So, you and I must pass through now, Little Sister, for the answers you seek lie within."

Fel nodded her understanding. At least, she thought she understood. She thought she understood as well as any girl looking up at a giant tree could understand. Stepping through the knotted doorway in the bark, she felt the ground change from sand to stone. It was black as pitch inside the tree, so dark that Fel could hardly see the hand in front of her. When her face met with a spider's web, she pushed through its gossamer strings. Then the golden glow of a torch met her and suddenly she found herself standing on stairway made of stone. It was as though she were in a castle, with walls of gray and white brick, but when she looked up, she saw no ceiling, only more stairs and beyond that … darkness.

Then a creaking sound echoed against the walls, and when she turned around, an old wooden doorway was opening before her. The Onier soared over her head like a lazy kite, a smoky shadow against the stone. "Come. For there is something for you inside," it said, flying through the doorway.

Fel stood there for a moment as the Onier flew through the wall like a ghost. When it was gone, she stepped over to the stairway railing and looked down. More stairs and more darkness. Finally, she followed the Onier through the door.

The stone of the stairwell met with old, wooden floorboards that creaked and groaned beneath her feet. When she was through, the doorway slammed shut behind her as the room shook in an unnatural tremor as dust and bits of drywall fell from the ceiling in a shower. She blinked hard as her eyes adjusted. Moonlight was streaming in through a window, and she could see an old, dust covered bed sitting in the corner. To her left was a wooden dresser that stood nearly twice as tall as her. Everything seemed strangely familiar.

Then the Onier entered the room, floating down through the ceiling in a cloud of black smoke and coalescing into shape atop the footboard of the bed. The Onier's giant wings were far too large for the room and so, as it landed, it had to fold its wings in on itself in a great crescent. Perched atop the bed, the Onier looked down on Fel with its long-beaked face.

"What do you see, Little Sister?"

What a strange question. Does it see what I see? Fel looked around the room once more. She noticed an old rug, colored crimson and gold, which sat beneath her feet, and she saw a second, narrower door next to the dresser. "We're in a room," she said. "And it feels familiar, but I can't place it yet."

The Onier did not answer. Rather, it turned its smoke filled eyes toward the window on the wall.

Fel looked out the window. They were on a hill at the center of a city that looked like Sindorum, but the buildings were all old, made of brick and mortar and stone. When she looked out to the Bay of Sardis, instead of sea water she saw a basin covered in salt. She turned back to the Onier.

"Where are we?"

"Inside of a memory that only you may know." Then the Onier pointed behind her. "Do you see the mirror?"

Following the Onier's pointed claw, she spotted a mirror sitting in the corner beside the door she had entered. Silvery metal and glass glinted in the moonlight as the mirror was the only thing in the room not covered in dust.

"Yes, I see it," she answered.

The Onier let out a sigh that sounded like a coming storm. "Look inside and tell me what you see."

The floor groaned beneath her feet as she stepped toward the mirror. Drawing herself parallel with the glass, it was not her reflection she saw. Inside the mirror was another world. A city of strange, moving, impossibly tall buildings and a guileless blue sky. The structures were shifting, morphing, changing form as she watched them. She saw two buildings slap together to become one towering spire, and then the spire grew branches like a tree. The tree-shaped spire held its form for a moment, and then it fell apart—like sand in the water—until it reformed itself into a domed arena filled with lights. There were many buildings like this that she could see through the mirror, all shifting and moving against one another, and all of them looked impossibly tall. Then a foot stepped on the mirror and Fel realized why. The mirror was looking up from the ground.

The foot lifted itself up, and then the mirror's viewpoint shifted, showing a man walking through an empty street. Only he wasn't just walking—he was sneaking, hiding from something she couldn't see.

And as he moved, the mirror followed.

The mirror followed him across the empty, cobblestone street and into an alleyway. Deftly, the man stepped around the puddles and the trash, careful not to make any noise. Halfway down the alleyway he stopped, briefly looked up at the sky, and then opened a door. Just as the man turned and stepped through the doorway, Fel caught a glimpse of his face. It was her father.

Then the door shut and he was gone. Only the empty alleyway looked back at her through the mirror. Finally, the Onier spoke.

"What do you see?"

"I saw my father," Fel answered as she stared at the mirror. "He was wandering around inside a strange city. It looked like he was hiding from something, but that he was looking for something at the same time. I don't know."

"Your father *is* searching, but not finding," the Onier replied. "No, he needs *your* help for that. If he is not careful, he will soon be lost. Or worse, he will find what is not meant to be found."

Fel turned around to look into the Onier's smoke-filled eyes. "And how do I help him?"

The Onier sighed. "Ah, that is the question isn't it, Little Sister? I can show you, but the way ... is dangerous."

"Please—" she started, but then another tremor shook the room and everything rattled.

"Ah," the Onier sighed again, "another memory..."

Someone was yelling. Someone in the next room. The voice sounded familiar, but the words were muffled through the wall. Looking for the voice, Fel could hear it was coming from the other side of the wall with the dresser and the narrow door.

She pointed at the door. "What's in there?"

"I cannot know, Little Sister," the Onier replied, "for it is your memory that was awoken. Not mine."

Stepping toward the door, she could hear the voice was angry, and when a second voice shouted back, Fel could hear it was an argument. Then, as she reached for the door knob, the voices fell silent. Pausing for a moment, Fel opened the door anyway. However, as she walked inside the only things she could hear were footsteps walking away, and then a door as it slammed shut. This room was even darker than the last, but then the door behind her slammed shut and a light flickered on with a snap and a buzz.

This second room had the same dimensions and furniture as the first. The bed in the corner, the window on the right-hand wall, and the dresser along the left. Only now everything was new. The floor was covered in blue and gold carpet, the bed was dressed in satin bedsheets, and she opened the dresser doors to find it filled with clothes. Her clothes. She was in her room.

What is this place? Where am I? Looking back to the door she had entered, she thought of the room she had just left. The abandoned, run-down copy of this one. *What did the Onier say? "For it is your memory that was awoken." If this is my memory, what am I remembering?*

There was something lying on her bed. Crossing the room, she found a children's chalkboard laying against the satin sheets and a piece of red chalk lying next to it. *"...it is your memory..."* Something was tickling the back of her mind like a half-remembered dream. She wasn't allowed to bring chalk into her room, because she had drawn all over her walls once when she was younger. If this was her memory, this had been after that. She could remember playing in her room with the chalk, but she couldn't remember why. Had she snuck it in? Or had her parents said, "Just this once"?

She picked up the piece of red chalk and the world shook again.

The light fixture rattled and the chalkboard fell off the bed. The doors of the dresser fell open and a drawer fell out, clattering and spilling clothes on the carpet. Then she saw something step in front of the window.

It was the face of a little girl. A little girl her age. It was her face. It was a copy of her that had stringy hair and sickly gray skin and eyes that looked back at her like black marbles.

Clutching the chalk in her hand, Fel spun around and ran.

Somewhere on the floor above her, a door slammed open and several pairs of footsteps scampered across the ceiling. Racing across the room, Fel yanked the narrow door open and leapt through. She could hear footsteps running behind her now as she threw the narrow door shut behind her. Ducking around the dresser, she ran across the wooden floor. Creaks and groans greeted her every step. Whoever was behind her knew exactly where she was. She reached the large, heavy door. Grabbing the handle, she leaned against its weight as it slowly swung open. The footsteps were right behind her. She heard the narrow door swing open behind her. Giving the door handle one last pull, she squeezed through the opening.

The stone stairwell met her on the other side as the large, heavy door slammed itself shut behind her. Backing away from the door, she could hear scratching on the other side, like claws scraping the wood, but the door did not open.

Turning around, instead of a wall she saw only darkness. Was this the way she had come? She took one cautious step into the black. And then another. And another. No cobwebs greeted her this time, but after a minute or so of wandering in the dark, an opening of light appeared before her and soon she was walking out the side of the tree and onto the sand. A wave crashed against the rocks and the ocean spray pelted her hair and her face.

Looking back at the Ulvus tree, Fel could see it had returned to its normal size. Just as everything had returned to normal. She could hear wind rustling through the leaves of the tree. She could hear people moving about the camp. Then the shadow of the Onier fell out of the mist and perched again atop one of the rocks.

"Where did you go?" Fel asked.

"Why, I was waiting for you here, Little Sister."

"Some bashers chased me. Bashers that looked like me. What were they?"

The Onier looked at her suspiciously. "The Otherworld has ... protectors? ... no ... guardians? ... no ... no, it has *aspects* of itself that it uses to keep itself whole and to defend against intruders."

Fel looked at the Onier sideways, not sure what to say. "It ... it what?"

The Onier stared at her hand. "What did you take?"

Fel held out the piece of red chalk.

"Ah..." the Onier said, looking it over, even as it made no move to touch it. "That piece is not what it appears."

"Then what is it?" she demanded.

The Onier shrugged its wings. "I do not know, Little Sister, but it will be useful nonetheless. Things from the Other have a way of finding their way back."

"Hrmph," Fel murmured, turning the chalk over in her hands. "Then do you know where I need to go next?"

The Onier's voice came out in a sigh. "I am afraid I am a poor guide, for I do not know for certain. It has been long since I travelled across the Here."

"You're right, you are a poor guide," Fel said as she stuffed the chalk into her pocket. "You don't even know what this knick-knack does, aye."

The Onier's beaked mouth twisted into a grin. "We are all poor in some fashion or another, Little Sister. What I do know is that you will travel with your family for now, for they will take you where you need. Then, if you still wish to help in this thing that we ask, then you must listen again for the music, and if you follow I will meet you along the way."

Then in a blink the Onier disappeared, leaving Fel alone in the fog.

PAR

Par went to see him before he left Vellus for Arc. His meeting with Rufus had left him with just enough time.

Par was several miles deep into the Low 28 now, Alba Calea's outer districts where the population got poorer and less civilized by the block. Traffic was light, since fewer and fewer residents on this side of the city could afford air transportation, but Par could see the streets and sidewalks below him were crowded. Then his navigator pinged and he turned his jumper off the line and aimed it down toward the street corner.

He had to steer around a crowd of prostitutes to reach the front gate of the storage facility. No one else was there except for a night watchman alone in his booth. The security guard gave Par only a cursory glance as he wheeled his jumper into the lot.

Unit 4B. Leaving the jumper outside, he picked a flashlight up off an old couch and shut the door behind him before he picked his way through the crowded unit. The place had been robbed once a few years ago. The thieves made off with nearly everything, forcing Par to refill it. The inconvenience meant less than the relief he felt when he found out the bandits had failed to uncover the storage unit's true purpose. He had asked Rufus, who owned the facility through one of the many business fronts the Alliance maintained, to up the security of the place after the break in.

Reaching the back of the unit, he pressed a hidden button on the wall. Stone grinding against stone echoed against the aluminum walls as a section of the concrete floor retracted, revealing a staircase leading downward. Flashlight on, he descended into the dark. He saw the three tiny lights ahead of him and as he reached the bottom of the stairs, he breathed a sigh of relief at their color: one blue and two green.

There he was, suspended in that chamber full of glowing blue fluid, chords and cables hanging from his arms and his back. The metal cylinder ran from the floor to the ceiling of the concrete room. It tugged at Par's heart every time he saw it. Eye's closed, the boy's face looked out at Par from the blue light of the chamber's window with a face not unlike his own. They had frozen him here almost one hundred and ninety years ago, when the boy had first fallen ill of the same disease that had felled his mother. Even now the disease ate at him, black and red splotches on the boy's feet and legs reminded Par of why he had placed his son in the cryogenic chamber.

Par made sure to visit every time he returned to Alba Calea. He did this even though his one and only son had remained in cryogenic sleep for nearly two centuries. Par told himself the visits were for the boy, but he knew they were more for himself, to remind him of the reason why he did what he did. It was a bargain he had struck with the Alliance, all those years ago. They had needed a Taker, Par had needed someone to take care of his son. And so, Par had bargained and negotiated with them until they had found a way to keep his son alive. Someone, somewhere within the Alliance had discovered how to use the same technology employed by starships to keep passengers safe and asleep during long, subspace journeys and then applied it to Par's mysteriously ill son. A cryogenic chamber had been brought here to Alba Calea where it was modified and augmented to keep his son frozen, aging at only a thousandth the normal rate.

All of that had been so many years ago. Par himself had been blessed, or cursed—it depended on your point of view—with the abnormally long life of a Taker. Those few who underwent the transformation to become a Taker often lived three, even four times longer than the normal human, as a Shade's nano-bots had ways of refreshing its hosts cellular structure. Even now, at two hundred and twenty-seven years, Par barely looked a day over forty. For Par, the elongated life of a Taker had worked out well in the case of his son. The longer he stayed alive, the longer he worked for the Alliance, the more likely that someone, somewhere, might find a cure.

Par knelt by the base of the cryogenic chamber and pressed a button on the control panel. A valve extended from the base and Par simply grabbed ahold of it with his hand. Then he closed his eyes and released his Shade into the machine.

Oh my. It has been a long time since we've come... He hushed his Shade and ordered it to visit his son. The tiny nanomachines swam through the fluid until they climbed inside the boy's mind. Par bowed his head as he listened, and then there it was. The music his son was dreaming about, the songs his sleeping mind was composing or remembering or rewinding in his head as he slept that frozen sleep. The music was slow, as slow as a clock that had been wound back and re-timed so that seconds were days and the days were years. That was the speed at which everything moved within the boy now.

The oboe, I still remember the oboe, and the songs that the instrument and I shared. It has been long, yes, it has been very long since I returned to this place... His Shade was busy within him, sending Par back feelings and images that his son had felt and dreamed while he was away. The Shade would absorb them, keep them, and make them a part of itself. In many ways, his Shade had become part facsimile of his sleeping son, a piece of his dormant consciousness that Par could carry with him wherever he went. Sometimes Par wondered if he kept his son here so that he could always have that piece of him with him, even if it was only pieces of shattered glass and stone from a long abandoned and wondrous castle.

Then his Shade passed him a warm and half-remembered dream of his son's long-dead mother, and Par felt the breath catch in his throat as he knelt to the floor and wept.

Par threw the camo netting over the jumper and tied the whole thing down. He hadn't counted on leaving Vellus so soon. When the Alliance called him to Alba Calea, it was usually for a few months. He would do surveillance, or counter missions, or follow-ups, or any number of other things they needed him to clean up for them here in the Republic's capital city. So, when he opened up the back ramp of his ship and ran a diagnostics check, he was not surprised to see that the reactor was still warm from when he had landed the night before.

Black as the aether in which it travelled, the *Nameless* resembled a dagger in its shape and form. The ship's hull was sleek and molded to foil radar and most other methods of detection. If the conditions were right, the *Nameless* could fly in and out of nearly any occupied area without being detected. Fast and agile, she carried an assortment of weapons, security measures, tricks and traps that Par had added over the years.

The ship was also the closest thing he had to a home.

Oh, he had *places* scattered throughout the galaxy. Places like the apartment in Alba Calea. Or the house he had on Umbrea Prime. Or the shanty on the moon colony of Pontus. But they were only places he stayed, assets that could be abandoned at any moment, and often had. The *Nameless* was the one place he occupied as a permanent resident.

He released his Shade as soon as he set foot in the cockpit, and he felt his companion compress itself and enter into the ship's cold storage unit where it would rest and recharge itself during their journey. The mission here on Vellus had not been overly stressful for his Shade, but the one ahead of them promised to be that and more. They would both need their rest before they reached Arc.

Par strapped into his pilot's seat and ran the *Nameless* through the rest of its pre-flight checks. When they were done, he fired up the engines and the *Nameless* purred like a contented animal. Taking off, Par guided the *Nameless* upward, and it rose through the clear, black night. Once he had cleared the planet's gravity well, his sensors found the next step in his journey orbiting the planet's moon: the Vellus Gate.

The giant metal ring was nearly a third of the diameter of the moon it orbited, but was only a few feet in thickness. In fact, if it were not for the lights attached to it, the gate would be nearly impossible for the naked eye to spot in the blackness of space.

The gates had been discovered, not built. No one truly knew where they had come from, or why they were there. Were they long lost artifacts of an ancient, dead race? Were they temporary tools that some other, more advanced race had left behind? It was a mystery that was still debated today.

The first gate had been discovered near Pontus, the backwater moon that sat on one of the Republic's far-flung borders. There were twelve gates in all, and while some were conveniently located near habitable worlds like this one near Vellus, others were located at more obscure locations, like the Gate of the Hourglass which had been discovered near a nebula of the same name. However, wherever they were, the gates had allowed the different nations of the galaxy to travel, communicate, and trade with one another.

When the *Nameless* was four minutes from reaching the gate's opening, Par saw the lights begin to shift and rotate along the ring. By the time he was two minutes away, the ring was in full spin. Less than a minute away, everything in Par's vision began to bend and blur. This was the part that always made him sick. Light flashed twice and then swirled as if caught in some great cosmic light-sucking vacuum. Then there was an audible *Pop!* and a ringing like a far-away bell as the entire ship was swallowed by the wormhole.

Par gripped the base of his seat so hard he could feel the ligaments in his knuckles begin to strain. Then a dizziness hit him and he swooned as he felt his stomach twist like someone were wringing a wet rag. The monsoon of colors began to rescind, and when Par could finally see straight again, he grabbed the bucket mounted to the wall beside him, yanked it off its magnetic couplers and emptied his stomach into it. Knowing he would be making a gate jump, he had purposefully not eaten much since his meeting with Rufus, but he managed to fill the bottom of the bucket with yellow bile anyway. He shut the lid on the bucket and then wiped the tears from his eyes and the spittle from his mouth.

Out the viewport, Par could see the swirling gray blue shadows that told him the *Nameless* had successfully entered the warped space-time of the wormhole. He sat there dumbly in his seat, slumped against his safety harness and staring out the viewport. Experienced spacers could shrug off a wormhole jump like a young nobleman having his first shot of liquor, but Par had never achieved that level of tolerance. For him a trip through a wormhole was like being hit with a hangover after a three-day bender, without the benefit of the good time.

His stomach churned and he pulled back the lid of the bucket again. This was only a dry heave mixed with bits of more green and yellow bile. He heaved twice more before his stomach finally settled. Finally, he stuck the bucket back against the wall and attached it to the drain.

Turning the controls to their automatic setting, Par left the cockpit. The *Nameless* could navigate the rest of the jump without him—there was nothing to run into or watch out for when traversing the length of a wormhole.

Located in a compartment behind the galley, the *Nameless* had four sleeper cells, though he had only ever used the one. The cell pulled out along the floor like a drawer in a morgue. Working the control panel, Par prepped the cell, checking the air levels and the power supply while he did. It would take the *Nameless* approximately three months of space time to complete the jump from Vellus to Arc. He set the cell's timer for eighty-eight days—he wanted to be awake when they hit normal time again—then climbed inside. Lying in the padded compartment, Par fitted the mask carefully over his mouth, checking and re-checking the straps and re-checking the air tank's level one more time before he activated the release. More than one solo pilot had suffocated in his own sleeper cell because he'd failed to secure his own air supply. When Par's consciousness finally began to slip away, he felt his Shade cozy up next to him as he heard the familiar voice of a young boy come through his mind.

I'm so glad you came. I've found so many dreams we need to share...

ATTICUS

Unifier's sleek, black form skulked over the blue-green planet like a lurking predator. The Coalition's flagship had rotated into a shallow orbit just above Arc's stratosphere as it prepared to make its first drop. Lieutenant Atticus Marius watched the clouds swirling below him as he strode down the center of *Unifier's* drop bay. "Sir, we're up," his platoon sergeant, Jonas Talor, called out to him from the other end of the catwalk. Atticus gave him a thumbs up in return, then pulled his helmet over his head, fastened his chinstrap, and stepped into his own drop-pod. He leaned back against the cushioned wall as the safety straps wrapped around him and the air supply attached itself to the side of his helmet. Then the inside of the pod filled with a thick, blue liquid that would cushion him from the turbulence as the pod fell from the sky. Atticus took a deep breath and let it out slowly, as he listened to his heart racing in his chest.

Finally, a tiny light on the inside of his helmet began blinking red, then yellow. The pod lurched in place, metal striking metal mixed with the groaning of gears. For a second everything was dark. Then the light in his helmet switched to green.

He heard a blast and a hiss and then nothing as his pod fell away from the ship and into the vacuum of space. Twenty-nine other pods joined him, falling away from *Unifier* and through the open vacuum. As the inertia carried them toward the swirling clouds, the only sounds Atticus could hear were his own breathing and the thundering in his chest. Then the atmosphere hit his drop-pod like a drumroll and quickly crescendoed into a roar. He could hear the stabilizer fins wrestling with the air, fighting against the current to keep his pod on an even descent. Minutes passed. Then he felt the rockets fire beneath his feet, slowing his fall as the pod began to break apart, pieces of it simply detaching themselves and falling away. He braced himself. Next, the rockets died out and there was an agonizing pause where his heart jumped into his throat and he felt his mouth go dry. Then there was no pod left around him, only the thick blue liquid, and then in an instant that too was gone. He was falling, falling, falling … then a jerk and a *wooooooshhh* and he was floating. His parachute had deployed. Twenty-nine other parachutes and the fullness of the night sky surrounded him. Nearly there. Looking down, he saw the valley. Right on target. As the ground rose up to greet him, he pressed his legs together, bent his knees, and pulled his risers to his chest, and then he was rolling on the ground.

Atticus had set their rally point near a tall white rock that shot out from the top of a hillside like the fin of a whale. All thirty members of Assassin platoon trickled in by ones and twos until he and Jonas had accounted for everyone. Then they were on the move. Atticus at the lead and Jonas at the rear, the platoon of soldiers marched single file over the hillsides until Atticus spotted the little ravine that was their point of entry to their target. Nearing the top of a berm, he pulled everyone into a halt.

He called up Thrace, his lanky radioman, and Marin, a red-haired sniper and one of his two female soldiers. Together they slid down the back side of the hill and then snuck up to the edge of the ravine where they lay on their bellies and, like wolves scouting a herd of sheep, looked down on the farmyard below. They watched through their night vision to see if anything moved. When nothing did, Atticus had Thrace call back for the rest of the platoon to move up.

The plan divided them into two groups. Jonas would take the sniper section—minus Marin—along with a pair of heavy gun teams and post along the ridgeline. Atticus would take the rest of the platoon and secure the target.

Atticus led his party down through stalks of bamboo to the base of the ravine where they found a dried-up stream bed that led them straight to the fence behind the barn. Far on the other side of the valley, a flare rose into the night sky. Another assault team had found their target. He called his men into a short halt to watch for movement again. Seeing nothing moving in the yard, Atticus signaled his men to move in.

Leaving the brush, they divided into five groups of three and began clearing the buildings. He took Marin and Thrace to clear the barn. Marin kept her rifle trained on the opening as Atticus pulled the creaky door open. Together they cleared the first room, and then he stayed to watch the door as Marin and Thrace worked the rest of the barn. The night was cool and he could feel his skin prickle in the dry mountain air. From somewhere to his north he heard a dog bark. Over the ravine he could see a lightning bug floating above the bamboo, like some ghost flitting among the tops of the leaves. He watched it hover there until it spun itself around and dove back into the bamboo and was gone.

"Sir!"

Atticus turned around to see Marin standing behind three disheveled figures. Civilians. This was why he had insisted they clear every building on the farmstead before they called up to *Unifier*. The mother and her two sons looked like most of the Duathic people they saw these days. Their clothes were little more than rags, they looked like they hadn't bathed in weeks, and they smelled like urine, dirt, sweat and everything else. This family had dark blue skin, black hair, and the yellow eyes that practically glowed in the dark, features that meant these three were likely from the central provinces here on Arc. If so, that meant that this mother and her two sons were a long way from home.

Atticus reached into his breast pocket and pulled out his hand-held translator. "Is there anyone else with you?" he asked.

The translator regurgitated his question into what he hoped was understandable Duathic, and the woman shook her head.

"Are you *sure*? We're not taking anyone prisoner and we're not going to hurt anyone. We just want to make sure everyone is safe, because we're going to blow this farmstead up in a few minutes. So if there's anyone else here, you need to tell us before we drop a big bomb on them." He kept his tone deadpan and matter-of-fact. They usually bought in better that way.

The mother's golden eyes widened as she listened to the translation and then her eyes met his. "*Yau'ma gaurna vest roame...*" She asked:

You're going to do what?

"Boom." He waved his hands in a mock explosion. "Now if there's anyone else here, we need you to tell us where they are so we can get them out. I promise that we're *not* going to hurt anyone."

She nodded as she listened to the rest of the translation. Then she turned around and walked into the next room of the barn. Atticus, Marin, and Thrace all followed and then watched as the Duathic woman grabbed an old shovel from against the wall and pushed away a pile of old, dusty hay in the middle of the floor. Then she reached down, put her finger through a hole in the floorboards and pulled open a hidden trap door. Below, sitting on a pile of grain at the bottom of the hidden room was a teenaged Duathic girl and a little boy no older than three. Both were of the same blue skin and gold-yellow eyes of the other three.

"Well shit," Thrace murmured.

"Fates, woman, how many kids do you have?" Marin said.

The woman frowned as the translator came through. "*Est tue, en varnuum leada pa...*" They are not mine, she said, this is my sister and her son.

"Oh, sorry." Marin blushed. Then she and Thrace helped the young woman and her boy out of the hidden granary.

"*Yau'ma halua, est nau varnuum. Inesta gaulle...*" It's okay, answered the older sister, you are a soldier, not a mother.

"That's right, no mothering for me," Marin laughed as she pulled the boy up on to the floor.

Then Atticus heard someone call him on the radio. It was Mako, one of his squad leaders. They had located their main objective.

Atticus turned to Marin and Thrace. "Marin, get these five back up the hill. Thrace, I want you to call Jonas and let him know she's coming."

"Roger that sir." Thrace replied as Marin gave him a thumb up.

Thrace followed him across the farmyard, where Sergeant Mako and the rest of their party had formed into two semi-circles around a pair of grain silos. Atticus gave his gaunt squat leader a nod as he walked between the two circular buildings.

There it was, on the south side of the silos, just as their intelligence reports had described it: a silvery metal ball around thirty feet in circumference. Atticus pulled a coin from the breast pocket of his uniform and, using his thumb, he flicked it at the metal sphere. There was a hollow clank, and then a wave of blue electric current rolled over the ball's surface and subsided. The sphere *thrummed*.

He turned to his radioman. "Thrace, get *Unifier* on the horn and then ready the signal rocket."

"Yes sir," Thrace said as he reached into his radio bag.

Mako stepped up beside him, his gray eyes studying the metal sphere. "What does this thing even do, sir?"

"Ops says it's some kind of electromagnetic receiver," Atticus said. "Command is worried about these things jamming our communications or something. *Unifier* says they are having a hard time getting a lock on anything down here and they suspect these things are the cause."

Mako looked the sphere up and down again. "But our radios are working fine…"

Atticus shrugged. "Maybe this one's not on."

The sphere *thrummed* again.

"It sure sounds like it's on," Mako said, his voice suspicious.

Atticus rubbed his chin and nodded. He had encountered more than a few mysteries during his two years at war, but never one like this. The thing looked like some menacing metal egg. Whatever it was, it wasn't theirs, and it had been placed in this village for a reason. Whatever the real purpose of these spheres was, Command had decided they were important enough to drop a half dozen strike teams from orbit to blow them up.

Thrace had mounted a small dish-shaped antenna to a tripod base and was aiming the antennae toward the southern horizon. The wiry soldier flipped a pair of switches on his radio pack and his mic buzzed twice. Then, using his compass, Thrace aimed the antenna at the southern horizon, adjusting it left and right until the readout on his radio lit up. Then the lanky radioman handed the mic to Atticus.

"There you go sir. I think I got 'em."

Atticus took the mic from Thrace. "Unifier Main this is Assassin Six, do you copy?"

He held the mic to his ear as the call came back clear. "Assassin Six, this is Unifier Main, go ahead."

He replied. "Unifier Main, we have secured target two alpha five, and we will be sending you the signal shortly, over."

"Roger. Assassin Six, send when ready, over."

"Roger. Assassin Six out."

He and Thrace fixed the signal rocket on a heavy tripod and aimed it at an eighty-degree angle toward the southeast. The rocket would mark the target for Unifier's orbital gunners and let them know that Atticus' platoon had cleared the area of civilians. He had Mako gather everyone else on the other side of the silos while Thrace armed the rocket and set the timer. Then all fifteen of them jogged back toward the ravine. Atticus bounded to the lead, and when he reached the fence line, he stopped and took a headcount of his soldiers as they ran past. The rocket fired right as the first few ran past him, taking off with a blast and then rising into the night sky with a trail of fire following behind it. The last two of his soldiers, the squad leader Mako and his radioman Thrace, were almost to him when something prickled his nose. The faint remains of a campfire.

Mako saw his face as he ran past. "What is it, sir?"

"I don't know," Atticus said as he looked about the trees and the bamboo for the source of the smell.

"Come on sir," Mako whispered, "the fire mission will be coming down in less than five minutes."

Atticus rose and as he stepped toward the fence he saw him. The blue face of a little Duathic boy was looking out at him from the bamboo on the other side of the barn.

"Mako, get them up the ravine," Atticus hissed. Sprinting toward the bamboo, he saw the boy duck back behind the stalks. "Hey!" He cried as he reached the edge of the bamboo and pushed a swath of the stalks aside. The little boy had been right there. "Come on! You've got to get out of here!" he yelled, but then someone grabbed him by the arm. It was Thrace, with Mako behind him.

"Sir, the payload is in-bound in four minutes," the radioman said. "We have to go now to get clear of the blast zone!"

Atticus took one last look at the bamboo and saw only darkness. His gut wrenched and twisted inside of him. Thrace was right.

"Alright," he said. "Let's go."

They made it to the back side of the hill just in time. When the orbital strike finally hit, it was a white-hot beam that shot through the clouds and hit the hillside like a giant spotlight. Then came the flash and a thundering explosion.

They came back as a platoon to walk through the blast zone. The crater was as wide as the farm had been, and there wasn't a single strand of vegetation for several hundred yards. Atticus flipped on his night-vision and walked over to where he'd seen the face among the leaves. Thrace and Mako both joined him as he circled the area twice, but the only things left were ashes and dirt.

Atticus pulled out his navigator and set their course for the north side of the valley. If the civilians kept a steady pace, they could reach the basecamp by sunrise.

TAYLOR

4.28.2388 – Planet Arc, Blackfriar Mountains

Taylor Caelynn picked her bra up off the floor and slid it back on while her lover was still lying on the ground beneath their blanket. His eyelids slowly floated up and down as he dozed in and out of the half-sleep that took him every time they finished. Gaius Ioma wasn't much for the closeness that other couples experienced after, and that worked just as well for her. It made it all the easier to leave. Even if their affair wasn't enough to get them into any kind of formal trouble—as they were both Republican officers of the same rank—if anyone ever found them out, there would be questions. And neither of them needed that.

Major Taylor Caelynn found the rest of her uniform, tied back her dark, braided hair into a bun so that it would fit under her hat, and then checked her complexion in the hand-sized mirror in the breast pocket. Taylor did not wear much for make up on her dark, mahogany skin— she was a wing commander after all, not a fashion model—but she did not want to walk into her command meeting looking like she had just come from a roll in the hay. The meeting was what had brought her to Arc's surface anyhow; the sex was just a scenic detour.

She was pulling on her boots when Gaius finally sat up, rubbed the sleep from his eyes, and looked her up and down as if he were just real-izing she was leaving.

"You … uhm … headed to the command tent?" Gaius asked.

"Yeah, my wing is running patrols for both the low orbit and the ground assault this time, and so the Consul needs me to present and keep everyone up on what the air cover is doing." She found her cap and stood up. "Are they keeping you busy today? You've got to be tired of managing supply lines and commo plans."

When he smiled back at her lazy-like and charming, she knew that was just the question that he had hoped she would ask.

"Oh, we'll see. I've been talking to some people," he said as he scratched himself. "I was hoping to get a little more command time under me before this is all over, and I have some friends who said that might be able to happen."

Always confident and cock-sure in everything he did, to Taylor, Gaius Ioma was like a card player who had stacked the deck in his favor and was now watching everything play out around him. Taylor had just made major a month ago, which at twenty-five years old was almost as fast as anyone could go. Gaius was six months younger than she and had already been a major for almost two years. The pace of his advancement wasn't just exceptional, there were rumors it had been illegal. She had heard from her friends that the people above him had pulled strings to move him up so quickly, strings that were not often pulled. Like so many young nobles their age, Gaius had entered the Republic's Officers' Academy on Menoa at 18, but then graduated a lieutenant at twenty, a year early. His time as a junior officer had been spent at the tip of the spear during the invasion of Troya. During that campaign, Gaius had made captain with 200 men under his command by the time he left that planet. Shortly after, someone had made him a major; he'd been evasive with her about who, and then stuck him into an XO slot. He had embraced his role as a logistical officer, always making certain the people above him came out well—and all the while he had collected favors upon favors and a heady network of friends.

And somewhere in there, the two of them had begun sleeping together.

They had met during the movement from Troya to the moons of Kanor Sol, back when they were both captains. They had met on accident while waiting in line at the officer's mess aboard *Unifier*, where he had clumsily knocked into her, spilling her tray. He had insisted on filling it up for her, grabbing her a double portion every time she told him to stop. He'd then held her food hostage as he brought her over to a table full of his friends. Grudgingly, she found herself eating and fighting back laughter as he held court among the other officers, recounting the bloodiest and funniest stories of his time on Troya. He ran into her again later that night in an officer's lounge, and he made a pass.

She turned him down. Taylor had been a different woman then, full of ambition and focused on her career. Nothing mattered more than the next mission. A year at Kanor Sol changed all that. Mission after mission of escorting logistical patrols between the moons, never shooting a round or firing a missile outside a simulator. The lack of action never dulled her skills—she still trained every minute as though her life would depend on it—but it *had* dulled something else.

For Major Taylor Caellyn, not only was she one of the best Raptor pilots in the entire Coalition, she had a family name as intimidating as any noble in the Republican Fleet. As a result, it was difficult to find men who were not inclined to treat her as either an object or a shrine, and she had long ago tired of both. And so, when a familiar face wearing a major's rank had walked up to her after a meeting and asked if she wanted to get a cup of coffee, she'd said yes. Gaius's casual and confident way with her was refreshing. Now, as the war was nearing its end, she often wondered how long it would be that way.

Taylor smiled as she put on her hat and adjusted her hair. "Well Gaius, I hope you don't get too bored running the camp. But if you do, I suppose you can always just wander your way to the front line. Just be careful if you do, things are going to get a lot more boring after this, and I'll need someone to keep me entertained."

He yawned and stretched, and the muscles on his shoulders tensed as he did. "Oh, don't worry. We're going to knock that city flat before anyone walks in there. Marius knows he has Teum cornered, so he's not going to risk losing any more men than he has to. We have them outnumbered, surrounded, and completely outgunned. They might have a half-dozen tanks in the entire city, and we have over two hundred parked just below this hill."

When he said this, she couldn't help but thinking: *If this is all such a foregone conclusion, then why does this King insist on fighting it out?* She tried to put that thought out of her mind. She wouldn't be on the ground, Taylor told herself; she would be thousands of miles overhead, but still the question lingered.

Gaius rolled out of the blanket, pulled on his pants, and walked over to her. "You know you don't have to worry about me." He grabbed her by the belt, pulled her to him and kissed her again. He closed his eyes as their lips met, but she kept hers open. She could see all of his brash confidence come to a halt and focus on her for that moment their lips met. There was always so much going on with him. Sometimes she wondered if she'd ever uncover a tenth of it. Other times she wondered if she even wanted to.

When the kiss ended, she pushed him away. "Have fun," she said as she smiled. Giving her lover one final wink, she walked out of the tent and into the early morning air.

They were old hands at this trick, sneaking in and out of each other's company. This time, Major Gaius Ioma was overseeing construction of the Coalition's base camp here in the Sinvoresse Valley. So when he heard that she had been invited to the Council of War meeting, suddenly there was an empty tent about a minute's walk from her shuttle's landing spot.

Crossing a beaten path, Taylor stooped as she walked beneath the awning of an open-air tent and emerged on a grassy causeway between two long rows of dark green ridge tents. Soldiers and junior officers were milling about, smoking, laughing, telling stories, cleaning weapons and playing cards. Taylor ignored the lust-filled stares and glances as she walked past. She was used to them, especially in the camps where the crowds were thicker and the women scarcer. The stares and glances had gotten slyer the higher she rose in rank, but not by much. Instead, Taylor tried to think of the meeting she was headed to and the briefing she was about to give, but instead her mind turned back the lover she had left back in the tent. Gaius' family, the Iomas, were a minor house on Alba Calea, one with so little money that they had not been able to afford to buy him a marriage. Instead, his mother had borrowed against the family's estate to pay for his admission into the Academy. To hear Gaius tell it, she had gambled the family's fortunes against his military career. And won. Now here he was, the second in command of the 88th Column, the most feared unit in the Republic's army, and a position normally reserved for a senior nobleman.

Taylor, on the other hand, came from a prestigious house. The Caelynns were esteemed for their political and martial service to the Republic. Her father was a Senator, as was one of her aunts, and she had another uncle who was a Margrave along the Voltine border. Before them there were too many positions and titles to count. She had little doubt that her mother would have a marriage arranged for her when she returned. That was another challenge entirely, one she did not relish facing. But such was the burden of a Senator's daughter.

She wondered again if her relationship with Ioma would last after the war ended, and then she wondered if she wanted it to. He was an enthusiastic lover, full of swagger and charm, but they made little conversation outside of work and gossip. She often just listened. His mind was consumed with intrigue and tactics and the social machinations of a young officer on the make, but little else. He occasionally asked about her family and she politely obliged. Neither of them talked about the future.

She crossed the long, flat rock that worked as the camp's makeshift landing pad and followed another beaten footpath down the hill's back side. The command tents were nestled there at the base of the hill among the pine trees. The path she followed was now flanked by torches, and Taylor found herself surrounded by aides and staff as she searched for the Consul's meeting tent. She followed the path around a grove of trees and there it was, an angular white dome with a wisp of smoke rising from its top that was nearly the size of a house. She pulled her notebook from the cargo pocket of her pants and entered the front flap of the largest tent.

The circular tent was full of more officers ranked both high and low, and the mood of the tent was loud and jovial. Taylor weaved her way through the crowds until she spotted the fire burning at the center of the tent where the eldest and highest-ranking were laughing and talking. There she saw the Consul Marius standing next to the pale, towering figure of Philemon Ieses. Not recognizing anyone, and not knowing where to go, she stepped to the side and pulled out her notebook from her cargo pocket to review her mission notes, but moments later a short, brown-haired aide found her and showed her to a chair about twenty feet behind the fire. There she sat, reviewing her notes and waiting for the meeting to start.

She was reviewing her flight paths when she felt someone sit down next to her. She turned her head and smiled at a familiar peer.

"Why hello, Lucian," she said.

A middle-aged man with flame red hair and a slight frame, Lucian Claudius was the youngest son of Scipio Claudius, the current speaker of the Senate and one of the most powerful politicians in the capital city of Alba Calea. However, despite his family's prestige, Lucian was still ranked major after nearly a decade of military service.

Lucian rubbed the stubble on his chin as he crossed his legs. "Good morning, Taylor. How has Admiral Thorus been treating you up there?"

"Very well, thank you." She smiled politely. "I am presenting today. The Consul and the Admiral asked me to fill everyone in on the air cover." The Claudian family had long been close friends of her mother's, and so she was not surprised that Lucian would visit her, but something behind his eyes told her he had sought her out for more than just pleasant conversation.

"Hrmmm." Lucian nodded as he rubbed his jaw again with his thumb. "I had heard you were in charge of the air cover. Rumor has it, Admiral Thorus gave you a Raptor wing. Is that true?"

"I have held command of *Unifier*'s alpha wing since my promotion, yes," she answered. "My wing will be flying both the atmospheric and the low orbit patrols tomorrow."

Lucian hummed and nodded again. "This war has treated you well, Miss Caelynn. You seem to have found a great deal of success with it."

Taylor gave this only a slight nod. "I have been fortunate." *This one is probing for something. He is trying to read me for some reason, and he's even keeping his eyes to himself. This is far too suspicious; I'll not give him what he wants.*

Lucian then turned to scan the faces of the people nearest them. She could see that his face was dour and wary, as if he did not relish the task he found before him. Finally, he leaned close to her as he spoke in a low and careful voice.

"I have someone who has asked me to ask you a question," Lucian said in a low voice.

Taylor raised an eyebrow and tried not to smile. "What is this? Middle school? Or are you playing at something, Lucian?"

Lucian shrugged as if he were talking about the weather. "It is … a small matter that has little to do with you or I … or so I'm told."

"Or so you're told?" Taylor crossed her arms. Unlike her lover Ioma, she had little time for games like this, but this had amused her and so she waited for his reply.

"Anyhow…" Lucian spoke cautiously. "What they're wondering is if you have any VIPs riding with you during this operation."

Taylor shook her head. "Not in the slightest. I haven't even had a request for one. I had supposed that anyone with a job would be down on the ground, but if someone wanted to ride with as an observer, then I'm sure we can free up a seat on someone's bird." She shrugged. "If they're interesting enough, I could even put them up with me."

Rubbing his chin again, Lucian nodded. "I will relay the message. And I apologize for the cloak-and-dagger, Caelynn. This is a … delicate matter, with many egos involved."

"Boys will be boys," Taylor said as she smiled and rolled her eyes. The delicate song of pride that her male peers danced to had always bemused her. Normally, she tried to avoid getting involved at almost any cost, but this day seemed to have other plans for her. She watched Lucian as he stood and walked away through the crowd to the back of the tent, where he joined a pair of other older officers and struck up a conversation. They were quickly laughing and joking and none of them so much as looked her way.

Taylor was staring at her notes again but pondering her conversation with Lucian when a pair of aides rushed past carrying a long wooden box. Weaving carefully through the high-ranking crowd, they stopped at the center of the tent, set the box on its end near the fire, and pulled out a holographic projector from its inside. The crowd began to hush as the machine hummed quietly and the green light shot out, producing a holographic image of the Sinvoresse Valley that filled the center of the tent. Consul Marius stepped up behind the box-like podium, and the tent fell into a hushed silence. Soon the only sounds in the tent were the crackle of the fire and the hum of the projector. The Consul let the silence linger as he looked out at the crowd, meeting each person in the eye. When his gaze fell on Taylor, she found herself catching her breath. Marius was a formidable man who stood over six and a half feet, square of jaw, with shock white hair and icy blue eyes that seemed to stare right through you. He was as trim and well-muscled as any rifleman at an age when many men were content to be dangling their grandchildren on their knees. He had served seven consecutive terms as Consul, three years each, and each term had been a new war to defend and expand the Republic. When his gaze had made the full tour of the room, he took in a shallow breath, held it, and finally spoke.

"We will strike an hour before sunrise." Marius gestured toward the hologram. "King Teum has his remaining forces gathered around the palace, and it is there we have focused our artillery." As if on command, the thunder of cannon sounded in the distance. "I want each and every one of you to know that I had planned for this war to be over by now. Long over. We won this war at Gravindi. We hammered our point home at Troya. And here on Arc, their homeworld, we have done nothing but march through them like paper soldiers. And yet…" He paused, scowling with disdain and contempt. "And yet, King Teum has repeatedly refused my terms of surrender. I have spoken to his wife, their Queen, concerning the care and wellbeing of those Duathic people who have been unfairly displaced by this conflict and wish to surrender—many of whom the Queen has assembled on the other side of this valley. Some few of you will be assigned to look after them, while the most of you will come with me to strike the final blow on this stubborn King and his brave people."

Then the Consul turned to the map displayed above him. "Now, to the business at hand."

Marius then took his time in highlighting the enemy positions, pointing them out on the map and discussing what they knew of their enemy's size and composition. He then briefly touched on each point of the assault, highlighting drop zones and entry points into the city for various units. Finally, he stood aside and called for the next speaker.

A procession of lesser officers followed, and each discussed their own obligations in turn: communications, radio frequencies, order of movement, logistics, and so on. After a portly intelligence officer waddled away from the podium, Taylor watched as the Consul tuned to look at her.

"Major Taylor Caelynn. If you would be so kind as to inform us of Fleet's plan for our air cover."

She stood and bowed toward Marius. "Thank you, my Consul."

The butterflies that she knew would be there welled up from her belly into her chest as she left her chair. Pushing the fluttering away from her heart, Taylor carried her notebook to the podium. Hundreds of eyes looked up at her as she flipped to the right page. Clearing her throat, she opened her notebook and started straight in. She needed to look down only twice, more from the simplicity of the plan than her own powers of memory. Her predecessor had told her that because the Consul could not directly control Fleet, Marius preferred Fleet to keep it simple and predictable. Because it was in both parties' best interests to keep things on an even keel, Taylor constructed her plan as just that: simple and predictable. Rotating patrols, four in the atmosphere and four in low orbit, each with direct communication to the Consul and Grande Admiral. As she neared the midpoint, she looked to Marius who gave her a subtle nod of approval.

Happy Consul, happy mission, she thought as she turned a page in her notebook.

Just then, the tent flap opened with a gust of wind that pushed a swirl of leaves into the crowd. An old, hunchbacked officer followed behind it, hobbling out of the morning light and into the dim shadows of the tent. His hair was a mottled mass that gathered into a widow's peak atop his head, and a scar ran from the corner of his mouth to the bridge of his hooked and crooked nose. Taylor could see an eyepatch covered his right eye and his left looked about the room like a frightened animal.

Everyone in the tent had gone quiet as the old officer stood there, frozen and flustered by the mass of people staring at him. Taylor heard someone behind her whisper.

"By the beard of Praegma, that's Droesus!"

She heard the old, hunchbacked officer grumble something inane under his breath and try to meander into the crowd gathered along the edge of the tent, but just as he looked ready to sit down Marius stood from his chair and held up his hand.

"If I may have a moment, Major Caelynn?"

Taylor bowed and backed away from the podium. "Of course, my Consul."

She had never seen or met him before, but she knew that Droesus was a Commander, one of five officers with a rank second only to the Consul Marius. Taylor also knew that Droesus himself commanded all of the armor in the Coalition's army. However, as Marius's gaze found him, Droesus cowered.

"Commander Droesus, do you care to explain your late arrival?" Marius asked in an even and stern tone.

Droesus turned and kneeled before Marius, his voice rasping. "A disciplinary matter needed my attention Consul. We caught a man stealing fuel. I apologize."

As the old officer kneeled, Marius drew his shoulders back and scowled. "The squabbling among your men tires me, Droesus. For an officer of your stature and responsibilities, this briefing is more far important than some petty theft."

Droesus appeared to become even smaller as his voice tightened, full of fear. "Again, I apologize, my Consul."

"You will see me after this, Droesus." Then Marius turned back to Taylor and nodded. "Major Caelynn, you may continue."

Taylor nodded back a solemn bow, her face acknowledging both the reprimand that had been leveled and the man who had just handed it out. *I feel like a meteorologist who's been interrupted by a news story about someone famous being murdered.* She put on her best smile and continued.

"Both the orbital and the atmospheric patrols will provide communications relay between ground units and *Unifier* should that be necessary." She pressed the button again to display her communications plan. "My pilots will be monitoring these frequencies to cover that contingency. You can see frequency A is for the atmospheric patrols and frequency B is for the orbital."

She kept the remainder of her presentation concise and professional. When she was done, there were only a few questions, which she easily answered, and then she returned to her seat.

The next speaker was a stout and muscular commander named Titus Agrippa who gave everyone a breakdown on how his drop troops would breach the city itself. While Commander Agrippa was highlighting his landing zones, Taylor stole a glance toward the back of the room. Droesus was now sulking in the far corner of the room with his arms folded and the sullen expression of a scolded child. She had heard about Droesus from Ioma. The man was a running joke among the ground officers who had coined him the nickname "the Old Crow" because of his gruesome appearance and the way he walked. After a moment, Taylor realized she was staring and turned her attention back to the center of the tent before the hook-nosed man noticed her.

The rest of the meeting was uneventful, and she found that little of it pertained to the job she and her wing were called to do, but she paid attention nonetheless, staring at each speaker attentively while jotting meaningless notes and drawings in her notebook. She had found that appearances and relationships were as useful as brains and ambition in the world of military officers, and Taylor had always been careful to cultivate both sides of that equation. When the meeting was finally over, she tucked her notebook back into her pocket and walked out the front of the tent with the rest of the crowd. She saw Gaius at the center of a half-dozen junior officers who were all laughing at a story he was telling. She smiled to herself and began walking toward the hill, but then something slowed her. It was like she could feel something creeping up the back of her neck. She turned around.

The crowd seemed to part, and there stood Droesus, staring at her with his one eye. She met his gaze and then, not knowing why, she nodded and waved meekly. He did not wave in return, but instead he grimaced, turned, and hobbled away in the opposite direction.

What an odd man. Odd and creepy. Perhaps he noticed me staring. Or perhaps he thinks I called attention to him when he tried to sneak in. She decided right then that was enough of the surface today. It was time to head back to orbit. Her shuttle would be waiting to take her back to *Unifier.*

Taylor had crested the top of the hill and was starting out across the great long slab of rock that was the camp's landing pad when she saw a lone figure stroll around to the back of the shuttle. Gaius Ioma. Somehow her lover had beaten her back to her own shuttle. Crossing the landing strip, she watched him lean up against the hull, his arms folded across his chest with a wide grin on his face. *How is it that he's so damned pleased with himself all the time?* She fought back her own smile as she neared the ramp.

"How did you...?" she began to ask, but he cut her off.

"Hey," he pressed a finger to her lips, and she stifled another smile, "I came to tell you I got your fighter wing assigned to the Gloriana for the ride home."

She gave him a curious look. "Are you telling me that you cut a deal to get us on the same ship and then rushed up the hill to tell me?"

He smiled and looked away. A gust of wind blew across the rock face and she turned her head to keep her hair out of her face. When she looked back, he took her face in his hands and he gave her a long, steady kiss.

"No, I made that deal a while ago," he said.

She punched him in the gut, and he keeled over, sucking air in through clenched teeth.

"You dumbass." She frowned. "You're lucky there's no one here but my pilots."

He laughed as he caught his breath. She put her hands on her hips and squared up to him.

"I've had enough of this surface stuff anyway. I was gonna say that if you want a visit again, you gotta come up to orbit and meet me next time."

He leaned one hand against the side of the shuttle. "It's better in zero-g anyway."

She scowled playfully and punched him again, this time in the kidney and then walked up the ramp. "See you later, Gaius. Don't get yourself killed. I'd hate to have to find another friend for the ride home."

She could hear him laughing behind her, and as the ramp closed behind her Taylor finally let herself smile.

ORTHO

4.28.2388 – Planet Arc, Blackfriar Mountains

Ortho Andronicus could not wait for the war to be over. He was reminded of this fact yet again when Marian, his fellow intelligence analyst, tapped him on the shoulder and pointed toward their superior's tent.

"Major Claudius wants a word with you," she said flatly.

Ortho did not like Marian. Not only did she have a tendency to treat him like a subordinate, which he was not, but he also suspected that she was sleeping with their commanding officer, Major Lucian Claudius, the very man she had just directed him to meet. This suspicion was only confirmed in Ortho's mind every time he was sent out on a detail. And Ortho was assigned to nearly *every* work detail involving a field mission. Ortho hated field missions. He hated the rain and the cold, he hated field rations, he hated trying to shit outdoors, and he particularly hated listening to the soldiers snicker at him behind his back as his short, pudgy, and un-athletic body attempted to keep up with the infantrymen, the scouts, the cavalry, or whoever else Major Claudius saw fit to inflict upon him.

So when Marian tossed her freshly curled blonde hair and pranced back to her desk, his first thought was that this figured. It was likely the final few days of this miserable war. Why wouldn't they send him out as the sacrifice yet again?

Ortho left his things at his desk and walked out of their tent to find the major just outside, sitting on a folding chair and smoking his pipe. Ortho stopped within a pace of the officer and then stood at attention.

"You needed to see me, sir?"

"You can relax, Andronicus." The major waved at him dismissively.

"We're boots on the ground. No need for that formality here." Ortho relaxed as Lucian took another puff on his pipe. "Apparently one of Consul Marius's aides broke both of his legs on the drop from orbit, and Marius came to me today and asked if I had anyone competent enough to keep up with him. Naturally I told him that Specialist Ortho Andronicus has more field experience than anyone else in my shop."

I have the most field experience because you fuck me every chance you get, you big, fat, arrogant, lazy prick, Ortho thought as he forced a smile on to his face. "Yes sir," he said. "It would be an honor to work for the Consul. sir."

"Good." Lucian smiled and pointed with the end of his pipe. "Then grab your gear and report to central command ASAP. The Consul's tent is at the bottom of the hill once you cross the landing strip right over there to the north."

Ortho bowed. "Of course, sir. I'll be right away, sir." *Right after I get done shitting on your bunk, sir.*

Lucian stood and stretched. "Good man. I'm sure the Consul will have lots for you to do." Ortho tried not to scowl as the major took another puff of his pipe. "If you make a good first impression, you might see yourself promoted before this whole thing is over. The Consul tends to take care of his own, you know."

I don't want a damned promotion. I want to go home, you fuck. Preferably in one piece. Ortho pushed his smile even wider. "I'll do my best, sir."

Then the major tapped him on the chest with his index finger. "Oh, and before I forget, if you could get that analytics report to me tonight before you get too busy, I'd appreciate it."

That's Marian's assignment you lazy, stupid, shit-fuck of an officer. I hope she gives you chlamydia. "Shouldn't be a problem, sir." Ortho swung his thumb back toward the tent and his desk. "I'm about half done with it anyway."

"Good man. Good luck, Andronicus." The major poked him with the stem of his pipe. "See you on the other side."

Fates, I hope you step on a land mine. Ortho saluted with a grin. "You too, sir."

It could be worse, Ortho thought as he walked away. *He could have sent me to a line infantry unit or one of the cavalry sections. The Consul of the*

Republican Army is unlikely to be at the very fore of the assault, and not even Marius would put himself in that much danger... Right?

Walking across the Coalition base camp, his ruck sack slung over his back with his duffle perched atop that, Ortho's thoughts wandered to the steps in his life that had brought him here. He had grown up the son of an accountant. His father and mother had encouraged him toward intellectual and creative pursuits, not athletics. As such, he played three instruments, was familiar with the works off all the great philosophers from Praegma to Carnegine, and even knew the religious texts that drove the Illyar and the Duathe. In school, he had excelled so highly at math that he had learned the finer points of calculus by age twelve, and by thirteen his father had taken to having his son look over his accounting work to check for errors. By the time Ortho had graduated school, he had a number of offers from different top universities, including the Institute of Alba Calea, but then King Teum had started blowing up Republican trade liners and Ortho was drafted into the Army.

He had graduated from the Military Intelligence school on Selteene and was thrilled to find out that he had been assigned to the Republican Army's central command. His talent at analytics quickly won him a job in Consul Marius' intelligence division, where his superiors immediately began fighting over who could take the most credit for his work. Ortho found he didn't mind this much. He wasn't there for advancement, and back then, every day at work was like a puzzle waiting to be solved.

He was also extremely grateful to be assigned to an office instead of a line unit because, quite frankly, the Fates had not granted him the physical gifts to excel at field work. He stood just over five feet three inches (in boots) and struggled to move with the standard armor, weapon, ammo, and rucksack that a soldier had to carry over long marches. His was shaped less like a powerball athlete and more like a potato. Obstacle courses were a nightmare. Shooting ranges had made him nervous and his hands often shook when he fired his rifle.

Ortho had lasted nine months at the Army's Intelligence Division before someone (he didn't know who) had decided he was too good at his job to be kept at a desk and he had been shipped off to Major Lucian Claudius' office. Major Claudius immediately recognized his talent and—unlike his previous superiors—had no time for anyone who actually knew what they were doing. The more competent Lucian's office appeared, the more work would be assigned to it, and Major Claudius had little time for anything as trivial as work. Once Lucian saw how motivated Ortho was, the major immediately solved the problem by sending his new specialist out into the field every chance he could.

It hadn't taken Ortho long to catch on to Major Claudius' game and respond in kind by taking no initiative at all, but even then, Ortho's name was still the first to come up whenever the major had to volunteer one of his men for a mission. And so, rather than sitting behind a desk and analyzing intelligence reports and mission debriefs, as was his strength, Ortho had been sent out on one miserable and horrifying mission after another. Over the ensuing months, he had lost count of the number of times he had been nearly killed, maimed, or utterly humiliated. The most terrifying firefight Ortho had participated in had been a twenty-minute shootout alongside a long-range reconnaissance unit while they were awaiting pickup on a mountainside. An entire company of Duathic light infantry had chased them up from the valley until they had Ortho and the recon platoon pinned up on a ridge. It was dark and Ortho's night vision had refused to work. He had fired blindly in the general direction of the enemy for most of the night, at times firing with his eyes closed. Once, near the end of the fight, he had simply held his carbine over the top of a rock and pulled the trigger until its magazine was empty. His main focus during the entire episode had been to avoid shooting anyone he knew (and from that perspective Ortho was very proud that he had succeeded), and more importantly, to survive. When the Strykers had finally swooped in and rescued them from the ridgeline, he'd done his best to not cry from relief, then failed at that and cried all the way back to base. He still shuddered from the memory of the reconnaissance soldiers laughing at him as he wept.

His legs ached as he trudged up a hill, and the weight of his belongings pressed heavily on his shoulders as he wondered what horrors and misadventures awaited him in the coming hours. Cresting the hill, he spotted the Consul's tent at the bottom, set amongst the deep blue colored pine trees that dominated this side of the Sindorum valley. He paused outside the tent, knowing that his meager rank meant that barging into the Consul's tent at an inappropriate time could mean a sharp rebuke, or worse. However, after looking around at the other tents and seeing no one who could help him, he realized he had little choice. Either stand outside and be chastised for not reporting, or push through and be yelled at for barging in. He chose the latter.

Pushing through the tent flap, a pair of tall and intimidating infantrymen stood to meet him. Ortho read their name tapes as they cornered him against the tent entrance. Brennen, the taller of the two, was a blond-haired and red-faced mountain of a man with a bored and uninterested look. Alek, the shorter guard, was still a full head taller than Ortho, and only a wisp of a black mustache decorated his otherwise hairless head. Both men were privates, a rank below Ortho.

Alek leaned down in glowering fashion as he addressed Ortho. "What are you doing here, Specialist?"

Ortho took a nervous breath and spoke quietly. "I was ordered to report to the Consul's tent. I'm from Intel."

The bald, mustachioed guard looked him up and down, reading his name tag and rank aloud. "Specialist Andronicus?"

Ortho realized he was almost cowering and then straightened himself. "Yup. That's me!"

"It's Siphone's replacement," Brennen yawned. "He's just early."

"I am?" Ortho asked, nervous. Was early good? It was better than late, but that did not always mean it was good. Brennen took him by the shoulders, spun him around, and pushed him back out of the tent.

"Here. Let me help you out so you aren't stuck in here with us." Leaning out the tent flap, Brennen pointed as he spoke. Ortho followed the big man's outstretched hand to a beaten path that lead to a much larger tent with a plume of smoke wafting out its top. "They're all in there having a big meeting. You need to go report to Sergeant Martin. He's in there, probably seated near the back. He'll get you taken care of."

Ortho immediately realized the two infantrymen were simply trying to get rid of him, so he conjured a protest. "Can't I wait here until they're done? It's not like they need little old me in a command meeting anyway."

Lazily, Brennen pointed at the tent again. "Naw, Martin said for us to send you to him if we saw you. Don't worry, just tell the guard at the door that you're with Sergeant Martin and you should be fine. We'll radio and let them know you're coming."

Ortho cursed under his breath as the two guards walked back inside the tent. He didn't want to barge in on an officers' meeting, but he also didn't want to wait around in awkward silence with a pair of guards who didn't want him around. There was no way around it. Sullenly, he trudged down the beaten path.

The guards at the next tent were holding the flap open for him as he arrived. They silently pointed Sergeant Martin out to him, and Ortho slunk his way through the tent with his best impression of a wet dog. Martin was a lanky redheaded man in his mid-twenties who sat straight up in his chair like a grade-schooler in the front row of an arithmetic class. Ortho could always tell a support soldier by his uniform. Where Ortho's was worn and faded from days spent out in the field in the sun and the dirt, Martin's was crisp and clean from a soldier who worked his days away in an office and took care of his appearance. Martin pulled up an empty chair when he saw Ortho coming, and Ortho gratefully pushed his bag between the chair's legs and sat down as discreetly as possible.

Martin leaned over to Ortho ear as he sat down. "So you're the Intel guy?"

"Roger that," Ortho whispered back.

Martin looked under Ortho's chair. "I see you brought your gear. That's good. The Consul will want to meet with you after the meeting, and the sergeant major will too, I assume, so you had better be squared away."

"I'll do my best," Ortho said.

"You had better. The sergeant major can be …. critical." Martin nodded at him. "I won't be going with you, but just listen here to the briefing so you have an idea of what's going on while you ride with the Consul. You don't have to take notes, just listen."

Ortho nodded and looked to the front of the tent where a young woman in a flight suit had taken the podium. Her uniform announced her as a Major Caellyn and she was a black skinned Illyari woman with a lithe and athletic figure who carried herself with the swagger of a successful fighter pilot. Listening to her talk about flight zones and air cover, Ortho could not help wondering if she was as uppity and condescending to her peers as Marian was to him. For some reason that he couldn't figure, he doubted she was.

The pilot was half way through her speech when Commander Droesus came barging through the tent flap, a blast of cold air following him inside. The crooked old officer even managed to look surprised when Marius noticed his late arrival and began chewing him out. Ortho frowned at the display. If Droesus had been trying to sneak into the tent, as Ortho had, he had gone about it all wrong. You couldn't pull out the flap like it was a book cover, as that always caused it to billow as the hot air escaped the tent. No, if you wanted to sneak into a heated tent properly (and *every* officer's tent was heated) then you had to push the flap in gently and slide your way sideways through the opening. However, as Ortho watched Marius chastise Droesus for his tardiness, he realized that officers rarely had any use for such tactics. These were the tools of the enlisted. The soldiers. Ortho did not excel at many things, but he knew how to stay out of trouble.

Shortly thereafter, the pretty major finished speaking and every male in the tent pretended not to stare as she walked back to her seat. From there, the rest of the meeting was boring and uneventful. No one else got yelled at and no more pretty women got up to speak. Just old, grizzled men who talked at length about plans and things that would have little impact on whatever role Ortho would play in this miserable affair. The meeting droned on and on, and he found himself regretting not finding a way to waste more time before showing up at Marius's tent. When the Consul finally adjourned the meeting, Sergeant Martin tapped him on the shoulder and pointed for Ortho to meet him outside. Happy to finally be leaving, Ortho hopped out of his seat and grabbed both of his bags and carefully weaved his way through the crowd of officers and orderlies.

Martin was resting his hands on his hips as he watched Ortho trudge out of the tent carrying one bag over his shoulder and the other on his back.

"Isn't there somewhere you could leave all that gear?" the redhaired sergeant asked.

Ortho tried to nod agreeably. He'd once had a group of tankers defecate in his boots while he was taking a shower. After he'd seen the guards at Marius' tent look at him funny ... well, he wasn't taking any chances. "Wherever you have that's safe, sergeant."

Martin looked him up and down and snorted. "I'm surprised Claudius didn't send us someone in better shape. You're travelling with the Consul himself, you know."

Fuck you, you pampered piece of shit, Ortho thought as he forced a smile. "Oh I know, sergeant. I wish I had more time to go to the gym, but Major Claudius keeps sending me out in the field."

Raising an eyebrow, Martin looked him up and down again. "I suppose. Follow me."

Martin led him back to the Consul's tent where the two guards, Brennen and Alek, were playing cards. Both gave him long looks as he re-entered the tent. Ortho realized that these men were likely part the Consul's personal security detail, and had been—and likely still were—sizing him up.

Martin pointed him toward the tent's far corner. "You can lay your stuff over there. The Consul's in another meeting right now, but he'll get you situated after that. He likes to personally see to all of his guys going out with him. He's like that. Cares about his guys. Brennen and Alek are with you, so there shouldn't be any problem with you being here. Just stay close so we can find you later."

Ortho gave him his best I'm-a-peon smile. "Thank you, sergeant. I'll just sit tight."

"Good man." Businesslike, Martin gave a gruff nod to Brennen and Alek, neither of whom seemed to want to acknowledge Martin's presence, and then walked back out the tent door.

Ortho sat down on his duffle in the corner and pulled out his book, *The Seduction of Reality,* by the prophet Carnegine. Turning to where he had left off last night, he could feel the eyes of the other two soldiers looking at him.

"Whatcha got there?"

Ortho waved the book's cover at them. "Just some philosophy. Carnegine actually, if you're familiar. I like to keep a book in my pack for when I get sent out. My boss sends me out on mission a lot. Dunno why. He just does."

The two burly soldiers looked at each other and Ortho got the distinct impression that his response had not won any popularity points.

Alek was shuffling the deck of cards while Brennen took a sip from his canteen and then smirked at Ortho.

"Sounds like something you read when women think you're ugly."

Ortho turned a page and pretended not to hear him. *Just because I know how to read…*

"Ain't gonna have time for reading tomorrow," Alek said with a condescending grin as he began dealing the cards.

"I expect not," Ortho replied. "I imagine we'll be pretty busy."

Brennen snorted. "Busy. Sure. You're from Intel, right?"

"Yeah." Ortho set his book down now and looked Brennen in the eye. He knew where this conversation was going next.

"And you said you get sent out a lot?" Brennen asked.

He nodded. "Almost every other week. Usually for a few days at a time. Although I'm sure that's nothing compared to what you guys do."

He knew better than to cross an infantryman's ego. Whether the infantryman in question was a machine gunner with a hundred kills or if he was a scrub assigned to guarding a water tank, an infantryman had signed up to fight. To kill. And possibly to die. An intelligence specialist like himself had not, and they almost always made sure he knew that. Even though nothing was being said out loud, Ortho knew that that was the topic at hand.

"You ever been in a tic, Specialist?" Alek asked flatly.

There it was. TIC stood for Troops in Contact. A firefight. Violence.

"A couple small ones," he said truthfully. "Nothing big."

Alek nodded with some small degree of approval. "Good. Then maybe you'll be alright."

Brennen snorted and picked up a card. "Siphone sure wasn't."

Alek tossed a card down onto the ammo crate. "That was just bad luck."

"Bad luck and a lot of stupidity," Brennen murmured.

Both men chuckled then as they continued their card game.

"That's alright," Alek said softly. "Intel's got some balls on him."

"See if he's still got 'em in a few hours," Brennen said a little louder. "See if they're still hangin' or if they suck up into his chest."

Ortho let the comment pass and turned a page in his book. The two soldiers laughed at each other. The next hour passed in relative silence.

The book served to take his mind off the tasks ahead, and he found his thoughts drifting to a common theme among soldiers of his rank: what life would be like once the war was over. His plan was to stack his resume with commendations, letters of recommendation, references, and contacts, so he could apply for the coziest desk job he could find when he got out. He liked the idea of becoming a data analyst for Republic Central Intelligence. It couldn't be that hard. He had aced their practice test, and they were known to recruit Intel grunts from the Army. However, failing that, he could always find a job with a contractor. Safeguarding mining shipments from bandits, or defending the Republic, it was nearly all the same to him. He just wanted an air-conditioned office and a fat paycheck. Perhaps one day he'd even have a secretary.

For now, he just had to make it through the day. Should the Fates be willing to see him through, he would be forever grateful. He had gotten quite cozy, perched on his duffle bag and reading his book in the heated tent. The words on the page began to blur and he felt his head begin to bob. Lying on his back, Ortho nestled his head against the back of his rucksack and the final thought that drifted through his waking mind was how glad he was that this would all be over soon.

ATTICUS

4.28.2388 - Planet Arc, Blackfriar Mountains

The two mothers, whose names were Mala and Lyre, had agreed to stay at the camp with her two sons. Initially, she had wanted to be released so she and her two boys could travel on foot to this refugee camp on the other side of the valley. However, when Atticus told her that the Coalition planned to bomb most of the valley on its way to the capital, she had changed her mind.

Atticus was signing and initialing the last few pages of the paperwork when Sergeant Talor came through the tent flap. Atticus' platoon sergeant was a broad-shouldered and barrel-chested man of middle age who had a perpetual grizzled shadow that crept over his face every day. Atticus gave his compatriot a nod, and Jonas grunted in response before folding his arms over his chest and watching a pair of clerks who were fussing over the two boys. All the while, Jonas held the irritated looked of someone who disliked being around other soldiers who were much cleaner than he was. Atticus quickly finished the last few pages, and then he and Jonas went looking for the nearest cook tent. Minutes later, they were eating potatoes and some local bird the cooks had grilled, when Jonas pointed his fork at him.

"You know that no one would have blamed you if you'd left them there."

Atticus nodded as he swallowed a potato skin. "Yeah, I guess I don't want anything like that keeping me up at night when this is all over."

"There's no helping that." Jonas managed to smile and scowl at the same time. Atticus wasn't sure how he managed it, but he did. Atticus' running theory was that it was the chewing tobacco the man consumed like candy. Years ago, Sergeant Jonas Talor had been an officer before someone had stripped his officer's commission. Atticus had never gotten the story out of the older man, and he had never found anyone else who knew it. However, when Atticus had arrived at Troya, his father, the Consul Marius, had personally seen to it that Sergeant Talor was assigned Atticus' enlisted counterpart. Nearly two years later, Atticus was still the lieutenant of a reconnaissance platoon and Jonas was its senior sergeant.

Jonas pulled out a piece of paper from his coat and handed it to Atticus. "And before I forget, you're putting Thrace in for a commendation, the same as he is for you."

Atticus grimaced as he picked the meat off a leg bone. "Commendations?"

"A bronze arch for him and a white star for you."

Atticus looked at the paper as he chewed another bite of meat. "He certainly deserves it. I'll get it filled out today. I suppose I couldn't' talk him out of filling out mine?"

"It's too late for that, sir." Jonas sucked the meat off a bone. "I had him turn it in while you were seeing to that family."

All Atticus could do was shake his head and sigh. Both men knew how much Atticus' peers hated him, how many knew he'd been given command of an elite combat platoon because he was the Consul's only son. Not that his job had helped him move up; he was still ranked a first lieutenant after a year of being eligible for promotion to captain. He and his father hadn't spoken much during the war—they never had, really, but everyone knew he was being kept in a combat position for as long as possible, and that fact had only served as another reason for his fellow junior officers, who were shuffled about and traded like game pieces, to resent him even more.

All this was more reason for Atticus to focus on his day-to-day. Mission after mission came down for Assassin platoon, each more dangerous than the next. He often wondered if his superiors were using him to impress his father, or if they were simply trying to get him killed. One week he and his platoon were dropped behind the enemy battle line to scout enemy artillery positions, the next they'd be sneaking up to Duathic camps, helping the snipers spot the command tents. He and Jonas had sent twenty-one soldiers home: thirteen to the hospital, eight in boxes. They had talked about visiting each one when they got back, and it was strange to think how close they were now, looking across the valley at the Duathic capital. They each finished eating and made their way back across the camp to find their men.

The Coalition war camp was centered on a flat clearing that jutted straight off the face of Mount Gedron, the smallest peak that bordered the Sinvoresse Valley. A long, flat rock nearly a kilometer in length served at the camp's landing pad, and Atticus and Jonas passed by just as a pair of box-like shuttles were landing. Atticus and Jonas had to shield their eyes as the backdraft of the engines pelted them with debris. They crested the peak of the hillside and followed a beaten path along the hill's northern ridgeline. Down below, Atticus could see where a column of tanks had parked themselves neatly on the northern side of the rock. Many of the tankers were lying in the sun, cooling themselves in the mountain breeze while they took their meal.

Descending into the valley, he and Jonas passed an Umbrean artillery line as they were setting up their guns. The Umbrean replicants had a queer fascination with the humans of the Republican army, and Atticus could feel the uniform line of men glancing at them as they passed. Each replicant was a male of average height and a muscular build. An Ieses nobleman, nearly three meters in height, his skin pale like ash and eyes like black marbles, circled among his troop of nearly identical men, softly giving orders in a calm and quiet voice. Beyond that, the gun line was eerily quiet as they always were. No crude jokes were being traded among the men—none of the soldiers were upset or frustrated, no one cursed.

When they had passed out of earshot, Jonas stole a glance over his shoulder and grumbled, "Damned strange, that lot." Atticus nodded and Jonas quietly continued. "I don't know about you, sir, but I've seen enough of these pale Umbrean noblemen. Give me a country without a king. I'll take my freedom with thinking included, thank you very much." He glanced back at the Umbreans again, as if he were paranoid they might be followed. "Your father, the Consul, should never have negotiated with them. Nothing good will come from honoring their claim to that damned temple. Just like nothing good came from their involvement at Gravindi."

"And what if we hadn't negotiated? We might be fighting them as well right now," Atticus quipped.

"And what if we were? I wouldn't mind putting a few of them down just the same as anyone else."

Atticus smiled and shook his head. The two of them had visited the same conversation before in many forms and the young lieutenant saw no reason to visit the debate again now.

They reached the base of the valley, and there they found the cave where the rest of their platoon had made camp. The cave was a hidden thing where a cleft of rock sat tucked behind a grove of pine, well out of view of anyone, friendly or otherwise, who might come nosing around. Just as Assassin platoon liked it. The sun was high overhead, but the cave was dry and cool, and their men had posted a rotating guard at its mouth. A stream, fed from the mountains, curved its bank not far from the cave mouth, and his soldiers were taking turns bathing in the cold mountain water before lying down.

Atticus was the last to tuck himself into his sleep sack where he fell asleep to the thunder of the Umbrean artillery. It was early evening when someone shook his shoulder, jostling him awake. He pulled the cap from his face to find one of his riflemen standing over him.

"Hey, sir..."

Atticus grunted as he turned over. "What do you need, Roman?"

"There's some guy from headquarters here to see you."

"What's Captain Barca need now?" Atticus sat up in his sleeping bag and looked toward the mouth of the cave. A short and bookish soldier in a sharply pressed uniform was standing there, a thick pair of glasses set on his nose. He held a clipboard at his waist. As Atticus was staring at him, the soldier shifted nervously and stepped out of the shadows, allowing Atticus to read the nametag sewn to his jacket. It read: "Ortho." "It's not our headquarters, sir, it's the Consul's man," Roman said in a low voice. "They want to see you in the command tent. High Command, that is. He won't say what for."

"Do they just want me? Or me and somebody else?" Atticus climbed out of his sleep sack and pulled on his boots. Anytime someone of his rank was called into High Command it was usually because someone was in trouble—or it was a big mission, which was just another word for trouble.

"No sir. Just you. He said you could leave Sergeant Jonas here."

"Well shit," Atticus sighed as he stood. "I guess you can let the old bastard sleep then."

High Command had made camp at the bottom of a rocky ravine covered in pine, and the trees and the rocks cast long shadows over everything below. Atticus followed the soldier to large tan tent flanked by a half dozen honor guard.

"You can wait here, Lieutenant," Ortho mumbled as he gestured to a fire pit that was dug in the earth next to the tent. Atticus took a seat on one of the folding chairs that were arranged around the pit and waited. The skittish little aide scurried off, leaving Atticus alone with nothing more to do than to watch the embers smoldering in the fire pit and look at the aides and junior officers that flitted about in ones and twos from tent to tent.

Then he heard someone inside the tent raise his voice. Someone was arguing. Atticus tried not to listen at first, but then his curiosity began to get the better of him. Like all junior officers he was fascinated by the inner conversations of his superiors, and soon he found himself sliding his chair closer to the wall of the tent so he could listen in. When he finally got close enough to pick out the words, the first voice he heard was his father's, the Consul Marius.

"Commander, I have reached the end of my patience. Your list of transgressions is baffling: You lost half of your fuel late in the invasion of Troya, leaving Ioma's company stranded in that mountain range. You travelled seventy-four klicks in the wrong direction after landing on Zietagen…"

"Your engineers blew up the wrong bridge on Acteum…" a voice of iron and silk cut in. Atticus guessed by the accent it was Philemon, the Umbrean Grande Admiral. "…you stranded my armor for two weeks."

"And you've made me apologize to the Grande Admiral more times than I can count," Marius continued. "It is my observation that you do not have difficulty taking orders—you are not insubordinate, rather, you have only difficulty carrying them out. You are consistently late, as you proved this morning, and so are your officers. Your soldiers are unruly and undisciplined. You have no tactical instincts, but you are even worse at logistics."

Philemon cut in again, "Remember when you accidentally dumped those armor-piercing rounds into Gravindi Harbor? I do. We could have ended the siege a week earlier if not for that stunt."

Even sitting outside the tent, Atticus could feel the towering Umbrean's steely gaze. He had only seen Philemon twice, but each time he had been struck by the Grande Admiral's intense demeanor.

Inside the tent, Atticus could hear Marius sigh, "I have tried to counsel you. I have tried to instruct you. As a last resort, I have even tried punishing you. Nothing has worked. Now, on the eve of us ending this war, I find I cannot trust you to lead my armor. Commander Droesus, I am not stripping you of your rank, because you are my friend— but I *am* putting a lesser man in charge of your column. Tomorrow, Major Ioma will be leading the Fifth Armored. By my command, he will retain you as his advisor."

A long pause followed, and Atticus sat still and silent. The guards who had earlier been trading jokes and stories moments now stood silent as they quietly shuffled their feet.

Finally, he heard Marius say, "Am I understood, commander?"

"Yes, I understand fully, my Consul." Droesus' voice—and part of his hip—had been taken from him many years ago, in a prior war, and Atticus had to strain to hear the harsh whisper he spoke in. "I have but one life to give to my Republic, and I give it freely. I will do whatever it is that our duly elected Consul requires. Long live the Republic."

"Then you are dismissed."

Atticus heard the shuffling of the old commander's feet as he limped to the front of the tent. *Shuffle-shuffle-step ... shuffle-shuffle-step.* Like some wounded animal crawling toward the door. Shifting his chair back toward the fire, Atticus tried to make himself as small as possible before he saw the tent flap move and the old hunchbacked officer lurched out into the daylight. Droesus spotted him anyway, and their eyes met as the old, crooked man gave him a wild and frightened look before he hobbled away in such a manner that Atticus felt he was watching an old dog that had just been kicked in the gut.

Atticus stood then, because he didn't want to be caught sitting by who-ever came out of the tent next. However, when the tent flap moved it was neither Marius nor Philemon who came out. The man was an Umbrean, that much Atticus could see plainly, but shorter than the others, just less than two meters in height with ashen gray-blue skin and white pupil-less eyes. The man stopped when he saw Atticus. He stood at the mouth of the tent, staring at him. He did not have a uniform, nor did he wear a rank of any kind on his clothing; rather, he wore a set of black cargo pants and a loose-fitting shirt of dark green with leather bracers bound tightly to his forearms. The man's stare forced Atticus to look away, and then look back. When their eyes met the second time the other looked away, shook his head, smiled, and walked away in the opposite direction of Droesus.

Then the flap moved again and the next man had to stoop low as he exited the tent. Philemon Ieses was the eldest son of Umbrea's ruling family. The Kingdom had been without a king since the beginning of recorded history. Instead, they were governed by the Family Ieses, who were—according to their holy text, the Manomena—appointed their nation's stewards by their ancient and nameless god.

The Grande Admiral drew himself up to his full height, nearly three meters, and towered over Atticus. An Ieses was different from the aver-age Umbrean. The Kingdom possessed many masters of genetics, and the Ieses had used their nation's expertise to alter their family's genetic framework. An Ieses was taller, faster, stronger, and more intelligent than a natural Umbrean. As a result, they also lived much longer, several hun-dred years on average. Their teeth were pointed, eyes black as marble, and while their skin was ashen and pale like other Umbreans, but it also had a leathery quality that made them look even more unnatural and inhuman. They could also consciously project pheromones that would alter the mood of any living carbon-based being around them, which only added to their terrifying presence. And so when the giant of a man looked at him, Atticus had to physically keep himself from trembling.

"Young Atticus Marius. I thought I might see you out here…"

"Y-yes, Grande Admiral." Atticus fought back a stammer. "I was called to meet with the Consul about something."

"Indeed you were." The towering Umbrean smiled down at him.

"I have been speaking with your father for much of the morning, and there's something I wish to tell you before you take yourself inside."

Atticus bowed as deeply as he dared. "Of course, Grande Admiral. I'm all ears."

"Indeed, and as you should be." Philemon took two giant steps toward him and got down on one knee as he looked Atticus in the eye. He spoke in a low, smooth voice. "Young Atticus Marius, I have some advice for you, boy, so listen and listen closely. I know you've been on reconnaissance duty for most of this invasion, sneaking around at night, calling in air strikes, gathering intelligence, and on and on; but now you're about to go to the front lines, as far out front as front gets. There is very little sneaking around out on the tip of the spear, and so here is a piece of advice from an old soldier who fought Teum back when we were both young. Ride swiftly and beware their ambushes, Young Marius. These Duathe never fight fair. From behind, from the sides, from above, but never face-to-face. And so be wary and watchful, for they will take you the moment you are not." Philemon slapped Atticus on the shoulder so hard that he nearly fell over. Then the Ieses stood and laughed, "Now sally forth, we're all waiting for you to make you father proud. He waits for you inside."

Then the pale giant stood and walked away. As Atticus watched the towering man moving through the ravine, he could feel the gaze of the whip-thin shadow of the man who had preceded the Grande Admiral watching him from somewhere he could not see. Atticus found himself looking at the ground then, thinking of what the giant had said to him. He took a deep breath and let it out slowly, before he finally put his head down and walked through the mouth of the tent.

The smells of leather, gun oil, and tea leaves hit him as the tent flap folded shut behind him. Near the back of the tent, Atticus could see the shadow of his father pouring himself a cup of tchai. Taking a deep breath, Atticus stepped to the center of the tent where he stopped and stood at attention.

"Come here Lieutenant, I need to speak with you." The tone Consul Marius spoke with was the casual commanding voice of a superior to a subordinate.

"Yes sir," Atticus said quietly as he walked to the rear of the tent.

"You may stand *at ease*, Lieutenant." Marius set the kettle back on the fire and turned toward his son.

"Have I ever told you the story of Consul Quintus Flavius?"

"No sir. You haven't, sir."

Marius propped himself on the corner of a wooden table and sipped his tchai. "Quintus Flavius was a Consul during the first Ribari uprising some six or seven hundred years ago, back when the Republic consisted of two continents on our homeworld of Vellus." The Consul propped his foot up on a chair as he took another sip of his drink. "He was a brilliant strategist, and so he easily put down the rebellion in a pair of battles where he took ten of the enemy for every man he lost. After the final battle, his subordinates lauded him a genius, and when he returned home, he was given every heroic title the Senate could foist upon him." Marius took a long sip of his tchai as he considered his story. "When it came time for peace negotiations, Consul Flavius demanded he be put in charge and the Senate entrusted him without question. After meeting with the Ribari rebels, Flavius promised that they could keep their lands and their men so long as they set down their weapons and promised never to rise up again.

"The next year the Ribari rose up in revolt again. The Senate immediately voted for Consul Flavius to again lead the war effort, which he did. Again, Flavius defeated the Ribari rebels, this time even more brilliantly than before. Again, Flavius was put in charge of the peace negotiations, and once again, despite the protestations of his closest lieutenants, he allowed the Ribari to keep their lands and their men.

"The next year the Ribari rose up again and again. Flavius was voted Consul, and again he dispatched them even more quickly than before. However, this time when he arrived at the peace negotiations, he found the tent empty. Sensing a trap, Flavius immediately ordered his men to turn around. However, to Flavius's surprise, his men did not turn around, and he saw then the weapons in their hands. That night, Flavius's lieutenants assassinated him and buried his corpse in the hills as they burned the Ribari province to the ground. And the Ribari did not rise up again for another five hundred years."

His father's face looked cut from stone as their eyes met. "Do you know why I tell you this story, Lieutenant?"

"I could only guess, sir," Atticus replied as he kept his face flat and attentive. He knew better than to finish his father's lectures for him.

"Because I want you to know that a kindness can mean weakness," the Consul spoke slowly and deliberately. "And you should never let your men think you are *weak*."

"Yes sir. I will remember that, sir," Atticus replied, nodding thoughtfully. He was unsure if his father's lecture had anything to do with his mission that morning, or if it had more to do with the conversation that had happened moments ago with Droesus and Philemon. Either way, Atticus made sure to look attentive, his eyes trained at the back wall. He found it easier to remain calm during these little talks if he looked at his father as little as possible.

The Consul took another sip of tea as he gestured to a map on the table. "I have a change of mission for you and your platoon. I want you to escort Droesus's tank column tomorrow. That old snake can't seem to catch a break with his ground escort. So I want you there to keep his armor clean of enemy infantry."

Atticus nodded at the back wall. "Yes sir."

Marius sipped his tea and studied his son. "It's a difficult assignment, but I have removed Droesus from command and placed Major Ioma in charge. You will be reporting directly to him."

Atticus nodded again. "Yes sir." His father's eyes narrowed as he leveled his gaze at Atticus. "You don't look terribly comfortable, Lieutenant," Marius said. "If you do not feel like you or your men are up to this task, I can give this mission to someone else."

Ever since he had become an officer in the Republican army, Atticus had yet to hear his father give him an order without issuing a challenge with it. Keeping his eyes straight ahead, Atticus nodded. "I have the utmost confidence in my men, sir."

"Your men are not what concerns me, Lieutenant. The question is, when the time comes, will you do what needs to be done?"

The question unnerved him, and Atticus glanced briefly at his father, meeting his cold stare. "Of course, sir. I will, sir."

His face like stone, Marius stood and walked to the far end of the table. "Do not disappoint me, Lieutenant. Report to Major Ioma immediately. Dismissed."

ORTHO

4.28.2388 – Planet Arc, Blackfriar Mountains

"Wake up, Intel!"

Ortho jerked awake just as someone kicked his duffle out from under him and his head dropped to the ground with a thump. He did his best not to appear annoyed as he looked up to see Brennan standing over him.

"Grab your gear. It's time for you to go." The burly soldier jabbed his thumb at the air. "The Consul is waiting for you outside."

Ortho rubbed the sleep from his eyes and rolled to his feet, but he made sure not to move *too* quickly. He didn't want this Brennan, or anyone else, to think he would jump every time he was rude to him. Hefting a bag over each shoulder, Ortho pushed his way out the front tent flap.

"WHAT-THE-HELL!"

The surprised and angry voice rang in Ortho's ears, and a shiver of terror ran down Ortho's spine as a singular question ran through his mind: Who was yelling? Looking up, Ortho searched for who the voice belonged to. There, standing before him, was the Consul Marius, all six and a half feet of him, dressed from neck to feet with the armor and weaponry of a light infantryman. Ortho could clearly see the legendary man's stoic jawline and the piercing eyes he was so well known for. However, the Consul was flipping through a palm-sized notebook and not even looking at Ortho.

"I *SAID*, WHAT-THE-HELL!"

Looking left, Ortho saw two more soldiers, both of specialist rank—the same as Ortho—who were standing shoulder to shoulder with dispassionate expressions, their eyes focused on the horizon. Now confused, Ortho began to wonder if someone was playing a trick on him. Perhaps some sort of hazing initiation into the Consul's entourage.

"GOD-DAMMIT SON!"

Sadly, he was mistaken. Stepping out from behind the two body-guards, Ortho found himself eye to eye with one of the shortest and angriest men he had ever laid eyes on. Red-faced, bald as a potato, and of roughly the same height as a bar stool, the stocky man was dressed the same as his taller counterparts. Ortho could see no name tag or rank, and so with no idea who the stocky man was or why he was so angry with him, Ortho dropped his bags and brought himself to stand stiffly at attention, training his eyes firmly on the horizon as the stocky man stomped up to within an inch of Ortho's face.

"Who the fuck are you?" the stocky man said in a voice like murder. "And why the fuck are you here?"

Well at least we're on the same page. Ortho kept his eyes aimed straight ahead and prayed he didn't sound as nervous as he felt. "Specialist Ortho Andronicus reporting for duty… er … uh …" Another shiver of terror ran down his spine as Ortho suddenly realized who this was: Sergeant Major Contus Sulla, the Consul's senior enlisted advisor. Somehow, Ortho had thought he would be taller. In the only picture Ortho had seen prior to this, the man had been smiling. That was not the case now. "… ah … Sergeant Major."

"I can read, dammit," the man hissed. "Why the fuck are you here and who the fuck sent you?"

While he could feel the man's breath on his neck, Ortho kept his eyes trained on the horizon. "Major Claudius from Intel sent me, Sergeant Major. He said the Consul needed a new analyst. He said I was it."

"We don't need a damned bean-counter, Specialist," the sergeant major snarled. "The Consul asked specifically for a radio operator."

Ortho swallowed hard. Hope sprung in his chest like a fast-growing weed. Perhaps they would let him go! He could think of a half dozen guys in the commo shop he could throw under the bus. He tried to think of who he disliked the most.

"Specialist, are you familiar with the TL-7500 radio pack?" the sergeant major asked.

"Haven't used one since basic training, Sergeant Major." It was an outright lie. He had used one two weeks ago while visiting an outpost, but he hoped that the more incompetent he could paint himself, the more likely he would be released.

"I don't give a shit about the last time you used it. I asked if you are familiar with the device, Specialist."

Fuck. A loaded question. Hope died inside him as quickly as it had appeared. "I'll do everything I can, Sergeant Major."

The sergeant major's voice lowered to a condescending growl. "You'll do everything you can? Well sheeeeet. I'll set up your goddamned radios, Specialist, while you watch and get yourself a refresher. Life ain't fair, Anto-ni-canamoose. If that's news to you, then you're in the wrong goddamned army, son."

Someone cleared his throat. Ortho chanced a glance toward the Consul.

"This is very entertaining, Contus," the Consul said as he checked his watch, "but if we're going to get this kid set up and stay on time, then we have to do so soon."

The sergeant major never took his scowling eyes off Ortho. "Agreed, Consul. I'll get him set up, and then we'll be on our way." Sulla gestured to the two bags on Ortho's shoulders. "You can leave all that junk inside the tent, Specialist. The only thing you'll be needing from here on is your gear and your rifle and this godsdamned radio."

Ortho ignored the sniggers of Brennen and Alek as he tossed his duffle and his ruck sack into the tent's back corner. When he re-emerged, the sergeant major stuck a pair of TL-7500 radios to Ortho's body armor with a belted pouch. The compact man then proceeded to give Ortho a brief, if very basic, profanity-fueled instruction on how to use the devices. Ortho did his best to play the novice, nodding attentively as the sergeant major spoke to him like a brain-damaged grad-eschooler. The Consul waited patiently all the while, leaning against a tree and reading his notebook. Finally, after Ortho had finished the last radio check, Sergeant Major Contus Sulla gave him an approving grunt, then walked back to the tent and stuck his head inside.

"You two ready to go, or are you gonna sit here all day playin' cards and airing out your dick holsters?"

Ortho couldn't hear the response, but Sulla appeared exceedingly pleased with himself as he walked back to Marius. After a minute of hurried shuffling and a few muffled curses, Brennen and Alek emerged from the tent dressed in full gear. Not another word was spoken as they followed Marius away from the tent.

The Consul led them all the way around the base of the hill and then into a wide gully that ran between two foothills. As they climbed the gully, Ortho could see the sun was high above the mountains now, and a waist-deep spring of water was running away down the center of the gully toward the valley below. Unlike the two taller and stronger bodyguards next to him, Ortho was fighting to keep pace with the long-striding Marius as they climbed, and halfway up the gully Ortho found himself nearly out of breath. As the sweat began to bead on his forehead, he heard the sergeant major grunt behind him.

"You sure you're up for this, Andronimoose? Or should I call over to the gottamned cook tent and ask them for a replacement?"

Ortho ducked his head as though something had been thrown at him. "You can count on me all the way, Sergeant Major!" Ortho yelled far more enthusiastically than he felt.

The sergeant major scowled. "All the way to what?"

Behind him, he heard Brennen snicker as he shouted his reply. "All the way to the end of the mission, Sergeant Major!"

Contus Sulla sniffed his contempt as he shook his head. "Claudius must have some twisted sense of gottamned humor."

They emerged from the gully on the wide, flat rock atop the hillside where all manner of aircraft were parked. They marched through a row of Strykers and then walked wide of a shuttle that was taxying its way into position to take off. Another dozen Strykers were lined up on the northern edge of the rocky landing strip. Ortho could hear the humming engines of the angular airships, and he could see they were filled to the doors with the lightly armored men and women of the 88th Column—the Coalition's elite, hand-picked air assault battalion.

Marius walked to the center of the airfield so that each Stryker had a good view of him, and with a glance and a crook of his finger, the Consul signaled for Ortho to follow him. Feeling small and out of place, the pudgy analyst walked awkwardly across the airfield to stand behind the legendary man.

Marius looked down at him with a face carved out of stone. "Call Commander Agrippa and ask if him and his men are ready to go. The eighty-eighth's net should be channel three. His call sign is Dog One."

Ortho pulled the hand-mic off of his shoulder. "Dog One. This is Eagle One Romeo, Eagle One actual is asking if you're ready to go. Over."

Ortho felt a shiver of nerves run down his spine as he waited for the radio to key up in response. Commander Titus Agrippa was a figure nearly as renowned as Marius himself. That this was likely Marius's last war was well known, and the question of his succession had been a frequent topic among the officers of Ortho's Intel shop. All agreed that Titus Agrippa was the most likely candidate.

The reply was quick and gruff and from Agrippa himself. "Eagle One Romeo, this is Dog One. We're up and ready if he is. Over."

Ortho heard Marius snort. "Tell that son of a bitch I was ready when I got up. And then tell that son of a bitch to give me and my men a bird to ride on."

Ortho held the mic in his hand for a moment, unsure if any of that was meant to be a joke on him and, if so, how or if he was supposed to play along.

Marius saw him hesitate and fixed Ortho with just the hint of a grin, "And make sure to call him a son of a bitch."

Okay then. Ortho thought as he keyed up the mic. "Dog One, Eagle One says that he's been ready since before you got up and wants to know where he's riding. He also adds that you are a son of a bitch. Over."

These guys are no different than a bunch of Privates with privilege, he thought. *Perhaps that's what they are. Perhaps it's all deliberate.*

The response came quickly with a voice that was droll and sarcastic. "Tell Eagle One we've got a spot for him in the eleven-oh-five with the rest of his platoon, but he can leave his smart-ass RTO on the pad."

Marius started walking to the third Stryker in the line. "You're catching on, Andronicus. Follow me."

Behind them, the sergeant major chortled. "Proper radio etiquette is important. Just remember who you're speaking for and don't let anyone push you around. You hear? Proper fuckin' attitude is important, Specialist."

"Roger that, Sergeant Major!" Ortho shouted. His nerves were still buzzing in his chest like a nest of hornets, but below that was a surging excitement that felt like pride. He followed the Consul and the sergeant major as they climbed up the back ramp of the Stryker and into a bay filled with soldiers. As they walked past the soldiers of the Consul's personal security detail, Ortho could hear Marius talking to them in the friendly manner of an old warrior.

"Glad you could make it this time, Corey. How's the leg? Good? Mean-looking gun you have there, Osseo. You gentlemen look like you're ready to fight. Alexander, you look excited, maybe too excited." Marius punched a soldier in the chest of his body armor and then playfully, with the flat of his palm, struck the helmet of a young woman. "Nice facepaint, young lady, glad you're here." And so on until they reached the front of the bay where three seats sat open right behind the Stryker's cockpit. Ortho sat down and pulled the safety harness over his head. When he looked at he faces around him, he realized that they were surrounded by the Consul's personal security team. Twenty-four men and women specifically trained to protect the Consul.

"Don't get too comfortable there, Intel. We aren't going that far!" Brennen gave out a mocking laugh.

"Aw hell," the sergeant major growled. "Your eyes are as big as saucers, kid."

Ortho replied with nothing more than a friendly smile as the roar of the Stryker's engines began to pick up.

"Don't worry, Intel," Alek pointed his finger from Ortho over to Marius. "Just stand behind the Consul if things get too hairy. Bullets bounce right off him. Makes all our jobs real easy."

Everyone around them laughed then, and Ortho even saw the Consul chuckle to himself. Ortho did his best to join in, all while trying not to look as nervous as he felt. Beside him, he heard Brennen say something else that seemed directed at him, but he couldn't hear him over the sound of the engines. They could think whatever they wanted of him. His two goals over the next twenty-four hours were to survive and to cater to the Consul's every want and whim. He would hopefully never see any of these other guys ever again. Finally, he felt the Stryker lift up off the ground and into the air. They were on their way.

ATTICUS

"WITH THE TANK COLUMN!" Jonas was incensed. "Are you kidding me, sir? We're under Droesus? We're a light infantry platoon! We don't ride around on the backs of tanks! We don't even have magnetic armor! This is what heavies are for, sir. What in the name of Fate were they thinking?"

Lieutenant Atticus Marius had brought his platoon sergeant, Jonas Talor, outside to discuss the mission they had just been given. Outside—and away from the rest of their men. Atticus had used the walk back from his meeting with the Consul, his father Arcos Marius, to digest their orders. Now, beneath the rustling leaves of an oak tree, he was listening to Jonas voice the same concerns that had been echoing through his own head.

Atticus shrugged. "I guess Droesus has just run out of people who will work with him."

"So your father sends us?" Jonas threw his hands up in disgust. "Bagh! This is insanity."

Atticus did not disagree. Unfortunately for the both of them, they had no choice. As second in command of their platoon, Jonas stood no higher on the food chain than Atticus did, and so no matter how much complaining either of them did, they were still stuck with the same mission. Glancing back toward the cave, Atticus could see a few of his soldiers were awake while the rest still lay asleep in their sleeping bags.

The young lieutenant shook his head. "I don't like it any better than you, but at least Droesus isn't in charge anymore."

Jonas barked a laugh. "That Ioma is no better. You know he left two platoons to die on Troya, right?"

"Not intentionally," Atticus said.

"You don't know that." Jonas pointed a finger at his lieutenant and then back at himself. "I was there, and I'm telling you right now that man is capable of anything."

Troya had been one of the great tragedies of the war. During the final days of the planetary siege, Atticus was fresh out of the academy and was stationed as a staff officer aboard *Unifier*. Ioma, then a captain, had led one of the strike teams that had breached Troya's defensive shield and then led the spearhead down to the surface. Hours later, his men surrounded, Captain Ioma had called *Unifier* for an orbital strike that wiped out over fifty of his own men and nearly half a planet. How Ioma had received authorization for a strike—or even if he had, or who'd fired the strike—was still shrouded in secrecy. What was known was that a shuttle returned Ioma and less than half his men back to orbit while *Unifier* gravity-dropped a second volley of bombs.

It was Atticus' understanding that Jonas had been there too, but the big man had yet to talk to him about it.

"Well … I wasn't there," Atticus sighed. "I don't know what he did or didn't do.".

"What we *do* know is that he had *Unifier* throw a rock down onto the planet," Jonas growled. "Right on top of his own men. It destroyed two continents."

"He probably had to," Atticus said flatly.

"And I had to take a shit this morning, but that doesn't mean I left it on somebody else's head. I put the damn thing down the well like everyone else," Jonas grumbled.

"C'mon," Atticus said. "None of this changes who we're taking orders from. Bloodthirsty or not, a Commander is still a Commander."

Atticus sighed and looked up at the late evening sky. He knew that he could no more win this argument than he could change his mission. Atticus wasn't even *trying* to argue. He just needed his platoon sergeant on board before they talked to the men.

"You *c'mon*," Jonas mocked. "We're on mission with a steaming pile of incompetence and a man so bloodthirsty he'd sell his own mother for a box of ammo. You know what happened to the last company that got stuck with Droesus? They got surrounded because he got lost. Eighty percent casualties. And they were heavies. Full head-to-toe power-armor."

"Yeah, I heard about that too. What do you want me to do? Go tell the Consul we're sitting this out because we don't like it?"

"Why can't we go back to Major Trajan? Ask him if he can't get us back into Captain Barca's company." Jonas looked like a man begging his wife for permission to go out with his friends. "Pullo likes you and his XO is really cute. All the guys like her. Why can't we just go back to doing stuff for our own company? Why are we getting shit on by the Consul of the entire goddamned Republic?"

"You *know* why we're getting shit on by the Consul of the entire goddamned Republic." Atticus spat on the ground as he let the implication go unspoken. They both knew his father purposefully made things harder on Atticus and, by extension, Assassin platoon.

Jonas sighed and looked up at the sky. "No offense, sir, but the Fates cursed me the day they made me your platoon sergeant."

Atticus laughed. "And I'm glad they did, old man."

"Fuck it." Jonas kicked the dirt. "Look sir, I know we don't know when we're leaving, but my friends in the artillery regiment were saying they have enough ammunition to last until noon tomorrow. So, if my gut's telling me anything, it's that they aren't setting off this dog-and-pony show until sometime tomorrow morning. So, my suggestion is to get the men as much rest as we can before then, because we don't know how long this shit-storm of an op is going to last."

Atticus nodded. "Agreed."

"And whatever you do, don't let this Ioma guy put us out front. We're a light recon platoon, not his personal shock troops."

Atticus shrugged. "We'll do what we can, I suppose. Whatever keeps you happy, old man."

Jonas grunted, "I won't be happy until I'm home with my wife and kids."

"Then let's get this over with," Atticus said with a dry and final tone as they both turned to walk back toward the cave.

Their platoon was quick to move once he and Jonas gave out the mission, and within minutes everyone had their gear on their backs. Leaving the cave, they found the armored column at the southern end of the camp. Here, the Fifth Armored Column had wrapped their Claymore tanks around the base of a foothill like an arrowhead aimed at the city Sindorum, as if demanding to be placed at the fore of the assault. There they found a grassy knoll near the rear of the column where his soldiers dozed and slept the rest of the evening. Not three hours before the dawn, most of Assassin platoon had slept their fill and were cooking coffee and their field rations while playing cards by flashlight. Then, an hour before sun up, a lanky, red-headed woman in a tanker uniform found them.

"I'm looking for a Lieutenant Atticus Marius," she said loudly with an air of authority that was reserved for officers.

Atticus stood. "Right here, ma'am."

One of his men shined a flashlight at her and Atticus caught a glimpse of her rank and name. Lieutenant Chastain.

"If you would follow me, please. The commander would like to speak with all of his ground officers."

Leaving his men where they sat, he followed Chastain to the tip of the arrowhead. Here, Atticus could look out over the entire Sinvoresse Valley. It was the dark before the dawn. The stars were high over the Blackfriar Mountains, and the ocean looked like an endless pool of black ink. Looking back toward the tanks, he saw Ioma seated atop the nose of a tank with a group of officers and soldiers gathered around him. The young major seemed at ease in the center of it all, handing out orders and advice with a ready and willing smile.

Short of the crowd, Chastain turned to Atticus and said, "I'll ask you to wait here, Lieutenant Marius. The major will see you once he's finished giving his operations orders to his tankers."

Atticus gave the woman a curt nod and sat on the grass next to a pair of soldiers who were seated atop a tarp where they had disassembled a heavy machine gun and were cleaning its inner guts by flashlight. Lying in the grass behind the machine gun were two sets of heavy power-armor. *Exactly the kind of armor you need when riding exposed on the back of a tank. Exactly the kind of armor my men don't have.* He leaned back against the nearest tank and looked out over the valley toward the city. Most of his men would be riding four to a tank. His mind had begun wondering how he would pair his men up when he noticed a crowd of same-faced men marching toward him.

They were Umbrean replicants, heavy infantry dressed in full drop armor, their helmets dangling at their hips and long rifles strapped across their backs. Atticus noticed a badge on their shoulders which marked them as Kodayene. Standing nearly seven feet tall, Kodayene were full-sentients, bred with strength and agility far superior to a normal man, and possessing an intelligence and self-awareness far beyond the half-sentients that the Umbreans kept as common GIs. Walking at the center of them was a man so massive that he even towered above the Kodayene around him. As the crowd neared, Atticus realized it was the same giant he had seen not a day earlier outside his father's tent—the Grande Admiral Philemon.

The last thing I need is to be noticed by this man and pulled into some larger conversation because of my last name. Looking around, Atticus realized he was surrounded by soldiers who were cleaning and prepping their equipment. Atticus quickly seated himself on a stack of ammo crates near the other human soldiers. Looking down at his rifle, he blew a spot of dust off it. Pretending to be displeased at the weapon's outer appearance, he pulled out a scarf and began polishing.

Despite the ruse, Atticus soon felt the towering shadow of the pale giant standing over him as a low but powerful voice grumbled, "What are you doing here, Lieutenant?"

Atticus got up to stand at attention and then saluted. "Just cleaning my weapons, sir, waiting for the Commander."

"Relax, Lieutenant." Philemon waved casually, and Atticus made a feigned attempt of being at ease. No man of Philemon's status truly wanted anyone to relax in his presence. Here with an Ieses within arm's distance, Atticus could feel the hairs stand up on the back of his neck.

The Grand Admiral scowled at him. "At this point in the day an officer should be inspecting the weapons of his men, not his own."

Atticus nodded, knowing full well that he had already done so, but he replied, "Of course, sir. I will do that, sir."

"Where is Droesus?" the giant growled.

"I do not know, sir," Atticus replied. "I have not seen him, sir."

"Hrmph," Philemon snorted. "Typical. Where is Major Ioma?"

"At his vehicle, sir." Atticus pointed through the dark toward the crowd of officers. "Just over there, sir."

"I see. Well take me to him, Lieutenant." Philemon ordered.

"Of course, sir."

Atticus noticed that the Kodayene, having received some wordless order from Philemon, stayed put near the ammo crates while he shouldered his rifle and led their giant master through the maze of tanks. The gaggle of junior officers parted before them when they saw Atticus and the towering Philemon walking toward the front of the tank column. Ioma was dismissing the last of his tankers when Philemon strode past Atticus.

"Gaius Ioma, how go your plans?" The Ieses spoke in a rumbling baritone and Ioma shot to his feet.

Ioma hopped off the front of the tank with a confident grin. "Grande Admiral! You have caught me off guard, your liege. No one of your stature should be able to get this far into my camp without someone spotting them and telling me."

"As if I didn't know how to sneak up on a tank column," Philemon boasted. "Who do you think I am, boy?"

Atticus sank back as far as he dared into the quickly disappearing crowd. Soon, there was no one left around him except for the soldiers cleaning the machine gun. Not sure if he had permission to leave or stay, Atticus leaned back against the nearest tank and waited. Then a shiver ran down his spine as he felt someone nearby, like a shadow he could feel but not see. Atticus turned around and there, leaning back against the aft of a tank, was the pale gray-blue Umbrean that Atticus had seen outside his father's tent the other morning. The man was casually carving a piece of wood with a pocket knife, and Atticus could see no other weapons on him. When the other felt Atticus staring, the Umbrean looked up. Atticus looked away just as quickly, but he could still feel the Umbrean smile. Awkwardly, Atticus tried to turn his attention back the conversation between Philemon and Ioma.

"Tell me, Major, where is that old vulture?" Philemon's voice boomed.

Ioma made a clicking sound with his tongue. "I am afraid I have not seen Commander Droesus since yesterday. I am, Grande Admiral."

"Don't be. Droesus has made a career out of disappointing people, and now he's finally finding out how the other side lives. Tell me, Major, is this tank column prepared to end this war?"

Ioma smirked. "We've been ready since I took over last night. In fact, I'm actually a bit worried we may end up waiting for *you* at the rally point."

"Ha!" Philemon guffawed. "You will never have to wait for me, Major." The Grand Admiral leaned down to put a giant hand on Ioma's shoulder. "Now listen closely, my boy. I expect you to be accurate like the cock at dawn. Not a minute early, not a minute late. Once my screening action is set, I cannot afford to have my cavalry left hanging, and it's impolite to arrive early at a party, understand?"

"Of course, Grand Admiral." Ioma bowed slightly. "Have I ever let you down?"

"No, you haven't, and that's why you're here." Philemon waved his finger at Ioma, "But if you let me down this time, I'll come back from my grave and strangle you in your sleep."

Ioma's smile was friendless while his eyes were full of hidden intent. "Don't worry, I'll be there."

"You had better be," Philemon said. He stepped closer, and Ioma tilted his head as the pale giant whispered in the other's ear. Ioma nodded, and Philemon stood to leave. However, before the pale giant walked away, he stopped to grab Atticus by the arm.

"Remember what I said to you earlier, boy."

Then the giant Umbrean nobleman waved to Ioma and walked off, his Kodayene falling in behind him. Ioma saluted and watched the crowd of men as they walked away. He noticed the man with the knife was gone as well, although Atticus could not pick him out from the crowd of men following behind Philemon.

Ioma called out for Atticus and all of the ground officers to gather around to review the mission's warning order. As all the other officers gathered around Ioma, Atticus stayed near the edge of the crowd, just within earshot, as Major Ioma began reading off his mission notes. The remainder of King Teum's army was likely holed up around the palace, he said, and while many of the Duathic civilians remaining in the city had turned guerilla, no one knew how many. *Unifier* was launching drop troops the moment their column was within a mile of the city. The

Consul himself would then arrive with the Strykers of the air cavalry. Ioma emphasized that the Consul's intention was to end the war today, at any cost.

Then Ioma's face fell as the crowd parted to reveal an old, hunch-backed man who walked around the corner of the nearest tank and hobbled toward the front of the crowd. Atticus recognized the old, one-eyed officer that he had seen outside his father's tent. It was Droesus. No one else in the crowd seemed surprised to see him and nearly no one acknowledged him except for a few who nodded their heads as he walked by. As Droesus came to bow before Ioma, Atticus noticed that the other officers—most of whom, not hours earlier, had called Droesus their commander—were looking at the man with naked disdain, as if the disgraced officer were nothing more than an unruly private.

"Major Ioma! I must speak with you!"

The crooked old man was nearly out of breath, and sweat beaded around his eye patch, betraying the fact he had likely ran a good way to catch up with his replacement. Ioma raised his eyebrows and crossed his arms as he faced the column's old commander.

"Please, hear me out." Leaning on one knee, Droesus held out his right hand as if to plead. "I know that I am late, but I have to discuss something with you, in private if we can. It is most important and it cannot wait."

Arms crossed over his chest, Ioma's tone was like a father speaking to a child. "Can you tell me now? Here?"

"Not in front of the men, sir. Please," Droesus pleaded.

Ioma frowned and his back to the older man. "No, Commander, you are too late for that. Whatever it is, it cannot be so important as to delay the mission. I will not let you keep *me* from being on time."

"Please, Major, I have only now just heard…"

Ioma waved his hand dismissively. "It is no wonder Marius sent me to take charge of your column. Your advice is likely as accurate as your schedule," said Ioma, droll and unamused. "I must finish my briefing and so I will ask you to dismiss yourself." Seconds passed in silence as Droesus stared at the young, dark-haired major in disbelief. Finally, Ioma clicked his pen and said once more in a tone covered in ice. "Wherever you dismiss yourself to is none of my concern, Commander, only that you do, so that I may keep this unit running on schedule."

With that, the old hunchbacked officer bowed his head and turned around to walk back the way he came. As Atticus watched Droesus walking through the crowd, he could see the fires of thought gleaming in the old man's one eye, but the commander never turned back.

When Droesus was out of sight, Ioma clicked his pen again before starting in with instructions for each part of the column. The new commander called on each of his officers in turn. Atticus saw Major Allereda, a balding and brown-skinned man, confirm the tankers' order of movement. A blonde, doe-eyed female lieutenant smiled brightly when Ioma called on her. She eagerly stepped forward to say that her engineers would be in the rear with the medics. Then, when Ioma announced that Assassin platoon would ride with him as his own personal strike team, there was a murmuring among the heavy infantry officers. When Ioma asked them if there was a question, a square-jawed captain with a scarred face raised his hand.

"If Assassin platoon is taking over, then where do you want us, sir?" Looking at the man as he said this, Atticus could see he had a set to his jaw that said his pride had been wounded.

"Don't worry, Arakin. I'll come to you and yours soon," Ioma smiled politely.

"Yes sir," the man called Arakin replied, and Atticus could see the muscles on his jaw tighten, causing nearly all of his face to go bright red—except for the scar that cut from the captain's left ear down to the corner of his mouth. When Atticus blinked, he noticed the sulking captain was glaring at him. Atticus looked away.

Ioma then finished outlining Assassin platoon's position, and Atticus sensed that the newly minted commander was enjoying Arakin's displeasure as he went into detail. Assassin platoon would stay with Ioma at the fore of the advance, just as Atticus had anticipated. No one, it seemed, wanted to keep the Consul's son in the rear where his options for glory might be limited. Jonas would be thrilled.

Their field meeting began to wind to a close then. An over-tired communications officer talked briefly about radio channels and call signs. Major Ioma was Reaper One. Atticus took note that the Arakin fellow was now Spiker One. The medics were all under the Halo call sign, and on and on. Atticus took relief that his platoon would retain the Assassin call sign, if only to save him from the bitching of his men. They had begged and pleaded to keep the name when he arrived even though it was tradition to change it whenever a new officer took the helm. He had eagerly relented. When Ioma's warning order was finished, the crowd quickly dispersed. The column was departing shortly.

Atticus had barely tucked his notebook back into his pant pocket when someone called out to him from the crowd.

"Lieutenant Marius!"

Atticus looked to see Major Allereda pushing his way through the crowd toward him. The balding man smiled warmly and extended his hand. "I look forward to working with you on this mission, Lieutenant. I was not aware that you had been reassigned."

Atticus bowed curtly as he shook Allereda's hand. "Neither was I until this morning."

Allereda held onto Atticus' hand for a moment as he leaned back to study him. "You had been with Captain Barca before this, am I right?"

"Yes sir." Atticus nodded politely. He knew what this was about. Another senior officer looking to curry favor with the Consul through his son. He had yet to see it pay off, but that had yet to dissuade anyone from trying.

Allereda finally released his hand. "I've heard good things about you. You know what they say about you?"

"No sir, I don't," Atticus lied. He knew exactly what was coming next.

Allereda gave him a friendly point and a wink. "Just like his father when he was a Lieutenant, they say. Strikes like lightning and disappears like the night." The other man laughed and Atticus did his best to smile back at him. "I'm not old enough to have known your father when he was your age, but if you're anything like they say, then I look forward to working with you, young man."

Atticus thanked him and gave him another curt bow as Allereda slapped him on the shoulder and walked away.

The column was moving into formation as Atticus made the walk back to his platoon. Crew chiefs, gunners, and drivers were climbing aboard their Claymore tanks. Heavy infantry soldiers in their jet-black power-armor hummed and whirred as they walked past him. Each

Claymore carried four soldiers, two on each side. Magnetic harnesses held them to the tanks' sides and as the 60-ton vehicles lifted themselves off the ground with a *thrumm* and a *hiss* as the shielding folded up from the sides to protect the soldiers. And so the Claymores began to roll into position. Two tanks side-by-side, and four to each section, the column began to take shape like a long black centipede curling its way between the foothills below Mount Gedron.

Returning to his men, Atticus found the soldiers of Assassin platoon were in the middle of donning their own magnetic harnesses. Jonas handed Atticus his harness and a mask that would filter out the dust and exhaust as they rode. These would be small comforts, but ones they were thankful for nonetheless.

Atticus found Ioma's tank still resting on the ground. The commander's tank had space for only three soldiers to ride as the tank's front right slot was occupied by extra radio and sensor equipment. Salentine and Thrace were already aboard, sitting against the tank's hull with their harnesses magnetically holding them in place. Thrace, Assassin platoon's radioman, was reading the last few pages of a paperback book. Thrace was a tall and lanky soldier in his early twenties with an overlong neck and a head shaped like an egg. The going joke within the platoon was that his mother had an affair with some overland flightless bird like an Eurochs or a Styrrich. Thrace claimed it was so his neck could support all the extra brain power. Atticus' money had always been on the latter.

Climbing into his own slot, Atticus saw the young, haggard machine gunner beside him was rolling a cigarette. Assassin platoon had gone through a lot of changes over the course of the war. Atticus himself was Assassin platoon's third platoon leader, the first having died on a jump while the second died to a sniper on Troya. Jonas, who had arrived the same time as Atticus, had become the platoon's second platoon sergeant. More than that, the platoon as a whole had gone through nearly a dozen wounded and KIAs since the start of the war. Through all of that, one thing had held constant: Salentine was the platoon's best machine gunner.

"You ready, sir?" Sal asked as he lit his smoke.

Atticus took the cigarette from Sal, stole a puff and handed it back. "I suppose I better be. You look like hell, Sal."

"That's on purpose, sir." Salentine held two fingers up to Atticus' nose. "Smell that."

Atticus made a face and pushed away the hand. "What?"

"I fucked a cook last night. She brought me to her tent and everything."

"And you didn't bathe like everyone else, why?" Atticus asked.

Thrace piped up from the other side. "He told me that he wants his corpse to smell like pussy, sir."

"Exactly," Salentine said cool and calm as he took another drag.

Atticus was chuckling when he saw Jonas appear below them. "Sir, I thought we were trying to avoid being put up front?"

"I tried," Atticus said as he shrugged.

"I'm sure Major Ioma has grand plans for us…" The grizzled sergeant grunted his disgust as he pointed at the lanky radioman sitting across from Atticus. "Thrace, I'm counting on you to keep an eye on these two. Don't let Lieutenant Marius go running off again like he did last night."

"Roger that, Sarge!" Thrace said enthusiastically.

Jonas looked at Salentine. "Sal, you look like hell."

"Got laid last night, Sarge," Sal answered with a bleary-eyed smile.

"Well, congratulations. Don't let 'em die virgins," Jonas grinned.

"Just doin' my part, Sarge."

Then Jonas pointed at Atticus. "I'll see you at the first objective, sir."

Atticus nodded and smiled as Salentine let out an animal-like howl. "BA-WOOOoooooo!"

As Jonas walked away, a pair of Raptors screamed overhead in a low pass over the column, and for a moment no one could hear anything except for the scream of their engines. Atticus looked out over the valley to see the artillery striking the city of Sindorum, flashing like distant light bulbs against a shattered horizon. Their Claymore lurched forward. The Fifth Armored Column was on the move.

TAYLOR

Major Taylor Caelynn spent most of the shuttle ride staring at her operation notes but never reading a word. Instead, her eyes stared blankly at the penciled text while her mind wandered back and forth about her lover, Gaius Ioma. On one hand, Gaius was charming, ambitious, and exciting. On the other, Taylor had long wondered if Gaius Ioma, the son of a disgraced and penniless nobleman, cared more for her or her family name. Back on Alba Calea, her father, Senator Caelynn, was one of the most influential men in the Republic, and his connections had been no small influence in Taylor's acceptance to the flight academy on Orsa Minor. She had taken her career in her own hands from there, but Ioma wasn't the first to be drawn to Taylor's last name as much as her looks. A girl had to be careful.

The puzzle occupied her mind while the shuttle docked, and it followed her as she walked the long journey through *Unifier's* halls. The war would soon be over and decisions would have to be made. Taylor had never been one to plan too far ahead, but now her mind was alight with the fires of uncertainty. She was still young, only twenty-five, but the pressures of career and family would soon be upon her. Whenever she returned home, she knew that the moment she stepped through the doors of her parent's manse in Alba Calea there would be people and factions waiting to pull her this way and that, a list that not least of all included her parents. All of this was swimming through her head as she took the final elevator down. Arriving at the fighter bay, Taylor managed to make it to her office without anyone stopping her, but as soon as she opened the door, her XO, Captain Josiah, stood to greet her.

"How was the surface?" he asked.

"Same as always," Taylor said as she set her clipboard on her desk, "but the Consul is happy with our plan, so we're good to go." "Did you hear about the unidentified objects that *Unifier* caught on her scope last night?"

"No, what happened?" she asked.

Josiah shrugged. "Some object or craft crossed along the outer ring of the system, then it turned and took off for Yenru Minor before they lost track of it."

"Really?" Taylor asked, skeptical.

"Yeah. The Ops guys I talked to tried to make it sound all creepy-like, but I mean it was probably just some comet or something that ran into something else. Anyway, I have some bad news for you." Josiah picked up a manila folder from his desk and handed it to her.

"What's this?" she asked as she flipped the folder open.

Josiah's voice sounded both bored and tired. "Four rookies arrived last night, and so Top took the liberty of re-assigning four of our veterans to another wing."

"What? They're in the Trawler wing? They stole four of mine to fill out the Trawlers and shoved four rookies down to replace them?" Disgusted, Taylor tossed the folder onto her desk. "What the hell, man!"

Josiah held his hands up in self-defense. "Don't look at me. I spent all day fighting it. Admiral Thorus said it's about need."

"It's about politics is what it's about." She pounded her finger on her desk. "Colonel Oleeda has been jealous of us ever since he got his command!"

Josiah shook his head in mutual disgust. "Colonel Hamster-Face is probably quite happy right now, but I don't think there's much we can do to fight this one."

Taylor flipped open the folder again. "Well at least they took Korta and Jo-Jo."

Josiah sat back down and kicked his feet up on his desk. "Sad to lose Baer and Killbrook though. They were fun to play cards with."

Taylor chuckled and tried to forget how mad she was. "You mean they were bad at cards and you took their money. Sometimes I wonder if you have too much time on your hands."

Her XO folded his hands behind his head. "I'm busier than you think I am."

Taylor shook her head. "No, you're not."

"You're right." He laughed. "But just so you know, I got the kids lined up outside whenever you're ready for them."

Taylor sighed. The last thing she wanted to deal with was putting rookies in starfighters on what might be the last day of the war. She rubbed her nose in annoyance. "How excited are they?"

Josiah laughed. "A couple of them look about ready to piss their shorts, and the other two are scared out of their wits."

"Well shit. Might as well make their day." Taylor picked up her clipboard and her pen and walked out the door. She found all four of the new recruits standing in a line, and they snapped to attention as soon as they saw her.

"At ease." Taylor waved her hand at them as the crowd of four relaxed their rigid stances. *Fates, I turn twenty-six next month, why do they look so young?*

"Congratulations, you made it just in time." Taylor tried to keep the sarcasm from her voice as she walked up to the crowd of young faces and flipped through the dossier. Four in all, they had arrived last night while she had been down on Arc's surface. She would have preferred to keep them grounded until after Sindorum, but Command had apparently decided differently. She flipped a page in the folder and stared down the rookies with her best attempt at an icy glare. "We have a mission today, and I need all four of you to fly because Command stole four of my veterans and moved them over to the shuttle wing."

Taking fighter pilots and turning them into taxi drivers indicated to her that some of her superiors lived in a different reality than the one she currently occupied. Why Command had taken her experienced pilots and replaced them with rookies at this hour was beyond her comprehension. Such was the life of a fighter wing commander.

She flipped another page in the folder and frowned. "Looking at your scores, some of you are quite talented, but don't let that get to you. This is not a simulator. This is not a training sortie. Today is going to be combat." She let her gaze wander from face to face. "As my uncle always said: 'Keep your head down and your chin up.' If you're confident, that's fine, but the Duathe are making their last stand. Don't let them make it yours." One of them had scored higher on the final than Taylor had, and the younger Taylor Caelynn had set records in her last year. Lieutenant Aerelli. To her chagrin, when Taylor matched the name on her roster with the name on the uniform, it was a baby-faced blonde girl. "Aerelli. Brannon. You two are working with me and Shale today. We're on the first patrol cycle, so you better be ready."

"Yes ma'am!" they both said at the same time.

Fates, do they have to look so proud and excited at the same time? Did I look that dumb my first time out? She glanced from her folder to the mission notes on her clipboard and focused on the printout before her face could betray her thoughts.

"Your Raptors are being fueled now. If I send any of you home to your mother, tell her not to blame me. I didn't let a bunch of teenagers walk out of the Academy with wings." She waved her clipboard at the other two. "Lorkin and Pah-choo… sha …the hell? … How do you say this?"

"It's pronounced Pa-cah-stoh-wall-ahh, ma'am," the tall, dark-haired man said.

"That's not how looks. What is that? Shaemish?" Taylor asked.

"I'm afraid so, ma'am." He smiled.

"I'm sorry about that. My grandmother was Shaemish and she was a cunt. I'm calling you Pac, because I'm only an eighth Shaemish and so I can't pronounce that mess of a name you have. If you don't like it, you can take it up with the Equal Opportunity office. They're in room 385A on the B deck." She looked him in the eye, her face deadpan as someone giggled. "Is that okay with you, Pac?"

The lanky youth's smile had broken into a toothy grin. "It's what they called me in flight school, ma'am. That'll be just fine, ma'am."

"Good, because you don't have a fucking choice, rook." She sighed as she looked at the flight schedule on her clipboard. "I suppose I'll put Pac and Lorkin on the third rotation so that you two can catch me before you leave." She pointed to the door behind her. "If I'm not in my office, I'm in my quarters."

Then she put a serious look on her face and pointed her clipboard at all four of them. "Now look. This last bit goes for all of you. If you have any questions about anything, no matter how stupid you think the question may be, I want you to find me and ask me. I normally don't like holding a Raptor pilot's hand, but I also didn't plan on throwing four kids into a major op at the last minute and I'm sure as hell not sending any of you home in a box if I can help it. Are we clear?"

"Yes ma'am!" they all said in unison.

"Good." She pointed her thumb to the wall behind her. "Now your call-signs and your birds are on the board behind me. The Consul is launching this op at a time of his choosing and we need to be ready when that call arrives. I will give you one final briefing when the call comes in. Before then, I expect you all to do a full pre-flight check on your equipment." She checked her watch. "It is… 13:37."

All four of them gave her one more "Yes ma'am" and then wandered away like a group of middle schoolers on a field trip. Aerelli, in her excitement, was almost skipping. Frowning, Taylor watched them for a moment as they gathered around the big marker board that adorned the hanger wall near her office. She decided that none of them looked too confused yet. Taylor had worked in replacement pilots before and she had quickly learned that it was easier making them come to her with questions rather than following them around. It was amazing what they could figure out if left on their own. And sometimes amusing.

Flipping her folder closed, she turned and walked toward the other end of the bay. It was time for her to check her own craft. She found her Raptor right where it should be. Bay 1A.

Pre-flight checks were a task she relished more than most. Taylor had managed to keep the same fighter for most of the war, and she had come to think of it like an old friend. Her first ship had been scuttled through no fault of her own. A mechanic had missed a coolant leakage on her fusion drive while it was sitting overnight on a hilltop landing pad on Mol. By morning, the radioactive coolant had made its way through both of her engines and several of the primary maneuvering thrusters, so the maintenance chief had simply cut it up and salvaged what he could for parts. At first, she had been upset—like any pilot she was attached to her first ship, but then fortune had smiled on her like a ray of sunshine when she learned that they had ordered her up a brand-new machine that afternoon.

And that's how she'd come to possess the *Wyvern*.

The *Wyvern*'s name was painted on her nose where it was coiled around the opening for the ship's main cannons. Behind cannon and name were four painted tick marks, representing the four kills she had earned at Naos Muani. No one in the fleet had earned more.

Unlike pure zero-g fighters, the Raptor series was a sleek ship designed for both space and atmospheric combat. Its nose was an arrowhead that held her cannon while a dozen missiles clung to her angular wings and rounded belly. Two barrel-shaped engines made up the bulk of the ship's body with wings that folded in and out as conditions demanded. The Raptor was fast. Faster than anything else fleet could offer. Air to surface missiles were affixed to the ship's belly, with air-to-air missiles on her wings. This war hadn't seen a Duathic fighter since the siege at Naos Muani, and it likely wouldn't see another. Because of this, some pilots had cut down from four dog-fighting missiles to the minimum two, or removed them altogether. Taylor had not.

Everything on her *Wyvern* checked out. She made her final radio check with *Unifier*'s operations center, then climbed out and locked her cockpit.

Knowing she had to wear herself out if she wanted any chance of sleeping that night, Taylor spent the next three hours at the gym. She had told everyone else that she didn't know when the mission would start. That was only partially true. The Consul had given everyone at the meeting they would kick off sometime tomorrow morning. She finished with a four-mile run on the treadmill. She hit up the mess hall on her way, but she didn't see anyone worth talking to, so she grabbed a to-go plate. Her quarters were a single room with a wash. After a shower, she folded the futon out into a bed and made herself a cup of tea. She fell asleep watching an old movie.

The call came in around 0500. Her first patrol cycle needed to be down on the planet by 0600. As she was pulling on her uniform, she buzzed Captain Josiah to get her pilots ready. Minutes later, she was making coffee in her office as she watched her pilots filtering into the fighter bay. Her coffee maker was still gurgling when she saw Shale walk through the door with Aerelli beside him. Shale said something to the rookie pilot, and her laugh was nervous and girlish. The coffee maker dinged. The office door opened and in walked her XO, Captain Josiah, who immediately sniffed the air.

"You made me coffee already? You're a really sweat girl, you know that?"

She glared at him as she fastened the lid on her cup.

Josiah grinned as he poured his own cup. "You're gonna make someone a really good wife one day."

"Jos, why don't you go stick your head in an oven," she grumbled.

Laughing, her XO grabbed a clipboard off his desk and walked back toward the door. "Because you need me to do roll call."

She grunted. The door swung open and shut. She waited in the office, sipping her coffee until she saw a crowd of pilots gathered around her XO before she grabbed her own clipboard and walked out the door. She was walking across the bay when she felt someone tap her on the shoulder. She turned around to see an aide from the Command deck standing behind her.

"Major Caellyn."

She nodded. "What do you need, Specialist?"

"The Admiral needs you to take an observer with you today," the aide answered. "He's a special VIP."

Oh look, another surprise for the fighter wing. She suddenly regretted everything she had said to Lucian at the command meeting. *Me and my big mouth, I guess I'll just have to saddle one of my pilots with someone completely unfamiliar to aerial combat.* She leaned in close to the specialist and spoke in a low voice. "Do I have to? Who's asking?"

"Admiral Thorus specifically instructed me to ask you," he said.

"I don't get it. Why can't they just scramble an observation shuttle?" She had meant the question rhetorically, but that subtlety was obviously lost on the aide.

The specialist responded cheerfully. "Maybe the Admiral wanted him to experience the capabilities of a Raptor first hand, ma'am."

Taylor grimaced, and to her satisfaction, the aide seemed to wince a little.

"Who is this 'him'?" she asked.

"To be honest, I don't really know, ma'am. He's from the ground though. That much I could tell." The aide pointed behind her. "I asked him to wait over by the door while I found you, ma'am."

Taylor frowned. VIPs were common during routine missions. Sometimes they were war reporters there to do a story. Or they were ground commanders who came up to familiarize themselves with Fleet's strategies and protocols. She had even had a pair of Senators who had travelled all the way from Alba Calea just so they could fly over Troya and see what was left. But this was different. This wasn't a routine patrol; this was a major operation. As she followed the aide, she wondered if there was any way she might still get out of this. Perhaps she could plead her case to the Admiral, put in a request for no add-ons to her manifest. However, as she came to the end of the hanger, she gave up all hope of avoiding her new charge as soon as she saw the hunchbacked man standing in the doorway.

"Commander Licinius Droesus," she said in her most cheerful tone. "Welcome aboard the *Unifier*."

Great. The creepy guy from the Consul's command meeting. Can my day get any better? She smiled as she stuck out her hand and Droesus stared at her outstretched arm with a surprised look before enthusiastically accepting her handshake.

"Major Caellyn, it is an honor to ride along side you," the hook-nosed man answered in a gravel-laden voice as he vigorously shook her hand. "I assure you that I will not be of any inconvenience whatsoever. You won't even know I'm here."

They all say that, she thought as she smiled and nodded. *He's enthusiastic at least, and polite, but there's something going on behind that one eye of his. Is that fear? Is it shame? What is he doing here anyhow? Doesn't he have a tank column to command?* She squared herself to him, which only seemed to make him even more uncomfortable as she saw him shift his feet nervously. *How is this guy a Commander? He's got all the confidence of an abused prisoner.* She cleared her throat. "We're always eager to welcome guests from the ground, Commander," she said. "But is there a reason you want to ride in a Raptor and not one of our observation aircraft? Perhaps a Vernal, or one of the modified Trawlers?"

The crooked old man stiffened and adjusted his eye patch. "It is my understanding, Major, that the Raptor's observation equipment is superior to both the Trawler and Vernal, or anything else that will be circling the valley today for that matter."

He's got that much right, she admitted grudgingly to herself. "I suppose I can't argue with that," she answered in a friendly tone. Taylor briefly thought about asking him why he was here and not on the ground, but something on his face made her think better of it. Instead, she smiled brightly and pointed over her shoulder. "Come with me, sir, and I'll get you taken care of straight away. I'm about to brief my pilots."

Droesus slunk behind her like a wary dog, looking left and right as they walked across the bay. To her, the crooked, one-eyed man looked paranoid, even fearful, as his eyes flitted about the bay. Taylor stored the information in the back of her mind, another puzzle dropped squarely on her lap. Debating whether she could put him in Shale's cockpit or her own, she decided that if her first patrol got too boring, she could prod him with a few questions.

Her XO, Captain Josiah, still had everyone gathered outside her office when they walked up. Taylor stopped to stand front and center before pulling the clipboard off the magnetic brace on her knee and readying her pen.

"Alright folks, listen up," her voice echoed against the hanger walls. "I need to get this briefing done before any more changes come from down from Top. As you know, we're running two simultaneous patrols around the valley to provide air cover and surveillance while our ground forces attempt to take the city. Each patrol will be comprised of two Raptors." She turned on her projector and a holographic map of the Sinvoresse Valley popped up between her and everyone else. "The Consul divided up our zone of responsibility into two zones, and I've assigned one patrol for each zone. That's one patrol for this inner circle around Sindorum itself and one patrol for the outer regions in the mountains." Now if you hadn't heard, Top took Misha, Cole, Kima, and Cully down to the shuttle wing and gave us four rookies as replacements. All of whom are flying with us today." Taylor pointed and everyone turned to look at Aerelli, Brannon, Pac, and Lorkin who were standing together in the back of the crowd. Pac waved awkwardly while Aerelli blushed. "Aerelli and Brannon are with me and Shale for the first patrol. Each round of patrols will last for two hours, at which point your replacements will arrive for the next round and you will return here, to *Unifier*, for re-fuel and re-supply."

She pressed a button on the top of the projector and it flipped to the next image, a metal sphere roughly the size of a small cottage that was mounted on a circular platform. "Top has informed me that these objects have popped up all over the Sinvoresse Valley in the last two weeks. Although we've yet to get a good look at who's setting them up, or even what they do, it's a good bet that they have something to do with Teum's last stand. If you spot one of these at any time, your rules of engagement are to check to see if any friendlies are in the area, and then you are clear to frag."

She saw Brannon raise his hand, and she gave him a nod to speak.

"Do we have to call in before we fire?" the dark-haired youth asked.

Taylor shook her head. "You're a big kid now. Just let Command know once the job's done. Welcome to Arc."

Vitrel, one of her senior pilots, spoke up next. "But if Command doesn't know what they do, don't they want to seize one at some point?"

"I'm told that Intel already has a couple that the drop troops nabbed this morning," Taylor answered.

"And they still don't know what they do?" Shale asked with a smirk.

"They think it might be some kind of jamming device. Might even have something to do with an E.M.P or something," Taylor shrugged. "Look, all we gotta do is blow the bitches up if we seem them. If that changes, Top should let us know."

A few chuckles were traded among the crowd of pilots and Taylor continued before anyone else could cut in. "And as a last minute FRA-GO from Top, we have a VIP, Commander Droesus, riding with us as an observer." When she gestured to the man standing behind her, she saw him twitch nervously. "I'll be taking him with me on the first round, and if the Commander hasn't had enough after that, he'll be jumping on with someone else once I return to *Unifier*."

She flipped her projector back to the map of the Sinvoresse Valley, clasped her hands behind her back, and looked out at her pilots. "I don't know how long this op is going to take, and so I don't know how many times each of you is going to have to go out. So, use the time you have between patrols to rest and keep fresh. Does anyone have any more questions?"

All she got back were nods. She gave them all a thumb's up and then checked her watch.

"Alright, everyone finish their checks. First patrol leaves in twenty-seven minutes. Let's bring this one home."

At that, the crowd broke apart as the pilots broke away in singles and pairs. Taylor had refrained from saying this would be their last patrol. It wasn't. There would be plenty of surveillance flights and peacekeeping patrols after this was over, but even so there was an air of finality among the pilots of her wing. This was likely their last "big op." The last time many of them would be in any real danger for a long time. And so, Taylor could feel a kind of loose seriousness and the passive tension bottled up in her pilots as the crowd dispersed and the pilots walked to their fighters.

She spotted her wingman, Shale, talking to Aerelli outside Bay 2A, where Shale's ship rested. Taylor sighed and rubbed her eyes. The girl had looked lost at first but now they were clearly flirting … in the middle of the bay … while everyone else was finishing their pre-flight checks. Shale was lanky, red-haired, freckle-faced and looked even younger than his twenty-three years. Taylor had kept him as her wingman for the last six months, and he'd yet to make a mistake worth remembering. Like many of the young men in her wing, he looked at her with a mixture of lust and respect. Now she was watching him flirting with one of the very pilots they would be flying with in less than an hour.

Taylor liked to keep her nose out of her pilots' personal business—the Fates knew she wanted them out of hers. *But I need Shale's mind on the mission at hand and not some rookie's ass who just showed up. Which is to say nothing about the rookie's mind which is, presumably, joining said ass in the rookie's first ever combat mission.* Taylor glanced over at the two pilots and saw Aerelli giggle as she batted her eyes at Shale. *I don't know what's worse, the fact that this little kid still has her face painted like a teenager going to a party, or the fact that I'm about to cock-block the same guy who has to watch my back today.*

Taylor cleared her throat. "Shale, Aerelli, have either of you finished your pre-flight checks?"

Shale at least had the decency to look embarrassed. The girl just looked at her with her mouth open.

"No ma'am," Shale replied.

"Alright then," Taylor said flatly.

Shale turned around and walked back toward his fighter.

Aerelli stared wide eyed like a deer while Taylor did her best to return a neutral stare. *It's just the wrong time to be flirting, kid.*

"Yes ma'am," Aerelli finally squeaked and then, like a scared mouse, the little blonde girl spun around and scurried away toward the bay of her own ship.

Taylor sighed and shook her head. *Perhaps I'll explain to Shale later.* She reminded herself that she didn't have time to worry about her co-pilot's perceptions now. Taylor checked her watch. She and Shale were set to launch in twelve minutes. She started making a second pass over her preflight checks and was double checking the firing mechanisms on the *Wyvern's* air-to-surface missiles when Shale walked up behind her.

"Ready to go, ma'am?" he asked.

"Do I look like I'm ready, or what?" she said with a smirk. It was likely the last time she would fly a mission in hostile territory. She had been anticipating and dreading this moment since she had woken up that morning.

"Yes ma'am," Shale smiled broadly before leaning in and, with a quiet voice, he said, "Sorry about the... uhm..."

She waved him off. "I don't care if you screw her. Just wait until we're not in the air." Shale blushed and laughed as she pulled her hair back and tied it off. "We leave as soon as I get our VIP seated. Get your equipment warmed up. The XO is getting him a helmet and then we'll be down the chute."

"Sounds good, ma'am." Shale glanced over his shoulder. "I'm all set. The other two are just about there, I think."

Taylor looked down the launch chute. The other wing wasn't ready yet either, and so the bay doors that connected the chute to the hanger still lay open, awaiting their first Raptor to arrive and request launch. Her mind briefly wondered if the civilian world would bring her anything resembling the feelings that were running through her right now. She always felt a mixture of excitement and apprehension before a mission, but now, thinking of the end of the war, the message from Lucian, and the prospect of another life—in that moment she felt afraid, uncertain and fearful of the change that would inevitably come. She was standing there, staring blankly at the nose of her fighter when she heard the shuffling, lurching limp of her guest approaching.

She spoke loudly without looking. "Commander Droesus, did Captain Josiah get you squared away?"

"Y-yes, he did," the tentative, rasping voice replied.

Taylor rubbed her eyes before turning around and forcing a smile. "Well then, let's get on with it. Shall we?"

Droesus did no more than grunt his approval, and she had him climb into the cockpit first. The Raptor was designed to be flown by a lone pilot, but a co-pilot seat was kept outfitted for surveillance and reconnaissance missions—or for an observer, like now. Taylor helped the hunchbacked commander fit into his seat, strap on his helmet, and fasten all of his safety equipment. On the odd chance that she did get shot down, she didn't want her guest splattered all over the ground because he didn't strap himself into the ejection seat properly.

Minutes later, she taxied the *Wyvern* toward the launch chute and found herself, unsurprisingly, the first one there. Major Taylor Caelynn liked being first; it suited her ego. She keyed up the mic and called the control tower.

"Unifier Control this is Rapier One. Requesting launch."

"Rapier One this is Control, you are clear for launch. Happy hunting."

DELEA

Delea hefted her backpack and set it down. It felt heavy to her. She thought of opening it again to see if there was anything else she could leave behind, but then it occurred to her again that this was it: all of her worldly possessions reduced to a single tan backpack. It was strange to think that her possessions, her life, was now reduced to the contents of one backpack. However, when she surveyed the rest of her tent and found it empty, she realized how little that would change anything. *What's changing is that there's not another camp. Mom's not taking us somewhere else to stay for a while. This is the end. I'm leaving our home and maybe never coming back.*

Delea still had no idea what her mother's plans were. When she asked her mother where they were going, the Queen had simply told her to get ready and be quiet. So Delea went and asked the captain of the guard, but Roake had only laughed and told her to ask her mother. Finally, she had gone to the bodyguards who were staying behind, but Dakko and Motya knew even less than she did. Now she was sitting in her tent, repacking her back for the third time and wondering if she was carrying too much or too little.

The tent flap moved and Motya's head poked its way inside. "Your Highness, have you seen your sister?"

Delea snapped her backpack up and slung it over her shoulders. "No. Why?"

"Because no one else has either," Motya replied.

"She's not in her tent?" Delea asked the obvious question as she walked outside.

"No, your Highness. That's why we're looking for her," Motya said as he gestured toward the mountains that ringed the valley. "And as you can see, time is of the essence."

Delea followed Motya's arm to look up at the valley's wall to see the fires still burning along the mountain ridgeline. Last night their enemy had landed, just as everyone said they would. Delea had been cleaning tents for the night shift when she witnessed the first wave falling across the clear night sky, dropping like comets and striking like meteorites on one of the Blackfriar's northern peaks. The camps had come alive then as people rose from their sleep to watch. Delea had joined a crowd of nurses gathered around the gazebo where they smoked. These were drop pods, Dakko had said, the first wave of the final invasion. There was a village up there, someone explained, but it had been forcibly abandoned by the King's soldiers and should now be empty. Minutes later an orbital strike struck, lighting the mountainside on fire. Over the next several hours, she watched the scene repeat itself until there were seven fires ringed like a crown along the top of the Sinvoresse valley.

Motya pulled open the front flaps of Fel's tent and Delea glanced inside to see a green backpack leaned up against an empty cot. "No one has seen her since oh-five-hundred when Thayne looked in on her."

Delea glanced at her watch. *That was nearly an hour ago...*

Motya shrugged. "But if you haven't seen her your Highness, then I'll..."

"Delea!" The Queen walked out from between two tents with Camus and Roake close behind her. "Where in the name of the Weaver is your sister?"

Delea shrugged and held up her hands.

Motya, morphing from frustrated to penitent, got down on one knee when he saw the Queen. "I just got done asking her myself, your Highness."

"Get up," the Queen snapped. "Keep looking."

Motya stood and hurried off into the dark.

Her mother's face was a mask of cold fury. "Your sister has picked a devil of a time to go missing."

Delea's shock was beginning to turn into worry as she watched her mother wave toward Fel's empty tent.

"Thayne and Motya were on duty and neither of them has an inkling of where she went or if she was taken!" Her mother managed to sound both furious and scared. "But this is useless talk now. Leave your bag and come with me."

Delea unslung her backpack and dropped it back inside her tent. Jogging, she caught up to her mother and the others at the bottom of the ancient stone steps that led halfway down the hill. Delea had not seen her mother this angry since the last time she had argued with her father. With Roake and Camus close behind, the Queen stomped straight over to the ruins of the palace's outer wall where the cooks were set up.

The only man there was Feleg, the head cook, who was stoking the first of his fires in one of the cooking pits. When he saw the Queen approaching he stepped away from the fire and dropped to one knee and bowed.

"Get up. I don't have time for that. Feleg, has my daughter been to see you this morning?"

The cook stood and dusted off his apron. "No, your Highness. I was about to ask you about her, because two of your other guards asked me the same question as I was walking here. When my cooks arrive, I may dispatch them to look for her as well, if you wish."

The Queen signaled for Roake and Camus to spread out, which they did, looking through the cook tents and fire pits as though they were searching for contraband. Feleg, as Delea saw, did not appear surprised or offended but waited patiently with his hands folded and his head bowed before the Queen even as the fire next to him died out.

"I do *not* wish for that, Feleg. I wish to keep this matter as quiet as possible, but if you can quietly ask them to keep eye out as they come in, that would be best."

"Of course, your Highness," Feleg replied.

Roake walked up and stopped behind the cook. "She's not here, your Highness."

Delea followed her mother's gaze as the Queen looked out at the surrounding tents, their colors still muted by the lingering dark.

"Then where do you suggest we look next?" the Queen asked.

Roake spared a glance back at Camus who was helping himself to a piece of jerky, and then bowed again to the Queen. "Since Kress and

Marental are already searching the gardens, I would suggest the fields to the west. The Princess played there often, and perhaps she met someone there to say goodbye."

"Then lead on, Roake," the Queen replied.

They were quickly off. Leaving Feleg and the cook fires behind, the four of them marched through the tents and toward the fields. However, not two minutes into their march, Delea heard a call come in over the radios. She realized then that she had forgotten her radio back at her tent with her pack, and so she had to wait and watch as her mother and Roake and Camus all listened as the call came in. Then Camus let out a laugh as he and Roake turned around and started walking back toward the hill and the ruins.

The Queen looked back at Delea with a frown. "They found her."

"Who?" Delea asked.

"Kress and Marental." The Queen shook her head in frustration. "She was walking up from the gardens."

They met Marental and Kress back at the Queen's tent where they were standing with Fel between them. Delea watched Fel stand and sulk while the Queen began interrogating her.

"What in the name of the Weaver were you doing?"

Fel hung her head. "Nothing."

Their mother's voice was full of serious anger. "Why did you sneak off? Why didn't you tell anyone?"

Fel sulked. "Dunno."

The Queen had her hands on her hips. "Were you meeting someone to say goodbye?"

"No. I wasn't meeting no one. I was by myself."

Delea quietly ducked out to grab her backpack and her radio from her tent. To Delea, it looked as though her sister had been caught without a good cover story and was now stalling to see if she could flip things in her favor. *But that's always been the difference between us. Fel has no sense of who she is. Of how important she is to her family and everyone else. She thinks she's just a regular girl, but she's not.*

When Delea returned, she listened to Fel admit that she had snuck away to say good bye to one of her friends, though she wouldn't say who.

When Fel was done, the Queen got down on her knees and hugged her youngest daughter tight.

Delea held back an annoyed sigh as Fel ran off to get her pack. Fel had always been a little different, but it had not been until the last few years that she had begun finding ways of using her strangeness to her advantage. It was beyond Delea why Fel had chosen now, of all times, to play a disappear-and-reappear game on everyone else, but if Fel had wanted to get away with anything strange, now was certainly the time to do it. When Fel returned with her backpack on her shoulders they were finally away, marching off into the dark in a single file line.

Roake took the lead, picking his way down the cliff and the rocks along the back side of the hill. No one from camp could see them here, and the crashing waves masked any sound they might have made as they marched down the winding path. The ground had turned to sand and Delea could feel the ocean spray from the waves crashing against the rocky shore below. Halfway down the hill, Roake brought them to a halt between two rocky crags. Delea was unable to see what hidden device Roake activated, but soon a rock slid aside to reveal a tunnel that led down into the sandy earth.

Delea pulled the flashlight off her backpack as she stepped inside the tunnel. Looking back, Delea watched Kress and Marental bow their heads and hunch their shoulders as they entered the rocky passage. A firm layer of hard-packed sand lined the floor, and Delea could feel her boots leave a print each time she stepped. But for the lights they carried, everything before and behind them was black as pitch as they marched downward, deeper into the earth. When the rocky passage leveled off, Delea's flashlight caught the opening to a massive room filled with grain and it was then she realized where they were. These were the storehouses that Empress Aelia had constructed beneath her palace, and the tunnel soon led them through several more of the cavernous storerooms that had been cut deep into the hill's bedrock. Then the tunnel branched and Roake took a right, leading them away from the storerooms and toward what Delea guessed was a north-easterly direction. Two succeeding sets of steps led them down, deeper into the earth. The air was old and impossibly musty here, and Delea had to hold her shirt over her nose as she walked to keep from coughing. Finally, after nearly half an hour of walking in the dark, the tunnel ended in a long set of stone steps that led up to a door, which lay flat against the ceiling.

Delea marched up the steps and climbed out of the doorway onto the surface, where Delea spotted an empty rowboat trapped in a pool of water between the rocks. Looking back along the bay, she guessed they were at least two miles from the camp. Looking back at the rowboat that was lolling against the rocks, Delea wondered if it was the same boat that had carried Noemi and her then-unborn baby across the Bay of Sardis.

Roake led them north across the open plain, and after an hour of marching, Delea saw a sliver of sun peek over the eastern mountaintops. Her little sister was walking next to her, and for a moment, Delea considered asking her what she had been doing that morning. Perhaps Fel had considered running away but had lost her nerve. *But what would be the point? We're running away from everything now as it is. Perhaps I can ask her once we get off planet.*Ahead of them, she heard Motya and Kress laughing at a joke that Dakko had told. They were walking through the short, bright green grass that bordered the shoreline, and only a hundred yards to the south waves were crashing against the sandy shore. Far to the north, Delea could hear the mechanical rumblings of the Coalition. All of them had seen the shuttles descending from orbit, ferrying soldiers and supplies to the Coalition's base camp that was nestled somewhere up in the foothills of the Blackfriar Mountains that ringed the valley. They were marching alongside a leg-deep stream, and Dakko was in the middle of another story when a rumble like an earthquake sounded from the mountains. Everyone went quiet and turned their eyes northward.

"It sounds like some huge metal beast," Fel whispered as the echoes trailed off into the mountains.

"If you speak of the Imperium, your Highness," Roake replied, "you're not far off."

"Why's that?" Fel asked.

Roake smiled at the question before he spoke. "I was on Troya when they came the first time, little princess. The replicants, they don't fight like other soldiers. There are few volunteers, and most of those are officers or nobles like the Ieses. There are no women in their ranks either. All men. No, most of their combat troops are replicants, genetically engineered for war." Roake stole a glance up toward the sky. "On Troya I fought them. They charge through gunfire. They ignore their dead. They fight wounded, often to their death. You rarely hear them speak or yell to each other, but they move as one. And out of all the replicants, the Kodayene are the strongest. Most of the other strains have minds like children to make them easier for the Ieses to control. However, a Kodayene is far stronger than any human or Duathe *and* can think like an adult, which makes them all the more dangerous."

Everyone else was quiet, and Delea saw Motya steal a glance back at Marental and Kress. The two towering women were the only female Kodayene ever produced, and they had been given to her father, the King, as a present from the Imperium during a more peaceful time. However, if the topic of conversation bothered either woman, they gave no notice.

Roake let the silence hang for another second before tussling Fel's hair. "But don't you worry, we're going to get the both of you off this planet before they arrive."

Fel looked up at him. "Will you keep fighting after they take the city?"

Roake smiled gently. "I will do as your mother asks."

Thayne snorted out a laugh. "We'll fight if we're able, child."

"I, for one, would love to fight," Motya said with an air of confidence.

Roake glanced back toward the other two. "You would not say that if you had a woman and a family to go back to."

Thayne rolled his eyes and smiled lazily. "You don't know that we don't, old man."

Then Roake's wrist beeped and he rolled back his sleeve to look at his navigator. "We're there."

Roake stopped them in the shadow of a small hill and they huddled in the tall grass. Everything around them was bathed in the gray light that only exists in those brief minutes between night and morning. Delea had often been awake at this hour, helping her mother and the nurses and doctors, and as she sat there on her knees with the leaves of grass brushing against her face, it hit her again how that was all over now. She was no longer a nurse or a medic, but someone else. This was the beginning of their exile. An exile that she and her sister would be beginning alone. Then she heard the *swish-swish-swish* of someone crawling through the grass and soon her mother and her sister emerged from the grass beside her. The Queen huddled the three of them together as she spoke in a low voice.

"Now listen, girls, because we may not see each other for a while now, and I can only tell you this once. The planet where you're going is called Linneaum. Neither of you have ever been there, but it sits on the border between the Imperium, the Republic, and us, though it belongs to the Imperium itself now. Before I was Queen, my aunt was married to the Margrave of Linneaum. She has always looked fondly on you girls, and she's promised to take you in as a favor. No one except for the people you see here know where you are going."

Miles away, another bomb exploded against the city, and their mother stole a glance toward Sindorum as a finger of black smoke began to rise into the morning sky. "I told your father to send only the pilots and aircraft to take you to the launch site, lest a soldier overhear your final destination and it somehow leaks to our enemies. I am sending Roake, Kress, Marental, Camus, and Thayne with you, just to be safe."

"But what about you, Mother?" Delea asked.

"Do not worry about me, dear." Her mother touched her cheek and smiled. "I have made my arrangements. I hope to join you on Linneaum someday. It just may be a while before that can happen."

Then a black shadow passed over the field, and the backdraft of the craft's engines washed over the grass in a wave as Delea looked up to see an armored troop carrier swing about, looping around them in a wide arc as it prepared to land.

The Queen grabbed each of her daughters by the arm, and Delea turned to meet her mother's gaze. "Remember who you are. Take care of each other. I'll be with you as soon as I can. I love you both."

They all said their final round of goodbyes as they embraced each other in the long grass. Finally, when the ramp of the first ATC lowered to the ground, their mother released them and pushed them toward the aircraft.

"Now go," she said.

It was easier than Delea had imagined it would be, grabbing Fel by the hand and running across the field. Running up the aft ramp, they passed a dark-green-skinned tail gunner wearing a pair of dark sunglasses with a cigar in his mouth. He saluted them as they passed, a toothy grin on his lips as he puffed his cigar.

Kress and Marental met them at the top of the ramp and helped them to their seats as the aircraft lifted off the ground. As the ramp closed behind them, Delea caught one last glimpse of her mother standing alone, looking up at them as they rose into the air.

There were well over forty seats in the bay of the aircraft, but only seven passengers and the tail-gunner, which left plenty of open space. Kress and Marental seated themselves near the back ramp with the tail gunner, while Roake, Camus, and Thayne sat near the front with Delea and Fel. Someone lit a cigarette and the smoke drifted into her face, burning her nostrils.

"Thayne! Goddamn it, put that out!" Roake yelled from the back.

Thanye stopped where he was, his hands frozen in midair. Fel looked up and wrinkled her nose at him. From the back, Delea saw Roake scowl.

"It's a ten-minute flight to the launch site. You can wait until then. Now put that out," the captain of the guard barked.

"Yes sir," Thayne mumbled as he rubbed the cigarette out on the bay wall. Thayne had a sleepy, hungover look about him as he gently pushed the burnt cigarette back into his pack. "Sorry sir. Just a little overtired."

Camus grinned. "Why you tired, Thayne? Something keep you up last night?"

Thayne smiled lazily. "Wouldn't you like to know, Cam?"

The ATC jostled and bumped as it rose into the sky, and Delea double-checked the straps on both her and her sister's harnesses. Once they leveled off, she saw Roake get up from his seat and walk over to them. The captain of the guard then grasped the webbing behind the seats for balance as he got down on one knee. "Your Highnesses, we are taking you straight to the launch site. When we get there, we will set you down and form a perimeter as you and your security team board the escape vessel."

Delea interrupted him. "And where is this escape vessel, Captain?"

"The backside of Mount Chernon, almost parallel in elevation to the palace. It's hidden inside the mountain, so we won't be able to see it from the air, but I'm told the King has a team in place and the rocket it ready to fire. All we have to do is get you there safely and—"

Delea interrupted him again. "Do you have the call-sign of the launch site team?"

"Yes, your Highness, it is Castle. We've contacted a 'Castle Four' already and confirmed..."

Roake was interrupted by the roaring engine of a passing aircraft and the ATC shuddered as it went by. From the wake of the blast, it felt as though the interlopers had passed right over their heads. Delea heard Camus curse under his breath.

"What was that?" Roake asked.

Thayne ripped off his headset. "Sir, the pilots say we have a pair of Raptors circling us!"

"Sonofabitch!" the tail gunner yelled from the back, and Delea saw him take aim with his weapon. With a grunt the gunner pulled the trigger and a stream of bullets flew out from the barrel of his minigun.

"Hang on!" Roake said as he hurried back to his seat.

No one spoke, and the only sounds were the ATC's engines and the air rushing by. Then Delea heard a distant whining scream that could only be a pair of starfighters soaring through the atmosphere.

"They're circling round on us!" Thayne yelled. "We're directly over the city now. The pilots are taking evasive maneuvers."

Everyone adjusted their safety harnesses and helmets and grabbed the safety straps that hung above their seats. Even Fel seemed to immediately grasp the situation, bracing herself against the wall with one hand and grabbing a safety strap with the other.

Delea felt their ATC speed up and rise higher in the air before falling into a dive. Looking through the window of a side door near her seat, she could see rooftops passing by just beneath the craft. She looked to the back of the bay where a viewport showed two specks on the horizon, swooping down from the mountains and growing larger and larger as they neared. Then two trails of smoke launched from the speck on the left and their pursuers peeled off, climbing into the sky and out of view. The next two seconds passed in slow motion. Holding her breath, she watched the two trails of smoke as they grew closer and closer. Her mouth went dry as she thought of her mother and father, and then she reached over and grasped Fel's hand. Behind them, she could see the missiles closing in and a sense of finality took hold of her. What would it be like to die in a crash?

The ATC slowed and lowered itself until it was no longer flying above the rooftops, but flying between them. Delea watched the shattered husks of houses and trees like burned skeletons fly by as the pilots attempted their evasive maneuvers. But somehow Delea knew it was all in vain.

Another furious second passed. They could no longer see the missiles approaching but everyone could hear the dull roar of their approach. The ATC swerved sharply, and something hard struck the craft's belly. Delea heard something snap, and everything shuddered. Then the explosion. For a fraction of a second everything in the bay was trapped in stillness before the shockwave hit them. Fire and smoke were everywhere as the ATC rocked like a boat in a storm and began to spin.

Everything swirled and a blinding light of many colors filled Delea's vision. Then nothing.

TAYLOR

4.28.2388 – Planet Arc, Orbit

Major Taylor Caellyn taxied *Wyvern* into the center of the metal pathway that was her launch chute. She watched a flicker of light shimmer across chute's mouth as the shielding dropped away and she felt a bump as her wheels settled into their grooves. Behind her, she heard Droesus clear his throat and she wondered if the old armor officer had ever ridden in a starfighter before. Then the bay doors closed behind them and they waited. Taylor heard all the air leave the launch chute with a quiet, steady *hissssssssss,* and then the hatch on the far end of the tunnel opened and the vacuum of space began to pull her ship forward. She fired the *Wyvern's* engines and her Raptor shot forward like a bolt of lightning.

The first time she experienced a vacuum launch in training, it had unnerved her so badly that her hands shook. Contrary to the entertainment media's portrayal, there really was no sound in space. Things simply happened as if you were watching a show with the sound turned off. As a rookie, that had unnerved her despite months of simulations. Now, after years of operating spacecraft, she felt at home out here in the vacuum. For Taylor Caelynn, launching into space was like putting on an old coat that always fit just right. An old coat full of silence and death.

Taylor put the *Wyvern* into a short orbit around *Unifier* while she waited for Shale and the others to launch. She had just pulled up a tactical map of Sinvoresse Valley when she heard the *Wyvern's* intercom crackle to life.

"Is this…" She heard Commander Droesus clear his throat again. "…is this thing on? Can you hear me? Are you there, Major? Can you…"

She pulled her mic to her mouth. "I can hear you loud and clear, Commander. How are you settling in back there?"

The cockpit vibrated as he shuffled in his seat. He was probably larger than he looked with the hunchback and all.

"Quite well, Major. Quite well." His voice sounded like a snake that had swallowed a mouthful of gravel. "The display is ... similar to that of a Stryker."

"It's familiar to you then?"

"Yes. Quite so, actually." He cleared his throat again. He sounded nervous to her. "I have one question, however. What is my call-sign while I'm back here? Do I even have one?"

"You can go by Rapier One Golf. That way they know who you're riding with and that you're a guest," Taylor answered.

"Thank you, Major. I will use that. Rapier One Golf..." he repeated.

Then Shale's Raptor shot out of *Unifier*'s maw and Taylor spun the *Wyvern* around in a tight 180 as she accelerated past her wingman. Moments later, the Raptors piloted by Aerelli and Brannon shot out one after the other. Taylor quickly got the four of them into formation and together they descended down toward Arc's atmosphere. She re-checked the settings on the *Wyvern*'s shielding in the minutes before they reached Arc's stratosphere, and she heard Droesus gasp as the fire began rolling over the cockpit. Less than a minute later, the flames receded and the clouds came into view.

The Sinvoresse Valley was still as quiet as Taylor had left it, but even from a thousand feet above the valley floor, she could see its peaceful state wouldn't last for long. Leading her little formation of four starfighters across the valley's northern edge, she saw that the tank column was already winding its way across the valley. For just a moment, she felt a pang of envy for whoever was leading the 5th Armored. He would be seeing combat up close, and although she did not relish the sight of dead bodies, she *did* miss the heat of the conflict. Missions for her fighters had been little more than escorts, recon, or patrol work like this. Things had gotten so routine that the newer pilots listened to music in their cockpits while flying, something unheard of in prior wars. But Taylor couldn't blame them. Their biggest worry was a surface-to-air missile, or maybe a lucky shot by a well-crafted drone.

They had crushed the Duathic Starfleet right at the beginning of the war. Marius had conceived a brilliant—if ruthless—bait and switch, where a pair of bomber wings were sent to bomb a few of the urban factories on Muani. The bombing was anything but surgical, and the haphazard destruction had done as much damage to the civilian population as it did to the factories. Wanting to protect their people, and thinking Marius had established a secret base somewhere in the Muani system, the Duathic fleet had reacted immediately, scrambling most of their fleet to secure the planet and then sweep the rest of the system. To their knowledge, they were simply beating Marius to the punch, as their intelligence had told them that Marius' Republican fleet was marshaling at Pontus. What they didn't know was that Marius had already snuck over half his fleet behind the largest of Muani's four moons.

The Battle of the Four Moons was Taylor's first and only dogfight. The entire battle had lasted all of ninety minutes, but she had managed to shoot down four enemy craft. One kill short of an ace. It was a fact that had dogged her for over a year after, until she had let it go when someone told her that she had the highest kill count of anyone left alive (there had been a Captain Nemek who had shot down six that day, but he disappeared months later while running a reconnaissance mission on Troya).

Looking down at her display panel, Taylor was pleased to see that Aerelli and Brannon had no trouble staying in precise formation as they came through the clouds and turned north. Travelling at a smooth seven hundred miles per hour, the water of the Auletin Ocean flew by beneath them. Four minutes later she could see the peaks of the Blackfriar Mountains rising up from the water's surface. She checked her tactical readout of the valley again. The tank column was half way across the valley now, and she could see tiny red dots scattered all over the city where Philemon's Kodayene drop troops had landed. Everything looked like it was going according to the Consul's plan.

She keyed up her mic, "Rapier Three and Rapier Four, this is Rapier One. You guys can start your patrol of the outer perimeter. Call us if you need us."

Aerelli called back with an affirmative and Taylor watched on her scanner as the two rookies took off toward the north. Once she saw they were on their way, she keyed up her mic again. "Alright Rapier Two, let's go do a quick fly-by of the city."

"Roger that, Rapier One."

She sped up as she aimed the *Wyvern* at the city. Pillars of smoke were rising into the sky as she came up behind Mt. Chernon and the city of Sindorum. Both she and Shale stayed up high for their first pass. No need to be flying low and give anyone on the surface a chance to catch them out with a lucky shot. She ran a quick sensor scan of the city as they passed by overhead. Nothing much was moving down there, but the air over Sindorum was as clear as a window.

Droesus's voice came through her earpiece. "Major, can you tell me how far out the tank column is now?"

She checked her scanner again. "They look to be about … twenty minutes from the city, sir."

"Hrm…" the older man grunted. "Ahead of schedule."

She wondered at his tone of voice for a moment. Was that approval she heard? Hadn't Droesus *lost* command of the tank column? Wasn't he being punished? Taylor had expected him to be bitter and brooding.

She adjusted the mic on her helmet. "Sir, there's something I've wanted to ask you, if you don't mind?"

There was a short pause before Droesus grumbled his assent. "Go ahead, Major."

"Did I miss something at the command meeting?" she asked. "Is there a reason you're here and not with your tank column?"

She could hear Droesus shift uncomfortably in his chair. "The Consul decided that, in light of recent developments, it would be better if I act as an observer." The old man wheezed nervously into the mic. "He put a … much younger officer in my place to, I believe, groom him for future endeavors."

Droesus voice trailed off then and Taylor said nothing, taken aback by the emotion behind his voice. The Consul had taken away his command? For who?

After a minute, Droesus's voice picked up again with a tone of false humor. "We old officers do not go out to pasture easily, but I suppose my time is nearer than I thought."

She nodded thoughtfully and they flew in silence for several minutes. The *Wyvern* cut quickly over the Blackfriar mountain range as she and Shale completed their first flyover of the territory surrounding the valley. The last of the mountains fell away behind them, and a call came in over the radio as they turned out over the Bay of Sardis: "Rapier One, this is Reaper One over…"

Was that Ioma's voice? She pressed the button to respond. "Reaper One, this is Rapier One. Go ahead, over."

"Rapier One, this is Reaper One. Our surveillance team has spotted a pair of suspicious structures atop the ridgeline to our southwest. They appear to be large, metallic spheres, and as per our guidance from HQ they are to be destroyed if possible. Because they are out of Longbow's range, I was wondering if you could find a shot. Over."

She keyed the mic to respond. "Absolutely, Reaper One. Just send me the coordinates. Over."

"Roger that." His voice was casual. "I'll have my crew beam you the coordinates now. Reaper One out."

So, her lover had taken the command slot from her wayward VIP. Her mind couldn't help chew over this as she watched the coordinates load on her display. Ioma had always been ambitious. She wondered what had happened—or what he had done—to move from a logistics officer to the commander of a tank column in the span of a few hours. Then she remembered what he had said the other morning: *I've been talking to some people. I was hoping to get a little more command time under me before this is all over…* She wondered what all that had meant for the officer in her back seat.

She sent the coordinates to Shale and they turned back toward the mountain range. Beneath them, the ocean's white crested waves flew by. Shale called her back right as the shoreline came into view.

"Rapier One, this is Rapier Two. Do you want this one, or no?"

She smiled to herself. The question behind Shale's question was, *Can I shoot it?* She keyed her mic.

"Naw, go ahead Two. It's all you."

There was a short laugh behind his response. "Hell yeah."

They swung in a tight arc around the southwest end of the Black-friars and, sure enough, there was their target, tucked behind a finger of a mountain ridgeline. Shale pushed ahead of her as he drew a bead on the structure with his Raptor. Taylor lased the target with her scanners as he fired. She was curious as to what Ioma had called her to blow up. Shale's air-to-ground missile vaporized the target just as the image pulled up on her screen.

It was a metallic sphere about thirty feet in circumference, and her sensors picked up a small electric surge that emanated from the sphere shortly before Shale's missile disintegrated it. *Strange,* she thought as she soared over the blast zone. *It didn't* look *like a weapon. What kind of tactical advantage is something like that gaining from being atop a mountain ridgeline?*

She called back to Shale. "Rapier Two, let's make one more pass over to confirm the hit."

She could hear the excitement in Shale's voice as he answered. "Roger that, One."

Can't blame him, Taylor thought as she brought the *Wyvern* back around. *We've done little more than recon and escort missions for the better part of a month. A little fire mission is just the thing to keep the appetite wet.*

A second pass over the ridgeline revealed little else. There were no life forms, no other buildings, structures, or equipment. For all she could tell, their target had been nothing more than an electrically charged sphere sitting atop a piece of rock.

She keyed the mic again. "Doesn't look like anything more. Nice shot, Two. Let's head back to the city to see if we can find any more trouble."

She flipped her headset back to the *Wyvern's* internal comms as they circled around the Bay of Sardis again. They were about a minute out over the water when her guest's rasping voice came through her headset.

"Major Caellyn, I was wondering if I could ask you a slightly more … personal question."

She shrugged. The radio chatter was mostly quiet and the tank column still several minutes from reaching the city. "Sure. Fire away, sir. Don't really have anything to hide."

Droesus's laugh was nervous. "I was trying to place your last name. Are you perchance related to the Margrave of Tue?"

She nodded. "I am his older brother's daughter. Why?"

"Ah, Senator Caellyn. You are Lady Fiona's daughter, then?"

"Yes, but … well …" She replied, taken aback. "I guess I haven't heard anyone call my mother by her first name in quite a while. Not outside the family anyhow."

"Ah, it is nothing. Your mother and I were acquaintances when we were younger. Nothing more." She heard him shift in his seat again. "I had heard she had married a Caellyn. I knew you looked familiar. You look … just like her you know."

What a strange man, she thought as the city came into view.

"Do you mind if I use the radio to call the tank column?" Droesus said. "I wish to give a small advisement to their commander."

And just like that, he changes the subject, she shrugged. "Sure, go ahead."

She heard Droesus flip his radio from internal comms to the command channel.

"Reaper One, this is Rapier One Golf."

Ioma's radio man replied. "Rapier One Golf, this is Reaper One Romeo. Will relay, go ahead. Over."

Droesus paused and then called back. "Ah … please relay that I recommend for your unit to advance with all haste on the city. Time is … of the essence right now."

There was a long pause before the other side replied. "Rapier One Golf, this is Reaper One Romeo. Reaper One says that he is well aware of his timeline and that he is actually several minutes ahead of schedule. Unless you have any reason that you can state for advancing with *further* haste, we will maintain our current pace. Over."

Droesus voice dropped to a sullen tone. "If that is Reaper One's prerogative, then I have no further guidance. Rapier One Golf out."

Taylor ignored the awkward silence from the man in her back seat as they made another pass over the city. Nothing much was moving. A few people on foot, but their Raptors were too high up to identify them as soldiers or civilians. They circled twice, and she was about to turn and fly southwest over the bay again when she saw a blip on her sensors pop up on the southern side of the city.

She called over to Shale. "You see that Two?"

"Roger that. Is that in our jurisdiction?"

"I don't see why not," she answered.

They U-turned and cut their altitude down to where Sindorum looked like a carefully made model of a city. Taylor aimed her sensors at the unidentified bogey and focused the target. She grunted in disappointment. It was an ATC, an armored troop carrier. Just what she had thought. Her fighter wing had shot dozens of them down over Gravindi to the point where it had almost become a game. She keyed her mic again.

"You want this one, Rapier Two?"

She heard Shale laugh into the mic again. "Roger that, One."

Closing in on the ATC, Taylor saw the tail gun spit a volley of bullets toward them. She shook her head at the gunner's futility. Even if the tiny gun had the range, there was no way a heavy machine gun could pierce the outer armor of a Raptor. A second later, a pair of missiles launched from Shale's right wing, telling her he'd already gotten a lock on the target before she'd called him. They pulled off together and she kept her sensors focused on the tiny craft as it ducked down below the skyline in some vain attempt at evasive maneuvers, as if there were anything a hovercraft could do to outmaneuver a pair of air-to-air missiles guided by a Raptor's fire control system. Shale's payload found its target and she watched the blip vanish from her sensor array. It did not appear again.

PAR

Par's first day out of the sleeper cell was spent in a stupor. Called aether lag by the experienced spacers, it was caused by the prolonged inactivity of lying in a sleeper cell while being sustained by machines. Par's sleeper cells aboard the *Nameless* had muscle activators and dream simulations to keep mind and body active during sleep, but the first day of aether lag was still there all the same. He spent most of the first day eating, exercising and reviewing his mission notes. Exhausted, he slept for another twelve hours.

Waking on the second day, Par made his way to the cockpit to check his instruments, his course, and the *Nameless'* internal readings. Everything was as it should have been. When that was done, he walked back to the galley and woke his Shade from cold storage.

Are we there yet?

The gray cloud of nano-bots swarmed out of the compartment and swirled around the galley in a kind of victory lap. Par asked if the reason for its impatience was boredom or anxiety.

Both? Yes, both. You would be bored too if you had to spend three months helping you dream. And yes, I did help. You see, the ship's computer asked me to because it said it did not have enough simulations to properly fill up all three months with constructive simulations, but I think it just got sick of me asking it for things to do.

Par told his Shade that they were only a few moments out, when they would arrive at Arc's gate. He asked it if it had reviewed the mission notes.

Of course. Many of the simulations I ran for you involved some version of the scenarios likely involved in our acquisition of the Queen and her two daugh-

ters. I took some liberties. I'll also have you know that I calculated our odds of successfully capturing all three alive.

And?

They are low, but I am optimistic. We've overcome long odds before.

Yes, we have.

I'm also encouraged by the ages of the two princesses. Not only because it will give us an advantage over them, but because it will be nice for me to have some company. It has been so long since I talked to someone my age…

It was no use reminding it of what it was. The Shade was only an AI, and though it had absorbed the personality traits of many of those people who had been close to Par over the years, over the last hundred years or so, it had come to think of itself as a teenaged boy.

The stars in his viewport began to slow, blurring across his vision in white streaks until finally they came to a halt and all was still again. They had re-entered normal space-time. His rear camera caught Arc's star gate falling away behind him. He activated the *Nameless'* main engine, and he sat down in the pilot's chair right as a bright light shot across his bow. He had met the blockade.

A score of starfighters and a Republican frigate descended into his view. The frigate settled itself less than a hundred meters from his bow, and it swung its observation light across his viewport again so that Par had to shield his eyes. When the light faded, Par noticed that his control panel had lit up with an incoming message. He pressed the receive button. The frigate wanted to know who he was.

Oh, and you'll be happy to know that I took another look at our transponder codes and touched them up a bit. Whoever thought it was a good idea to label us as a diplomatic envoy was overthinking. We're a free trader. Nothing more than a guy with a ship hauling much needed medical supplies to some rich merchant on Arc's southern continent. Diplomatic envoys get military escorts to their destinations. Free traders don't. Once they've scanned us, they won't even give us a second glance.

Par transmitted the codes and a few minutes later his Shade was proven right. The frigate signaled for him to move forward as it pulled away. Par saw a predetermined flight path load into his navigation computer and he set his auto-pilot to follow the course. The blue globe of the planet Arc soon came into view.

An hour away from Arc's gravity well, Par asked his Shade to run some calculations. When they passed behind the dark side of the planet, Par re-aimed his ship and cut off the power to everything but the *Nameless'* emergency life support. His inertia and Arc's gravity could pull him in from here. He wanted to keep his energy signature as low as possible, and he knew that the *Unifier*, the most powerful ship in the Republican fleet, was out there somewhere within Arc's orbit, lurking, waiting to detect any deviants like himself. He ran silent all the way until he hit Arc's stratosphere, where he flipped on his maneuvering thrusters and aimed his ship toward a giant thunderhead over the ocean.

He turned on the *Nameless'* shielding right as the air resistance began to pick up. Fire and thunder passed over his hull, and the ship shivered and shook in the turbulence as he flew into the thunderhead. Par manipulated his maneuvering thrusters, once, twice, and then they were steady. Moments later, the storm clouds parted and now he was over the ocean, dark and roiling in the storm. Here was the dangerous part. If any Coalition ships were out on the waves within fifty clicks of his descent, they'd have him on their scanners and he would have to run. He flipped on his engines and the *Nameless* soared downward until Par pulled it up sharply and leveled off about thirty feet above the angry waves. He kept one eye on his sensor display as he aimed his ship northeast. An hour passed. Nothing showed. Ninety minutes later the sun broke over the horizon, illuminating the shadowy peaks of the Blackfriar Mountains.

His antennae picked up the signal a mile from the coast, an infrared beacon shooting its beam in a conical pattern over the waves. He traced it back to an enclave along the cliffs. Whoever was there knew what they were doing, since the short wave beam was about as discreet a signal as could be sent. Par was pleased. He signaled back and it promptly disappeared. He landed the *Nameless* on a flat, dry rock beneath the cliff face. He asked his Shade to join him as he unstrapped his safety-harness, and the cloud of nano-bots collapsed in on itself and crawled back inside of his body. Then he turned on the *Nameless'* active camouflage and climbed out of the cockpit. When Par reached the bottom of the ramp, his ship's exterior had changed its color to reflect the black and gray rock that surrounded it. It was not a pure cloaking device, but no one would see his ship unless they stumbled right up to it.

He saw her step out from behind an outcropping as his ramp slid shut behind him. She was a replicant. He recognized the face as one he'd seen before many times. She was a common model, likely from the servant class, plain but pretty with brown eyes and dark brown skin. He noticed that her head was shaved bald and covered in tattoos shaped like thorny vines, likely signs of the religious penitence that all replicants were programmed to have for the Ieses, the ruling family of the Umbrean Imperium. There was a grace to her gait as she came to stand before him, and he noticed a hint of a smile as she bent her head in a slight bow.

"You may call me Saithe, a name I've taken as our makers give us none. I'll save you from my real name which is no more than a series of numbers."

He bowed in return. "You may call me Par."

She laughed softly, girlish and warm. "Par ... this is a Ribari name? I have never met a Ribari Taker."

"Met many Takers, have you?" he asked dryly.

"More than you might guess," she said, humming as she spoke. "But most of them are dead now." She looked at him sideways, humming still, her voice taking on a musical and eerie tone. "Come, follow me and I will get you suited for the day ahead."

He nodded, and she led him down a rocky path that took them down to the base of the cliff where the mid-morning sun was rising over the mountains. She stopped them at a nook in the path where it turned through a batch of bushes. Reaching behind a bramble of thorny flowers, she produced a black duffle bag.

"Here," she said, handing him the duffle. "This is your cover for the time being. You are an aid worker with the Imperium."

Par took the bag from her and unzipped it. There was a uniform and a small case of medical equipment.

She cocked her head in a way that could easily be construed as seductive. "I trust you know enough first aid to manage?"

He nodded. "I should."

Saithe kept a look out on the path as Par dressed himself behind the bushes. When he was done, he left his old clothes in the bag behind the bush. Then he followed her as they continued down the path. Cresting a rise in the earth, the open plains of the Sinvoresse Valley opened up before them, and the tattooed woman gestured to the northwest.

"About a mile ahead of us are the Gardens of Eire. Queen Anyse has set up her refugee camp there." Her voice purred as she spoke. "The Coalition detachment should be arriving within the hour."

The clothing she had given him was a light gray medical uniform that was only a half-size too large. His shoulders bore the insignia of the Umbrean Imperium, the same as hers. Her uniform was a slate gray and fit her snugly, placing every curve of her body on display. Though the only jewelry she wore was a bracelet on her wrist, she had an unmistakable elegance about her that, judging by the way she walked, Par guessed was all completely intentional.

"Where is your camp?" he asked, trying to keep his eyes on his surroundings.

She glanced over her shoulder. "I came down from the Coalition base camp this morning. I've been working there as a supply assistant for the last three months."

He finished the thought for her. "And you were assigned to work in the refugee camp, but then how did you get down here before the rest of them?"

"I borrowed an air bike from one of my lovers. I have it parked right over here." She winked and smiled again as she waved for him to follow. "If you're nice to me, I'll give you a ride."

Par gave her a questioning look. "If you were assigned to the refugee effort, how are you here by yourself? Why aren't you coming in with the rest of them?"

"Because I wasn't really assigned to begin with," she answered. "My name was only added to the list of workers. As was yours."

He was impressed. His first mission with a replicant from the Imperium, and it appeared she was a professional. At least, professional enough to accomplish everything she just said. "And how did you manage to pull all *that* off?"

She smiled bashfully and even blushed a little. "My other lover works in operations. He did me a favor."

Par doubted that anything about this Saithe woman was bashful or shy, but he had to admit, he was impressed all the same. The ability to form and utilize relationships, romantic or otherwise, was a mark of skill in their profession.

"You have more than one officer as a lover?" he asked.

"Had." Her smile turned rueful. "My logistics officer suffered a heart attack this morning. It's a pity too, as he was the kinder one. The other is cruel, as most of the Ieses are."

He couldn't help but let out half a chuckle. "Why didn't you kill the cruel one and keep the kind one?"

She shrugged. "What's one more lover? Besides, the kind one also happened to be the smart one. Here's my bike."

He couldn't see it at first, but then she pressed a button on her bracelet and the brush beside the path morphed into a black, metallic tarp. Saithe pulled the tarp away to reveal a sleek, black, military style air bike.

She smiled at him as she swung her leg up over the seat. "If you hop on, I can give you a ride."

He ignored the implication and climbed on behind her. "So, forgive me for being blunt," he said, "but I've never worked with one of your kind before. Do you mind if I ask you something more … personal?"

She laughed, girlish and inviting, as she fired up the bike's ignition. "Of course not."

"What kind of … model are you? Like is a servant class, or …"

Saithe looked back over her shoulder, glanced down at his belt, and then winked at him with a gleaming smile. "Pleasure model." Then she kicked the air bike into gear and they sped away down the path.

Saithe kept the bike at ground level, hovering over the graveled path at a moderate speed. Holding to her waist, Par could feel the taut muscles beneath her uniform. The grass of the open plain flew past them as Saithe guided the bike through the low ground along the shore, staying out of view from the rest of the valley until the grassy plain opened up into a small ravine. They were a quarter of a mile from the camp when she turned up the ravine and stopped. Parking her bike at the bottom of a creek bed, they dismounted as she threw her camouflage cloak over their ride.

Par left Saithe at her bike and climbed to the top of the embankment and pulled out his binoculars to look at the camp. Tents of every color sprung up before him, standing in contrast to the blue-and gray-skinned Duathe he saw moving around the camp. He focused in on the tents at the top of the hill. That was where his brief had said the Queen and her two daughters were camped. He was zooming in on the nearest batch of tents, looking for any sign of his quarry, when the voice of his Shade snuck into his head.

You know that woman is flirting with you? I've not seen a woman flirt like that in ... like ... maybe never. I can't say it hasn't affected me. Can you say the same?

Annoyed that he hadn't turned off his Shade when he first touched foot on the ground, he sternly told it to deactivate itself.

Fine. But even I know old widowers need to get laid every now and again. No one ever said hunting wasn't supposed to be fun.

He felt the AI leave his mind as he tucked away his binoculars. Climbing back down the ditch, he found Saithe leaning back against a tree, sipping from her canteen.

"I could have told you that the Coalition's team isn't due for a few more minutes." She held up her wrist, pulling back her sleeve to reveal her bracelet. "I'm still patched into their comms." She had a satchel slung over her shoulder and she opened it to produce a data pad. "I see that you have been assigned as a medical technician. Your name is Neunal and you are a Fenling."

"A Fenling?" He was taken aback. The title did not sound appealing.

"An Umbrean commoner. A non-replicant who is not a part of the ruling class."

That sounded anonymous enough. The last thing he wanted to do was stand out among what he assumed would be a mostly Umbrean crowd. There was little difference between an Illyari human and a normal Umbrean human. It was the Ieses family who were different. In the three hundred years they had governed, the Ieses had expanded the Imperium from their home-world of Umbrea Prime to include a dozen planets. They had also taken control of the Imperium's superior cloning and genetic manipulation technology, programming all replicants to worship them as gods, while altering their own genetic structure to make them taller, faster, and smarter than the average human.

"And what about you?" he asked. "What is your job?"

"Logistics. The same as before. Though I have no official position or duties. We both report to the same man." She studied her tablet. "Captain Derleus."

"What happens if Captain Derleus comes looking for us?"

"He won't. He does not have our names, I've seen to that—though everyone else does."

He nodded. "Good. Then we can just play it off as a clerical error if anyone catches us and brings us to him."

He heard something exhale in the sky, and when he looked up, he saw a pair of Coalition shuttles setting down on the other side of the camp.

"Here we go," he said as he hefted his bag over his shoulder.

They walked across the open field and circled around the camp, passing through the trees and then along the beach, staying out of sight and away from the tents until they reached the far side of the camp where the shuttles had landed. Both craft were sitting side-by-side in an open field below a hill that seemed to be the camp's eastern border. Par could see two more shuttles approaching over the horizon, while the two that had landed had lowered their ramps for hundreds of gray-uniformed aid workers who were now milling about.

The two of them walked casually along the northern base of the hill, carefully staying out of view from the shuttles until they were close enough to be considered part of the crowd. They then stopped next to a stack of crates that were being unloaded by a pair of burly, green skinned replicants who paid them no mind. Par leaned back against the stack as if he had been there the whole time, while Saithe pretended to study her tablet.

The third shuttle was landing now. When it lowered its ramp, more aid workers disembarked. Most wore the same gray uniforms, but a few wore blue uniforms with Republican insignia on their shoulder. When the fourth and final shuttle landed, it opened to reveal soldiers, nearly all of them replicants. Walking at their head was a tall, pale white figure dressed in dull black armor. His hair and eyes were as black as opal, and he stood a head taller than even the augmented Kodayene that were walking beside him.

"That is Mnemander Ieses," Saithe said quietly from behind him. "Fourth son of the Teth Gideon by his concubine Cymbaline. His older half-brother Philemon commands the Imperium's army for the Coalition."

He glanced back at Saithe. "Did you know he was coming?"

Her face wore a worried look as she shook her head. "He was not on any of the manifests that I saw. I can't tell you why he is here, but I will say that such a man is not sent lightly."

Par nodded solemnly as he watched the tall, pale man lead his soldiers toward the camp. *Is he here for the same purpose as we are? And if so, what will he want with the Queen?*

Plans and contingencies began running through Par's mind. If this Mnemander Ieses were to seize the Duathic royal family before he did, then his job would grow much more complicated. And much, *much* more dangerous. Par counted at least fifty soldiers walking behind the pale giant. How many of those would be dedicated to guarding the Queen and her daughters? Where would they take them? And would he be able to follow them once they left?

Par began keeping a checklist in his mind to report back to Rufus once this was all over. That Saithe had not known about Mnemander's presence was alarming, and Rufus would want to know everything he could about their new Umbrean allies.

Saithe tapped him on the shoulder. "All of the replicants are grouping. I'll be expected to be with them. I have to go." She began walking toward a crowd of replicant women that all looked eerily similar to her. Some of them even had similar tattoos. "I'll see you inside the camp."

Par gave her a curt nod as she fell in with the other replicants. He noticed that Saithe managed to sneak in with the small group of her own model as the entire crowd of replicants fell into a rank and file formation behind the soldiers. All four of the shuttles had been unloaded now, and everyone in a uniform was grouping together. The replicant workers formed military-style columns and ranks to the front while everyone else milled together in a crowd in the back. Par fell in with the other native Umbreans as they wandered at the back of the procession. His crowd was the first to stop at the garden's outer gate where they began unloading their equipment and returning to the shuttles for more. His head down, Par left the other Fenlings and pushed on through the crowd. Keeping his eyes on Mnemander, he followed at a safe distance behind the towering pale man and his crowd of soldiers as they marched into the camp.

He reached into his mind and awoke his Shade.

I was wondering if I was going to be involved today.

The camp carried the stench of when people lived too close together. He could smell urine. He could smell campfires and the meat being cooked. There was sweat and mud and smoke mixed with the smell of the trees and the flowers all around them.

Now halfway into the camp, it was clear Mnemander was searching for someone or something. He paid no mind to the crowds of destitute Duathe who were staring at him as he marched down the graveled path. The towering giant was marching with such purpose and haste that the crowd of regular soldiers were a dozen paces behind, and it looked to Par that even the dozen Kodayene behind him were having to trot at times to keep up.

The Queen wasn't here to greet them, and now Mnemander's headed straight for the tents on the hilltop, right where Anyse and her daughters had set up their tents. You need to get ahead of them if you're to have any chance of getting to the Queen first.

Saithe was nowhere to be seen, as she had been swept away with the formation of replicants that had split off for the southern end of the camp. He was on his own, at least for the time being, and a plan was forming in his mind as he followed Mnemander. If Par could find at least one of the girls before Mnemander did, he could take the one and kill the others, either now or later. If he found only one now, he could have her out of the camp and on his own shuttle within the hour. The towering giant and his entourage had pushed through the tents and were now marching up the hillside. Par turned at the base of the hill where a dirt path led down into an irrigation ditch. He jumped down to the bottom of the ditch and took off at a run, climbing the slanted concrete up the hill.

His was a messy plan, and Par disliked messy things, but there was little helping that now. He reached into his bag as he ran and found his case of injectors. The first injector he readied was Mersis, which would place a grown man into an eight-hour coma. The second was Ghamedes, which stung like a hornet and brought near instant death. If he could find Saithe to help him before he reached the tent, he could give both princesses Mersis. If not, he decided that he would seize the younger daughter and leave the Queen and her eldest for the Umbreans to find. The younger princess would be the easiest to carry.

He began to prepare himself mentally as he neared the first tent. Reaching into his pocket, his right hand grasped the Mersis injector as he pushed the tent flap open with his left. Empty. Nothing but lonely cots. He glanced again in each corner before moving on.

Halfway toward the next tent he released his Shade, and it slithered down his body before hovering an inch above the ground, fanning its tiny nano-bots in every direction. He asked it to keep a look out behind him. The last thing he needed was to be caught red-handed and unannounced by Mnemander and the small army he had behind him.

The next tent had a dozen cots, each with a sick Duathe refugee, but only a startled nurse stood to greet him. He waved her off before she could speak, and then he hurried back out the flap. He could hear Mnemander's party searching the other tents nearby, and he heard his Shade's whisper in his mind.

They're only a couple rows behind you and closing fast. I don't think they've found the Queen, but there's a lot more of them than there are of you.

Par ducked inside the next tent in the line. There were about a dozen cots in this tent, but only two held Duathic patients. *You've got one coming now. It's the giant.* It was time to play his cover. Par pulled a thermometer from his duffle and walked up to the man who was sleeping. The tent flap flew open behind him.

"What are *you* doing in here?"

The voice was like acid over ice. Par turned around. He had never come this close to a full blooded Ieses before. The dark onyx eyes of Mnemander Ieses stared down at him, and Par could feel his heart begin to race. He had heard that among their many genetic modifications, the Ieses possessed an ability to control a set of heightened pheromones that could inspire everything from love to fear in those around them. Right now, Par had to guess that Mnemander was inducing fear.

"Fenling, I asked you a question." The pale giant's voice was filled with unspoken threats.

Par swallowed hard and gestured toward the cots. "Just scanning some vitals, my lord, as you ordered."

Mnemander Ieses leaned closer to Par's face as if to study him closer. He growled in a low voice, "I ordered no such thing. Now tell me again what you are doing here."

Par could feel the hairs on the back of his neck stand up as a breath of fresh fear ran through his chest like a cold breeze.

"I apologize, my lord, I must have misunderstood my order. I was wondering why I was the only one here." Par took a deep breath and fell into a kneeling bow. "I will accept any punishment you have for me. I only ask that you forgive me."

"Hrm …" Mnemander growled as he stood straight up. His head pushed at the canopy of the tent as he arched his back.

Par kept his head bowed but from the corner of his eye he saw two Kodayene replicants armed with rifles step through the tent flap behind Mnemander. However, when he looked back up, the pale giant seemed to relax.

"It is not likely that you are to blame, Fenling," Mnemander said. "I will see to your superiors once our task here is complete. For now you will come with me and aid us in our search."

Not what he had hoped, but it sure beat the alternatives. Par shoved his medical equipment back into his duffle as he hurriedly followed Mnemander and the two Kodayene out of the tent.

"W-What are we looking for, my lord?" Par made sure to add the right amount of penitence and awe in his voice as he stuttered. This was not hard as his heart was still racing with adrenaline.

"It is not *what* Fenling, but *whom*," Mnemander growled as he stomped toward the next tent. "My brother has given me orders that I am to ensure the safety of the royal family, so we are searching for King Teum's wife and two daughters."

"A-And why is that, my lord?" Par chanced the question, purposefully wincing as Mnemander turned back to look at him.

"Now *that* is one question too many, Fenling."

Par bowed deeply as Mnemander turned back to enter the next tent. "Yes, my lord. I will be quiet, my lord."

Par waited outside while Mnemander and the two Kodayene stepped into the next tent. He could see other Kodayene soldiers walking in and out of the other tents around them. It seemed to him, as far as he could tell, that no one else had found anyone either. Mnemander emerged after only a few seconds to growl at him again.

"And stop that groveling. You're giving me a headache." The pale giant shook his head as he stalked toward the next tent. "This is why I had all of your kind stay below. The sniveling and bellyaching does nothing but make me cross."

Par held his tongue and—taking a cue from the replicants around him—made himself busy with searching. Over the next hour, Mnemander and his squad of over-muscled replicants barged through the rest of the tents. Reaching the end of the final row, they found a set of tents that were completely empty. The rest of the tents atop the hill had been full of sick or injured Duathic refugees, cots, and medical equipment. These tents were smaller, personal spaces that were arranged in a semi-circle near a fire pit with logs and folding chairs circled around it.

Par knew it in his gut before the words of his Shade echoed in his head. *If I were a betting man, I'd say our little queen has decided against turning herself in.*

ATTICUS

The tank rattled to a stop as the top hatch yawned open and Major Ioma rose up from its armored belly. Pulling on his headset, his sharp, black eyes surveyed the distant ridgeline as he keyed his mic. "Alteric, put me through to Rapier One. I need her to come take a look at something Longbow spotted …"

Strapped to the side of Ioma's tank, Atticus turned in his magnetic harness to look behind them. Only Salentine, himself, and Thrace fit on the side of Ioma's tank, as half of the tank's left flank was fitted with extra communication and sensory equipment. Major Ioma had positioned his tank near the front of the column, and only a handful of tanks rode ahead of them. Now, looking behind them, Atticus realized that not only had they stopped, but the entire Fifth Armored Column had stopped as well. Atticus could see his first squad, led by Sergeant Mako, riding four to a tank on each of the two tanks behind him. Atticus saw Mako turn his way. The gaunt squad leader gave Atticus a questioning look that seemed to ask, *Why are we stopped?* Atticus could only shrug in reply.

Turning back around, Atticus brought up his rifle scope to look at the ridgeline before them. An hour earlier they had left the Coalition's base camp and descended Mount Gedron. The foothills of the Blackfriar Mountains were jagged spurs of brown-black rock that jutted from the earth like spear points. The Fifth Armored column had crossed halfway through the jagged hills before Ioma had ordered a halt. Now, as Atticus looked up at the sharp, black rocks, he saw the craggy ridgelines that curled toward each other, forming the Prophet's Doorway, the main pass that led from the mountains to the wooded flatlands of the Sinvoresse Valley.

Looking through his scope, Atticus spotted the gleam of metal flashing behind a rocky outcropping. When he focused in on the cliff, he recognized the rounded metallic shapes. *More spheres. Strange that they weren't all destroyed last night,* he thought as he lowered his rifle. *What makes them so important that Ioma calls the entire Fifth Armored to halt?*

Not twelve hours earlier, Atticus had listened in as the Consul Marius, Atticus' father, had stripped Lucinius Droesus of his position as Commander of the Fifth Armored Column and given it to Major Ioma. Immediately after, Marius had placed Atticus under Ioma's command. Since then, the major had shown himself to be very comfortable as acting Commander of the Fifth Armored Column, and Atticus had watched as Ioma ordered everyone about like he had been doing it his entire life. *To be a king, one must act the king,* Atticus' father had once said. *If you want the respect of your men, you must first act like you deserve it.* Growing up, his father had often talked to him about leadership, and whatever the young major's other failings might be, Atticus knew what he was looking at in Ioma. *The Major knows he belongs here …*

Above him, Atticus heard Major Ioma key his mic again. "Rapier One, this is Reaper One. Our surveillance team has spotted a pair of suspicious structures atop the ridgeline to our southwest. They appear to be large, metallic spheres, and as per our guidance from HQ, they are to be destroyed if possible. Because they are out of Longbow's range, I was wondering if you could find a shot. Over."

Ioma had apparently decided against wearing his helmet, and his dark hair waved in the breeze as he cupped the headset to his ears. When he was done listening, he keyed his mic again. "Roger that Rapier One. I'll have my crew beam you the coordinates now. Reaper One out."

Beside him, Salentine whispered in Atticus' ear. "What the hell is going on sir?" Atticus turned around to face his machine gunner, Salentine, whose unlit cigarette was hanging from his mouth as he spoke. "There's like … two hundred tanks here. What the fuck we need to stop for, sir?"

Thrace, the radioman seated on the opposite side of the tank turret, pointed his thumb toward the cliff. "The Major is concerned about something he sees up on that ridgeline. He just called our air cover to deal with it. More spheres I think."

"Shit," the machine gunner mumbled. "I thought we blew all them fuckers up last night."

Atticus shrugged and shook his head. "Apparently not."

A pair of Raptors screamed by overhead, a trail of vapor following in their wake as they flew over the mountain pass. Less than a minute later they circled back and one of the Starfighters launched a pair of missiles that shot downward and exploded right where Atticus had seen the metallic glimmer of the spheres.

Atticus heard his platoon sergeant call through his head mic, "Assassin Six, this is Assassin Seven, what's our situation? Over."

No doubt the rest of the platoon is wondering the same thing. Atticus keyed his mic to respond. "Seven, this is Six. Unfortunately, I know about as much as you at this point." Keeping his voice low, he stole a glance up at Major Ioma who was still studying the ridgeline with his binoculars and talking into his headset. The Raptors screamed by overhead again. "It would appear that Reaper One is concerned about our passage through this last mountain pass, and he's coordinating with our overhead cover right now. Beyond that, he hasn't communicated anything with me. Over."

Jonas replied that he had little more to add, and both men agreed that Assassin platoon would simply have to keep pulling security until they finally moved. Once Jonas hung up, Atticus looked down at his watch. *Back at camp, Ioma made it seem like he was going to keep a tight schedule. If we don't move soon, we'll miss our rendezvous with the Umbrean Cavalry.*

Atop the tank, Ioma appeared irritated and annoyed as he shifted to look back toward the rear of the column. "Alteric, where are those engineers? I thought they'd be here by now. Call them, get their ETA, and then tell them we don't have this kind of time to waste..."

Ioma's voice trailed off as a support vehicle crested the hill behind them. Zipping along the column of tanks, the boxlike craft looked almost like a toy as it hummed to a stop next to their Claymore. Then the side doors swung open and two technicians got out, the first a gray-haired sergeant and the second a shapely female lieutenant with blonde hair and a uniform that looked about a size too small. Atticus spotted a pink decal stuck to the top of her helmet as she skipped past him, and he abruptly realized it was the same doe-eyed engineering officer he had seen at the field meeting. The gray-haired sergeant opened the vehicle's back hatch and together they pulled out a metal crate that, sitting on the ground, stood about three feet in height. Atticus strained to see what they were doing as the gray-haired sergeant opened the top of the crate to reveal a control panel.

Engineers? Is this why we stopped? Or was it the spheres? Atticus looked up to the black smoke wafting over the western ridgeline. *Or perhaps both?*

Then Salentine leaned up to whisper in his ear as he finally lit his cigarette. "Is it just me, sir, or is that blonde giving the Major a pair of the ol' 'fuck me' eyes?"

Atticus stole a glance at the lieutenant as she extended an antenna from the top of the crate while staring at Ioma with a gleam in her eye. *Sal's not wrong.* When he looked back toward Ioma, the major was pointedly looking the other way.

"I could get used to working for the Major if the scenery is going to look like this," Salentine mumbled as he took his first puff of tobacco. "That's no common barracks whore. That right there's a noblewoman. Top shelf."

The gray-haired sergeant had returned to the front seat of his truck, where he was smoking a cigarette and working at a computer screen. Behind him, the blonde lieutenant was punching commands into the crate's control panel. Atticus caught a look at the nametag on her chest. Antonia.

Not one of the largest houses on Alba Calea, but one of the richest, that's for sure. And here she is, working for a man belonging to one of the poorest. He saw that Ioma was still listening intently to his own headset with eyes closed. *I wonder if its just chance that she's working for Ioma. Somehow, I doubt it is…*

While Atticus knew many of his peers had affairs while on deployment, he had never had the time or the energy for such things. Assassin platoon's mission schedule was far too busy. They were never in camp long enough for him to have more than a single conversation with any woman, let alone a woman of equal rank. There were two women in his platoon, but they were his subordinates and he had never allowed himself to look at them as anything more than professionals. Beyond that, he would never risk the wrath of his father on something so trivial.

"Lieutenant Antonia," Ioma said, finally looking directly at the woman. "How many of them are there?"

She brushed a stray hair back as she batted her eyes and smiled. "We should know in a few minutes, sir. We're releasing the nano-bots now."

Antonia extended another antenna from the top of the crate and punched at the controls. Two minutes later, she keyed in a final command and backed away. A doorway, a foot in diameter, opened at the base of the crate as dozens of metallic locusts scurried out and launched themselves into the air in a silvery swarm. The locusts weaved back and forth through the larger vehicles before rising into the air and disappearing over the top of the western ridge of the Prophet's Door.

Antonia returned to her control panel and studied the screen. Ioma leaned down from his tank hatch to peer at the readout.

"Are they stable? Or are we in for a show?" the major asked over the hum of the tank.

A deathly chill though ran through Atticus as he realized what they were talking about. He thanked the Seven Fates for whatever intelligence Ioma had heeded. *Tac-nukes. They are disarming a cluster of tac-nukes that were set here as a trap.*

Below him, Antonia shrugged. "They seem stable enough, sir. It shouldn't be a problem." The control panel beeped and she looked down. "Looks like we got it right sir. Two of them. Enough to open a hole in the ground large enough to fit the entire column."

Ioma whistled. "You're a clever woman, Antonia. What would I ever do without you?"

She smiled mischievously at him. "Well then maybe you shouldn't, sir."

The look she then gave Ioma was anything but professional, and Atticus looked away, pretending to check the safety on his rifle. He felt Salentine lean in next to him. "It's not often, sir, that I'm jealous of you officer types, but that blonde there is about the best-looking woman I've seen since we left *Unifier*."

Atticus said nothing and suppressed a laugh as the gray-haired sergeant emerged from the support vehicle's front seat to help Antonia lift the crate back up into the vehicle's hatch.

Ioma, still perched atop the tank's turret hatch, cupped his hands over his headset again. "Alteric, who is Rapier One Golf? ... Droesus? How did he manage to get himself on a Raptor? ... What in Fate's name is he saying? ... Halt again? He must be mad. We can't stop again, we'll miss our window. Blow him off. ... I don't know, tell him I'm coordinating a..." Ioma scowled as he looked back toward the ridge.

"No, I don't want to talk to him. What is he saying? … That we should go around the pass? That's ludicrous, we are up against a timeline and that could add twenty minutes…" Ioma shook his head and sighed as he listened. "…I don't have time for this. Just get rid of him, and if that old crow calls again Alteric, just blow him off."

Atticus found himself looking back up toward the black rocks of the Prophet's Doorway. Behind him, Salentine flicked his cigarette out into the grass.

"What do you think that shit's about sir?" the machine gunner mumbled as his eyes flickered toward Ioma. "You think we're about to get fucked? It's been a while since I got fucked sir. I wouldn't mind a little action if it came along."

"I don't know…" Atticus' voice trailed off as the engineer's vehicles sped away toward the back of the column.

Below them, the tank's engine picked up into a low growl as they lurched forward, and above them the turret hatch swung shut as Ioma disappeared down into the tank's belly. Like some big, slow centipede, the tank column began crawling forward with the tanks lined up two-by-two. The Fifth Armored Column was on the move again.

The slope of the earth leveled off and the grass beneath them fell away to reveal red, dusty soil that kicked up into clouds of dust as the tanks hovered over. Atticus looked once more to the smoke drifting up from where the Raptor's missiles had struck the spheres.

We're still nearly an hour from the city. What in Fate's name could they have been for? Atticus wondered this as their tank hovered down the open hillside. *It's little matter now, but you have to wonder why no one destroyed them last night. Did* Unifier *not see them sitting atop a ridge?* He pushed the thought out of his mind as their tank passed between the two towering, black peaks that formed the Prophet's Doorway.

Beside him, Salentine checked the feed-tray on his machine gun to make certain it was loaded. The machine gunner was a crack shot and had one of the quickest wits in the platoon, both traits which had persuaded Atticus to keep Salentine close at hand for this mission.

A tank cannon thundered from ahead of them as a rocky cliff splintered into a thousand shattered stones. The impact echoed against the rocky cliffs as the explosion hung in the air for just a moment until a hail of gunfire followed in its wake.

"Oh shit!" Salentine shouted as a bullet ricocheted off the Claymore's cannon.

Machine gun fire peppered the tank line, bouncing off the armor and buzzing through the air like a thousand angry bees. Atticus released his magnetic coupling and leapt from the side of the tank, and when his feet hit the ground, he rushed toward a pile of rocks and cupped his radio mic to his mouth.

"All Assassin elements dismount and find cover!" he shouted into his radio as he hit the dirt and hunkered next to the nearest rock. Then he pulled the scope of his rifle up to his eye and focused in on the rock face above them.

A dozen gun nests littered the rocky hillside below the cliff. They were dug bunkers covered with branches and grass, and each nest boasted a handful of weapons, all of which were now blasting gunfire down on them like a shooting gallery. Atticus lowered his rifle as Salentine fell in beside him, pressing his back against a jagged stone that rose up from the ruddy earth like some unruly weed.

"What did I tell you, sir! We're about to get fucked! Look at that shit right there!" Salentine laughed as he pointed toward the front of the column.

Atticus kept his head low as he turned to look, bullets hissing past him from every side. Every tank in front of them was smoking or on fire. Two of them had been blown to pieces, now no more than empty husks smoldering in the dirt.

Salentine squeezed off a long burst, took a breath, and then squeezed off another as a rope of tracer rounds flew from his barrel and up into the ridgeline. All around them, the rest of Assassin platoon was scrambling for cover between the rocks. Atticus raised his rifle, took aim at the nearest gun nest and fired twice. Then he shook his head at the futility of it, as the embankment was nearly six hundred meters away.

Then a pair of tanks pulled up behind them, humming to a stop in a cloud of red dust. Both tanks' turrets thrummed as they swung their cannon to face the hillside and fired. Atticus winced as the heat from the dual blasts brushed up against his face. The tanks then alternated their cannon shot, creating a rhythm that churned the hillside like a farmer tilling the earth. When the two tanks finally went silent and Atticus uncovered his ears, he realized that not only were they no longer taking small arms fire, but the neighboring hillside was now several feet lower at its apex.

When the last echoes of the tank cannon died away against the cliffs, Atticus suddenly realized that the only sound was the scattered gunfire of his own men. "CEASE FIRE!" he shouted above the din as he waved his arms at the men around him. Seconds later it was quiet as everyone's eyes were still aimed at the hills above them. Nothing and no one moved—not among his men, not below the cliffs, not along the hillside. The only motion in view was the smoke and dust that drifted up from the shattered rock above them.

"Well shit. We should ride with these tanker fellows more often," Salentine mumbled beside him. "I'm afraid they took all the fun before I could even get through my first belt."

"I wouldn't worry about that," Atticus answered quietly. "We have a whole city ahead of us."

Then something did move. Two brown blurs that jumped out of a ravine not a hundred meters from where he and Salentine sat. At first Atticus thought they were some sort of animal, but then he saw that they were in fact two Duathic boys—their skin blue like the sky, their clothes tan and gray like the rocks around them. They were running away toward the south end of the pass.

Salentine swung his machine gun over the rock and took aim through his scope, but then he immediately lifted his finger off the trigger and glanced toward his lieutenant.

"Sir, do you want us to fire?" the soldier shrugged. "They ain't got no weapons."

Atticus frowned and brought up his own scope. He could see nothing threatening on either boy, and their backs were to him as they ran away. They had on grey pants and shirts, not uniforms—neither looked older than adolescent.

"I don't..." he started, but then he saw that the taller boy was holding something in his hands. Right then, the radio mic on Atticus' shoulder crackled to life. It was Major Ioma.

"Assassin Six, this is Reaper One." The words were harsh, the voice clearly frustrated. "If you have eyes on those dismounts, I want you to open fire."

Atticus keyed his mic. "Reaper One, this is Assassin Six, they appear unarmed."

The answer was immediate. "I don't care. Light them up. If those two enemy combatants get away, I will personally see to it that you are stripped of your commission."

"Fuck it, sir," Salentine thumbed his safety off and let out a long, even burst. Both boys fell to the ground as Salentine's bullets ripped through them. The first rolled to a stop and then lay still on his back, while the second fell in a heap and then thrashed wildly against the earth.

"Shit," Salentine mumbled. "Got him in the spine."

The machine gunner spat in the dirt and readjusted his aim. He let out a long, slow breath and squeezed the trigger again. The machine-gun's report echoed against the stony peaks, and a second later, the boy's spasming stopped and his body lay still.

The echoes were still ringing against the rock when Ioma called him back. "Good, now have your men mount up, Assassin Six. We have a timeline to meet. Reaper One out."

Numbly, Atticus switched his radio back to his platoon's internal net and ordered them all to remount. He and Salentine climbed behind the armored plating and, once they had reattached their harnesses, the machine gunner pulled two cigarettes from his shoulder pouch, placed one in his mouth, and handed the other to his lieutenant. Atticus looked down at the rolled stick of tobacco before reluctantly accepting it.

"We gotta smoke to keep the evil spirits away, sir." Salentine's grin was sardonic. "Especially after something like that."

A crash echoed against the rocky cliffs as the tank ahead of them collided with the smoking husk of its destroyed fellow. Metal groaned and screamed as the live tank pushed its dead brethren out of their path.

Salentine took a long drag as they passed near the bodies of the two boys. "Them kids shoulda stayed in that gulch, sir. Ain't nothing we coulda done about that after." The gunner pushed the smoke out the corner of his mouth. "The Major ain't takin' no chances."

Atticus said nothing as the lead tank collided with the next smoking wreck. Metal was screeching against metal as he strained to see what the second boy had been holding, but the body was laying with its back to him. The boy had died with his shoulders hunched and his lifeless arms curled tightly to his chest.

FEL

The first vision came to her while they were falling. Shadows and light. Light and shadows. A kaleidoscope of colors flew through Fel's vision as they hurtled through the sky, spinning, spinning. She clutched to the handle on the wall next to her seat as the ATC hurtled toward the earth. Then, in the last instant before they crashed, a shadow rose up from the floor and enveloped her in the emptiness of its shadowy wings, and then all was darkness.

When Fel came to, she was hanging awkwardly from her harness and everything around her was white. No doubt some sort of safety measure, a foamy sea of white had engulfed the bay of the ATC. Brushing away the foam around her, Fel found it was soft but dry, like a thick, pillowy cushion. Now the cushion was receding, disintegrating, collapsing in on itself, and soon the sea of white had dwindled enough to reveal the rest of the bay. They had crashed, and the ATC was laying half on its side and at an angle, so that the viewport on the back ramp was aimed at the ground. To her left was Camus; he was still suspended in his harness, and she could see the bodyguard's eyes were closed. Looking toward the back ramp, Fel spotted Kress and Marental fighting with their harnesses and readying their weapons. Kress held her massive rifle in her lap, and then she swept away the foam and reached for the charging handle, chambering a round with a *clack-clack*. Then the giant woman pulled the release on her chest strap and rolled out of her seat.

"Fel! Are you okay?"

Her sister's voice called out to her as wave of foam rolled aside and Fel saw Delea swimming toward her through the sea of white. Feeling along her harness, Fel found the release and pulled. With a snap, she fell away from the wall and into the foam. She sank slowly up to her neck as her sister swam toward her, but by the time she was able to reach out to touch her sister's hand, the foam had receded enough for Fel to stand awkwardly on an empty seat.

"You must stay inside, your Highness!" Marental shouted from the back of the bay. "We are securing the perimeter and will return shortly."

Then Kress opened a hatch on the ceiling, and the two giant women climbed out into the daylight, their weapons in hand. A flurry of gunshots followed and then the hatch slammed shut.

"Fel! Are you alright?" Delea gasped as she pulled herself up next to her little sister.

Fel frowned. "I'm fine Del. Calm down, hey."

"Calm?" Wiping the foam off her shoulders, Delea looked at her like she had just laid an egg.

Gunfire rattled like rain against the outer armor of the ATC. Fel looked out one of the side viewports to see if she could recognize where they were, but there was only dust and smoke. The last bits of safety foam were slowly disintegrating into a layer of sandy dust along the floor of the bay as she jumped down off the seat. Then Fel heard something clank against the hull above them and a moment later, light streamed down onto their heads as a lithe and agile form fell from the ceiling and landed in front of them. It was Motya.

The foam dust flowed over his boots and down the floor as he climbed up toward them. In his left hand, Motya carried a metal case, and Fel could see a worried look on his face as he neared.

"You're both awake? Good. We're about to be surrounded if we don't move soon. Hold still, Roake wanted me to check you both over before we move."

"What happened?" Delea asked.

"We think a Raptor shot us down." Motya set the case down on the seat next to them and opened it, revealing a full medical kit. "We're somewhere in the third district, right in the middle of the war zone. Both of the pilots are dead. Roake's setting up a perimeter with Thayne and Kress and Marental..." Fel could see the bodyguard's hands were shaking as he fumbled with the medical tools. "Roake sent me back here with the med kit to see if there was anything we could do for Camus. We're … in a lot of trouble."

"Camus?" Delea cried out as she looked at the unconscious man hanging behind her. "What happened to Camus?"

"The crash knocked him out. I think he didn't put his harness on the right way or something." Hands still shaking, Motya flipped through the kit until he finally pulled out a syringe. "Don't worry, Roake and I checked the both of you before we made for the cockpit. You should both be fine, no worse for the wear, provided that we avoid getting either of you shot." He readied the syringe and aimed the needle at Camus's shoulder.

"He's dead," Fel said.

She knew because she had been beside him the entire time, but he hadn't moved or even breathed since she'd woken up. When Motya heard this, he slowly lowered his hands until the syringe rested in his lap.

"Oh," Motya's voice trembled as he set the syringe back into the case.

"What about him?" Fel said as she pointed to a still form lying near the back ramp.

All three of them turned to look. There, still strapped in his harness, was the gunner who had greeted them when the ATC had first picked them up.

"Oh-my-goodness," Delea said as she grabbed the syringe from Motya and climbed down the side of the bay. Seconds later, all three of them were gathered around the unconscious soldier.

"What's that?" Fel asked as she pointed at the syringe.

"It's called a spike," Delea replied. "I don't know what the official medical name for it, but it's likely our friend here has a severe concussion and possibly some internal bruising, and a spike accelerates the healing process, cushions the brain from further injury, and best of all…" Delea said as she emptied the syringe into the unconscious soldier's shoulder. "…it's got little adrenaline."

Delea took the case from Motya and replaced the syringe. As she snapped the case shut, the ceiling hatch opened again and Roake dropped down into the bay.

The captain of the royal guard climbed down to where they were.

"Motya, we have to move. Thayne and I have scouted an escape route, but if we delay any longer, they'll have us surrounded. How is Camus?"

"He's dead," Delea said. "But we have the gunner right here."

If Roake reacted to the news of Camus's death, Fel missed it. Instead, she saw him frown at the unconscious soldier lying before him. "We'll have to carry him I suppose." Then the captain reached down and pulled the release on the soldier's harness and Motya caught the unconscious man as he fell from his seat. Roake dropped down next to him, and together the two bodyguards carried the unconscious soldier to the back ramp.

"Is a spike supposed to wake him up?" Fel asked as she followed behind.

"It is," Delea replied. "But it may take a few moments to take effect."

"We'll have to carry him until then, your Highness," Roake said as he pushed a button on the wall. "We don't have time to wait around." With a snap and a hiss, the back ramp of the ATC opened and lowered itself to the ground.

Nearing the ramp, Fel heard a bullet ricochet near her feet. It caromed off the walls of the bay until she saw it embed itself into the duraglass of a viewport. Delea grabbed her hand, and together they ducked through the metal doorway.

A mountain of rubble greeted them as they scampered down the ramp, hand in hand with her sister, Fel could hear bullets snapping and hissing off the rock pile as they ran past and then dropped down between a wall and a pile of loose brick. Looking up, Fel could see their ATC had crashed into the side of a building, and part of the wall had collapsed on top of it.

"Everyone ready?" Thayne was sitting near the top of the rock pile, and in his hand was a small, black control box. "Hold on to your hats. Here it goes!"

There was a small explosion, almost like a firework, and Fel watched as the air around the crashed ATC crackled like lightening. Then a wave of static washed over everything as a cloud of gray smoke billowed out of the wreckage.

"MOVE!" Roake shouted.

Fel felt her sister's hand pull her to her feet and Fel glanced to see a pistol in her sister's other hand, though where Delea had gotten the weapon, Fel could only guess. Kress was the first to walk out from the shelter of the ruined building, and Fel watched the giant woman spray down the side of an adjacent building with her massive rifle as the rest of them leapt up from their hiding spots and ran past. Pushing through the smoke, another ricochet snapped next to Fel's feet as they crossed through a courtyard and then dashed into an alleyway. Somehow, Delea and Fel ended up at the fore of the party, and as they neared the end of the alleyway, Fel kept a tight hold on her sister's off-hand while Delea kept her pistol ready in the other. The two sisters stopped at the mouth of the alley, and a hand reached out and touched Delea on the shoulder. Roake was behind them.

"Wait," the captain of the guard said.

Here, the alleyway met a wall and a haze of smoke still hung in the air above them, clouding their view of the buildings around them. Seconds of tense silence passed before Fel heard footsteps running across the rubble on the other side of the wall. There was the metallic clink of armor and equipment as the soldiers ran past, and as the footsteps faded, Roake stepped past Fel and Delea, glanced over the wall, and then waved the entire party forward. Crouching low, the captain led them along the wall until it ended in yet another pile of rubble, where Roake stopped them again. Inching around the pile of concrete, the captain of the guard peered into the street. A few moments later, Roake signaled them with another wave, and they followed him around the rock pile and out into the next street.

The street was filled with craters and potholes and debris from the battle, and Fel clutched her sister's hand tight as they weaved around the obstacles. Then the report of a machine gun echoed, and as the asphalt kicked up around them, Fel looked up to see the back of Roake's head burst open like a melon. His lifeless body fell to the ground in a heap.

Shocked, Fel stared, her mouth agape. *Is he dead?* She had never seen someone die from a gunshot before. She couldn't move, only stare dumbfounded at the limp form lying in the street. Then someone tackled her like a powerball player. Her sister's arms wrapped around her, and together they tumbled down to the bottom of a deep crater. Bursts of gravel and asphalt rained down them as the machine gun strafed the earth above them. Fel ducked her head into her knees as the dirt and the debris fell around them. Closing her eyes, Fel silently said a prayer to the Weaver, the father of the universe, to grant her wisdom, for that was what she felt she needed the most.

And then another vision came.

Shadows. They crawled over the edge of the crater and slithered down over the dirt. They appeared in midair and climbed down from the sky. They grew out of the ground, from the bottom of the pit to curl around her like tendrils made of darkness. They were everywhere about her now, watching her with shadowy eyes, grasping at her with their shadowy limbs, whispering, murmuring, sighing and mumbling in her ear. The shadows were crawling out of her pockets and into her hair. They were slithering around her head, whispering into her ear, and she could feel them grasping and slithering against her skin. They were cold.

And then in the distance ... she heard trumpets.

In an instant, the shadows disappeared, vaporized into nothing, as a loud *CRACK! CRACK!* pierced the air, echoing over the machine gun and everything else. Then it was quiet again.

A pair of hurried footsteps trod up to the edge of the crater and the tall, intimidating shadow of Kress stood over them, her long rifle in hand.

"There were only two. It is safe now," the towering bodyguard said as she reached down toward them with an arm like a tree trunk. Delea hoisted her sister up first, and soon Kress had pulled both sisters up into the street. Fel spared a glance toward the lifeless body of Roake lying next to the curb.

"He is gone, child," Kress' deep voice spoke softly. "We can only move forward, and with haste."

Fel noticed that Kress' side was sticky with blood, and the bodyguard's shirt clung to her side. Then Delea grabbed Fel by the hand again and pulled her toward the next alleyway. There, they met up with Thayne, Motya and Marental. As she sat down against the wall, Fel saw the tail gunner's unconscious body lying between her and Motya, who was troubling over a hand-held navigator.

"Where the hell are we?" Motya cursed again under his breath as he nervously poked at the navigator's controls.

"May I see?" Delea asked, extending her hand.

Grudgingly, Motya surrendered the device, and Delea finally let go of Fel's hand as she accepted the navigator. Then Motya shuffled along the wall and settled down next to Fel as his eyes nervously studied the rooftops around them.

Sitting against the alley wall, the sound of scattered gunfire all around, Fel's memory returned to the night before, when she had snuck out in the dark of the night. She remembered the music that led her down to the river. She remembered the Onier rising out of the water, a spirit made of shadow. She remembered the strange cabin and the mysterious argument going on inside. She remembered the shadow that had wrapped around her during the crash—the very same shadow that found her cowering at the bottom of the crater. And finally, she thought of the trumpets she had heard sounding in the distance.

I need to listen for the music, she remembered. *The Onier said it would return.* Closing her eyes, Fel offered up another silent prayer to the Weaver, asking again for wisdom, safety and guidance. *And so it may be,* she finished, ending the prayer.

Someone coughed. Looking to her left, Fel saw the tail gunner they had rescued from the back ramp of the ATC. He sat up, bleary eyed, and looked around.

"What the fuck?" he said, squinting at the sun. "What the hell happened?"

"Shhhh," Motya whispered as his eyes nervously shifted from the gunner to Fel and then back to the rooftops. "We crashed and we're surrounded. Now be quiet, we're trying to figure out where we are."

"Aw shit," the gunner whispered back.

Fel could see he was a smallish man, shorter even than Delea. Scooting along the ground on his butt, the tail gunner slid up next to Fel. He glanced nervously to her, then to Motya, and then up at the sky. "Where the hell are we?" he murmured as he pushed his hands against the ground and stood, craning on his toes to peer over the wall behind them. Then something sharp cut through the air and struck the gunner just above his breastbone and flew out of his back. His body fell to the ground next to her with a sickening thud, the soldier's lifeless eyes staring back at Fel like a doll.

"Shit-shit-shit!" Thayne hissed as he jumped around Motya and hurried over to the body. Quickly checking over the soldier's neck and head, Thayne grabbed the body and dragged it behind a doorway.

It had all happened so quickly that Fel was still realizing what had happened. Her eyes kept moving from where the soldier's body sat and the red spot on the opposite wall. Part of her mind kept waiting for him to stand and start moving again, but the other part of her kept staring at the blood and bone. Then Marental walked up behind them in a crouch and knelt down next to Motya.

"What happened?" she asked.

Motya shook his head in disbelief. The two bodyguards whispered quietly to one another, but Fel tuned it out. She was listening for something else, and for a moment she thought she was close to hearing it. Closing her eyes, she could hear the hummingbird engines of a Coalition aircraft thrumming overhead. An explosion rattled a nearby building. She listened deeper . Someone, a woman perhaps, shouted out a warning and behind her, somewhere, was a baby crying. Still, Fel listened deeper. She knew it was there. It had to be—the Onier had said that it was, and so she listened as hard as she could—and there, deep below the earth, she heard it. A slow, rumbling rhythm, like drums upon the deep.

Then someone grabbed her by arm.

"You okay, your Highness?"

Fel opened her eyes to see the dark face of Thayne looking down on her.

"I said, are you okay, your Highness?"

As he grasped her by the arm, Thayne was looking at her as if she were made of glass and might shatter at any moment. Fel chewed her lip for a moment before answering.

"Yeah, I'm fine, hey!" she said as she pulled away from him.

Then Delea came around the wall. Her sister grabbed her by the other arm and yanked her to her feet. Fel cried out as she yanked her hand away. "Let go! I can make it on my own, sis, hey!"

"Fine," Delea frowned. "But you have to keep up on your own then. We're making for one of Father's safe houses."

Both Thayne and Delea backed away as another aircraft flew low over their heads, the very air shaking from its engines. Then another spat of gunfire came from the street behind them, and a few rounds caromed off the walls at the far end of the alleyway. Ducking her head, Delea turned around to face everyone else in the alleyway.

"Alright, we're ready to go," she shouted. "Everyone follow Mary!"

They sprinted across open streets and jogged down alleyways as Marental led them on a winding path through the buildings. Twice, Marental paused the party's advance as Kress lined up a shot with her long rifle; twice the long rifle spoke, and no one shot back at them as they sprinted across another open street.

Fel followed behind Thayne all the while, and for his part, the dark-faced soldier stayed close to her. Several blocks later, their party was huddled between two apartment buildings when the eerie screams of starfighters ripped through the air above them. Circling back, the starfighters screamed overhead a second time as a deafening explosion shook the earth. A wave of fire followed in the starfighters' wake, shooting up over the rooftops and dropping debris on their heads.

"Mary, are we almost there?" Delea asked.

"Not far now, your Highness," Marental replied as she double-checked the navigator.

Then the towering Kodayene woman turned around and jogged to the other end of the alleyway. Speeding into a sprint, Marental put her shoulder through a door. It gave way, flying open with a loud *crack*. Everyone quickly got up and followed her through the shattered doorway, which took them into a courtyard. A dusty water-less fountain and a few tattered lines of laundry greeted them, but the only doorways Fel could see led into the surrounding buildings. Then she watched Marental walk over to a corner of the courtyard where a piece of rebar stuck out from the ground. Marental grabbed the rebar and pulled open a panel in the ground, revealing a hidden set of concrete steps leading down. Pulling out her flashlight, Delea led them down into what looked to be a cellar, and soon they were descending into the dark room. As Marental closed the metal door behind them, Fel could hear the starfighters scream past again, and another wave of fire enveloped the sky as the doorway swung shut.

Someone found a light switch and a single bulb snapped on, bathing everything in a dim, golden glow. Fel settled down between a pair of metal wire shelves that were stocked with cans of food. Waiting there in the dark, she closed her eyes and listened, hoping to hear a note, a word of song, a rhythm, anything like what she had heard up on the surface. But now there was only silence. Sitting there in the dim light, huddle against the wall, she found herself clutching the inside pocket of her coat.

PAR

The fury was plain on Mnemander's face as he searched the last remaining tents. The pale giant was pulling the canvases right off the poles and tossing them into the breeze.

"Why have we not found them? Where is the Queen?" he raged. "Search everything!"

The replicants and their master had searched every tent on the hilltop and still not a single member of the Teum family had been found. When Par had first encountered the towering commander, Mnemander had been testy and impatient. Now, the failed search for his quarry had made him even more cross. Par could see that the replicants around him were clearly affected by their master's rage. Even the burly Kodayene looked meek and penitent as they bustled about, searching again through places they had already explored. All the while, Mnemander seethed and stomped about, clenching and unclenching his fist as he fought to contain his anger.

Taking a cue from the replicants around him, Par stayed busy. Searching through the tents at the south-western edge of the hill, he noticed that they were completely empty—very much unlike the ones they had searched earlier, which were full of medical patients, cots, and equipment. He also noticed that there was a fire pit nearby with logs and folding chairs circled around it. These tents were clearly not like the others. His Shade seemed to agree.

These tents are for living, not medical stations, and they're further back from the medical tents than the other living spaces we've seen. So, if we're looking for clues, I think we're getting warmer.

Par circled around the fire pit, looking for anything that might provide him evidence of his quarry. Then he caught a glint of metal winking at him from the ashes of the pit. He stole a glance back toward Mnemander, but the pale giant had his back to him. Reaching deftly into the cold remains of the fire, his fingers closed around a piece of metal. Blowing off the dust and ash, he saw that he held a pendant made of silver and gold. He stuffed it into his pocket just as he saw Mnemander smash a chair to splinters with his boot.

"Where is the Queen?" the giant bellowed. "Why is she not here?"

"Because she has fled, uncle."

The voice was smooth and calm like honeyed wine. Par, Mnemander, and everyone else turned to face the voice as a man in a black jumpsuit walked out from behind an ancient wall. He was bald and athletic, and though he was of average height, he had the pale skin of an Ieses. He stopped a few steps from Mnemander and pushed his hands into his pockets as he studied the larger man with a calm and steady gaze. "Philemon asked me to check in on you, uncle, and so I thought I would show up a little early to see if I could help, but I'm afraid that we are all a bit too late, aren't we?"

I've studied the pendant and I can say that it's the royal insignia of the Teum family. If my data on the Duathic customs is correct, the only ones allowed to wear these are members of the royal family themselves.

Par noticed that everyone around him appeared distracted by the new arrival, so he took the opportunity to wander further back from the crowd. Leaving the fire pit, he circled behind a pair of ancient stone walls. He saw a tree standing alone near the cliff's edge. Its massive canopy swallowed the light as he stepped beneath it, and a breeze off the bay rustled its rust-colored leaves. Crouching next to its trunk, Par noticed the grass here was torn and matted down, and that there were dark stains on the tree roots.

Is that blood? I think we need to take a look at this...

Par bent down and scooped up a handful of blood-stained earth. A host nano-bots crawled down his arm like an army of ants before studying the pile of dirt sitting in his palm.

Okay, I have enough. Analyzing now...

Dumping the dirt onto a root, Par stole a glance back toward the two Umbrean men.

Mnemander's face had gone icy cold as his eyes studied the other man. "If you are already so ahead of us, tell me this, nephew... How long ago did our royal party leave?"

"Likely sometime just before dawn." The bald man nodded out toward the rest of the camp. "I've taken the liberty of looking around a bit already, and I've surmised that whether by coincidence or by design, there seems to have been several large parties who left the camp this morning, each in a different direction. I've spent the better part of the morning trying to figure out which party included our Queen." The bald man sighed. "She's my problem now, I'm afraid, which is all the worse for her. I doubt Philemon or the Consul will have much mercy or patience for a woman who goes back on her word so quickly."

Mnemander's voice was emotionless as he turned and walked away. "I'll leave it to you, then."

"There is *one* thing I'd ask you to do for me." The shorter man smiled to himself as he waited for Mnemander to stop. "If you would be so kind as to search this camp from top to bottom for any clues to where she might have gone, I would consider it a great favor."

Mnemander's voice remained flat and his face betrayed not a hint of emotion. "As you wish, Sader."

We need to get away from him.

Par's Shade crawled back inside of him as he snuck away from the tree and along the edge of ancient wall. Relieved that no one seemed to take any more note of him than before, he simply walked away, slipping through the crowd and then through the tents. Minutes later and he was walking down a set of ancient stone steps on the west side of the hill. The base of the hill was surrounded by crowds of Duathic refugees who were gathered around their multi-colored tents. Par passed by a set of cook fires and then walked a few rows into the tents before stopping to collect his thoughts.

That guy was a Taker.

Par nodded in agreement. He looked back, searching the hillside to make certain no one had followed them.

I had to switch to Passive the moment I saw him, or we would have been made. I'm searching my database right now to see what we have on a "Sader" from the Imperium, but nothing has turned up yet.

Par doubted that anything would. If his Shade's database knew anything, then Rufus would have known, and it likely would have been discussed back on Alba Calea. And Rufus had said nothing about any Takers from the Imperium. The Ieses were thought to be incapable of bonding with an AI and becoming a Taker. Something about the genetic modifications they had undergone over the last three hundred years now prevented them from being compatible with being bonded to an artificial intelligence composed of nano-machines. However, while Sader possessed many of the traits common to the Ieses family—such as the pale skin and the black, opal eyes—he had also been quite different from his counterpart, Mnemander. For one, he was shorter; nearly the same height as Par. Though he had clearly been younger than Mnemander, the taller, older Ieses had treated Sader as an equal, perhaps even a superior.

If there's one thing we need, it's to find Saithe and find out who this Sader is. Because whoever he is, he's already ahead of us, and if we follow him, we run the risk of him detecting us and turning around.

And the last thing they needed was a duel. Especially not a duel with a Taker under commission from the Imperium. Win or lose, the fallout could potentially be enormous. What he needed to do was to find another angle, someone or something that would tell him where the Queen and her daughters were going. Then, with a little luck, he could beat them there.

I found Saithe. She's back near the shuttles, helping set up. You know she's a lot less flirty when she's not around you. Which is nice. Even if you're not going to do anything about it, I can still dream. You know I've never had a girlfriend before. Always wondered what that would be like…

Par tuned out his companion. There were times his Shade had a hard time remembering it was an AI and not an amalgamated concoction of the personalities Par had interacted with over the years. A Taker's AI was one of the few machines truly capable of self-awareness, but being self-aware did not allot it a personality. No, those were developed, absorbed, and grown over years of experience and interaction with other sentients via the AI's host—and Par had been a Taker for a very, very long time.

Par headed northwest next, weaving through the tangle of tents and campfires as he circled back around the base of the hill toward where the Coalition shuttles were parked. There was a nervous energy about the camp now. Many of the Duathe watched him suspiciously as he walked by, as if some darkened motive had spurred his travel. The people he heard talking spoke in quiet, hurried whispers. Everywhere he looked, he saw groups of the replicant soldiers walking about, searching, looking. And then somewhere up ahead of him came the voice of a woman calling out in the voice of a preacher.

"Woe! Woe, oh great city. The hour of your sorrows is at hand. Once you were glittering gold with scarlet pearls, and now you are like a victim lying naked and bloody with enemies all around you."

Par wound his way through a patch of blue and orange tents to an open area where a crowd of people were gathered. There, standing head and shoulders above the center of the crowd was a Duathic priestess of some kind. She wore an animal skull atop her dark-haired head, and her green-skinned face was painted with red stripes. Her steely eyes glared out at the crowd as she spoke.

"With great violence our city will be torn down, never to rise again." Her voice bit through the warm afternoon air. "There will be no music here. There will be no work. No shelter. No trade. No love."

Circling around the crowd, Par spared her another glance and by chance he caught her eye. For the briefest moment, Par felt her eyes look at him from beneath the animal skull, and it was as if she looked *into* him before her gaze turned back to the crowd.

"Fallen, fallen is Sindorum the great. Never to rise again. She will become a home to demons that will haunt her and fill her temples with madness. The foreign kings, these invaders, they will rape her and strip her bare and leave her lying on the rock as nothing but a corpse."

Par sped up to a fast walk until he had passed through the crowd and put its strange orator well behind him. As the woman's voice trailed off behind him, he found himself walking through the last few tents along the edge of the camp. Beyond that was the open field where the Coalition shuttles were still unloading. Saithe was mixed in with a crowd of replicants that looked almost exactly like her, leaving Par to stare dumbly at the crowd, wondering which one was her until he saw her smile and wink. Then she re-assumed her mask of servitude as she walked over to him.

"Is there something we can do for you, Mister Malcus?" she said as she bowed, her face a docile mask.

"Yeah, I, uh… We need one more to help with this crate." He gestured toward an adjacent shuttle.

Saithe trained her eyes on the ground as they walked, the perfect servant. Then, when Par was certain they were out of earshot, he leaned over and whispered into her ear. "The Queen and her two daughters are gone." Touching her arm, he steered them toward the tents. "And the Coalition has sent a Taker to hunt them down. An *Imperium* Taker."

He emphasized the last words to make certain she understood his implication. Matters involving the Imperium were supposed to be her area of expertise. That they were being surprised from her end this early on did not reflect well on her. To Saithe's credit, if any of this had surprised or rattled her, she did not show it. She simply nodded as he let go of her arm.

"Sader Morgan. That is most likely who they have sent." She whispered through gritted teeth. "No one lesser would be fit for such a quarry. Where is he now?"

"He was up on the hilltop last I saw," Par spoke quietly as they walked. "For all I know, he could be hot on their trail by now, though it looks like the Queen has covered her tracks well. Our friend Sader ordered Mnemander to search the camp for any more clues."

Saithe eyes flashed with anger. "He is not my friend, nor should he be yours. He is an assassin of no conscience whatsoever."

They were several rows into the tent city now, and Par could see soldiers walking through the camp in packs of four. Though these soldiers were clearly replicants, each face eerily similar to the next, they were not the towering, burly Kodayene that Par had encountered on the hilltop. Those men seemed assigned to accompany Mnemander only. No, Par recognized that these soldiers were of the Brevan strain of replicants, which were a typical Imperium military creation, physically augmented but mentally stunted to make them easier to control. Par doubted these search parties would be turning up any truly promising leads.

"So where do we go from here?" Saithe asked.

"If this Sader Morgan fellow is who you say he is, then we'll need to find a way to either get around him or get ahead of him." Par nodded toward the hilltop. "I gathered that the Queen and her daughters had made camp up there along with the camp's medical staff. I figure if we can find anyone who worked with them or saw them before they left, we might find our lead."

"That is if the Ieses have not gotten to them first," Saithe said as they watched a group of Imperium soldiers herding people together on the side of the hill. "Do you have any idea of where we should look?"

And this is the moment where we impress the pretty girl with telling her we have a lead...

Par held up his hand for Saithe to stop as he waited for his Shade to finish the thought.

I have finished analyzing that bit of dirt and blood we lifted from the hilltop. You'll be relieved that it wasn't anyone from the royal family, at least not according to my records. However, its also not normal blood. It's afterbirth. Whoever was beneath that tree has just given birth. All we need to find is a newborn.

Par turned to Saithe. "It's only a guess, but one of them may have helped a woman give birth last night."

The tattooed woman put her hands on her hips and bit her lip. "Well I don't know where that's going to get us, but at least it's a place to start. You're lucky that I happen to know where they've been keeping the new mothers."

Saithe led them back toward the west side of the hill, near the ancient stone steps where a pair of the burly Kodayene stood guard. Looking up, Par could see the hilltop was crowded with soldiers in blue and gray uniforms, all with the same build and features. He followed Saithe past the cookfires to where a block of tents was circled around the ruins of an ancient tower.

A Duathic nurse approached them with a humble bow. "Is there something I can help you with?"

Saithe bowed in return. "Are these the tents the Queen assigned for the new mothers?"

"Yes, they are," the nurse said.

"Then we are looking for any new arrivals you may have had in the last day."

The nurse's reply was nervous as she glanced at Saithe's tattoos. "Has there been some … trouble?"

Saithe's smile was warm. "No, no trouble at all. We're only looking for someone who used to work here."

"There was only one who arrived yesterday," the nurse nodded, "but the mother has passed. Would you like to speak to them?"

Saithe smiled again. "Yes please."

The nurse gestured for them to follow, and she led them to a blue and orange tent that was strung from the base of the tower. Par paused outside, thinking over in his mind how he would interview the family, but then Saithe pushed past him and strode into the tent. *Well, I hope she has a better plan than I do,* he thought as he ducked his head through the door.

An elderly woman, thin and rawboned, stood as he and Saithe entered the tent. Beside her, Par could see the babe clinging to the breast of a younger woman while a third woman, the youngest, sat in the corner where she was hugging her knees. Her eyes were red from grief.

"I apologize for intrusion," Saithe said, bowing her head, but Par could see there was no warmth to her smile. "We understand that you've only just arrived?"

The old woman lifted her chin defiantly as she looked Saithe in the eye. "This is true. We arrived here yesterday morning. Is there something we can do for you?"

"Yes. Quite." Saithe's eyes had a predatory gleam. Her smile was almost threatening. "We understand that you may have seen Queen Anyse or one of her daughters yesterday. It seems they may have … left unexpectedly."

All three Duathic women exchanged glances, and Par noticed the woman with the baby at her breast swallowed hard. Saithe noticed it too.

"Are you the child's mother?" the replicant woman asked the breast-feeding woman.

"No, I'm only a wet-nurse."

"The mother has passed," the old woman said, her voice shaking. "She died of poison from a snakebite while in labor. Thankfully the child's life was spared. Though we may have seen one of the Queen's daughters, we are not certain, and we certainly do not know where they went."

The old woman had kept her defiant look, her chin raised and her shoulders square, but Par could hear fear in her voice.

Saithe raised a suspicious eyebrow. "I would … request … that you remember carefully, as there are far more unpleasant people than I who are looking for them." She turned again to the nursing woman. "You worked as a nurse for the Queen's medical corps. Did she give any indication to where she might be headed? Or do you know of anyone with whom we may speak who might know of her whereabouts?"

The baby looked to have fallen asleep, but the nurse was so focused on Saithe that she didn't seem to notice. "No ma'am. She did not even say she was leaving. We just woke up this morning and she was gone. Left with her two daughters and all her bodyguard."

Par coughed softly as he interrupted. "How many guard?"

The Duathic nurse noticed the baby was asleep, and so she pulled up her shirt. "I think about eight or nine, sir."

Inside his mind, Par's Shade was doing the calculations. *Eight or nine… We've fought longer odds before, but we were better armed and more prepared.*

Though he and his Shade had been alone for that battle, Par remembered. And that had been decades ago.

No matter what, the faster we find them, the better our chances, I say…

Saithe put her hands on her hips as she focused on the wet nurse. "What time would you say they left?"

The wet nurse shook her head. "I can't say. Sometime in the early morning. The last I saw any of them was late last night at a cooking fire while we all had supper. The Queen, she used to feed us every night."

"Last night, did you see her after that?" Par asked with a gentle voice.

That seemed to scare the wet nurse as her eyes went wide for a split second before narrowing. "N-No sir. I don't believe I did."

She's lying. I can see her eyes moving up and to the left, as she's accessing the creative part of her brain. We already knew she was at the fire last night, but now we know they didn't leave right away.

Saithe looked back over her shoulder at Par, as if to ask him if he had any other questions. He shrugged. Both he and Saithe made to leave the tent, but just as Par was ducking his head, the young girl in the back corner spoke up.

"Do you … you … you said there were people worse than you looking for them, and that they may come for us. What did you mean?"

Saithe gave the young girl a final, predatory smirk. "The Ieses are here, girl. And they will be very interested in you, I think."

Par pushed through the tent flap with Saithe beside him, and they made their way back toward the hill. Par could feel the unease of the people around him. The Duathic people he saw were quiet, watchful, and few seemed to be straying far from their own tents. He understood why when they passed a squad of Umbrean soldiers, all replicants, their weapons held at the ready as they walked.

"Well, I'm afraid that got us little headway," Saithe said as she pulled the hood of her uniform over her head. "Where do you want to go now?"

"I have an idea." He pointed to the stone stairway. "We just have to get back to the top of the hill."

It was mid-morning now and the hillside was even more crowded now with replicant soldiers standing guard at nearly every tent they walked past. Par sent his Shade out ahead of him to scout the way, and he was pleasantly surprised to see that the tent he sought was still un-guarded. The soldiers thankfully paid them little mind as he and Saithe circled the outer edge of the medical tents to the east side of the hilltop. There, they slipped inside a tent with a dark, heavy shell. Inside, Par could hear the hum of the air conditioning units that kept the tem-perature much cooler than it was outside. The thick tent blocked out most of the sunlight, and Par pulled out his flashlight. Saithe let out a surprised gasp as the light flicked on.

"Is this what I think it is?" she asked.

The beam of his flashlight swept across the tent, revealing dozens of empty cots. "If you're thinking of a morgue," Par replied, "then yes." He spotted two cots near the center where the corpses lay hidden be-neath white sheets, still as stones. Par pulled the sheet off the first cot, revealing an old man. Covering the old man again, he walked over to the other cot and pulled back the sheet to reveal a young woman.

"Why are we here?" Saithe asked.

He leaned down over the dead woman's body. "I need to do an interview."

Par opened the woman's eyelids and he aimed his flashlight down into her lifeless eyes. Then he called his Shade to him, and the AI swarmed through the tent flap and filled the air like a host of flies before they landed on the dead woman's face as the tiny nano-bots climbed into her eye sockets. He could only hope it was not too late, that her brain had not decomposed too far. Now inside her skull, the nano-bots began hooking up to the dead woman's brain, firing what synapses still worked while they rooted around in her short-term memory for anything she might have seen or heard before she died. Visions, sounds and shadows flooded into the AI and echoed through Par's mind as his Shade searched what remained of the dead woman's memory.

The young mother had died beneath that tree, just as the old woman had said, from a snakebite the girl suffered on the rocks along the shore. Par saw that a young girl, no more than seventeen or eighteen, had rushed down the cliff to help her. He caught a glimpse of the would-be savior and recognized her immediately. It was Delea, the older of Teum's two daughters. The young, pregnant woman had been panicked and gone into labor as the poison flooded into her system. The mother-to-be had known she was dying, and something primal within her had begun pushing the child out. The young princess and the other refugees had carried the young woman up the rocky hillside.

Par began to despair, wondering if anything of use would come from his efforts. He did not know where he would go after this. Spy on Mnemander? Try to follow this Sader Morgan? Then he saw it. A glimpse, a shadow on the hillside. The path that wound down from the backside of the hill, as it wound down among to the shore, there among the crags was a door, hidden among the rocks. It was only a guess, but it was the best guess he had found since learning the Queen and her daughters had disappeared.

Par opened his eyes and recalled his Shade from the dead body. The nano-bots crawled out of her eyes and ears like roaches and then swirled once more around the tent before disappearing back inside of him. Par turned back toward Saithe who was staring at him, slack-jawed, in a mixture of fear and awe.

"I think I know where to go next," he said.

ORTHO

4.28.2388 - Planet Arc, City of Sindorum

Kneeling in the courtyard, Ortho heard the Stryker's engines winding up as it took off behind them. They had landed on the mountainside, on the western edge of the city, where a grassy field bordered the Temple of Dusk. A blast from the Stryker's engines blew a swirl of dust past Ortho as he saw the Consul Marius stand up beside him and begin marching toward the temple. Ortho heard no commands exchanged but the entire security team rose with the Consul and followed him wordlessly.

All around them, Ortho saw the soldiers of the 88th rushing around as they secured the Temple of Dusk. He could see now why the 88th were given such important missions: Commander Agrippa's soldiers moved like lightening, running about—even sprinting—in full armor. Orders were shouted crisply and clearly, and strong points were secured with ruthless precision. Ortho had never been a part of such a large-scale operation, and he could only imagine what the 88th would be like in a battle.

The Duathe had built their Temple of Dusk at the highest point in Sindorum, and the mountain looked down on them as they walked. Ortho followed close behind the Consul as Marius and his team crossed the grassy field. Here the temple yard was adorned with shrines of loose-stacked stone with many-colored flags and ribbons that fluttered in the mountain breeze.

The radio pack had quickly grown heavy on Ortho's shoulders. They were not half way across the field when his collarbones began to ache and his breathing became heavy as he fought to keep pace with the Consul.

"Intel!"

Sergeant Major Contus's voice struck Ortho's ear like a wasp shot out of a cannon.

"Yes, Sergeant Major?" he answered, panting.

"Have you conducted a radio check with our friends from the Kingdom yet? Or do we need to stop and let you catch your breath first?"

Ortho heard the soldiers around him snigger as he grabbed his mic. "Negative, Sergeant Major. I'll do it right now."

"Don't make me remind you again, Specialist," Contus growled.

Ortho switched his radio to the Kingdom's central net and was greeted by a Zealot One Romeo, who sounded as bland and robotic as Ortho would have expected from a replicant. Ending the call, Ortho reported his success to the sergeant major and was promptly ignored.

They passed a dozen craters with black drop pods at the center. This was where the Kodayene, replicant soldiers from the Imperium, had already landed. Cresting a berm, Ortho could now see the near-identical soldiers standing in the windows and on the roofs of the many smaller buildings that encircled the temple grounds. The Imperium had joined the war shortly after Ortho had graduated basic training, and he had read all of the news feeds about them. Fraternal clones, these replicants were bred for combat, possessing greater strength and speed than a normal human and with just enough genetic variation to allow for a minimum of individual thought.

They were nearing a high stone wall where two of the Kodayene held open a silver gate adorned with ribbons of blue, yellow, red, and gold.

Marius stopped to stand before the gate. "Where is Philemon?"

Both Kodayene stood a full head taller than Marius, who was himself nearly a head taller than any of the men behind him. They were burly men with heavy brows and wide jawlines that looked hewn from stone. When Marius spoke to them, the guards each dropped to a knee and replied in unison.

"The Grande Admiral told us that he awaits for you in the temple sanctuary, Consul."

"Very well," Marius answered and walked through the gate.

Ortho followed the Consul and everyone else through the gate. Here the earth leveled off and an artificial lake spread out before them. The lake was perfectly square, its edges set by jagged black rocks that wrapped around the lake and then formed a bridge that led out across the glassy water. Passing beneath the stone archways that adorned the bridge, they reached an empty island made of the same black, rough-hewn stone. Ortho could see no building or structure here—only flat, open rock. Following the Consul, Marius led them to the center of the island and soon they could hear stone grinding against stone as a hole opened beneath the Consul's feet, revealing a stairway that descended down into the rock.

They went single file down the steps.

Ortho heard Alek grunt behind him. "The last time I was inside something like this, Brennen, your mother was calling my name."

"Yeah, she told me about that the last time I called home," Brennen answered. "Smallest dick she's ever seen, she said."

"She must get a lotta big, fat cocks then, don't she?" Alek guffawed.

"Not as much as you do, she said," Brennen answered.

"Haw!" Alek laughed. "You sound jealous. Doesn't he sound jealous, Intel? He does, doesn't he?"

Ortho shrugged, but before he could reply, Captain Pansa turned around and pointed at both Alek and Brennen. "Sew it up you two. This isn't the cook tent."

The smell of burning incense met Ortho at the bottom of the stairs and he passed through the doorway and into a candlelit sanctuary. Windows lined the walls, revealing the waters of the lake outside and throwing watery shadows all along the sanctuary's floor and ceiling. A ring of candles sat at the center of the sanctuary's stone floor where a statue of the Duathic goddess stood on one leg, a cloth over her eyes and her arms outstretched toward the heavens. Four priests, dressed in plain gray robes, sat kneeling at the base of the statue. Two of the heavily armed Kodayene stood guard above them. The ash-blue faces of the Duathic priests were solemn and their heads were bowed—whether in penance or prayer, Ortho could not tell—but as he followed the Consul closer, he could see that the priests' arms were bound behind their backs.

A pale-faced Ieses man walked out from behind the statue. He was shorter than most of his peers, standing just a hair shorter than Marius, and was dressed in a jet-black jump suit. When he saw Marius, he stopped and gave a deep bow.

"Consul Marius, welcome to the Temple of Dusk."

"Sader Morgan," Marius looked down at the silent priests. "Tell me, why are we detaining priests now? Were they interfering with you at all?"

"Actually, they were," Sader said smoothly as he stepped with an eerie grace to stand beside the Consul. "We have reason to believe that Queen Anyse and her daughters passed through this temple on their way to escape the city. These men were obstructing our search."

Ortho stayed close behind Sergeant Major Contus and Captain Pansa as the rest of the soldiers dispersed throughout the sanctuary. Something made Ortho want to keep as much distance as he could between him and this man Sader Morgan.

"The Queen was *here* and not at the refugee camp?" Marius sounded astonished as he studied the Duathic priests kneeling before him.

"I'm afraid so, Consul," Sader Morgan said quietly. "I spent all morning tracking the Queen's movements and I am happy to report that we have taken her captive. Her daughters, on the other hand, have evaded us. Though I am reasonably certain that someone here saw them."

Marius fixed the priests with a thoughtful gaze. "Then I will understand whatever measures you feel you need to take."

"By your will, Consul."

"And where is the Queen?" Marius asked. "I wish to ask her why she chose to break from our agreement."

Sader Morgan bowed again. "Grande Admiral Philemon has taken her for his own questioning, my Consul."

"And where is Philemon?" Marius asked.

Sader pointed to an ornate door at the far end of the sanctuary. "He is in the antechamber, reading from the scripts and meditating."

"Come with me Andronicus," Marius said as he stomped toward the door. "The rest of you can stay here."

Hefting the radio pack on his shoulders, Ortho followed the Consul across the sanctuary and toward a doorway of blackened wood in the corner. The walls here were windowless, and the shadows were dark. A soldier emerged from a hallway to pass directly behind the Consul, and Ortho had to stop quickly to avoid running into the man. Ortho offered a word of apology and the soldier mumbled something back before he disappeared down another hall. For a moment, Ortho wondered who the man had been, as he did not recognize him from the rest of the Consul's security team. However, the Consul was already through the door, so Ortho shrugged it off and followed.

The antechamber had been long ago converted to a combination of study and library. Bookshelves filled with books, scrolls, and ancient tomes lined three of the walls while the fourth wall harbored a door in one corner and a desk facing a window in the other. The center of the room was occupied by a long table made of stone and encircled by high-backed, wooden chairs. Ortho sat down on a bench along the wall where he unstrapped the radio pack and laid it at his feet. Sitting on the bench, his shoulders ached from the memory of the weight. Then the door creaked shut behind them as Ortho noticed the pale giant of a man sitting in the corner, his back bent over a reading desk.

The towering form of Philemon Ieses filled the antechamber as he stood. The pale giant was half a foot taller than the ceiling, and he had to stoop to move around the room. Ortho could feel his own anxiety rise as the candlelight threw the giant's shadows across the room. He had heard that among their many genetic modifications, the Ieses could produce pheromones to evoke different emotions in the normal humans around them. This was useful for the stewards of the Imperium of Illyer, because each Ieses was often in control of over hundreds if not thousands replicants. Ortho felt the hairs on his neck prickle. When the pale giant glanced at Ortho, for that moment, the only thought in his mind was fear.

If the Consul felt anything like what Ortho did, he did not show it. Instead, Marius smiled warmly as he sat down on a wooden chair.

"Greetings Grande Admiral."

Philemon gave a slight bow with his head. "I greet you in the name of the Prophet and the Father Above."

"I trust you are enjoying being the first of your family to return to the Temple of Dusk," Marius said.

Philemon breathed in deeply and let it out in a long sigh. "There is … a certain majesty to this place that I had forgotten. It is a shame that Teum has kept it from us for so many years."

"And I am honored to see it returned it to you," the Consul said. "Now, to the matter at hand. I am told you have captured our wayward Queen."

Philemon's chuckle of laughter rattled the ribs inside Ortho's chest. "As you ordered. This morning, I sent my cousin Mnemander to meet with their Queen at the ruins to the south, but she was not there. Mnemander searched the entire camp for the better part of the morning but found neither the Queen nor her children. Then my Kodayene and I landed here to find the Queen fleeing along the temple's southern wall. I'm afraid the girls have slipped from our grasp, for now. My men have tried questioning her, but she has remained silent on their whereabouts."

"I would like to speak with her, if I could," Marius said.

Philemon bowed his head again. "Of course, my Consul. She is only just in the next room. I will have them bring her in now."

Philemon did not move from his chair, nor did he shout out an order or call on his radio, but moments after he said the words, the side door of the antechamber swung open and a towering Kodayene soldier stooped through the opening and held the door.

Next came a Duathic woman, dressed in simple khakis and a travelling coat, but Ortho would have guessed her a queen no matter the circumstance. For one, she was a beautiful woman, though she was well past Ortho's age, with light blue skin and dark blue—almost black—hair that fell well past her shoulders. For another, she moved with a grace that could only have been born through a life of public appearances. When her eyes locked briefly with Ortho's, it was with the gaze of a ruler, and he could tell that she was a woman who looked up to no man.

The Duathic Queen sat politely in the high-backed chair closest to the side door, and as she locked eyes with Marius, the corner of her mouth twisted upward in the hint of a smile. The giant soldier behind her left the room, swinging the door shut behind him with a thud that echoed through the chamber. When the echoes faded, a silence hung in the air like ice as Queen and Consul stared each other down.

"You have negated our agreement, your Majesty," Marius said without a hint of irony.

"And for that I am sorry, Marius. I had hoped things would not play out this way, but my little schemes are but nothing before the will of the Weaver."

Ortho sat still and silent behind the Consul. He could see the muscles on Marius' jaw clench and unclench as he glowered at the Queen.

"Though I do not share your … superstitions, your Majesty, I am curious as to what caused you to put so many of your people at risk by fleeing like a thief in the night."

The Queen cocked her head like a lecturing teacher. "I had every intention of honoring our agreement until last night."

Marius raised an eyebrow. "And what, pray tell, happened last night to change your mind?"

"I learned that someone is trying to kill my daughters." Her eyes flickered to Philemon and then to Ortho, then back to the Consul. "And though I cannot tell you who, I have taken every step since then to see them safely away before turning myself over to you."

The Consul let out a chuckling laugh that filled the antechamber. "My little Queen. My friend the Grande Admiral tells me his men caught you and your guards slinking away behind the outer wall."

The Queen raised her chin defiantly. "I am not yet done."

"Done with what, your Majesty?" Philemon's baritone voice echoed across the table.

The Queen gave the Ieses a sidelong glance. "Securing the safety of my daughters."

Marius chuckled in disdain as he shook his head. "If you were so concerned with the safety of your children, you would simply have turned them over to me. Now, I cannot give you any such assurances." Marius then waived his hand dismissively. "Call our basecamp, Specialist, and tell them to send a team to take our little Queen up to *Unifier*. I will deal with her once this day's work is done."

"Of course, my Consul," Ortho said as he picked his bag up with both hands and lugged it toward the corner. The window here looked out to the nave of the temple where a skylight opened upon the clouds. Setting his radio pack on the desk, he extended the long-range antenna and pushed its tip right up against the glass. He knew that he did not need to be precise, as the radio wave would push right through the glass and up into the sky until it bounced off Arc's ionosphere and travelled back down to the Coalition's basecamp on the other side of the valley. He made the call. Operations answered that they would dispatch a shuttle shortly. Shoving the antenna back down, he hefted his pack back over to the bench by the antechamber's main door.

The Kodayene guard had returned and was escorting the Queen back out the side door. When they were gone, and the door closed, the Consul rapped his knuckles against the stone table.

"She has essentially signed her husband's death warrant."

Philemon nodded in solemn agreement. "And if that is what she wants?"

Marius shrugged. "Then it's no concern of ours. Their kingdom is lost. What are we to worry over the petty squabbling of the exiled and deposed?"

"As you say Consul. What would you have of these priests?"

"What of them?" Marius asked. "These ... local witch doctors are not our concern—unless you think they hold something of value to us. Have they said anything important?"

"My interrogator has spent the last hour questioning them, and so far they have been entirely hostile to us." Philemon smiled a wicked smile. "They seem to suffer from the belief that their King is summoning a spirit to drive us from the city."

"Ha!" Marius let out a hearty laugh as he sat down on a high-backed chair. "The Duathic superstition amuses me. I wish I had the time to sit and listen to their threats myself."

"Indeed. It was amusing for me until Sader asked me to leave. He said that they were so angered by my presence that he would be unable to garner anything of value from them until I left." Philemon picked up an ancient tome from a stack of books on the table and flipped it open. "And so now here I sit, reviewing the very texts they were quoting to me as they made their threats."

"And what passages are those?" Marius asked.

Philemon flipped to the back of the tome, searching through pages until he stopped and read. "And as the white horse walks upon the first city again, so the first seal shall be opened and the ground shall give way, striking upon them with a fire from the deep."

Marius laughed. "I would hope that any horse that survived our bombardment has had the good sense to leave the city. However, if some horse drops an orbital strike upon my army, well then so be it. Teum deserves to win."

Ortho held his hand over his mouth to suppress a snort as Marius and Philemon laughed together. When they were done, Philemon's voice was deep, almost mournful. "Their religion was corrupted long ago when they broke from us." Philemon bowed his head, as if remembering. "But that was ages ago."

"So it was," Marius said, standing. "And now I must go. I will finish this business with the women and children another time. For now, I have a king to kill."

"Then I will see you after." Philemon stood again, stooping his giant form below the ceiling, and the two men shook hands before the Consul turned and reached for the door. Ortho followed, hefting the radio bag back over his shoulder and rushing after Marius as the Consul returned to the temple sanctuary.

"Captain Pansa!" Marius voice echoed as he entered the cavernous room. "We must away! Our armor is nearing the inner district and I wish to observe their advance. We must away at once!"

Their Stryker was already humming when they walked out the temple's back door. Ortho climbed back into his seat, and by the time he was pulling his harness back over his head, he felt the Stryker lifting them off the ground and into the air.

TAYLOR

4.28.2388 - Planet Arc, Stratosphere

Taylor Caellyn was on her way back to *Unifier* when the message came in. She was ascending through the wispy clouds of Arc's upper atmosphere when she spotted the light on the *Wyvern's* dash. Taylor double-checked her settings to make sure only she would hear the message and not her passenger. Commander Droesus seemed harmless enough, but Fleet business was Fleet business—oftentimes, the less the people on the ground knew, the better. Taylor pressed the button to receive the message. It was a simple one: Admiral Thorus wanted to see her as soon as she docked.

Taylor ran through the odds in her head. They were in the middle of an operation. She had a VIP in her co-pilot's seat. The Admiral of the entire fleet wanted to personally see *her* in the middle of all *that*. The over-under favored bad over good.

The *Wyvern* emerged from the clouds and cut through Arc's stratosphere as Taylor took aim toward *Unifier*. The Coalition's flagship had moved into a deeper orbit as it cut behind dark side of the planet. Taylor called her wingman, Shale, to let him know she had a meeting upon their return. Setting her autopilot to intersect with *Unifier*, she sat back and was again wondering why the Admiral wanted to meet with her when her passenger keyed up his mic.

"Is there something that may keep you detained when we return, Major?" Droesus asked, his voice polite and accommodating.

Taylor shrugged. "I don't know yet, sir. I'll have to see when I get back."

"I suppose we both will then," Droesus replied.

To her surprise, Commander Droesus had taken more of an interest in her than he did in the mission or the battle below. He had asked about her time at flight school and the officer academy on Orsa Minor. He was curious why she had chosen to be a pilot, and a fighter pilot to boot. And even further to her surprise, she had not minded. Lucinius Droesus struck her as a warm and caring man, the kind you wanted to work with. It all made her think back to the Consul's meeting in the tent. Major Taylor Caellyn knew plenty of officers who got by more on personality than competence. What could Droesus have done to fall so far?

They found *Unifier* in the shadow of Daellor, the smaller of Arc's two moons. In that darkness, the long, black ship was nearly invisible to the naked eye. However, as soon as Taylor called in their approach, guidance lasers shot out from the great ship's control tower, and a few minutes later they were back inside the fighter bay.

She glanced back at Droesus as she pulled off her helmet. "You can wait in my office if you'd like, Commander. I don't know how long this will take."

"Actually, Major, if I could request a shuttle back down to the surface," Droesus said as he carefully undid his chinstrap and harness. "I have only just now become aware that there is some … shall we say … urgent business that I must see to before the day is over. That is, if you do not mind."

Do I mind? Oh, you have no idea. One less thing for me to worry about. She smiled in a way she hoped was polite. "Not hurting my feelings, Commander. Just let my XO know you need a ride and he'll give the shuttle wing a call."

Taylor climbed down the ladder from her cockpit and onto the bay floor. Breezing through her office, she caught her XO, Captain Josiah, working at his computer. After telling him about Droesus, she asked him about the Admiral, but Josiah knew even less than her.

The lift to the Admiral's operations center ran along the outer shell of *Unifier's* hull. The great ship was a veritable city in space—over three hundred levels of living quarters, logistics offices, hanger bays, weapons bays, and every other function a flagship fulfilled—and she could see it all as the glass capsule soared through the lift tube. Taylor was the lift's only occupant as it rose out of the fighter bay and through several more levels of maintenance. Stopping briefly at pilot's quarters, it picked up a pair of staff officers who chatted quietly about office politics while the lift soared past a half-dozen of *Unifier's* greenhouse levels—lush, verdant gardens that were maintained by a small army of drones. The staff officers got off at an observation deck, a wide-open expanse of a room with glass viewports three stories in height. Next, the lift picked up a crowd of engineers in berthing, young men who fell curiously quiet when they saw her standing in the back corner. The lift carried the engineers to stowage, and as the doors shut behind them, Taylor heard one of them let out a whistle. Finally, the lift rose past the command shuttle bay and stopped at level 285. Operations.

This was *Unifier's* nerve center. Every radio call from the surface or from its patrols came here. Operations was where every Fleet mission was conceived, approved, and cancelled; where every report was taken in, poured over, or ignored. It was also home to more useless personnel, both enlisted and commissioned, than Taylor could find anywhere else in Fleet. If you had enough rank and competence to avoid a dishonorable discharge, but you were lazy, annoying, or dumb enough to upset your chain of command, then they sent you Ops. Taylor knew that her career path would eventually bring her here—every fighter jockey who wanted to advance had to do their time in Ops and Logistics, but she wanted to put that off for as long as possible. Taylor Caellyn belonged in the sky and the vacuum, not in a padded swivel chair behind a desk.

She picked her way through the gray-black hallways and the staff officers carrying binders and clipboards and bored looks on their faces until she found the door to "Central Operations." There she ran into the Admiral on the other side of the hall. Miranda Thorus had been a fleet Admiral for just over two years, having taken over for her predecessor, Admiral Shone, shortly after their final victory at Troya. A formidable woman standing just under six feet tall, Admiral Thorus kept her hair cropped in a high fade with a part to the side, making her look almost like a man from the back. She beat Taylor to the door.

"Are they fueling your Raptor, Major?" Admiral Thorus asked as she swung the door open.

"Yes ma'am, why?" Taylor replied.

"I hate to do this to you, Major, but we have to send you back out. Step inside and I'll show you why."

Taylor stepped through the door. A massive display panel on the opposite wall bathed her and everything else in a blue-green hue. Aides and staff officers bustled about in every direction, hustling to and from the room's four terminals located in each corner. Sitting at the center of it all was a circular table of liquid blue light with a holographic display of the solar system rising from its center.

Taylor joined Admiral Thorus beside the table. The stubby shadow of Master Chief Swinney stood opposite them, his bald, olive-skinned head peering down at the table below. Admiral Thorus typed in a command and the hologram zoomed in on the solar system's asteroid belt. Highlighted amidst the rocks were two arrowhead units marked as "unknown."

"We picked these two unidentified objects about an hour ago," Admiral Thorus said calmly, but Taylor could sense the nervous tension in the room. "As of now, we don't know if they are vessels or some kind of unexplained astronomical phenomena."

"Could be anything," Master Chief Swinney grunted.

Admiral Thorus nodded. "The red flag to me were the energy signatures. When these ... *objects* came in on approach, they looked like a pair of stars shooting through space." She harrumphed as she zoomed in on the arrowheads. "Now? As soon as they came in range of our central array, they went as dark as rocks. The only reason we can pick them out from the asteroids is that Specialist McCleaon kept a lock on."

"And they haven't moved since?" Taylor asked.

"Not an inch," Swinney said in an ominous tone. "Civilians don't act like that."

"Typically, no," Thorus agreed.

"Whatever they are, they're looking for trouble," Swinney said. "Gods damned pirates if you ask me. They'll spook if you get too close, Major. I guarantee it."

"In any case, we don't want you to get any closer than you have to, Major," Thorus said. "Whatever they are, they are not our mission here. Just get a good look at them and come back. We'll decide what to do with them when we know what they are."

"Roger that, ma'am," Taylor answered. "May I see what you have on them?"

Master Chief Swinney waved a finger to a man seated behind a control panel. "Petty Officer Haimes? Front and center with that print-out my good man."

A portly man in a baggy uniform pulled a stack of papers off his control panel and walked it over to the table. Taylor picked up the stack and began flipping through the pages. Admiral Thorus had not exaggerated when she had said they looked like stars shooting through space. The first printout showed two massive energy signatures that had appeared roughly a light minute outside of the solar system. *Unifier* had detected electromagnetic pulses that the equivalent of a small star coming from each of them as the anomalies approached. And their speed. They had moved at a third of the speed of light until they had stopped, like a bird landing on the ground, right inside the asteroid field. There they went dark, two celestial candles that snuffed themselves out where they now sat, unmoving pieces of slag floating amongst the rocks and debris.

"Spooky, isn't it, ma'am?" Haimes said quietly.

Taylor nodded as she flipped to the next page. Close up scans revealed a pair of blackened objects that looked like three arrowheads fused together, their points bent down like the beak of a hawk. If the vessels had weapons or anything else, it was impossible to tell since most of the scans were blurry. However, she found one where the scan had come in clear. Only part of the hull was visible because an asteroid blocked half the vessel, but she could see the hull looked like the charred tip of an arrow.

Well that's not creepy at all. She turned back to Admiral Thorus. "What's my objective, ma'am? Do you just want me to do a recon? Or am I moving to contact?"

Swinney interjected with a grunt. "Damned right it's a movement to contact."

Admiral Thorus glanced knowingly at her Master Chief and then back at Taylor. "Recon first and if no credible threat presents itself, we'd like to make contact if we can. I'm not bringing *Unifier* or any other capital ship into weapon range of something capable of producing that kind of energy signature."

But you're sending me and Shale, oh joy. Taylor picked up a photo and held it up to the light. "So you want me to call them?"

"No. Once you're in weapons range and have a good eye on them, we'll call them from here while you get a couple close range scans. If you need us to cover you, we can have *Growler* throw a slug at them."

Growler was a gunship, specially designed around a giant magnetic rail gun that could throw metal slugs at nearly half the speed of light. It could "cover" them from half way across the solar system. If Admiral Thorus wanted Taylor to scan the unidentified vessels with her Raptor, that meant pinging them with her weapons array, something that could easily be perceived as a threat.

"No need to worry, Major," Swinney grunted from across the table. "The Admiral and I already have *Growler's* crew on standby. Fingers on their triggers too. One word from you and we blow them out of the damned aether."

Admiral Thorus nodded gravely. "Indeed. If anything gives you trouble, you just run back to us. That's an order. There's a reason I'm sending you and not some observation shuttle. If these things, whatever they are, give you any trouble, I want you to be able to get yourselves out."

"Yes ma'am," Taylor said as she restacked the pages. "On approach, I'll do radio checks every half hour?"

"Make it every fifteen," Admiral Thorus said.

"Roger that," Taylor said.

The Admiral picked up the picture and handed it to her. "Take that printout with you to show to your wingman. Fly safe, Major."

Tucking the dossier under her arm, Taylor made for the hallway and the lift. She kept to the elevator's back corner to make certain no one could look over her shoulder as she flipped through the pictures. When she walked back into her office, her XO stood to greet her with an agitated look on his face.

"Hope you didn't have any plans with that Commander Droesus, ma'am," Captain Josiah said.

She set the dossier down on her desk. "And why's that?"

"He grabbed one of the new kids and together they somehow grabbed a shuttle and headed back down."

"New kids? Which one?" she asked.

"Pack-a-walla-walla or whatever his name is."

Taylor raised an eyebrow. "The Shaemish kid? He's supposed to be third rotation."

"Yeah, they're supposed to be pre-flight right now, but he's not here. I had to call Major Rice and ask for a replacement," Josiah complained.

"And what did he say?" Taylor asked.

Her XO gave her an exasperated shrug. "We're lucky ma'am. He had some guy named Cleo who just got off sick leave."

"Well tell Cleo and Rice that they have my thanks. We'll deal with Pac's insubordination or whatever it is when this is all over. I told the Commander that you would hook him up with a ride. Perhaps he just misunderstood." Taylor shook her head as she flipped through the dossier. "As for my briefing ..." She tossed the dossier onto her XO's desk. "We've got more immediate things to worry about."

Josiah flipped open the folder and his brow furrowed as he studied the first picture.

Taylor sighed. "Apparently, the Admiral wants Shale and I to check out a pair of unidentified intruders instead of managing my fighter wing in the middle of an operation. So, I need you to have some kind of plan to fill in our slots in case that Shale and I don't make it back in time."

Josiah let out a frustrated snort. "Why doesn't she send some of Rice's pilots out? Why us? Why you?"

Taylor grinned sardonically. "Probably because of how badly Rice botched things at Arvod."

Josiah rolled his eyes. "If it's all the same to you, ma'am, I'll just have the whole wing on standby to move up in the rotation. I don't think there's anyone else we can tap."

"Do what you have to Josiah. I've got to go." Taylor walked toward the door. She heard Josiah call out as the door shut behind her.

"Happy hunting, ma'am!"

Hunting it is, she thought as she walked across the fighter bay. *Happy it is not.*

ATTICUS

Atticus crouched at the edge of the crater, his left hand over his rifle and his right pressed to the ground as he prepared to spring forward. His entire platoon, all four squads, were crouched close behind him, ready to follow. Spots of dirt kicked up in front of them as the enemy machine gun sprayed the mouth of the alleyway where their crater lay. Before them was an open lot full of weeds, destroyed vehicles, and more craters. Beyond that was their objective: an abandoned government building hiding a pair of anti-armor cannons, the same cannons that—mere minutes ago—had ripped through a dozen of their tanks back on the road.

They had travelled only a few miles into the city when Sergeant Jonas had watched the two tanks behind him disappear in a storm of fire. Dismounting their tank, Jonas and the sniper team ran to the second floor of an empty apartment building to get a better view while the remaining tanks maneuvered. Malin quickly spotted a group of Duathic men with rifles crouched atop an abandoned municipal building on the other side of an empty lot. When the window below the guerillas flashed like thunder, Jonas had immediately called it in.

For reasons Atticus could only wonder at, Ioma had ordered Atticus' lightly armored Assassin platoon to assault that same municipal building. This was despite the glut of heavy infantry mounted to the tanks behind them. Atticus had needed to ask Ioma twice if he had heard him correctly, to which the major had responded by pointing and growling with his most intimidating glare. "Did I stutter, Lieutenant? I want you to take that building and destroy whatever is shooting at my tanks. Now move."

Peeking over the top of the crater's edge, Atticus could see it was a plain building, like so many on the outer edges of Sindorum—black and gray brick with a few small trees scattered around it. Surrounding the building was an asphalt parking lot that had been battered to bits by the artillery. Craters, rubble, and dead cars lay everywhere.

A burst of machine gun fire peppered the mouth of the alley again and Atticus bit his upper lip as clumps of dirt bounced off his helmet. *Any sane officer would have called* Unifier *and ordered a narrow target orbital strike from one of our gunships. Instead, Ioma sends his only light infantry platoon head-first on a flanking run. I'm not sure if he wants me dead or covered in glory—or both.*

He felt a tremor and again peeked a look over the crater's edge to see a pair of Ioma's Claymore tanks rumble into the open lot. Peering over the crater's edge, Atticus watched as their cannons rotated in unison as they took aim at the municipal building.

"There they are!" Atticus shouted to the soldiers behind him. "Follow me!"

He leapt from the crater a split second before the tanks fired. *Boom! Boom!!* The shells screamed across the open lot and exploded in twin fireballs not twenty feet from the building where they had struck something invisible. The blasts hit Atticus in the face and he stumbled, recovered, and pushed forward into the cloud of dust and smoke. He emerged from the other side of the smoke cloud running at a full sprint and caromed off the bottom of an overturned bus. He spun around to see the soldiers coming behind him.

One by one, his soldiers collided with the bus as Atticus slid along the bus's belly to peer around its front bumper at the municipal building. *They must have some kind of shield up there that we can't see, because I can't see anything between here and the building.* He aimed his rifle around the bus's front bumper and drew his sights on a shadow in a second-floor window. He squeezed the trigger twice and the shadow disappeared.

Across the parking lot he saw the other half of his platoon bounding through a cluster of burned cars. All according to their plan. His platoon sergeant, Jonas Talor, was leading them around to the back of the building while Atticus led the assault on the front.

Atticus swung himself back behind the bus as the last of his soldiers emerged from the smoke cloud to land against the bottom side of the bus. Two of his soldiers, Mav and Oxan, were carrying a third man, Lollen, between them. He ordered them to stay with the wounded man and to follow inside once the first few rooms were clear. Then he had Salentine and Graide lay down covering fire from the rear of the bus while everyone else formed up in a stack behind him to rush the door.

"On me!" he shouted before he jumped out and ran toward the gray brick building.

He could hear the enemy gunfire pick up as everyone dashed toward the door, but someone had thrown a pair of smoke grenades—he wasn't sure who—and a thick white cloud of smoke billowed up before him. He charged through at a quick jog until the wall jumped out at him. He hit the gray wall of the building, and slid along its side through the smoke until he ran into a doorway.

"*Door!*" he shouted to the men behind him. "*Over here!*"

Sergeant Raef was the first to fall in beside him, and Atticus waited as the rest of his soldiers formed a stack behind the squad leader. When Raef squeezed Atticus' shoulder, he pulled the door open as Raef and everyone behind him rushed past. Atticus counted each one as they entered the doorway. All nine had made it from the bus, and as the ninth rushed passed him, Atticus followed through the door. Inside, he could hear the gunshots echoing against the brick walls.

Raef and Joric had been the first two men through the door, and so they were the first two men to be shot. Sexton and Drake were next and managed to kill a man each before the remaining guerillas fled further into the building. When Atticus arrived in the room, Joric was dead—a bullet hole through his right eye—and Raef was recovering from the shock of the two rounds that had struck the front plate of his armor. Mav was laughing at Raef, his squad leader, and calling him a lucky son of a bitch as the other man was rolling on the ground and cursing. Atticus tried not to stare at Joric's lifeless face.

Mako's squad claimed three more guerillas in the next room, and Atticus got a good look at the bodies as he passed through. None of these Duathe were wearing full uniforms. The first two guerillas were lying face down on a rug in the center of the room while the third was slumped against a desk along the back wall. His face was smooth and full of youth, and Atticus guessed that the young Duathic boy had only just tasted puberty. *Fate is a cruel mistress.* He looked down at the boy's dead eyes. *But it is a mercy when Fate meets you quickly.*

These were the guerillas he had been hearing about. Men and women who were convinced they needed to defend their city against Marius's and Philemon's Coalition. The Duathic army itself had been so thoroughly destroyed at Actium that when King Teum returned to his capital, he had no more than a thousand soldiers left with him. With the Coalition army still very much intact, Teum had done what he could to even the odds by telling Sindorum's remaining population that the Coalition was going to raze the city to the ground. Atticus had seen the reports. Prior to Teum's return, Sindorum's garrison had been overstocked on weaponry but devoid of manpower. Now, the intelligence division said the garrison's arms room was empty and its barracks were full. The numbers were uncertain, but if his father's intelligence division was sure of one thing, it was that the people of Sindorum were ready to fight.

Atticus met Jonas in a storeroom stacked full of office chairs, and just like that, the first floor was clear. Their conversation was brief. Jonas's section had taken no casualties while killing four guerillas on their way in, but they had seen at least a dozen more escape out the back. When Atticus told him about Joric, Jonas cursed and spat.

"Another man in a body bag and it's no sense. It's a damned mystery to me why Ioma sent us here, sir," the grizzled sergeant snapped. "The heavies would have blown through this building like a paper bag and not lost a man. Between you and I, sir, the higher the body count, the happier Ioma is." Jonas spat out another line of chewing tobacco, his mouth twisted in a snarl. "I know how he is."

"You know better than I..." Atticus let his voice trail off as he looked toward the hallway behind them. Sergeant Mako was rallying his squad to push up to the second floor as gunshot echoed down from above. "I figure we have about a dozen more upstairs, give or take. Whether or not they'll fight it out, I don't know."

Led by the squad leaders Raef and Mako, Assassin Platoon began fighting their way up the stairs. As the platoon's lieutenant, Atticus took the familiar position of directing traffic from the rear of the assault. His sergeants rarely allowed him to stay in the lead of any attack for long. Atticus fell in at the back of the zigzagging line that the soldiers had formed. It was an open stairwell that ran from the first to the third floor. Moving carefully from step to step, Atticus kept his rifle aimed upward as the guerillas shot down the stairwell at them. He saw a head poke out over the railing while two arms and a submachine gun sprayed a dozen bullets down at them. Atticus shot twice, bouncing one round off the railing and striking the man in the neck with the other. His enemy disappeared behind the ceiling and was not seen again.

An explosion shook the second floor and dust fell on him from the ceiling. Shouts and gun blasts followed as the zigzagged line of soldiers hurried up the stairs. They lost their second man here—Khale, one of Mako's riflemen who took a pair of rounds through the neck. Mako and Mav pulled him back down to the first floor, but Khale had bled out before Doc Vansa caught up to them.

Atticus raced ahead then to catch up with the vanguard of his platoon, but by the time he caught up with the front of their assault, the second and third levels were clear. Four guerillas were lying dead in the hallway while Raef and his squad had lined up two more captive guerillas against the wall, their hands cuffed behind their backs. Mako's squad found the two anti-tank cannons on the second floor. Atticus ordered Mako to set the cannons with demolition charges, then he returned to the hallway and descended the stairs to the first floor.

Raef and the other squad leaders had rounded up all of the remaining guerillas into the building's main lobby. There were twenty of them, fifteen cuffed and on their knees in the center of the room, while the other five were wounded and on stretchers. Atticus noticed that while none of them had a full uniform, most had jackets or pants or boots. *Likely taken from some storeroom and distributed so they could identify each other. The weapons, too. Teum has more equipment than he has soldiers right now.*

Most of the Duathic guerillas were men over forty or boys just starting puberty, but there were a few women as well. The Duathe stared at him with their yellow eyes as he walked past, their faces either full of fear or hate. He found Jonas and Raef in an office at the corner of the lobby with one of the prisoners.

As Atticus shut the door behind him, he saw Jonas, hands folded across his chest, standing over a kneeling Duathic man.

"How many guerillas were here?" Jonas asked, his voice stern, and then waited as the electronic translator on the desk relayed his question in Duathic.

"Eva-nuum par unuu-um. Su edruum, es tauliss ..."

When the electronic translator had finished, the prisoner, a Duathic man with blue skin, stayed silent, staring up at Jonas with cold, yellow eyes. Raef coughed and the prisoner's eyes flicked from Jonas to Raef then to Atticus and finally back to Jonas.

"Why are you fighting us?" Jonas asked.

No answer.

"We have no quarrel with you, only your king," Jonas said. "He's the reason we're here. Not you. Where did you get your weapons? Your uniforms? The army?"

No answer again. Atticus could see that this wasn't going anywhere. He looked back out the doorway at the rest of the prisoners sitting in a row with their faces to the wall. *It's unlikely we have time for all this. The Major will be calling any minute.* Atticus walked back toward the hallway. *We need to deal with the roof.*

As if on cue, Atticus' radio crackled to life. "Assassin Six, this is Assassin Six Romeo, over..."

That was Thrace, his radioman. Atticus grabbed his mic and responded. "Assassin Six, I'm up here on the roof with Assassin Six and there's something you need to see. Over."

He took the stairs to the roof. When he stepped through the doorway onto the roof, Thrace was right there to greet him. "Right this way, sir," the lanky radioman said as he gestured for Atticus to follow.

Sitting together at the center of the roof were two dissimilar devices. One was a generator of some sort with electrical coils that spilled out its sides and ran along the rooftop and down the backside of the building. The second was an antenna no taller than a man with a small box and two blinking lights at its base.

"This thing," Thrace pointed at the bulkier device, "is a particle field generator. That's what deflected the tank shells earlier."

"Really?" Atticus asked. "A particle field?"

"Yes sir," Thrace nodded. "All it is are a bunch of nano-bots floating around in the air, and whenever they sense a projectile coming, they bunch together to strike it."

"How do they know when something's coming? Why didn't the nano-bots stop us?" Atticus asked.

Thrace shook his head. "Some kind of magnetic shield that the nano-bots maintain, but we were okay because the nano-bots only stop inanimate objects."

Atticus got down on his haunches to look at the generator. "I didn't know that the Duathe had such a thing."

"Neither did I, sir. I've only seen one before and it was a prototype." Thrace shook his head in wonderment and then stepped forward and flicked the antenna with his finger. "But this thing is almost as curious at the generator."

"How's that?"

Thrace smiled. "Well, sir, it's a sub-space beacon!"

Atticus jaw dropped. "What?"

"Yup!" Thrace grinned. "I've only read about these. This thing is so old that the only way to find another is in a museum! These beacons were used to help spacers navigate across uncharted star paths before we discovered how to use the Gates."

Staring at the antenna, Atticus wondered why such a device was here on a rooftop in the middle of a warzone. Where the guerillas using it for something else? It wasn't hooked up to anything except the power generator. *Perhaps they didn't know what it was...*

The door burst open behind him and a furious man in black heavy infantry armor pushed his way through the door and onto the roof.

"What in the hell are you doing up here, Lieutenant?" the new-comer demanded.

Atticus could see the scar on the man's face burning with anger as he stomped toward him. Captain Arakin. The man looked no happier now than he had this morning during Major Ioma's warning order. More of the black armored heavies followed behind Arakin, each man turning sideways and stooping low to fit through the doorway as they plodded onto the roof. Arakin made a beeline for Atticus, leaned right into his face, and snarled.

"Goddamn it, Lieutenant, I asked you a question."

Atticus leaned back and blinked to keep the spit from hitting his eyeball. The scar on Arakin's face, running from ear to chin, was turning red; the man was so furious and Atticus had no idea why.

"I was ordered to take the building by Major Ioma," he said as calmly as he could.

The captain's gauntleted finger thudded against Atticus' chest. "Why the fuck would Ioma tell a bunch of lightweights like you to take a target like this? Huh?"

"I'm sorry sir, but..."

"Shut the fuck up, Lieutenant. I had all my men lined up to hit this building when you raced in front of us out of nowhere. Had my men with their armor cleared this building, we wouldn't have taken a single casualty." The captain moved his gauntleted finger up to poke him in the chest like a parent scolding a child. "How many men did you lose taking this pile of shit?"

Atticus swallowed. Being a captain, Arakin was a full rank above him, so Atticus knew he had to take the abuse for as long as the scar-faced man wanted to dish it out. *But something here doesn't make sense. Ioma gave me orders...* He tried not to stammer as he answered. "Two KIA and two wounded, but they can both still make mission. I'm sorry if..."

"Shut the fuck up." Arakin jammed his finger in Atticus' shoulder again. "And how many did you kill or capture?"

"Uhm..." Atticus tried to think. They were still counting the dead when Thrace called him to the roof. "Eight dead and then I think we have about a dozen in cuffs downstairs."

"Eight?" The captain scowled again as he stepped back and spat a line of black tobacco juice over the ledge. "That almost makes up for the two dozen you lost out the back because you didn't have enough men to properly cordon the building." Captain Arakin shook his head and looked up at the sky. "Shit, son. I had an entire company of heavies on its way and you hit this thing with a recon platoon. What the hell were you thinking?"

Atticus held up the palms of his hands. "Honestly, sir, Major Ioma ordered my platoon to take this building after we were attacked ..."

Hands on his hips and the scowl still on his face, Captain Arakin cut him off with a glare and another jab of his gauntleted finger. "Like hell he did, Lieutenant. We called our position in to Reaper One the moment we were hit, requested to assault the building, and he gave me the all clear. When I saw you get ahead of us, I called him and he told me that he'd ordered you to back off. I know Major Ioma from back at the academy. We graduated together. You're just trying to show off for your old man." Arakin shook his head and pointed toward the doorway. "Now get your men and get the fuck out of here. This is our objective."

Atticus said nothing more as Arakin walked away. The crowd of heavies were already clearing Atticus' men off of the roof. He and Thrace were the last to leave, filing through the doorway and descending the stone stairway.

"Sir?" Thrace asked from behind him. "Did I hear that Captain right? Are we supposed to be here, or no?"

"Apparently not…" Atticus shrugged as he glanced back at the doorway to make sure no one else could hear. "…but I asked the Major twice to confirm this building was the target. If there was any miscommunication, I don't think it was on us."

And that was all he could say. Disagreements between officers were often no less petty than arguments between those of lower rank, but no one benefitted when enlisted soldiers were pulled into an officer's quarrel.

Jonas met them on the first floor. Behind the burly sergeant, a squad of heavy infantry had taken over and were guiding the prisoners through a bronze double doorway on the far end of the lobby.

"What the hell is going on sir?" the pepper-haired platoon sergeant growled.

Atticus sighed. "It's their objective now, I guess."

The command network on Atticus' radio crackled to life as Major Ioma's voice came through his earpiece. "Assassin Six, this is Reaper One. I need you to ex-fill from your position now and allow Spiker One and his element to take over. Do you copy?"

Atticus keyed his mic. "Copy that, Reaper One. We're ex-filling time now. Over."

Jonas spat out a line of tobacco juice. Aside from Thrace, the platoon's RTO, Atticus' platoon sergeant was the only other person in the platoon with access to Ioma's command network. "Well, I wasn't exactly expecting to pitch a tent here, but I thought he'd at least let us…"

Jonas fell silent as Ioma came over the radio again. "Good. See that you're back with the column in five. Reaper One out."

Jonas shook his head and spat again.

Atticus ordered his men outside and as his squad leaders began leading everyone out, he leaned toward Jonas again. "At least he doesn't sound angry. I don't know what happened here, but he told me twice to hit the building, you heard him…

"Don't speak too soon, sir. You don't know this cunt of a man like I do." The wad of tobacco exaggerated Jonas's frown as he chewed thoughtfully. "You know what sir?" Jonas unplugged his headset with a violent yank. "Since Doc Vansa is taking care of Joric and Khale, I'm gonna catch up to her and make sure that's taken care of. If anyone asks for me, tell them my radio's malfunctioning."

Atticus nodded solemnly. "I'll tell them I sent a runner."

"Yeah, I know the tank commander on my ride from our time on Troya." The barrel-chested platoon sergeant spat again as he walked away. "He'll catch us up when we're done."

Assassin platoon was quiet as they marched back to the road. Absent was the bluster and joking that usually followed a fight, and the silence permeated them all the way back to the column. Atticus couldn't help but think of Joric's lifeless face, or the blood gushing from Khale's neck. No one said a word as they came clear of the buildings and stepped out into the street.

A pair of Strykers were landing next to Major Ioma's tank as Atticus approached. Looking through the bay door of the nearest Stryker, Atticus could see a dozen soldiers with impeccably clean uniforms and heavy weaponry. Watching the soldiers dismount the Stryker, he spotted their unit patch. His father's security detail. Walking around the back of Ioma's tank, Atticus encountered the imposing figure of the Consul Marius talking with Major Ioma.

"Well done Lieutenant!" Ioma said with a cheery smile. "That was a most … difficult assignment, but you came through. I hope your men are saddled up, we'll be moving along shortly. The Consul wants to talk with you…"

Atticus gave Ioma a deferential nod. "They are returning to their positions aboard their tanks now, sir."

"Excellent," Ioma replied, smiling widely. "Well, I'll let you two talk. The Consul simply wanted a word while he's here."

Is this why I had to assault that mess of a building? So he could show me off in front of my father? Or is there some other game? As Ioma climbed back aboard his tank, Atticus turned his attention to his father.

"I understand you've lost some men?" Marius' tone was neither warm nor unkind.

"Yes sir." Atticus tried not to look down at his feet, failed, and then forced himself to meet his father eye to eye. "Two, sir. Joric and Khale."

"Hrmmm…" the Consul of the Army of the Republic grunted as he looked up at the sky. "Then you have seen the wounded beast face-to-face. Teum has seen his defeat but he will not go down easily."

"Yes sir." Atticus nodded as he gestured back toward the government building. "We found some … older equipment inside the building sir. A particle field generator and some kind of subspace transmitter that we don't fully understand why it's there."

The Consul waved his hand dismissively. "Further indicators of Teum's desperation. He's a cornered man with few resources. Report your findings to Ioma and see to your men." His father made to step away before pausing to grasp Atticus' shoulder. "And remember, Lieutenant, what I said about kindness and weakness. The time for reflection will be later. Today we end this war."

"Yes sir," Atticus replied as his father walked away.

The Consul signaled his security detail to follow as he walked back toward his Stryker. Atticus saw a chubby radioman hustling behind his father as Marius climbed aboard the armored aircraft. Moments later, the two Strykers lifted into the air and soared off to the northwest.

Atticus climbed back atop Major Ioma's tank. He was pulling his harness back on when Salentine held a cigarette in front of his nose. The tank hummed as it began moving forward. Atticus looked at the white stick of tobacco for a moment, then pushed it away.

"No thanks, Sal. I'll pass for now."

On the other side of the tank, Thrace let out a laugh. "How about you give me one of them things, Sal. I'm pissed as hell."

Salentine wordlessly handed the cigarette over the tank's hull to Thrace and then offered the lanky radioman his lighter. Thrace was letting out his first puff as the top hatch opened and Ioma emerged.

"By the way, I didn't want to say anything while the Consul was here, but you took the wrong objective, Lieutenant." Ioma's face was deadpan, emotionless, almost bored. "I told you to take the building across the street and to set up a base of fire for Captain Arakin." Ioma pointed behind them to an apartment building straight across from the municipal building they had just assaulted. "Don't worry. I have already apologized to Captain Arakin for infringing on his mission. I told him that in your eagerness you must have misheard me." Ioma looked him straight in the eye as if he had done Atticus a great favor.

Atticus swallowed hard. *I know this drill all too well.* "I understand sir. Thank you, sir. I'm sorry that I messed up sir."

Looking down on him, Ioma nodded gravely. "You must have misheard me, Lieutenant. I won't reprimand you this time, but I'll have to include the incident in my post-op debrief. There are zones of control on this battlefield and we must respect them. See that it doesn't happen again."

"It won't, sir. I'll be sure to listen more carefully next time, sir," Atticus replied, his head bowed.

"Good." Once the hatch closed and Ioma was gone, Atticus held open his hand in front of Salentine. The machine gunner wordlessly pulled out another cigarette and offered his lighter. Behind them, Thrace let out a long drag as he looked up toward the sky. Together, the three of them smoked in silence.

The city Sindorum rolled by. Fits of gunfire forced them to stop twice more, but Assassin platoon stayed mounted and shot back from the road until the enemy retreated. Other times they simply let the rounds bounce off the tanks' armored plating as the column drove past.

ORTHO

4.28.2388 - Planet Arc, City of Sindorum

Kneeling on the sidewalk, a gust of warm air struck the back of Ortho's neck as the Stryker lifted off and rose into the sky behind him. The Consul's security team had just set their feet on the ground, and they were spread out in a wide circle that reached to either side of the street. It was the bright mid-afternoon now, and Ortho rested one knee on the pavement as he kept his eyes on the windows and rooftops.

Marius had ordered the Stryker's pilot to set them down near the center of the 88th's formation. They were in the heart of the city, surrounded by abandoned apartment buildings and houses with sharply peeked roofs and the smartly placed corner shops that had serviced Sindorum's now-vanished residents. Ortho could hear the song of battle being sung all around him. The constant, irregular rhythm of small arms fire that was punctuated with the explosive staccato of the air support or the random thud of a distant grenade. Hunkered against the wall, Ortho watched a platoon of soldiers, the red and gold emblem of the 88th Column on their shoulders, bounding across the nearest street. He had never been in an engagement of this scale, and he found himself wondering: *If this is how the outer edge of a battle sounds, what does the front line sound like?*

"INTEL!"

The sharp voice sent shivers down Ortho's spine and he snapped his head around to see the sergeant major stalking toward him with an expression mixed of both anger and amusement.

"Hey Andronimoose!" The stocky man snapped his fingers at Ortho. "Gottamn! Are you with us yet? Or did you leave your mind back on the bird? Where the hell is the Consul?"

Ortho pointed toward the other side of the street. "Right over there,

Sergeant Major."

"Put your fuckin' hand down. I know where the hell he is." Sergeant Major Contus Sulla stopped a foot from where Ortho was kneeling against the wall and looked down at him with a cruel grin. "What I'm wondering is why the fuck you're over here when he's over there?"

"Roger, Sergeant Major." Ortho felt his heart jump into his throat and he leapt up and took off toward the Consul.

He could hear some of the other soldiers sniggering as his stunted, pudgy legs broke into a trot. The weight of the radiopack jostled and bounced against his shoulders as he jogged across the street. Something exploded in a nearby apartment building, sending rock and glass into the street. Ortho instinctively ducked and held his head as he ran. It sounded like a gunfight was developing about a block away. By the time he reached the sidewalk, the sound of the gunfire was so loud that Ortho could have sworn that someone was shooting at him. It sent his heart racing so fast that it felt like a rabbit was trying to escape from his chest. He found the Consul kneeling at the corner of a gray brick house, and Ortho took a knee behind him.

"Andronicus, I'll need you next to me as we move now."

"Of course, my Consul." Even though Marius had said this casually, like a father speaking to a child, Ortho felt his stomach twist against itself. Looking back at the other soldiers, he was surprised by how calm and certain they all looked.

Marius's eyes watched him as he took a sip from his canteen. "Andronicus, tell me, what is the status of the armored column at this time?"

"I've been listening to their channel and ours ever since we left the temple, sir." Ortho swallowed a deep breath to calm his nerves. "They've encountered some light resistance from what they've been calling 'non-uniformed irregulars'. But from what I've heard, it's nothing they can't handle, sir."

Ortho heard the *thrum* of Littlehawks and looked up to see two of the heavily armed aircraft soar right over the gun battle on the neighboring street. Swinging around in a wide arc, they angled for a second pass, as they returned at nearly the exact same angle, but this time the rocket launchers on their bellies roared like angry dragons. When the rockets impacted, the explosions shook the earth beneath Ortho's feet.

Marius pointed toward the blasts and spoke loudly above the din. "And what about this ahead of us? Who is Titus dealing with?"

Ortho adjusted his headset. "Much the same, sir, if I hear them correctly." He hoped he looked calmer than he felt, but the rabbit was still frantically beating at his chest like it would burst forth from his sternum at any moment. "This should be Bravo company ahead of us, sir. They're saying they've cornered some guys who were shooting rockets at them. I don't think this is the Duathic army they're fighting sir. They've been calling them guerillas. I think it's just people from the city with guns."

Marius nodded grimly. "Yes, or they're army dressed like civilians, or they're civilians thinking they can be army. Whatever they are, we were told Teum had been arming the locals against us. It is fast becoming apparent that whoever King Teum has left is more willing to fight than I had hoped. Either way, we shall see how long they last." Marius's gaze then turned to the soldiers around them. "Captain Pansa! Let us away. I wish to catch up to Titus before he reaches his objective."

"Right away, sir," Pansa called back and then turned to his men. "Ready up?"

After each squad leader had given him a thumbs up, Captain Pansa gave a whistle and the entire platoon moved as one. The Captain himself took the lead, walking at the very front of the formation while Marius and Ortho stayed to the center. Unsurprisingly, Ortho saw the sergeant major fall in directly behind him. Ortho did his best to walk confidently, hoping the correct posture would encourage the severe man to leave him alone.

Captain Pansa led them around the gun battle, and Ortho felt great relief when they came no closer than a block and a half of the building where the battle was raging. Ortho stole a glance and watched a squad of Bravo Company soldiers dashing across the street, where they kicked in a door and stormed the building. A violent exchange of rifle fire erupted in their wake, but by then Ortho had passed the corner and could see no more.

The security team travelled quickly and the next dozen blocks passed by with little violence. Ortho, however, fought to keep up with the torrid pace that Captain Pansa had set. In fact, everyone was marching so quickly that he had to hop into a jog every few steps to keep pace with the sergeant major and the Consul. Soon, he was breathing heavily as the sweat began building on the back of his neck.

"Intel, you gonna be able to keep up?" the sergeant major grunted. "Or do I gotta ask one of Pansa's boys to carry that pack for you?" The stocky man sounded almost happy that he had noticed Ortho's discomfort. Trotting again to catch up with the Consul, Ortho silently swore an oath that he'd not let the man see his fear or fatigue. He tried to keep his voice cheerful.

"Negative, Sergeant Major. Just have short legs is all, sir." However, in his mind he was cursing the man behind him. *Here we are in the middle of a battle and all this guy can find to do is bitch at me for breathing heavy? No one trained me for this. What does he expect?*

By the next block Ortho found his second wind. Whether it was anger—or the stamina that he had built over the dozens of random missions that Major Claudius had sent him on the months prior—he had no idea, but he suddenly found himself keeping pace.

Captain Pansa was leading them on a winding path through the city, always turning to avoid the nearest patch of fighting. They slipped down an alleyway to avoid a gun battle, but when they came to a street blockaded by burning tires, the captain backtracked to another street. No matter how many detours and turns Pansa made, however, Ortho noticed that the direction of their travel never wavered for very long. They were headed southeast, toward the center of the city.

Ortho turned down the volume on the armored column's channel so he could listen closer to the 88th's net as they walked. The more he listened, the more it became clear that Sindorum's few remaining Duathe were fiercely fighting the 88th with all they had. What was more, Commander Titus Agrippa was having a hard time pinning the guerillas down. One group of irregulars on a rooftop had fired a volley of rockets down at Charlie Company, but by the time Charlie had responded and cleared the building, it was empty. Titus had immediately told Charlie's commander to avoid chasing the enemy next time. They had a schedule to keep, he said. Minutes later, another group of fighters had jumped out of an alleyway to shoot at Bravo Company, but after they had broken and fled, Bravo Company's captain had asked—nearly begged—Agrippa if he could pursue. But the commander's answer was no. When a third attack struck Alpha Company from the rear, Ortho heard the Consul chuckle.

"Watch now. Titus will drop the hammer soon."

The soldiers behind him laughed and Ortho did his best to smile and chuckle along with them. Whatever adrenaline he had found before was beginning to wear thin. Captain Pansa's pace still had not slowed and Ortho's lungs were beginning to burn. His head was beginning to ache and his left foot was going numb. He adjusted the straps that were digging into his shoulders. However, he forced his face to remain stoic. The last thing he needed now was the other soldiers laughing at his discomfort.

Someone called out behind him. "Hey Intel, who they fighting? Are these them guerillas we been hearing so much about?"

Ortho looked over his shoulder to see a pair of riflemen, one squat and one thin, walking directly behind him.

"Yeah, who is it?" the thin one said. "It's not every day you get to shoot at untrained civilians."

Ortho took a second to pick out the nametags on their uniforms: Mercos was the squat one, and Kraus the thin one.

"Well, Bravo Company killed a couple I guess, and they said they didn't have much in the way of uniforms." Ortho shrugged. "So yeah, they might be guerillas, I guess."

"Hell yeah," Mercos said. "We're gonna end this war with some target practice. Intel, let me tell you, civilians can't shoot for shit. This is gonna be fun as hell."

The gunner, Kraus, shook his head at his friend. "Mercos gets a little too excited about doing his job."

Ortho gave them both a friendly smile. "Nothing wrong with liking what you do."

Another fit of small arms fire flared up ahead of them. As the pot shots became a firefight, this time it was the voice of Titus Agrippa that came over the 88th's net. "All Dog elements, this is Dog One Actual. Be advised, we are calling in close air support on the building at coordinates 58006 by 29947. Over."

Ortho called out to Marius. "My Consul, Titus is calling in an air-strike time now. We should see it strike to our south." Not seconds later, they heard the whine of Raptor engines come at them from the southern sky. *They must have come from the bay,* Ortho thought as he covered his ears. *They're flying incredibly low if they're this loud.*

The air trembled as the Raptors raced overhead like a pair of gigantic black darts. Then the earth shook as two fiery plumes rose above the skyline. As Ortho uncapped his ears, he heard Marius let out a hearty laugh.

"Ha! There's the hammer!" the Consul said. "Andronicus, let me know how many bodies they find."

"Of course, Consul," Ortho said as he pressed the headphone against his ear to listen. It didn't take long for Bravo Company's captain to call back to Dog One. They had found corpses inside the shelled building, but not as many as they had thought. Ortho looked back toward the Consul. "No more than a dozen, sir. Bravo Company sounds a little confused."

Then Marius yelled to the other side of the street. "Pansa! Find a place to halt. It's time I called Titus and let him know I'm here."

"Yes sir," the young captain called back.

The platoon stopped at the next intersection and the security team spread out into four small groups that posted at each street corner. Ortho followed the Consul as they stepped inside the open doorway of an abandoned bookstore.

Marius tapped him on the shoulder and held out his hand. "Let me see your hand-mic, young man."

Ortho pulled the hand-mic off his shoulder and handed it to the Consul. As Marius made his call, Ortho looked over the store. The doorway looked as though it had been kicked in, and it looked like looters had thoroughly searched the desk and the register. However, many of the books were still on their shelves—even the display windows were intact. The store's good condition stood in stark contrast to the many other buildings he had seen that had clearly suffered from looting. Ortho mused between whether a bookstore made for poor looting, or if the looters had left it alone out of some kind of reverence or respect. He was trying to read the titles on the nearest shelf when the angry voice of Sergeant Major Sulla came to his ears.

"GOTTAMN IT INTEL!"

Ortho felt his stomach drop into his intestines before he snapped his head around to see the sergeant major glaring at him from across the street.

"What the hell are you so busy looking at, son?" the sergeant major's voice was a mix of outrage and hate. "And what the hell is so important that you aren't pulling security?"

"Roger, Sergeant Major," Ortho said as he affixed his gaze again at the rooftops and windows around him. He felt his face flush with embarrassment as he heard the soldiers chuckling on the other side of the street. Then Marius pressed the hand-mic back into his chest.

"There you are young man." The Consul said as Ortho took the hand-mic. Marius then called out across the street again. "Ready up Pansa!"

"Yes sir!" The captain called back.

Ortho adjusted the straps on his shoulders again as he stood. He could feel the weight of the radio pack's digging and burning against his collarbones. *Thank the Fates I haven't had to carry one of these the whole war,* he thought as he started walking. *It's like carrying a small person on my back.*

A blur of motion caught his eye as he stepped away from the door as a half-dozen men in street clothes ran out from the alleyway with weapons at their hips. The next few seconds happened in a terrifying blur. Someone, somewhere was shooting, and bits of concrete were flying off the wall and peppering Ortho's face. He tried to duck for cover, but for some reason he felt as though he were trying to move underwater. The ground swam beneath his feet. Bits of shrapnel bounced off his helmet. Someone was yelling. Then Ortho felt two hands grab him and yank him back inside the doorway, tossing him like a doll. Ortho grunted as he hit the stone floor back first. Rolling over onto his hands, he pushed himself to his feet in time to see Marius slide up to the doorway and pull up his rifle. The Consul fired four shots down the street and then ducked back inside as a return volley battered the outer wall. A choir of gunfire was singing in the street now, as Ortho scrambled over to kneel against the other side of the door. Glancing out a nearby window, Ortho found his view blocked by a cloud of dust. Then he heard Captain Pansa's voice yelling above the din.

"CEASE FIRE! CEASE FIRE!"

Ortho snuck a glance out the doorway as the young captain was waving his off-hand to signal the cease-fire. A machine gunner fired one last burst over the bodies lying in the street, sending a spray of red blood over the concrete. As these last gunshots echoed against the empty buildings, Ortho could hear the *thump-thump-thump* of his heart racing in his chest.

Pansa called out for a status report, and after a few seconds of hurried yelling, his squad leaders shouted back. Every squad was up, no one was hurt.

Leaning out the doorway, Ortho stared at the nearest dead man. The gray skinned Duathe was lying against a wall, his rifle clutched in his hands while his dead, yellow eyes stared at the ground. Ortho had never seen the product of violence so up close before. Out in the street, the other solders were gathering to move out. Ortho did not move. He was still staring at the face of the dead man who had tried to kill him.

Someone punched him on the shoulder.

"They always look prettier when they're fresh." Sergeant Major Contus Sulla pointed a knife-hand at Ortho's nose. "And they'll be sayin' the same about you if they catch you, Intel. Remember, if you ain't lookin' for them, they're lookin' for you."

"Roger, Sergeant Major," Ortho said as he again shifted his shoulders against the weight of his radio pack.

Behind the sergeant major, Mercos was checking the safety on his rifle. "Goddamn, I thought we'd gotten rid of you for a second there, Intel."

The sergeant major punched Mercos in the shoulder as he walked away. "Nice shootin', Merc."

Ortho laughed but said nothing as his eyes turned again to the dead man lying against the wall. Searching his feelings, Ortho could only feel relief. He was glad the other man was dead. Finally leaving the doorway, he fell into the formation behind Marius and ahead of Mercos. They were on the move again.

DELEA

"Victory Main, this is Sentinel Four, over." Marental released the radio's call button and waited for a reply, but the only answer was static.

Marental and Motya had been calling for help ever since they had hidden in the bunker, and per Delea's request, they had turned up the radio's volume so that everyone could hear. Motya and Marental had tried everything they knew. Tried every frequency. Called every call sign. Boosted the signal every way they knew how. Still, no matter what they tried, the only reply they had garnered was static echoing against the bunker's walls.

They were hiding in what Marental had called a "safe house." Delea's father had a dozen of these spread throughout Sindorum, hiding places that he or any other dignitary could use in case of an emergency, though the term safe-*house* seemed more title than description. To Delea, the place looked more like a bunker, the walls were bare concrete with canned food sitting on the shelves and a pile of cots sitting in the corner. Everyone was quiet, listening to the radio static or to the battle above. According to her watch, they had been down there for a little more than an hour, though for Delea it had felt much longer than that.

Thayne had been injured during the crash; he had a concussion, and a fracture on his lower leg. Delea had splinted his leg and hoped the spike she had given him would take care of his head. Then, somewhere during their flight from the crash site, Kress had been shot. Mercifully, the bullet had travelled straight through her abdomen, and so Delea had spent the first few minutes in the bunker applying quick-clot and bandaging the entry and exit wounds. She was wrapping up the tape on her bodyguard's back when Kress grunted in pain. Something was broken. Delea felt along the giant woman's ribs to find two of them broken. Sighing helplessly, she sank down onto her knees. Not only was she ill-equipped to treat such an injury, but if there was any internal bleeding, it was well above her medical level.

I guess we'll just have to try some painkillers. Reaching into her med pack, Delea found the theranol and loaded it into her syringe. She would need to double the dose for the Kodayene woman. As she stuck the needle into Kress' back, she caught Marental's eye and gave her a nod.

"Try the radio again, Mary," she asked softly.

The radio mic looked like a toy in the giant woman's hands. "Victory Main, this is Sentinel Four. Requesting assistance, over."

Silence and radio static hung in the air for half a minute before Motya finally spoke, his voice trembling ever so slightly.

"Why won't they answer?"

Minutes of silence and static followed as they stared at the radio and each other. The light hanging from the ceiling flickered as a bomb struck nearby. Thayne pulled out a cigarette and grunted his disapproval. "Shit. You gonna get us a ride there Princess, or what?"

For a moment an uncomfortable silence hung in the air as Thayne pulled out his lighter. Then Kress drew herself up and Delea could see an angry set to the woman's jaw. "No smoke," the giant woman snapped.

Glancing sideways, Delea saw that everyone had frozen in place, waiting to see what Thayne would do. She could practically feel the tension hanging in the room as the naked flame of Thayne's lighter licked the open air. Finally, the wiry bodyguard let a wry smile touch his lips as he held his cigarette to the flame.

"No smoke?" Thayne chuckled as he inhaled. "Fuck that."

Kress took a step forward as Marental held out her arm to hold her sister back, while Thayne brazenly took his first drag.

"What does it matter?" Thayne said as he blew ring of smoke. "There's gotta be a foot of concrete between us and the street."

For the next half second a flurry of thoughts raced through the young princess' mind. *This is all hanging by a thread now. These four bodyguards sworn to protect me and Fel, but three men are dead, including Roake, who was in charge. Thanye and Kress are hurt, and you have to get them to safety before anyone else dies …*

"You want to get twisted in half, little man?" Kress said with a snarl. "We are trying to hide."

"Fine," Thayne said as he rubbed the cigarette out on the wall. "I ain't fightin' no wounded apes like you, that's for sure."

"Good. And watch your tone around the royals," Marental added.

"Fine. Fine." Thayne raised his hands in mock surrender and then—while still seated—managed to bow toward Delea. "I forgot myself your Highness. Sorry for being an ass. It won't happen again."

Now is my chance to smooth things over. Delea quickly stepped forward before anyone else could speak. "Apology accepted Thayne." She gave him a slight bow in return. "You have been wounded in my service and I owe you a great debt already. I will do everything in my power to see that both you and Kress and anyone else are given the medical attention you need as soon as possible." Then she turned again to Marental. "Can you try the command center again?"

"Of course, your Highness." Marental kneeled down by the radio again as she keyed up the handset. "Victory Main, this is Sentinel Four. Do you read me, over?"

Empty static filled the bunker again and after a few seconds of agonizing silence, Marental sighed. "This is getting us nowhere, your Highness. We could come up with a plan to get to the crash site, and then…"

"What?" Motya cried as he pointed up toward the ceiling. "Are you suggesting we go back up there?"

Marental shrugged as if she were talking about running an errand. "It is either that or we wait down here until we are discovered and captured."

"You can't be serious!" Motya's voice shook again, whether from anger or tension, Delea couldn't tell. "There's an entirely hostile army marching through the city right now. Oh, and by the way, unless the King has pulled off a miracle, they're probably winning."

Marental's deep baritone echoed against the concrete walls. "And they will be there tomorrow as well."

"Yeah, but at least it won't be a city-wide gunfight," Motya replied. "Besides, this is as good a place as any to call for a medivac."

Instead of responding, Marental turned and spoke to Delea. "Your Highness, I am afraid tomorrow will bring us less luck than today. Perhaps by tomorrow the Coalition will have won and the King is surrendered. Then perhaps there will be no one to reset the launch."

Another realization washed over Delea as she listened to Marental. *Without Roake or my mother here, there's no one else in charge—except for me. But the plan is in ruins and there are so many things we don't know. Will our escape vessel still be there? How far has the Coalition advanced? How far behind enemy lines are we? We're not only trying to escape now. We're trying to survive.*

Up above, the battle had quieted, making the dimly lit room feel even more isolated, and Delea found herself looking around the room for her little sister. She spotted Fel tucked between two shelving units, her head leaned back against her backpack. *Fast asleep. At least one of us isn't worried.*

Indecision needled its way through Delea's nerves as she tried to think, and instead she found herself wishing that her mother was there.

Then the radio crackled to life.

"Sentinel Four, this is Victory One Romeo. Victory Main is no more, and we had to displace due to contingencies. What is your status, over?"

Marental snatched up the handset. "Victory One Romeo, this is Sentinel Two. We are on the ground. Repeat, we are on the ground. Our ATC was shot down and we have wounded. We need a pick up if we are to make launch time. Over."

The reply was quick. "Sentinel Four, what are your coordinates?"

Marental pulled out the navigator and read off the coordinates. After a brief silence, the answer came. "Copy that Sentinel Four. Birds are risky right now as the Coalition controls most of our airspace at this time. From what we can see, the enemy advance is nearly right on top of you. I don't know that I can get anything safely to you right this second…Hold one, Sentinel…" Then another voice came on behind the speaker, and they could hear a muffled conversation happening in the background. When Victory One Romeo returned, his voice was disappointed but stern. "Sentinel Four, I am being advised here that we can simply move back the launch time. If you can either sneak your way out of the city or find a place to hole up for the night, then we can reset the launch time tomorrow evening, and by then there should be an outside chance I can get you a ride. Do you copy? Over."

"Well ain't that a bitch," Thayne said as he re-lit his cigarette. Kress frowned at him from across the room this time, but said nothing.

Marental re-keyed her handset. "Copy that, Victory. We'll call you back once we've talked it over."

Marental set down the handset as another nervous silence fell over the room. Delea studied the faces of her companions. *They can move back the launch but they can't get us out. We must decide now—stay or go, and commit to our plan.* Delea knew that if she was going to say something, it needed to be now. Taking a deep breath, she took a step forward into the middle of the room.

"Listen... I know neither my mother nor Roake are here to tell us what to do, but it's clear to me that we can't stay here. Two of us are wounded and need proper medical treatment. They say that they can move back the launch, but they cannot get us there. We're losing this battle. No one can pretend we're not. Once the Coalition controls the city, how long until they find the launch site? If we don't leave now, we may never get off this planet. We cannot wait until the battle is over. We have to move now."

Kress and Marental both stood and acknowledged her with deep bows of respect. When Delea's eyes turned to Motya, the bodyguard dropped to one knee.

"As you command, your Highness," he said. "Take no care for my life, as it is yours to command."

Delea fought back a swell of pride as she nodded to her bodyguard. "Well it is my command that we all outlive this mess, Motya. We are all in this together."

Behind her, Kress sat back down against the wall with a grunt. "Don't make any special trips for me, your Highness. This is not as bad as it looks."

A noble lie, Delea thought. She had seen Kress coughing earlier, and what she had wiped off on her uniform had been too dark for phlegm or mucus. Finally, Delea turned to look at Thayne, who was finishing the final drag of his cigarette.

"Shit," he said. "I don't mind movin', but where we gonna go from here?"

Motya nodded toward the gunner. "Thayne has a point. Though I am not in favor of leaving, I *will* eagerly follow your orders, your Highness. However, where *do* we go from here? Do we simply make for the city's edges on foot?"

Kress laughed. "Ha! You worry too much, little man."

Delea smiled but shook her head. "No, Motya's right. We should have a plan. May I see the navigator?"

Delea's mind raced as she took the navigator from Marental. *Where can we go from here? We're not that far from the palace. If there was a way safely to get across the river, we could reach my father's forces...* And then she remembered. Working through the navigator's maps, it took her only a few clicks to confirm where they were as the plan began to take shape in her mind.

"We're only a few blocks from the Vilmaer Mansion!" she said excitedly. "If we can make it there, I might know of a way to get us out of the city in one piece, and if we do it right, we'll avoid most of the fighting!"

"And how is that, your Highness?" Motya asked.

"The catacombs," Kress said with an unfriendly grin.

Thayne blew a puff of smoke at the ceiling. "The catacombs? Sindorum has catacombs?"

Delea nodded toward the surface. "A thousand years ago, back when the city streets were dirt and everyone still rode around on horseback, the city was so crowded there wasn't any room for the commoners to bury their dead, what burial plots remained were very expensive. They would have to carry their deceased friends and relatives out of the city. However, when the merchants bought up all the land outside the city, then this too got very expensive. So, people began digging tombs in the caves beneath the city. And every year, as more people died, more tombs were dug. This went on for hundreds of years and eventually people began digging tunnels to connect the tombs and caves." Delea sighed. "Which brings me to the Duke of Vilmaer and my father. You see, the Duke was a close friend of my father's and one of their shared hobbies was restoring the catacombs. The two of them talked about their project extensively, and if I'm not mistaken, the two of them had the entire network mapped out. The Duke's mansion is abandoned now, and if we're lucky, we might be able to find a map there."

"And what if we find no map?" Motya asked.

Kress hefted her rifle and gave a throaty laugh. "Then you get behind me, little man, and we shoot our way out."

ATTICUS

4.28.2388 – Planet Arc, City of Sindorum

He had expected Sindorum to be a ghost town. Instead, he saw faces staring at them through the windows as the tanks rolled past.

Lieutenant Atticus Marius waved a gloved hand at a group of Duathic children staring at him from the shattered window of a battered apartment building. Only one of them waved back. None of them were smiling.

The Duathic people on this side of Arc were mostly blue-skinned, but he had seen plenty of grey, red, and green faces as well. He had expected an empty city, but now they were driving past buildings and houses and yards full of people. At Gravindi, the city had been abandoned by the time he had arrived. Nothing but empty shops, empty houses, and empty yards. That had been Atticus' first big city of the war, and so he had expected Sindorum to be the same. Now, nearly an hour into the city, he guessed that perhaps half the population was still here. Most of them were hunkered down indoors. Abandoned belongings littered the alleyways. Sandbags lined the doorways. Boards covered the windows. These were people ready for a siege or an occupation. Preparing for a life under foreign rule.

Their entry into the city had been costly. The Fifth Armored Column had lost three tanks to an ambush on the city's outskirts. Atticus had lost two soldiers of his own assaulting the same guerillas who had attacked them. Khale and Joric. Their bodies were now in bags at the back of the column waiting to be shipped home to their families. Atticus had tried not to think about that. After all, they had a war to end.

The ambush had been nearly an hour ago, and the Fifth Armored Column was on the move again, pushing its way further into Sindorum.

Ioma had kept himself and Assassin platoon in the center of the column now, perhaps having grown cautious from the morning's ambushes. Atticus and the soldiers of Assassin platoon had stayed wary and alert, keeping a sharp eye on the rooftops and alleyways as they drove past. Some of the soldiers ate energy bars and drank water as they moved. Others, like Salentine, simply chain-smoked cigarettes.

"Man, I wonder what that hot piece of ass Lieutenant is doing right now," Salentine said wistfully.

Thrace laughed. "He's sittin' right next to you, Sal. Go ahead and say hi if you like."

Salentine winked lustfully at Atticus. "How *you* doin' sir?"

Atticus suppressed a laugh.

"You thinkin' about them tits too, sir? I sure am. That top she had on was barely big enough for a gradeschooler, let alone someone as—" Salentine cupped his hands in front of his chest "—well-endowed as that young lady."

Behind them, Thrace let out a laugh. "Sal, is ass all you think about?"

"Sometimes," Salentine answered as he glanced back at Thrace. "That and murdering moolies like them kids over there." The gunner playfully pointed his machine gun at a group of Duathic children staring at them over a fence. When they saw the barrel of Salentine's gun, they disappeared. The machine gunner lowered his weapon and let out a satisfied grunt. "Sometimes I think about all the money I'm gonna spend when I get back."

"On what?" Thrace asked.

"Booze. A new air bike. And some more booze. Then some girls. And then I gotta get *them* booze. Then I'll probably have to buy some condoms."

Thrace groaned. "Sal, you don't have a brain, you have a second dick stuck in your head."

"Probably. That's probably why I'm so good at killing people. I got two of them guerillas back at that ambush. The other guys hit 'em too, but I hit 'em first. Got one on the way in and one in that stairwell."

Thrace shook his head, laughing to himself. "I didn't hit shit."

"I know you didn't, but that's why you got that radio, man." Salentine pulled out another cigarette from his shoulder pocket. "Cause you a smart guy. And I ain't. Smart guys can't shoot so good because they got so much shit in their heads. All I got is a big fat second penis I can't use." The machine gunner lit his cigarette and let out a short puff. "That's why I'm so horny all the time, and that's why I get pissed off and kill people."

"You get to shoot at people because you're in the Army, Sal," Atticus said, rolling his eyes.

"And a good thing too, or I'd have blue balls every damn day!" Salentine poked his lieutenant on the shoulder. "Shit, I got blue balls now just thinking about that Lieutenant and her ass!"

Thrace gave Atticus a sly look. "Hey sir, do you think the major is hittin' that?"

Atticus shook his head and held a finger over his lips. "Of course they're not. That would be improper. They're in the same chain of command."

"Shit. Fuck that." Salentine made an obscene gesture with his hands and his hips. "He better be. I would. I'd have her down inside the tank right now."

Atticus rubbed his eyes as he tried to think of a way to change the subject. He didn't know what kind of soundproofing these Claymore tanks had, but if he had to guess, Ioma or his crew could probably hear them, and that was the *last* thing he needed right now. Deciding it was time to change the subject, Atticus asked Salentine what kind of airbike he wanted to buy. The machine gunner let out a thoughtful puff of smoke as he contemplated his reply.

And that's when the first impact hit.

The earth shuddered as a white-hot burst of fire shot into the sky. Atticus instinctively ducked behind the tank's armored plating a half-second before the shockwave hit them in a mighty gust of wind that rattled them against the tank like dry bones in a coffin. When it had passed, Atticus peeked over the top of the shield to see a mushroom cloud climbing over the rooftops like an angry god. He could see the impact had been about two blocks ahead of them, but even at that distance the sound had been painful to his ears. *A lot of people just died, and if I were a betting man, we are about to head straight into it.*

Ioma did not emerge from the hatch this time. Instead, their tank simply sped up and raced past the rest of the column. Atticus had to grab onto a safety handle to keep from falling off the side. The rest of the column whipped past as their tank raced toward the blast zone.

Salentine spat his cigarette into the wind as he thumbed off his machine gun's safety. "This is about to be some shit now, sir!"

Atticus turned to Thrace. "How far are we from the Temple of Inception?"

Thrace looked at the display on his wrist computer. "Less than half a mile."

The first thing they noticed was the crater. It was as if some giant trapped beneath the earth had thrown apart the ground in an effort to escape. The crater itself was nearly as wide as a city block, leaving Atticus to wonder how wide the blast zone had been. One tank was perched upside down on the ruins of a house, and the remains of two other Claymores were scattered across the edge of the crater. Pieces of heavy infantry power-armor were strewn about like shrapnel.

Their tank rolled to a stop at the edge of the crater, and the top hatch opened. Major Ioma climbed down to the ground, and Atticus quickly unfastened his harness and jumped down beside his commander. Walking along the crater's edge, they came to an overturned support vehicle. It was a mule outfitted with extra sensors and commo. Ioma yanked open the driver's door. Atticus saw a pink smiley face painted on the top of a helmet. Her face was ashen grey. Ioma bent down to feel for a pulse. Releasing her limp hand, it flopped against the seat. He then rose and shut the door.

"Get your men down here Lieutenant and set up a damned perimeter!"

Atticus signaled for Thrace and Salentine to dismount, and then called Jonas and the rest of the platoon.

"I needed to fuckin' piss anyway," Salentine whispered as he hopped off the side of the tank.

Major Ioma walked slowly back to his tank, his face grim as he spoke into his handset. "Reaper Three and Reaper Four, this is Reaper One. I want you to bring your sections forward to my position and each of you set up in a semi-circle around the crater. Immediately. Over."

The rest of their tank section had caught up to them now, and Atticus spotted his platoon sergeant climbing down from a nearby tank. All of Assassin platoon was soon on the ground, and Atticus had his men find positions in the buildings and the piles of rubble near the crater. Atticus was leaned up against a broken wall when Jonas walked up behind him.

"That's about the biggest crater I've ever seen sir." Jonas' face was calm but Atticus could feel a sense of unease in the grizzled man. "I haven't seen our armor chewed up like that before, and there's what? Four or five Claymore tanks lying here?"

Atticus nodded as he surveyed the scene. A torso of heavy power-armor lay not twenty yards away, and he could see bone and blood hanging from the arm socket. A haze of smoke and dust still hung in the air.

Jonas let out a long sigh as he pulled out a wad of chewing tobacco from his breast pocket. "And Thrace tells me we're only two blocks from the Temple of Inception. This does not bode well for the remainder of this operation, sir. A bad omen, if you will."

"For the record, I don't disagree with you, but…" Atticus glanced warily back toward the crater. "I also don't think the fighting capacity of our enemy is our only concern."

"What do you mean, sir?" Jonas murmured as he turned to look.

Major Ioma had climbed atop another tank. The Claymore's commander was leaning out of the hatch, listening as Ioma was coolly pointing toward a nearby building. When Ioma had finished, the tank commander nodded and then climbed back inside as Ioma hopped back down to the ground. The tank then rolled slowly forward until it was aimed squarely at a three-story apartment building across the street. The Claymore then lowered its cannon and fired, flame spouting from the end of its barrel as the blast shook everything around them. Fire, dust, and rubble flew out from the windows of the apartment building as the Claymore fired a second time. Then the tank turned around and rolled away.

"Lieutenant!" Ioma's voice called to him like a hammer through a window.

"Yes, Major!" Atticus sprung up to face his commanding officer, who was walking toward him with hurried, angry steps.

"Listen up, Lieutenant, I have something of actual import for you to do." Ioma waved his hand toward the destroyed apartment building. "Take your men, search that building from top to bottom. My remaining engineers tell me the triggerman was hiding near there. You have my permission to kill anything and anyone you come across." The major's face was a mask of cold fury. "In fact, that's an order."

Atticus gaped for a second before he caught himself. "Yes sir."

"Don't look so shocked, Lieutenant," Ioma said with a snarl. "These are guerillas we're fighting here. Civilians with weapons. Nothing more than common rabble. This is all about what you're prepared to do and doing what needs to be done. If we show the resolve to respond with enough violence, they will simply stop fighting."

"Yes sir," Atticus replied.

Major Ioma then stomped off back toward his tank, walking with the hurried gait of a man looking for something to fight. When their commander was out of earshot, Jonas leaned close in to Atticus' ear. "You don't have to admit I was right about him, but I was right, wasn't I, sir?"

"I'm afraid you were," Atticus solemnly agreed.

Walking along the perimeter of the crater, he and Jonas quietly rounded up their soldiers and gave them their orders. The general reaction was that of apprehension, but when Atticus told their medic, Vansa, that they would be clearing the destroyed apartment building, the blonde girl's set her jaw with a look of determination.

"Good." Vansa said as she tucked her hair up into her helmet. "I was hoping to get a look inside. It will be easier to fill out the report later."

Atticus sighed and rubbed the dust from his eyes. He hadn't even thought that far ahead yet, but Vansa had a look of furious anger that Atticus had rarely seen out of his medic. The blonde-haired girl had little time for senseless killing, and he had no doubt that she intended to do just what she said.

"You do what you gotta do, young lady," Jonas grunted. "You know we're not stoppin' you."

"Agreed," Atticus added, looking over his shoulder, "but lets get this platoon through the next hour first."

A sense of dread filled Atticus as the platoon neared the shelled-out apartment building. The grass and trees outside were burning, a pair of holes as big as trucks adorned the outer walls, and the smoke and the dust was still funneling out the windows out as they approached. Then they heard the screams.

Breaking into a trot, Atticus reached the broken doorway first. It was a four-story apartment building and he could see how the first shell had punched through the front door and ripped through every room on its way to the building's back wall, which was now fully collapsed. Dust and smoke hung heavy in the air of the caved-in hallway. A doorway to his right was miraculously still intact. He opened it. The dead bodies of an entire family were strewn about the living room. The man and his daughter on the couch, a boy and his mother on the floor. Dust-covered blood was still dripping from their eyes and their ears. They had been watching out the window. Atticus walked back out into the hallway, shutting the door behind him.

His soldiers were pulling a pair of young boys from beneath a slab of concrete. The first boy was fine, but his brother had his leg twisted so badly that his foot was pointing the wrong way. Then a woman crawled out of the dust and Atticus picked her up; with her arm over his shoulder, he brought her out and set her on the curb of the road where she sat there weeping. Back inside, he found a man and a woman who were locked in each other's arms with a young girl between them, all three of them crushed beneath a slab of concrete from the ceiling. They found maybe a dozen others in much the same way. No one else was alive.

He walked back to the curb where his medic, Vansa, was checking the woman's vitals while working on the boy's leg. She had Mav helping her, bossing him about like she always did with her help.

"Just give her an IV. I'll look at her again after I set this kid's leg," the blonde-haired medic said as she dug in her aid bag. "And when you're done I need your help here. This damn splint takes three hands to put on properly, but it's all I've got."

Mav nodded dutifully as Vansa handed him a bag of intravenous fluid. Vansa looked up at him as she began unpacking her splint, and it was then that Atticus realized he was staring.

"Is everything okay, sir?" she asked.

"Yeah..." Atticus rubbed the dust out of his eyes again. "It looks like those two are all there is for now. I'm going to go find the Major and report."

Vansa's face twisted into a furious glare. "I'm not going to forget this, sir."

"I expect not," Atticus answered as he walked away.

He found Ioma's tank parked near the crater and the major leaned up against the backside of the machine with a map in his hands.

"What did you find, Lieutenant?" Ioma asked as he folded up the map.

Atticus wiped the dust from his face. "There's nothing inside but civilians, sir."

"Civilians? No weapons? No arming devices?" Ioma's voice contained only cold disappointment.

"No sir. Just families. A lot of children and women. Most of them are dead and I'm afraid that the ones who aren't are pretty messed up, sir. There area couple of kids who are pretty bad. My medic's looking at them now. I think we should ..."

"Leave them," Major Ioma simply talked over him. "Our air cover spotted some people on foot running into a park approximately two blocks to our northeast. I want your men to head over there and investigate immediately. I'll send a pair of Claymores with you."

Ioma stared at Atticus impassively as he waited for his lieutenant to answer. Atticus looked back toward the apartment building and then at the people sitting at the curb where Vansa and Mav were tying off the splint on the boy's leg. Then he looked back at Major Gaius Ioma.

"I understand sir, but ... are we...?" Atticus gestured toward the apartment building.

Ioma cut him off again, his voice flat. "None of that matters right now. Set your feelings aside, Lieutenant. It's collateral damage. We're here to do what needs to be done. Nothing more."

Something cold and hard climbed up inside Atticus' chest, and it sat there next to his heart like a lump of rusted metal. He stared back at Ioma with a blank look until the major put an edge into his voice.

"Now move, Lieutenant. We have a war to win."

FEL

Her sister was being bossy again. Fel knew her sister liked being bossy, even if she never wanted to admit it. From the moment they had stepped foot in the bunker, Fel had been subjected to her older sister ordering Marental to man the radio, and then ordering Motya to help her, and then ordering Thayne to guard the door. Thankfully, Delea had left Fel alone. Fel had never liked being around her sister when her sister was being bossy. So Fel had sat down between two shelves of canned food, leaned against her backpack, and closed her eyes. She had kept the pack strapped to her shoulders in hopes they would not stay hidden in the bunker for long. However, the more she listened to the others talk, the more she wondered how long they would stay.

Glancing around the room, Fel noticed that no one was really paying attention to her. They were all too busy bickering. Carefully, her fingers found the buttoned pocket on the inside of her coat. Unfastening the button, she reached in and pulled out the piece of red chalk. She thought, for a moment, about drawing something against the wall to see what would happen. Then she thought better of it and stuffed the chalk back into her coat, buttoning the pocket again.

Leaning her head against the wall, Fel focused her ears on the rattle and thrum of the battle above. Soon enough, her eyelids began to droop as the fatigue of her ordeal washed over her. Then the voice of the Onier came back to her as she drifted into a dozing half sleep. *Things from the Other have a way of finding their way back...*Ever since fleeing the crash site, Fel had listened for the music. She was sure that the chain of events had brought her here for a purpose. So she had not been surprised when, shortly before arriving at the bunker, her ears had picked up an eerie drumming that sounded like it came from deep below the earth. Now, as she lay dozing against her backpack, her mind drifted to and from the waking world as another pocket of sounds found her dreaming mind.

Trumpets. A choir of horns blowing a single, slow-building note. Fel could hear them sounding from the same deep place as the drums, and though she could count seven horns, the sounds that they made were like no mortal tune. The first sounded like hail and fire and blood. The second sounded like a mountain being thrown into the sea. The third sounded like bitterness and regret. And the fourth sounded like darkness. Then came the fifth trumpet, and though she knew it was smoke, she could not smell it nor hear it so much as taste it in her mouth. The taste she felt was death.

And finally, she didn't know how, but she knew the sixth and the seventh trumpets sounded like silence, for their wielders had not used them yet.

Then someone shook her by the shoulder and she was awake.

"You doing okay there, little miss?" She opened her eyes to see Thayne's charcoal face looking down on her. "We're fixin' to move on from this place here in a bit, Princess."

Fel yawned and stretched her arms. Wiping the sleep from her eyes, she saw Marental packing up the radio while, on the other side of the room, Motya and Kress were getting ready to open the doorway back to the surface.

"Yeah, I guess, hey," she yawned again and took Thayne's arm as he pulled her to her feet.

The doorway creaked loudly as Kress pushed it open and everyone made for the stairs. It was a warm afternoon now, and the sun was shining bright overhead. Navigator in hand, Marental led them north out of the bunker and their party of six wound through the ruined alleyways and the broken buildings. Sindorum had originally been founded in a depression along the mountainside that was created by an avalanche thousands of years ago. As the city had grown, miles of rock had been cleared, carving a "bowl" into the mountain's face. As a result, much of the city was built on gently sloping rock that gave way to steep, sharp cliffs along the city's edges. Here, they walked amongst red thatched rooftops and alleyways so narrow that the two giant Kodayene women had to walk sideways to get through.

Fel stayed close behind Thayne, and she marveled how the grizzled bodyguard's eyes flicked constantly from rooftop to window to street. Ever watchful, ever alert.

Cresting a hill, Fel stood on her toes to gaze north over a fence. The silvery dome of the palace winked at her in the sunlight and she could just pick out the statue of the Duathic demi-goddess, the Silver Lady, that stood at its peak. For that moment, Fel's mind drifted back to the day they had left the palace. She saw her father standing at the top of the palace steps, tears in his eyes as he waved them goodbye.

Then a hand grasped the back of her shirt and pulled her down behind the wall. It was Thayne, and he held a finger to his lips as he mouthed the words: They're here. The wall began to vibrate behind her head, and Fel could feel the enormity of the thing moving behind her. Thayne mouthed another word to her: Tank. And the wall rattled as the thing passed behind them. Then came another. And another. When the fourth one had passed, the vibrations faded into the distance and all six of them sat there, backs to the wall, until the sound had faded.

Then Fel saw Thayne cough into his hand and wipe it on his pant leg, leaving a tiny red streak on his thigh.

"Heya man! You hurt?" Fel asked.

He looked at her defensively. "What?"

"Are you hurt?" she asked again.

"Aw... just a little, but it ain't nothin." He waived his hand nonchalantly. "Bit my lip or something, I think."

Then Marental called to them from the other end of the wall. "Ready up!"

Up and moving again, Fel clung tightly to the straps of her pack as Marental led them down the hill and across another road. Soon, the battle was all around them again. She could hear bursts of gunfire flying over their heads, hummingbird engines soaring through the sky, and the distant voices of men as they called out to one another over the din.

Their tiny party was crossing an open lot now, overgrown with weeds taller than Kress or Marental, so tall that to Fel they seemed like trees. She kept close behind Thayne, who seemed not to mind. Staying low, their party had slowed to a walk, picking their way through the towering weeds. When they came to a fence, they stopped again and Fel saw Delea sit down next to Marental to study the navigator's screen.

Crawling behind the fence, Fel studied her surroundings. She knew they were deep in the residential section of the Fourth Ward now. There were apartments and penthouses with a view of the river and the historic city center. Fel had no idea what was left here after months of bombing, but the Fourth Ward had been a very beautiful place before the war.

Then a gate on the fence flew open and a crowd of people ran past them through the reeds and then north across the lot. A dozen in all, Duathic women and children mostly, Fel struggled to understand the jumble of hurried voices and shouting as they ran past, but one word stood out to her. *Tank.*

A thunderclap sounded and the world shook. Across the fence, Fel saw an apartment building shudder as bits of mortar showered down into the weeds.

"Shit!" Thayne cried out as he grabbed her by the hand and pulled her to her feet.

They were running again, all six of them, parallel to the fence as another thunderclap struck the apartment building behind them. A wall collapsed. Then screams of agony and terror. Angry cries of pain that burned into her mind as they faded away behind her. Fel did not look back as she ran. Soon they left the empty lot behind and, after crossing another road, they ran into a park. More of the towering stalks met them here as Marental led them deeper into the park. Thayne had finally let go of her hand and Fel could hear the bodyguard's heavy, ragged breathing. Twice he coughed into his hand before wiping a bloody streak on his pants.

Marental shouted for them to keep up as she ran along the graveled path that led them down a steep slope. *This is the park that borders the mansion's backyard,* Fel thought as they passed by a grove of apple trees. *We're almost there.*

Then her foot hit a rock and she tripped, flying face first into the dirt. Rolling over onto her belly, she froze as a shadow passed directly in front of her. It was not a shadow of one of her companions, nor was it a shadow of a bird or some animal. No, it was a shadow all unto itself, moving by its own will across her path and then disappearing into the weeds. Spitting the dust from her mouth, she looked up to the horizon to see more shadows flitting through the air, circling like crows around a set of sharply rising steeples that jutted up above trees of the park. *The mansion.* Then someone grabbed her by the back of her shirt and dragged her off into the weeds.

"We're cut off, little miss. We must hide." The deep voice of Kress whispered in her ear as the towering woman set her gently down on the ground. Then, taking Fel by the hand, Kress led her down a muddy slope and into the water and the reeds. The hulking woman held herself low against the water, and Fel did the same, lowering herself down until the water came up to her neck. The pond smelled like mildew and bugs and stagnant water, but Fel held herself still. Beside her, Kress' hulking, muscled form rippled in the water and her golden eyes watched the pond's shore as they waited.

Fel stole a glance over her shoulder and spotted the mansion's spires not a hundred meters behind them. She wondered if perhaps they could make a run for it, but when she turned around she saw why they could not. Soldiers. They were walking in a line, as if they were looking for something. Their heads and eyes turned side to side as they searched. In the chaos and the smoke, Fel had not seen their enemy as they had fled from the crashed ATC, but she could see them now. These were humans, all of them. Their faces were all different, so she knew they were not replicants. It had been so long since she had seen a human up close that she had almost forgotten what they looked like. Their skin tone ranged from pinkish white to tan and brown and then to black—but not charcoal black like Thayne, but black like a rock.

Beside her, Kress' eyes were flicking back and forth, tracking the soldiers as they approached. Fel sank deeper into the pond so that the water was now up to her chin and her breath made tiny ripples on the water. Impossibly, Kress' had hidden her hulking frame in the same manner as was slowly inching her way backwards between the reeds as a small crowd of soldiers passed by the pond. Fel followed her bodyguard as they sneaked away through the reeds. But the soldiers were fanning out, unknowingly surrounding the pond and cutting off their escape.

A chill went through Fel as the nearest soldier lit up a cigarette. How long would these soldiers stay? Were they looking for them? Or were they on some other mission? She felt Kress' hand on her back, signaling for her to be still as the smoking soldier told a joke to one of his fellows. He had light brown skin and a joking demeanor about him. He slung his weapon onto his back, turned, and unfastened the front button of his pants. A trickle of water hit the pond, and it took a moment before Fel realized what was happening. Kress' arm struck out like a snake, and she grabbed the pissing soldier by the front of his uniform with one hand as her other hand clamped over his mouth. Then she pulled him into the reeds and together they disappeared below the water with hardly a splash. Fel had seen the soldier's face, twisted in a silent scream of surprise and terror as Kress pulled him down. He died without another sound. When the water moved again, it was only Kress. She took Fel by the shoulder and, moving in a low crouch, they crept up out of the pond and through the mud, right past where the soldier had been standing. Her rifle on her back, Kress was so low she was nearly crawling, one hand against the ground and a knife in the other. Fel could see a trail of watery blood across its blade.

Following her giant bodyguard, Fel tried her best to not disturb the grass and the weeds around her as she marveled at how seamlessly Kress seemed to do the same. The giant Kodayene woman seemed to move like a jungle cat, slipping through the grass and the weeds with nary a bent leaf. With Kress in the lead, they crossed the graveled path and slipped back into the grass and the weeds. They climbed up another short slope and through a patch of thorny bushes, and then suddenly there was the rest of their party sitting quietly along the path. Behind them was a black iron gate that was nearly as tall as a one-story house.

"What happened?" Delea whispered, leaning forward toward Kress.

"She fell," Kress whispered back as she sheathed her knife. "We are fine now, but we should go. I had to take one to get away."

Delea glanced at her and Fel could see her older sister's face was full of worry and frustration. Fel bit her lip as she fought back a retort. Motya opened the gate and it creaked as he swung it open. Beside him, Thayne kept watch on the path behind them.

"They're looking for the body already," Thayne said quietly.

Then, without another word, the six of them passed through the gate and followed the path toward the black spires of the mansion.

ATTICUS

4.28.2388 - Planet Arc, City of Sindorum

"Keep your eyes peeled for tripwires, gents!"

Sergeant Talor shouted the order as the soldiers began marching through the tall grass. Minutes earlier, Major Ioma had ordered Assassin platoon and a pair of tanks to search a park for the saboteurs who had fired off a bomb, destroying a section of the 5th Armored column and killing dozens. The park they were searching was several city blocks strung together in a straight line with a graveled path running down its center. Atticus had asked the two Claymores to stay to the gravel while his platoon fanned out into the grass on either side. Their anti-gravity motors humming, the two tanks were directly behind Atticus as he marched.

We'll sweep the place down and back and be done with it. I see little reason to put much risk into chasing down a group of guerillas who likely know this city better than we. Atticus looked at all of his remaining twenty-eight soldiers fanned out in the grass. *They know the drill.* Somewhere behind him, Atticus heard Salentine telling a filthy story. Something about a girl and her dog that he had met on leave. A few of the others were even laughing.

Their air cover didn't even have eyes on their quarry anymore, meaning that they were likely gone—unless they were hurt and couldn't move. If that were the case, caution would be even more important. There was nothing more dangerous than a wounded enemy.

Deep in his chest, Atticus could still feel that cold piece of anger shifting and scraping inside him. Before ordering the search, Major Ioma had retaliated to the bombing by destroying an apartment building full of civilians. Atticus had left a pair of riflemen to watch over the survivors. He could still see the eyes of the little boy looking at him as they walked away.

"Hey! Over here!"

Atticus turned around to see that Marin, one of his snipers, had stopped near a grove of trees and was bent over the ground. He followed her as she stood up and walked around the grove of trees where they found a glass building half-covered in vines.

"Hold up," Atticus said as he held his fist in the air.

Everyone behind him stopped. Raef's squad was gathered on the road near one of the tanks. Both Claymores had stopped, hovering with their cannons pointed out. Mako and his squad formed a half-circle around a pond thick with reeds. While third squad and the snipers each took a knee in the grass on the other side of the road, Jonas and Sergeant Clarke, the sniper section leader, met Atticus where Marin was stopped on a small path that branched off from the road. The short, red-headed woman had dropped to one knee and was studying the ground.

"See something?" Jonas asked.

"Two sets of footsteps, Sergeant Talor. Right there," Marin said as she pointed at a muddy spot in the path. "One of them's small, like a kid. The other's an adult, probably male. And over there..." She pointed at the grass as she stood. "You can see where two other people were pushing through the field. If you look closely at those two, you can see where one of them might be limping."

"No shit." Jonas let out a laugh. "Who taught you all that?"

She shrugged. "Uhm... sniper school? That, and a little from Sergeant Clarke."

Clarke smiled wide. "Just a little, though. At this point, she's probably better than I am."

"Nice work, Marin," Atticus gave the flame-haired sniper a friendly punch in the shoulder.

"Thanks, sir," the red-haired woman said, smiling shyly.

"Now for the real question," Clarke said, his voice proud. "How long ago did they pass by?"

"Minutes, Sergeant," Marin replied. "Five at most. Whoever they are, they must be close by."

But how close? Atticus thought as he searched the clouded glass panes of the greenhouse. Beyond the decrepit greenhouse, the path sloped downward as it met a pond and a gazebo before it wound back upward, over a hill and through a grove of trees. He looked back to his red-haired sniper. "Do you think you can follow them?"

"You mean track, sir? Of course, I…"

Her voice trailed off at the sound of a distant shout. Everyone looked toward the pond as they heard the *swish-swish-swish* of someone running through the grass. It was Hoc, one of Mako's riflemen, jogging up toward them with a pained expression on his face.

"What's wrong, Hoc?" Jonas asked in an anxious tone. "You look like a dog stole your dinner."

Hoc looked straight at Atticus. "Salentine's dead, sir. Someone snuck up and stabbed him."

The cold, hollow, rusted thing that had crawled up inside Atticus' chest now moved again. He felt his hands begin to shake and he pushed them back onto his rifle, gripping it tightly. He looked Hoc in the eye and asked him where.

Hoc pointed with his thumb. "He's over by the pond, sir. They had to pull him out."

Jonas pointed at Clarke and Marin. "Stay here. Follow those tracks."

Together, Atticus and Jonas followed Hoc to the pond where they had laid Salentine out on the grass. The gunner's eyes and mouth were open as he lay on his back, and for a fraction of a second, Atticus wondered if Salentine was just out of air, or perhaps unconscious. Then he saw the knife wounds. The attacker had stabbed him twice at the base of the neck, just inside the clavicle, and then a third slice across his neck to get the jugular. There was a spot of blood under Salentine's left shoulder, and when Atticus lifted his dead friend's arm, he discovered two more stab wounds just inside the armpit. Atticus knew enough about knife fighting to know this was not an untrained guerilla. These were textbook attacks. Salentine had died quickly.

"How the hell…?" Jonas murmured.

"I don't know, Sarge," Mako said as he stepped out of the reeds and pointed at a gazebo on the other side of the pond. "I was over there by the fence. Sal and Mav were over here by the water. Sal was taking a piss and smoking, and Mav said he wasn't looking at him 'cause he was pulling security to the north. Then Mav said Sal went quiet for a bit, and when he looked back, he found him lying here in the reeds. We pulled him out and rolled him over, thinking he'd just fallen in, but then we saw all them knife wounds. That's when we got Doc."

Mako was Assassin platoon's most senior squad leader, and one of the most even-keeled men Atticus had ever met. However, as the gaunt sergeant recalled the scene of Salentine's death, Atticus could hear the grief and regret.

"Where's Doc?" Jonas asked.

Mako pointed his thumb back toward the road. "Once Vansa saw he was dead, she said she couldn't look at him no more. She went to go get a body bag."

"Shit," Jonas mumbled.

"Whoever did this, you can see where he crawled out over there." Mako pointed to the other side of the pond. "Show him, Corrin."

"Follow me, sir." Corrin waved as he walked around the pond, and Atticus followed. When they reached the other side of the pond, Corrin pointed to where the reeds had been bent and broken from someone crawling their way out of the water. Atticus circled the pond to the broken reeds to take a closer look. He could see the drag marks and footprints of two people—one small and one gigantically large—pulling themselves through the mud and then crawling away into the grass. Turning back around, he could see a crowd of his men had gathered. Everyone was staring at the body. Atticus could feel the hard and painful thing in his chest slowly turning from cold to hot.

Walking back to the gazebo, he looked to his platoon sergeant and spoke quietly. "Jonas, get everyone else back on line, but find Marin and bring her back down here. We're taking Mako's squad to track these sons of bitches down, and then we're going to kill them." He gathered Mako's squad around him in a huddle as he took a knee. "Now listen up, here's the plan..."

FEL

4.28.2388 - Planet Arc, Sindorum

The shades had followed her.

The front door of the mansion thundered shut as Fel walked through the foyer and onto the green tile floor of a great dining hall. The northern wall of the room had windows two stories high, their glass cloudy with dust and grime and half-covered in vines. Even so, Fel could see the ghostly shadows in the sky outside, flopping in the air like untethered kites. They were circling the mansion's front yard, as if waiting for an invitation to come inside.

The music had returned as well. It had joined her shortly after they cleared the gate, but now the tune had changed again. The trumpets she heard before were replaced by a slow drumbeat accompanied by the hollow whine of a single, anxious string. It was eerily similar to the song she had heard last night, and to Fel it sounded like fear and terror sung to life. However, she had pledged to follow it anyhow, despite the uneasy feeling it created in her gut. Standing there amid the dusty tables and chairs of the abandoned dining room, she looked up at the shadows swirling outside the vine-covered windows. It felt almost like reflex when she reached into her coat pocket and pulled out the piece of chalk.

"What's that?"

A chill of surprise ran down Fel's spine as she saw her sister staring at her hand.

"It's nothing," Fel replied. "I found it while I was wandering down by the beach before we left." She kept her face flat and her voice even. It wasn't exactly a lie, even though it felt like one.

"Is that why you disappeared before we left?" Delea asked.

"No," Fel stuffed the chalk back into her coat. "Like I told mom, I just wanted to say goodbye to some of my friends."

Delea's eyes narrowed. "Which friends?"

"Does it really matter now?" Fel shrugged. Her sister scowled at that, and Fel could see her sister's eyes were suspicious now, flicking back and forth from Fel to her coat. *Why is she even mad about that? I'm not the reason we're here. I didn't make us crash.*

Then Marental walked up behind Delea and touched her shoulder. "Your Highness, the map…"

Delea nodded and then gestured toward Thayne. "Can you keep an eye on my sister while we search the mansion?"

Thayne agreed, and Delea left the dining room with Kress, Motya, and Marental. The wiry bodyguard pulled out his pack of cigarettes and, as he put one in his mouth, he caught Fel's eye and nodded toward the stairwell at the back of the room.

"We need to keep an eye out to see if any of them soldiers decide to follow us," he said as he sparked his lighter. "And we'll have ourselves a better view from the second floor."

Fel glanced back toward the vine-covered windows before she followed him up the stairs. The shadows had disappeared, though she could still hear the drumbeat and the shivering string singing their dirge. Then, as they were climbing the stairs, Fel saw a shadow, black and feathered, flit through the rafters. Reaching the second floor, Thayne took up a spot in the shadows near a window that looked out at the mansion's backyard. There he could see the gate where they had entered and the park beyond. She waited for him to get settled, pretending to look at the faded paintings hanging on the wall, while he set down on the floor between a broken chair and a curtain. She watched him take a long slow drag on his cigarette as he peered out the window. Then, when she was sure he wasn't looking, she tiptoed down the hallway to a door that was standing half open. Quietly, she slipped through and went onto a balcony that overlooked the dining room below.

Here on the balcony, the towering windows of the dining hall stared back at her. Through their dusty panes and tangled vines, she could see there were no more shadows outside. Then her eyes moved again to the rafters and she spotted something walking along one of the beams. It was a Kotling. It stood up on its haunches and sniffed the air before dropping back down on all fours and waddling back into the shadows.

Glancing back out the doorway, Fel saw Thayne's attention was still fixed on the window and the yard outside. Closing the door, she pulled off both of her shoes and left them on the carpet. Careful and quiet, she climbed atop the balcony railing and stood, her head rising above the rafters. A twenty-foot drop opened below before her. Extending her arms, she stood on the railing, balanced on the balls of her feet. Then, arms outstretched, she fell forward and caught herself against the nearest rafter. Wrapping her arms and legs around the wooden beam she pulled herself up and sat with the beam between her thighs. Using her knees and elbows, she climbed her way along the beam to the outer wall until she stopped next to a giant window. Sindorum's Fourth Ward spread out before her. City and mountain rose before her against a pale, cloudy sky. The palace looked down on her from the very top of the city, which was about half way up Mount Chernon, and below that were the strings of firey gunfire and the scattered explosions that burned and flashed between the buildings below. She could see how the fighting was moving closer and closer to the palace as their enemies closed in on her father.

Fel found herself wondering how her mother and father were. Had her mother made it out of the city? Was she even trying to escape or had she gone to find Teum? Was her father still alive? Suddenly she felt very afraid. Silently, Fel closed her eyes, bowed her head and prayed to the Silver Lady to keep both of her parents safe.

Opening her eyes, Fel saw her breath misting in the air. A cold shiver climbed up her spine and into her chest where it grabbed a hold of her lungs, and that's when she knew the Onier had found her again. Looking up, she watched the black and brown wraith fall through the ceiling. Two massive wings, with feathers of drab brown, filled the space between the rafters as the Onier descended to sit before her on the wooden beam. The Onier's smoke-filled eyes looked down at her, and Fel met its gaze as the voice came into her head like a friendly stranger.

"The music has brought you here, Little Sister, just as we said it would. Now we just have to find out why." Fel knew then that it was the same Onier as before; she could tell by the shape of its wings and the way its voice sounded like the creaking hinges of an open coffin. Then the Onier's smoke filled eyes turned to look at her right arm. "Do you still have the small treasure we found?"

Reaching into her coat, Fel pulled out the piece of red chalk.

"That is good. You have done well, Little Sister, to bring it this far. Because you have asked and because we must know, I have found some clues to what our treasure is and what it does." The Onier's wings slowly folded and unfolded as it spoke, passing intangibly through the rafters as they swept back and forth. "It is an artifact, made by one of the Children. So it is a thing that can pass between this world, the Here, and the Other, where you must go. Though why it was in the that room, I can only guess."

"But what does it do?" Fel asked.

"Ah, child…" The Onier sighed as the edges of its beaked mouth twisted in a smile. "That is what we will have to find out."

"Do you know what happened to my mother? Is she safe?"

The Onier shook its head. "That I cannot say, for she has travelled out of my view. I am but a visitor to the Here, and so there are many things I cannot see, including your mother." The Onier's smoke filled eyes turned to look out at the city. "As for your father, it is him I have watched. As you have seen, he has gone down into the thing beneath this city. One of our bravest followed him until he came to a narrow door, but there our agent had to stop. For through that door is a dangerous place. And now we fear what he will do, for we can hear their voices. We can hear their music. They call to us the same as they call to you."

"Who are *they*?" she asked.

The Onier shrugged. "That I cannot say, though we know they play the songs." The Onier's head snapped back around as it looked toward the balcony door. "Your friend approaches and you must go, for danger is coming to you like wolves in the dusk. So, I tell you now where you must go. The place you seek is here, in the garden. The music will guide you. Mark the sign of the Weaver as it lies in the shadow of the Thief."

ATTICUS

4.28.2388 - Planet Arc, Sindorum

Lifting the latch, Atticus cracked open the gate and slipped inside the fence. The grass and the weeds were thicker here, as if they were building up inside the fence so they could burst forth when it fell. Atticus stayed low, crouching as he held the gate open. Mav, Mako and the rest of first squad quickly crawled through the gate and fanned out through the grass and the weeds. His red-haired sniper, Marin, was last and he shut the gate behind her. Then, Atticus slowly raised himself even with the top of grass as he studied the mansion through the scope of his rifle.

Built with red brick and topped with a black, shingled roof with four towering spires at each corner, the mansion was an impressive building. The invasion had given it one scar—a hole in the east side of the roof that appeared, to Atticus, the product of an artillery strike. Looking lower through the mansion's multitude of windows, he could see no lights. The only thing Atticus saw moving was a raven that crossed the yard and alighted atop the mansion's northern chimney. Then, just as he was about to put his weapon down, he saw something move behind a first story curtain.

He dropped back down into the grass and crawled over to Mako. "There's someone in there."

The gaunt sergeant nodded, and Atticus could see the cold fury in Mako's eyes as he signaled the soldiers behind him. One by one the squad began to move, silently weaving their way through the brush and moving with such care that they hardly stirred the weeds and the grass. Including the wiry sergeant, Mako's squad counted only six now, and the squad leader himself took the lead. He was followed closely by

Graide and Harrick, each heavily muscled and among the strongest in the platoon; next was Hoc, Salentine's best friend who had been with him at the pond; Joric, Mako's pot-bellied grenadier; and finally Sexton, Mako's lone remaining machine gunner.

The plan was for Mako's squad to flank from the east while Raef's squad approached from the north. The rest of the platoon, led by Jonas, would be spread out along the fence between them to provide a base of fire.

Marin fell in with Atticus as they followed Sexton at the rear of the party. The sniper's eyes flickered from the yard to the mansion and back again as she stalked through the grass. The mansion's black spires loomed above them as they weaved through the weeds and the brush. Mako cut south through the yard, leading them around to the backside of the mansion. Following behind Sexton, Atticus could see the shadows of his other soldiers crouched just outside the black bars of the fence, and he knew that Raef's squad was moving parallel to Mako's along the front side of the house. In less than a minute, their prey would have nowhere to run.

The weeds opened before them to reveal a cobblestone path and that led them through the towering weeds. The red evening rays were shining through the thick, green stalks as they neared the back of the mansion. When the weeds parted altogether, they opened into a grassy yard that met with a walled veranda on the west wing of the mansion. Mako called a halt and everyone came on line, staying hidden in the weeds.

Mako snuck over to Atticus and pointed to the right. "I saw a second door on the other wing of the house, sir. If you want, we could split up and meet in the middle with Raef's squad."

Atticus nodded. "I'll take Marin, Harrick, and Hoc and we'll go around this wall, while you take the rest of yours and head that way."

"Yes sir," Mako said quietly as he waved to the others. "C'mon. Let's go kick in a door."

Atticus watched the four of them disappear into the long grass. Then, staying low, he jogged to the remaining three and repeated the plan. Gathering Harrick, Marin and Hoc next to him, they waited at the edge of the brush while Mako and his team circled around toward the other door. When they were halfway across the back yard, he waved his team forward and they approached the wall of the veranda in a wedge formation. Atticus fought back the memory of Salentine's lifeless, mud-stained face lying in the grass as he readied his rifle. His heart was pumping in his chest as he neared the corner of the wall. Then a blur of black and brown flashed before him. He leveled his rifle and fired.

DELEA

The door, of course, was locked. Delea could not explain why the Duke of Vilmaer would have left a door on the second floor of his mansion locked, other than it fit with the rest of the bad luck they had endured so far. She holstered her pistol and leaned down to look closely at the door handle. There was nothing jammed or otherwise obstructing the latch that she could see. The Duke had simply, for whatever reason, left the door locked. She stood up straight again and examined the rest of the door for anything that might help her identify the room behind it, but there were no discernable clues she could see.

"You think that's the room?" Motya asked from behind her.

She shrugged. "I think so, at least I'm pretty sure it is, but it's locked for some reason. We haven't found any keys anywhere, have we?"

Her bodyguard shook his head. "No, your Highness, but if we need to get in there, I think I can help."

"Please do," she said, stepping back.

Delea watched as Motya slid the shim between the door and the frame, right where the latch should be. Then he pressed a small black button on the shim's handle and it began to vibrate. Then, grabbing the shim's handle, he pushed it down hard with both hands as both the latch and the bolt sheared cleanly off. Finally, when Motya pulled the shim out, the doorway swung open, revealing a room lined with bookshelves and a dark wood desk that sat facing them along the opposite wall.

"It's a small wonder the room was still locked," Motya said, sliding the shim back into his bag. "Most of the other rooms have been looted."

"Thank the Fates for small mercies, I suppose," Delea said as she walked into the room. Walking up to the desk, she was relieved when the first drawer slid open easily. Thankfully, the Duke had not bothered to lock the desk with the room.

"Fate?" Motya set his pack and his rifle on the top of the desk. "You're not religious like your father?"

"No," she answered as she thumbed through a drawer full of index cards. "I remember when the Magister said that our cause was just, and that our King, my father, was guided by the holy hand of God and that his guidance during the conflict would be as wise as the great prophets. Well, then Troya happened, and that Magister changed his tune. And so did I."

Motya nodded as he opened a file cabinet. "I remember that. Didn't he die in a bombing or something?"

"He did." She shook her head as she opened another drawer. "Not long after that, my father started going a little crazy. He was paranoid that there was a spy somewhere. If there *was* a spy, I doubt he ever found him. Later on, he stopped sleeping and he would get really … angry for days at a time until finally my mother took me and Fel away. She kept us busy by looking after our people."

Motya shut one file cabinet and opened the top drawer of another. "I had heard a few stories from the other guardsmen, but not much. I did not know that was why you left the palace."

"Yeah, my father and this war took away any belief I had in a higher power," Delea answered as she flipped through a stack of folders.

They searched in silence for a few moments. The only sounds were the flipping of pages and the sliding metal drawers. Then Delea flipped open a folder and pulled out a lacquered printout that had been cut and folded into four pieces.

"There!" she exclaimed. "I think I found it!"

Then the door to the hallway swung open and Marental leaned her head into the room. "Your Highness, we are in danger and must flee immediately."

"What?" Delea asked as her heart jumped up into her throat. She hurriedly folded up the map and stuck it into her pocket. Wasting no time, she and Motya followed Marental out into the hallway.

"Kress and Thayne have both spotted soldiers approaching the mansion," Marental explained quietly as they jogged down the hall. "If we are not quick, we may be surrounded before we can escape."

"Where is my sister?" Delea demanded as they reached the stairwell.

"Thayne is bringing her," Marental replied. "I told him to meet us in the garden."

Reaching the bottom of the stairs, they passed by an ornate bay window and Delea looked out to see a pair of shadows stalking through the weeds outside. Behind her, she heard Motya take in a sharp, hissing breath as he saw them, too. Dashing across the carpeted floor, they reached the end of the hallway where a plain, white double doorway swung open before them. Kress met them there, holding the door open as they dashed inside the kitchen.

"We must make for the back gate, it is our only chance," Kress said as the door swung shut behind them.

Kress took the lead now as they pushed through the kitchen. Following the others through the countertops and ovens and stoves, Delea remembered the soldier's face that she had seen through the muddy glass. *Humans, not replicants.* She did not know how she knew it, only that she did—and a sense of unease washed over her as she followed Kress and Marental through the kitchen. *Kress had to kill one of them back in the swamp. If Kress had killed an Umbrean replicant, they probably wouldn't care, but no, these were human soldiers, and the dead man had a name.*

The backdoor of the kitchen opened to a walled veranda overgrown with vines like dark green fingers. Kress had taken the lead now and when she leaned out to look around the wall, the crack of a gunshot echoed through the air. A snap of dust caromed off the wall.

"By the Weaver!" Kress cursed as she spun behind the wall. "They're lined up in the weeds!"

A chorus of gunfire came at them from the yard and everyone took cover behind the wall as bits of concrete flew from the brick and bullets ripped through the mansion behind them. Falling to the ground, Delea crawled up between Motya and Kress as the gunfire thundered around them.

"We're surrounded," Motya said, his voice was full of defeat.

"Not yet, little man." Marental pointed to Motya and Delea and then to the corner of the wall. "You and the princess will hide yourselves here while we lead them off." Staying crouched below the wall, the giant, purple-haired woman walked over to the corner of the veranda and pulled up a grate from the floor. "Down here," she said, pointing with her gloved hand.

Behind them, Kress held her rifle over the top of the wall and fired blindly, launching a flurry of gunshots into the garden. Then she ducked down as a thundering chorus came back in reply. Again, a volley of bullets ripped through the mansion's walls, shattering windows and peppering the veranda.

Holding the grate, Marental shouted above the din. "Hurry Princess! I will close it behind you."

The gunfire all around her, Delea climbed down into the hole. Nearly five feet deep, it looked to be a storm drain. Her feet met a layer of water and sludge as she lowered herself down. The water soaked its way up the hem of her pants as she sat down on her haunches. Leaning on her knees, she spotted a pipe, nearly four feet in diameter. Then she heard Motya's voice shouting above her.

"Why am I staying with her?"

"Because you're the only one who fits!" Marental yelled back. "Take the navigator. Someone must take the princess to the launch site once this is done!"

"Fine!" Motya snatched the navigator from Marental as he lowered himself down into the hole.

Delea pressed herself against the wall as Motya's lanky form dropped down into the water beside her. As Marental was lowering the grate shut above her, she began to wonder what had befallen her sister.

FEL

Mark the sign of the Weaver as it lies in the shadow of the Thief. The Onier's words echoed in her mind as its shade disappeared before her, collapsing into a wisp of black smoke. Then the balcony doorway opened behind her with a creak and a yawn.

"Your Highness, we have to go..." Thayne's jaw dropped as he looked at her through the doorway. "What in the name of the Weaver are you doing up there?"

Before he could get in the way, Fel stood and launched herself from the rafter beam and landed in a rolling somersault on the balcony carpet. Bounding to her feet, she slipped past him and ran through the doorway.

Stopping in the hallway, she turned around. "You ready?"

Thayne looked from her to the rafter and then back to her. Scratching his head, he nodded. "You're an odd girl, miss."

Together they ran down the hall and descended the stairs. Reaching the bottom of the stairwell, Thayne took her by the hand and led her into the dining hall. "Come, your Highness, the others are headed toward the back."

Weaving through the dusty tables and overturned chairs, they crossed the dining hall, and Fel stole one last glance out a window to see shadowy shapes moving through the weeds outside. Then Thanye pushed them through a swinging double door, and they were gone. They were jogging through a carpeted hallway when the *click* of a door latch echoed against the empty walls. They stopped. A door swung open.

Holding her by the arm, Thayne pulled her through an open doorway. He let her go as they entered a room filled with dusty boxes and junk. Thayne eased the door shut behind them as Fel crept around a pile of trash bags. Long ago, a bomb of some kind had struck the adjacent room and scattered bits of charred wood over top the boxes and bags, and there was a gaping hole in the corner of the back wall. Climbing over a stack of boxes, Fel stopped to look back at Thayne, who was still standing near the door, listening with his rifle ready. She sat on her knees behind the boxes and, staying still as a stone, she listened to the hallway.

Creeping and quiet, the bootsteps entered the hallway. One by one, Fel heard the doorways begin to open and close. The soldiers were searching for them. Silently, Thayne backed away from the door and crawled behind an overturned bookshelf so that he was completely out of sight from the doorway. Seconds later, the doorknob turned and the door creaked open.

Crouched behind a large, sagging box, Fel held her breath as a pair of bootsteps walked into the room. Seconds of terrifying silence passed, and Fel could hear the soldier's breathing as he stood there, a few feet inside the door. Then a gunshot echoed from the other side of the house, and everything froze. Someone outside was shouting. Fel thought she heard Kress' voice cry out, and then the gunfire retuned in earnest. Fel could hear the bullets ripping through the far end of the house. Then the door closed and the bootsteps hurried away down the hall. As the gunshots echoed through the mansion, fear gripped Fel in a way it never had before.

Then the gun battle died away almost as quickly as it had begun. Seconds later, hurried bootsteps clattered through the mansion in every direction. More gunshots followed, but they were scattered and random. And then there was no sound except for the quiet that lasted for a moment, then stretched into minutes. As the quiet settled over the mansion, the only sound Fel could hear was the breeze whistling through the empty building.

"Are they gone?" she whispered.

"Shh," Thayne said.

She looked back toward the hole in the wall where the evening redness was leaking through. Outside, she thought she could hear someone walking through the weeds. Were those voices? Briefly, she considered pulling out her translator to see if she could pick up what they were saying, but then a breeze picked up and she wasn't sure. Slowly, the fear and terror deep inside her began to fade away. She sat there in the dusty room, listening and waiting. Another breeze rattled through the mansion and Fel heard the roof creak and moan in the wind. Then a sound. A note.

Soft and stealthy, the music came to her ear, a single string shivering its eerie tune.

ATTICUS

"Ceasefire! Ceasefire!"

Atticus waved his hand as he shouted the order. They had been shooting holes in the brick walls of the veranda for over a minute, and if Lieutenant Atticus Marius knew anything about free-for-alls, it was that they were likely shooting a lot and hitting little. *Besides,* he thought as he looked across the yard, *it's not like we can really see the bastards, can we?*

As the gunfire died down, he thought he could hear voices arguing from the other side of the brick wall that wrapped around the veranda. Then, just as the last of his soldiers stopped firing, he heard a door open and close.

"They've gone back inside!" he shouted as he stepped out from behind his tree. "On me! Now move!"

Waving his men forward, Atticus rushed across the yard. Grabbing his radio mic, he called his soldiers on the other side of the mansion to tell him he was moving in. Then he called Jonas and told him to keep the building surrounded. With any luck, their enemies would have no route to escape. Atticus had half his platoon surrounding the building, snipers and machine guns on every side, while two squads swept through the building. If their enemies tried to flee out the windows, they'd be shot. If they tried to hide inside, they'd be found and cornered and shot. If they tried to fight, they'd be shot. Someone in that mansion had killed Salentine, and whoever it was was going to pay.

Mako's squad was right behind him as he crossed the mansion's back yard. Rounding the corner of the wall, he swept the area with his rifle before making for the back door. Whoever they had seen on the veranda had turned around and gone back inside. Atticus' hand grasped the door handle when Mako's voice called out behind him.

"Sir, over here!"

Turning around, he saw Mako standing over a grated storm drain. The lanky squad leader pointed his rifle down and turned on his tac-light as he peered down into the grate. Then he let out a snort of a laugh and reached down and pulled up the grate.

"Come on out," Mako said. "Game's up, man."

Atticus stepped over and looked down inside. Sitting in about a foot of black water was a Duathic soldier dressed in a gray and brown uniform that Atticus did not recognize. The Duathe raised his right hand in the air in a sign of surrender before setting his rifle down on the ground with his free hand. With the barrel of Mako's rifle aimed squarely at his head, the Duathe climbed out of the storm drain.

The rest of Mako's squad had encircled the veranda, and two of them came forward to take the prisoner. They tied him up in flex cuffs and sat him down on the ground, facing the wall with a pair of riflemen standing guard.

"Anyone else down there?" Mako called out as he shined his tac-light in a sweeping circle around the drain. Atticus leaned over the hole again. Following Mako's light, he could see holes in the muck where the Duathic man had been walking around. Mako's light caught a drain-pipe along the wall, and the sergeant tried to angle his flashlight to look inside. Then gunshots rang out from inside the mansion, and Sergeant Jonas' voice came to Atticus over the radio. "Assassin Six, this is Seven. We have two more hostiles up on the second floor. Over."

Grabbing his hand-mic and turning toward the door, Atticus called back and told Jonas that they were entering from the mansion's west side. Behind him, he heard Mako order Corrin and Graide to stay with the prisoner. Then Atticus held open the door as the remainder of Mako's squad filed through. Stealing a final glance back at the prisoner's back, Atticus followed his men inside.

Moving in single file, they swept through the kitchen and then down a hallway. Following the gunshots, Mako led them through a double doorway and into a grand ballroom with a towering ceiling and a railed catwalk along the second floor. Tables and chairs were strewn about, and on the far end of the room was Jonas's squad, their weapons pointed up toward a catwalk and the second floor.

"They went up that way, sir," Jonas said, pointing up.

"How many?" Atticus asked.

"Two of them, we think," Jonas answered, his eyes and rifle still pointed at the catwalk. "Two big guys, from what we saw. Heavily armed, too."

"Well they're cornered now. We've got the place surrounded," Atticus said as he studied the catwalk. "Alright, here's the plan…"

Then Atticus' earpiece buzzed to life and the stern voice of Major Gaius Ioma came into his ear. "Assassin Six, this is Reaper One. Where are you right now?"

Atticus felt his heart sink into his stomach as he rubbed his eyes with his fingers and let out a deep sigh. He could hear the ominous tone in the major's voice. He pulled his radio mic from the hook on his shoulder, but as he brought the mic to his mouth, his voice died in his throat. Seconds passed in tense silence until the major's voice came back a second time, this time with more than a hint of anger and contempt.

"Assassin Six, this is Reaper One. What is your position? Do you copy?"

Across the room, Jonas scratched the stubble on his chin and made a face. "Sounds like the game might be up, sir."

Atticus nodded reluctantly and slowly brought the mic to his mouth and pressed the button, "Reaper One, this is Assassin Six, I read you. We're still in pursuit of your triggermen. We've lost one of ours, but we've captured one hostile and I think we're closing in on the rest of them now. Over"

There was a short pause and Atticus could practically hear the major's snort of contempt before he answered. "How did you lose your man?"

"He was stabbed," Atticus answered. "Over."

The answer came back the second Atticus released his mic. "What's done is done, Assassin Six. Change of plan. I need you and your men back with me with all available haste. Reaper One out."

FEL

The music was calling to her, just as the Onier said it would. The string and its song had snuck into the dusty room and slithered into her ear. But still Fel hid behind the boxes. She had not moved, not yet, for the sake of fear. She was afraid for her sister. She was afraid for their bodyguards. She was afraid for herself, that she would leave and be lost to her sister and everyone else. But then she thought of her father and how the Onier said she could help him, and so she crept away. Slipping past the dust-covered boxes and crumpled bags, she crawled over to the hole in the wall. With the pack on her back, she had to lower herself down onto her belly, but once she was through she found herself in the mansion's back yard surrounded by the tall, leafy weeds that seemed to be everywhere. She leaned down to listen through the hole, and she could hear Thayne desperately whispering her name. It was okay, she told herself, she would be back before they left. She had no intention of parting company—this was just an errand she had to run.

She ducked into the weeds.

The sound of the shivering string reverberated in her ear as she walked, buzzing through her skull like a hornet until it faded and slipped away, beckoning for her to follow—and so she did, sneaking cautiously in a crouch through the weeds until she came to a cobblestone path, which she followed as it wound and curved its way through the yard of overgrown weeds. The path crossed beneath an archway and then opened up into a stone pavilion with a fountain.

"Mark the sign of the Weaver beneath the shadow of the Thief." The Onier's words echoed in her head as she looked around. The pavilion was

encircled by a hedge that had long grown unruly, branches and overlong leaves jutting out from its sides. The stone tiles of the pavilion had a simple circular pattern carved into each one, but no imagery that she could see. Certainly nothing that looked like a Thief.

That left the fountain. From looking at it, the pavilion's centerpiece had long gone dry as streaks of dirt and dried mud decorated its basin. Its center was shaped like a tower with a miniature statue of the Silver Lady at its peak, her staff in her hands and her eyes toward the horizon. Twice she circled the fountain, but Fel could see nothing that resembled a Thief there either. Leg over leg, she climbed inside the thing. There it was. On the upper lip of the basin where someone had carved a figure wearing a hooded cloak.

Footsteps coming down the path. The others were looking for her. Whatever she needed to do here, she needed to do it soon. Sitting down against the fountain's tower, she pulled out the piece of red chalk. Quickly, she drew a circle and then five curved lines that arced outward around it. The sign of the origin. The sign of the Weaver.

The fountain cracked, opening up below her like a mouth, and before she could jump out of the way, she tumbled and fell as the earth swallowed her whole.

At first, it felt like she was falling, but darkness had swallowed everything and soon she wasn't sure. After a minute or so, she was almost certain she was flying upward, not down.

She landed on a mattress, a soft and pillowy thing that hit her in the face, and then she bounced, flailing through the air before she landed again, this time with a thud. Rubbing her face with one hand, she found the floor with the other, running her fingers through a thickly woven carpet. Fel picked herself up and sat on her knees. She could see nothing, only the blackness that came from complete absence of light. The darkness around her was so total that she couldn't see the color of the floor or the walls or even the hand she held before her face.

Then a gentle wind found her as a pair of giant, feathered wings wrapped themselves around her shoulders and she heard the Onier whisper in her ear. "Welcome back, Little Sister."

Fel stared blankly at the darkness. "Where are we?"

"Where?" The Onier sighed as its smoke-filled eyes blinked at her through the darkness. "A place that is between spaces, between the Here and the Other."

"Between?" Fel asked. "How can it be between?"

"We travelers call this place the Staircase. It is ... a pathway with many doors. Some that lead back to the Here, many others that lead down into the Other."

"Is my father here?"

"No," the Onier sighed like a gust of wind. "But if we find the right door, we may find him yet on the other side."

"So, my father is somewhere in the Other? How did he get there?"

"He found a doorway, though he did not know to where he was going ... and that is why he is now ... lost."

"He's lost?" she asked the pair of eyes in the dark. "Where is he trying to go? What was he trying to do? How do we find him?"

The Onier blinked. "To your father's ... intentions, you will have to ask him yourself. As to finding him ... well ... I have brought you as close as I can. Though I know not, cannot know, exactly where he is."

"I don't understand," Fel pleaded, "how can you bring me close, but not exactly close?"

"Because there is no *exactly,* I'm afraid. The Downside of the Here is a moving, changing thing that shifts against time and space, like a puzzle box trying to solve itself, though it never really can."

The concept sounded strange and exciting and terrifying, all at the same time. Fel tried to imagine such a place, found she couldn't, and finally decided she didn't care. Looking the Onier in the eyes, she stated she was ready.

"Ah, but of course you are, Little Sister." The Onier blinked again. "You'll find your surroundings familiar, as the Other is largely composed of reflections of the Here, from where you just arrived, from where you've lived your whole life. So, whatever you see, your father likely sees as well, though not always. And that, Little Sister, is all I'm allowed to tell you."

Then the two golden eyes of the Onier opened before her and Fel tried to stammer out a question. "But why..."

To which the Onier only said, "Good luck, Little Sister. And let there be light."

And light there was. A blinding glow so bright that Fel had to shield her eyes from it until they adjusted, and then, finally, she could see. She was sitting in a living room with white walls and beige-colored carpet. A bay window looked out at a freshly cut lawn covered in sunlight. Beyond that, a wide, two-lane road stood before a row of near identical houses. She adjusted the straps of her backpack as she stood. Then, from somewhere above her, she heard a doorlatch open. She walked up a set of carpeted stairs, running her hand along the white railing as she did. Six white doors met her at the top, but only one of them stood open. Carefully, she pushed the door open and walked through.

She stepped out into a hallway—a corridor, really—with white walls and doors, many doors, and a dark red carpet flecked with gold. It all looked very familiar. The words of the Onier came back to her. *...the Other is largely composed of reflections of the Here...* It was the Palace. She was standing in one of the main corridors, though she couldn't remember which floor. *Where am I? And more importantly, where is my father?* Walking stealthily down the hall, she kept her ears peeled. Every door looked the same, cream white with a brass knob. She stopped to press her ear to a door that she remembered as leading down to a cellar, but the only sound she heard was emptiness. She stopped again at the door of a guest room but heard only emptiness again. Stopping at the next door, she looked in to see a study, but the only things there were books and shadows. Then a door opened at the other end of the corridor and her father walked out.

Dressed in robes of gray and brown, he looked part-man and part-ghost in the dim light of the hallway. The father she remembered had always been clean-shaven, but the man before her now had a thick and tangled beard of white. For a moment, their eyes locked, and Fel could see anger, fury, and fear twist across her father's face. Then he turned around and ran back the way he came.

The door thundered shut behind him.

"Papa!" she yelled before she sprinted down the corridor. Reaching the door, she found it was a thick wooden thing with iron bandings, and Fel had to press her foot against the wall and lean back with all her might to pull it open. She finally slipped her way through and it slammed shut behind her. Far ahead, she could hear her father's footsteps echoing across a hardwood floor.

She was standing in a ballroom filled with empty tables and chairs and six pillars that ran from floor to ceiling, nearly three stories high. She found him, a shadow weaving and zigzagging through the tables and chairs, making for another doorway at the room's far corner.

"Papa!" Her shout echoed through the great room. "Wait!"

He looked back once but never slowed. So Fel launched herself after him, weaving through the tables and chairs so quickly that she had nearly halved the distance between them when her father slammed the door shut behind him again.

Fel pushed through the doorway and found herself standing on a gallery overlooking a great hall. When a flicker of movement caught her eye, she spun to see her father's shadow running past the railing and around a corner. She raced after him. Rounding the corner and through a door, she chased his footsteps down a spiraling stairwell made of stone. Dimly, in the back of her mind, she knew that this was not how the palace was laid out at all, not as she had known it, but all of the places looked familiar, even though they were all out of order somehow.

The thundering echo of another door rolled up the stairs. Reaching the bottom, Fel again found a heavy wooden door. She had to lean against the door to pull it open and then squeeze herself through the opening. The next room was a bathhouse filled with steam. She could hear mumbling voices as she ran through the mist, but she paid them no mind as she could still hear her father's footsteps racing ahead. The bathhouse opened into a stable where Fel could smell the hay and the musky, sweaty smell of the animals. Running across the hay covered concrete, she reached yet another doorway. This time, when the door swung shut behind her, she found herself standing on a rooftop, flat and wide and made of stone. Up above her was a canopy made of night and stars.

Her father was nowhere to be seen.

Cautiously, she took a step forward on the shingled roof. Then a second step. Then a third. Something felt off balance to her, but she couldn't say what. Then a gust of wind struck her and everything seemed to teeter, as even the sky above her seemed to shake and ripple like a piece of paper. Dropping down onto her belly, she grasped the shingles with her fingers, trying to hold on. When the shaking stopped, she looked up. Shadows were creeping across the roof. Creeping toward her.

Her first instinct was to leap up and run, but when she glanced behind her, she found the door she had entered had disappeared. So she froze. Clinging to the shingles with her fingertips, she watched the shadows creeping across the roof. There were seven that she could see. Five on her left, and two on her right. They were walking slowly, each in a crouch with their hands held out beside them as though for balance. As they got closer, Fel could see their heads turning side to side. They were searching. Perhaps they did not yet see her.

The roof itself was not flat and even; rather it rose and fell in gradual peaks and valleys. Fel was lying next to a peak. She watched the five shadows on her left descend into a valley as the two on her right weaved around a smoking chimney.

Are they searching for me, or for my father? Either way, she would have to run soon. The two on her right were headed straight for her, and she had less than a minute to make up her mind. Where had her father gone? Was this what he was running from?

It was now or never. Jumping up from the roof, she spun around to duck back through the door she had entered, but there was nothing there. Footsteps running after her, pitter-patter across the roof. Spinning around again, she ran.

She took off at an angle, putting the pair directly behind her while cutting across the five to her right. Leaping over the peak where she had hidden, she ran down into a valley and then up again. She could hear the pair racing behind her, and with a glance to her right, she saw the five running in a crowd. Shadowy girls, each one of them, with long, stringy hair blowing in the wind as they ran.

She ran around a pair of dormered windows and leapt over the next peak. Here the roof dropped again before leveling off. Glancing back, she saw the shadows close behind her, two and then five as they jumped over the peak.

Racing through a cloud of chimney smoke, an open field of shingled rooftop opened up before her. *How big is this thing?* Then, as if in response, the roof began to narrow and tilt. She leapt over a valley gutter as the flat roof tilted on itself, and an abyss opened up to her right. A few steps later, it had become so steep that she had to get down on all fours. Her hands clawing against the sand covered shingles, she scrambled up to the nearest peak.

Hanging one leg to either side, she could feel her heart thundering and her lungs burning in her chest. Below her, she could see seven gray-skinned girls, all with black, dead eyes, clawing their way up the roof with dirty, blood-cracked fingers.

Throwing her leg over, she slid down the other side. Her backpack skid against the sandy shingles as she slid down the roof. She felt her pant leg rip as she hit the valley gutter. This valley was flanked by window dormers, eight in all. This was her chance. Quickly, she scurried over to the nearest window, pulled it open, and climbed inside. Pulling the window shut, she flipped the locks and closed the blinds.

Darkness.

Slowly, she backed away from the window. Feeling with her hands, she found a door and let herself through. Still dark. The smell of dust and age met her on the other side. Feeling with her hands, she bumped something with her shoulder and then heard it crash. Dust flew up around her and she coughed, waiving her hands as she stepped through the cloud.

The dim light of a candle came to her, rising like an orange beacon in the dark. She crept her way toward it. As the light grew around her, she found herself standing between bookshelves filled with books and covered with cobwebs.

I'm in a library, she realized, *but which one?*

There were a number of libraries in the Sindorum Palace, but none that looked like this. Columns of bookshelves spread out before her, all of them ancient and filled with dust-covered tomes. Stopping at a shelf, she looked at the titles, but the words were written in a language she didn't recognize.

Then someone grabbed her, one hand on her backpack and the other by her shoulder, yanking her between a pair of shelves. Before she could scream, a hand covered her mouth while another pulled back a hood—and there, in the shadows, was the face of her father leaning down with a finger over his lips.

"Shhhh, child. Shhhh, my little Fel. Do not worry, your father knew it was you. He only wanted to make certain you were alone."

His breath hit her nose, smells of sweat and sour breath flooded her nostrils all at once, and she winced. The worn and dirty cloak he had covered himself with made him look foppish and small. There were bags beneath his eyes, and his face seemed worn, as if he'd aged ten years. His hair, once glimmering blue, was now a shock of white, wild and un-kempt, that stuck out atop his head and wrapped around into a tangled, white beard that Fel could see was filled with dust and debris. When his eyes—wild and desperate—met hers, she could not help but wonder what had become of him in the months since she had seen him last.

"Where have you been, Papa?" she whispered.

"Where? Heh." He chuckled giddily as if she'd told a clever joke. "Down here, of course. And before that, I was looking for down here and how to get here and once I got here, I started looking, looking and looking and I've been looking ever since, really."

"What are you looking for?" she asked.

Her father blinked as he looked at her, as if he were not expecting the question. "Why ... the keys!"

"What keys?"

"The keys to the throne room!" the King hissed. "That's where the doorway is, but they've locked me out, the little devils."

"What doorway...?"

She started but then he held a finger over her mouth and they looked up toward the ceiling. All she could see were bookshelves and the wood paneled ceiling of the library. Seconds of silence passed, and then a tremor shook the room, rattling the books against their shelves and knocking a few to the floor.

"What was that?" Fel whispered.

"Nothing, heh. Just an old memory come to visit, but they're too late." Her father let go of her and stepped out from behind the wall of books. "Come now, little Fel, we must go."

She followed her father through the aisles of books and then out a side door that led onto a wide-open lawn covered in night. Walking across a carpet of blue grass, Fel turned to look at the building they had just come from. If it was the palace or not, she could hardly tell. A blurred mass of towers, walls, and windows rose to her left, formless and hazy to her eyes, like a half-remembered dream. Like the city she had seen in the mirror, towers seemed to rise and fall, walls appeared and then collapsed, swallowing doors and windows with them. When they had finally crossed the lawn, her father led her to a doorway where he stopped and put his hand on her shoulder.

"Shhh…" he said as he furtively searched their surroundings, "… listen."

Fel drew a breath and held it, closing her eyes and straining her ears against the dark. A gust of wind blew past, billowing her hair and rushing through the leaves. Then she closed her eyes and peeled away the sounds, one by one. She heard the wind whistling through the windows and the doorways behind them, and she peeled that away. She could hear rain sprinkling, pitter-pattering against the plants and the windows, and she peeled that away too. And then, finally, she could hear them. Footsteps walking softly on the wet stones of the roof. When she opened her eyes again, she saw her father staring at her, his eyes white with fear.

"They're coming!" the King hissed as he pulled the door open.

Quiet and careful, they slipped inside. It was a waiting room, complete with coat racks and sofas. Drawing the blinds shut, they hid behind the furniture.

Claws scraping on the roof. She heard one of them shimmy down a gutter. Another slid down the wall. Several more simply jumped off and landed with a thud in the yard. Fel tried to count, but soon lost track. There were far more than seven, dozens perhaps.

Long moments passed in silence as they waited.

Her father's voice squeaked with fear. "Have you seen them?"

She nodded.

"They all look like you!"

"Where are the keys you're looking for Papa?"

He let out a sigh. "The gatehouse. In the concierge. The guardsmen kept a set of master keys there. If we can find that, if it's still here, we can make our way to the throne room and open the door."

"What door is that Papa?"

"The wide and the narrow, my little Fel, the narrow and the wide."

The white-haired man that was her father then peeled back the corner of a curtain to look outside.

"The yard is empty," he said. "Now's our chance."

They first made for the outer wall. There were no trees or shrubbery here, only bare grass and open lawn, nothing that anyone could hide in—or so her sister had once said, so long ago. Thankfully, nothing met them as they dashed across the yard, and nothing met them again as they reached the wall. This version of the wall looked much the same as the original. Made of stone and mortar, it encircled the entire palace, and guard towers marked it every hundred yards. They followed it until they saw the twin peaks of the gatehouse roof rising above them.

"Wait," her father said as he held out his hand. "Watch. Listen."

They waited in the shadow of the wall, listening and watching. For long moments, they did not move, and nothing else moved either. Finally, her father drew back his hand.

"Okay."

The grass was wet here, though Fel had not seen it rain. By the time they reached the gatehouse, she could feel the wetness on her socks, which made her remember how it had been raining back in the real world. However, she had been completely dry until now. Had she really been here that long? Or had something else happened?

Two peaks, one for the gate and one for the house, rose up from the wall. The door was unlocked and her father swung it open wide. However, he did not enter right away, but peered first through the window.

"It's empty," he whispered. "Come, let us fetch us the keys."

Inside, it smelled of smoke and wood. When they were both inside, the hearth lit up with a crackling flame, throwing firelight all over the room.

"Do you see that?" her father breathed.

She nodded.

"Pay it no mind, as it is only a projection of our collected memories," he said this to reassure her, but his voice shook with fear.

Fel looked to the walls. "Where are the keys?"

The gatehouse was only one room, a hearth with a table and chairs for the guards standing duty. Hooks and shelves lined one of the walls where the guards could keep their equipment. Windows and bare walls marked two others, while the fourth wall held the hearth and ... a lockbox.

It was a thin, metal thing with a key in its latch, and the door gave a little whine when her father pulled it open. He reached in and pulled out a ring full of keys, large and small.

"Look at that," he said, flipping through the keys, "we found them. Just like that, heh. I wonder which one..."

Claws on the roof. No, it was footsteps. Fel ran for the door as her father let out a cry and followed right on her heels. Grabbing the handle, she flung the door open and leapt through just as something fell down from above. She landed on the grass in a tumble, springing to her feet as she heard metal strike stone behind her. Looking back, she saw the gatehouse was covered in a cage, as if someone had dropped it from the sky. Her father was standing in the doorway, shaking the bars with one hand and holding out the keyring with the other.

"Quickly, my daughter! Quickly, you must take them and go!"

Grabbing the keyring from his hand, she saw fear wash over his face as he looked behind her. Spinning around, she saw shadows racing across the yard. Shadows shaped like her.

"Quickly now! Run!"

Her father shoved her away from the doorway and she ran. Sprinting around the gatehouse, she found the gate, but it was closed. Not breaking stride, she took off along the wall. Perhaps there would be a tree or something that could help her get over the wall. Looking over her shoulder, she saw her doppelgangers racing toward her. Some were behind her; others were cutting across the yard.

A blur of black and gray leapt out of a flowerbed with a hungry hiss. Black marble eyes and cracked fingernails leapt out at her, grasping. Fel ducked her head and dove. The ghoulish girl's legs struck her in the back as her doppelganger tumbled over top of her and collided with the wall. Rolling back to her feet, Fel took off again. She didn't dare look back; she could hear the footsteps close on her heels.

The outer wall was a wide half circle, arcing away from the cliff and the river. Fel cut straight across, from the northern gatehouse to the garden along the southeast.

Running through a flowerbed and leaping over a shrub, her feet met a paved path that led straight for the Palace Temple. Or, at least what Fel hoped was the Palace Temple. The fuzzy, shifting walls of this version of the palace rose up before her, and she spotted a doorway along the nearest wall.

Reaching the wall, she ripped the door open and slammed it shut, right in the faces of two of her doppelgangers. She could hear them clawing at the door and she threw the latch shut. Before they could react, she ran over to both of the windows and forced the locks shut on them as well. Her own angry face met her at the second window. Furious, black-marble eyes looked back at her as her other-self let out a rage-filled, blood curdling scream.

"WAAAAAGGGGGHHHHH!"

Several of them were still clawing at the door, shaking the doorknob and kicking at the locks. Looking out the window, she saw a crowd of her doppelgangers throw open another door and file inside. They would be to her soon. Looking around, there were two other doors in the room, but she saw no way to lock them.

What do I do? For a moment, she panicked. Then her hand found her pocket, and she remembered. *The chalk!*

She still had it, though it had broken into several pieces and her pocket was full of dust. She pulled out the biggest piece. The chalk had gotten her back here. Could it get her out?

Footsteps running down the hallway. They were almost here.

She sat down on the floor below the window. Cracked fingernails were scraping along the glass. She heard a door open behind her. Quickly, she put the chalk to the wooden floor and drew a circle around herself.

The lacquered wooden boards opened up like a mouth and she fell into its gullet.

All of the light vanished. Again, she flew upward into the darkness. Tumbling up through the black until she landed, again, on a mattress. She bounced, landing in the dirt. This time the light was immediate.

The faint, red glow of evening was shining down on her through the tall, leafy stalks of the weeds. She was back in the garden, just outside the mansion. Picking herself up from the ground, she pushed her way through the heavy stalks until they parted, revealing the dry, empty fountain.

She stared at everything in amazement.

"What the hell, girl!"

Thayne grasped her by the shoulders as he kneeled down and looked her in the eyes. "By the Fates! What has gotten into you? You're shaking! You look like you've seen a ghost!"

I have, she thought, *and the ghosts were all me.*

"I'm … I'm fine," she said. "I was … I was just looking for something. I'm sorry I ran off."

"Hell!" Thayne cursed and spat. "Well come on, then. The soldiers are gone now and we need to find the others if any of them are left." Her bodyguard took a deep breath and let it out as he released her.

She nodded and waited for him to give her a final, frustrated glance before he walked away down the path.

"Come on. We have to go."

"Okay. I'll follow you," she said.

She waited until his back was turned before she finally checked her coat pockets. She had dropped the last piece of chalk she'd used, but she could feel the other remnants sitting in her inside pocket. With her left hand, she found the keyring. Briefly, she pulled it out. It was a wide, metal ring nearly as thick as her fingers that held over a dozen keys of all shapes and sizes.

I'm coming back, Father, she thought to herself as she flipped through the keys. *I won't leave you there. I promise.*

Thayne stopped and turned around, his eyes cross with annoyance. "Hey! You coming?"

"Aye," she nodded, shoving the keys back into her pocket. "I'm right behind you, mate."

PAR

"We're almost on top of it now," Saithe said as she tapped the brakes on her airbike. "It will be easier if we walk from here."

Saithe shifted her airbike into park and the machine lowered itself to the ground. Dismounting the bike, Par studied the rooftops and windows for signs of life or danger, but the only living things he spotted were a murder of crows perched atop a crumbling bell tower. Rubble and craters decorated the street while shattered apartments and crumbling condominiums loomed over them as Saithe followed her navigator and Par followed her.

Back at the camp, his companion had donned an overlarge brown coat that seemed to accentuate her lithe and athletic frame. But more than her clothing, the tattooed woman's demeanor had changed as well. No longer around her fellow replicants or their pale masters, the Ieses, the docile and submissive nurse had been replaced by a woman who walked and spoke with the air of a ship captain, all of which made Par wonder who the replicant woman was back on her own homeworld, wherever that was.

Saithe studied the screen of her navigator. "The coordinates place the crash on the other side of this block."

The late afternoon sun was bright overhead as they entered an alleyway littered with garbage and debris. Shell casings and bits of shrapnel were mixed with the trash and Par spotted a dead body lying in a doorway. The soldier wore a Republican uniform with a Coalition patch on his arm, and the blood that covered his nose was dried and crusted.

They had been tracking the Queen all day.

Par had found the Queen's trail just outside the refugee camp on the backside of a hill. Next, his Shade had found the latch for the hidden doorway, an electronic latch disguised as a rock. That had led them into the tunnels beneath the hills where the earth was soft enough for footprints. There, Par had counted the footsteps. A dozen people accompanied the Queen, which meant at least ten guards plus the two princesses. Par had faced longer odds, but not by much. Tracking them through the tunnels had led them to another doorway hidden on the open plain, and a few miles from there, he and Saithe found the burn marks in the grass where the shuttles had landed. Two shuttles. Five minutes apart. What that meant, Par could only guess.

It was there that Saithe had revealed her worth again. Through her affair with the Imperium intelligence officer, she had acquired access to the Coalition's intelligence mainframe aboard their mothership, the *Unifier*. A few keyword searches on her data pad told them that only one Duathic aircraft had been spotted all day. Spotted and shot down. She had even found the coordinates.

"There." Saithe pointed to the end of the alleyway where a wall had collapsed and they could see a wingtip resting atop the pile of rubble. Walking around the pile, they found the downed aircraft half buried in the base of the building. It looked like a squared-off hornet with flat, angular wings, and Par could see the furrow where the vessel had crashed into the ground, slid, and collided into the building. The back ramp was lying open, so they walked inside. The vessel was tilted against the side of the building and the stale stench of death hit Par in the nose as he spotted another dead man hanging from a safety harness at the front of the passenger bay. Par climbed up the bay's walkway to study the corpse. The dead Duathic man wore a non-descript uniform and had a rifle slung around his shoulders, but more importantly, his body appeared whole. Par released his Shade and the AI flew out of him in a black and gray swarm.

Behind him, he heard Saithe let out a nervous laugh. "Just so you know, Mr. Riordan, that was just as unsettling as the last time."

Par grabbed the dead man by the jaw and pulled his mouth open. His Shade circled once and then swarmed into the man's mouth and ears. Par closed his eyes as the nano-bots crawled through the dead man's head and into his skull. There, the AI settled into the brain's sulci and began to stimulate its electric synapsis.

"Never mind, that was even worse," Saithe whispered.

What is she going on about?

Par told his companion not to worry about it, or her.

What do you mean, 'Don't worry about it?' We haven't spoken to a woman that attractive in years. Are you kidding me? Look at her! How am I supposed to not worry about her?

Par closed his eyes so that Saithe would not see him rolling them. There were times he regretted programming his companion with the mind of pre-teen boy. Par could not blame his companion for being distracted by Saithe. His replicant partner was a striking woman, mahogany skinned with brown-black eyes, and while her head was shaved bald, this served only to give her an even more exotic look. When she moved, it was with a dancer's grace and all the seductive charm that came with it. She looked every bit the "pleasure model" she had described herself to be when they had first met.

Anyway, you'll be happy to know that we've stumbled onto a royal bodyguard. He was with the two girls, but not the Queen who apparently went another route by herself. Par's mind received images of a moonlit march out of the camp and the open field where he saw the Queen hugging her daughters before they climbed aboard the aircraft. Then they were flying and then he saw a bright flash and everything shook. Suddenly, they were falling from the sky and then nothing. *Apparently, this guy's neck snapped on impact, and so he has no idea where anyone went from here. Sorry.*

His Shade left the corpse, the nano-bots crawling out the dead man's mouth and nose and ears like ants leaving an ant hill. Behind him, he heard Saithe take in another sharp breath.

"What did you do to him?" she asked, drawing back.

Par gave her an inquisitive look as the black cloud of nano-bots circled around him once and then melded back inside of him.

"I mean..." Saithe stuttered. "How does it all work?"

Par shrugged and rolled his shoulders as the last of the nano-bots sank beneath his skin. "Our brains store memories by grouping neurons together." He pointed at the dead man's forehead. "Short term memories are stored in the frontal lobe, while the memories we store for the long term are converted further in the back. I usually don't have to reach that far. This one had everything we needed up front." Par gently reached up and shut the dead man's mouth. "Let's check out the cockpit and see if we can figure out where they were going."

He did not bother to interview the two dead pilots they found seated in the cockpit. He just let his Shade sneak into one of the terminal ports of the main control panel where it came back with a pair of coordinates aimed directly at the backside of the mountain. Not knowing what that could mean, he recited the eight-digit number to Saithe.

She bit her lower lip as she punched the coordinates into her navigator. "Well, according to the Coalition's database there is nothing back there, but all that means is that they know as much as we do."

"But no other Duathic aircraft have been spotted?" he asked.

Saithe shook her head emphatically. "No. None."

He climbed out of the cockpit. "Which means they left here on foot."

Par returned to the bottom of the ramp. Boot prints in the dirt. Shell casings lying in the rubble along the wall. A ricochet mark on an alleyway door. Bullet holes in the concrete. Whoever had survived the crash had met a fight. The trail would be easy to follow. They went back for the airbike and Saithe set it to follow them as they walked.

The bike was trailing behind them, and Saithe fixed him with a curious look. "So how does someone become a 'Taker'?" Her voice had hummed when she asked this, and Par wondered to himself if it was something she did intentionally or if it was just part of her biological programming. He thought a long moment before answering.

"You have to have the gift first," he said. "Not everyone can bond with an AI. They're not sure why, but it has something to do with your subconscious and whether or not it's willing to accept a symbiotic relationship with an artificial intelligence."

She sped up to walk next to him and looked up at him with her eyes large and dark. "And then what?"

"And then?" He shrugged. Did her faction back in the Imperium ask her to find out as much about him as she could? Or was she just genuinely curious? He decided to play it straight. There was little to be lost on something that was common knowledge in the Republic. "If you're lucky you might get some training."

"Were you trained?" she asked.

He shook his head. "No."

"Then how did you learn?"

He shrugged again. "I asked it what it could do and it told me. We work together and we learn together."

"You can talk to it?"

He nodded. "Unfortunately."

"Are you talking to it now?" she asked.

"No. He's keeping an eye out, and I need to concentrate." He stopped at an intersection and studied a set of footprints in the dirt. "I'm still trying to figure out how many we're dealing with."

"There are seven of them," Saithe said confidently. "The two girls and five of their guard." When he looked at her sideways, she sighed and rolled her eyes. "One of them is carrying a Tech-8A heavy long rifle. It's an oddly … specific weapon for anyone other than a specialist to carry, but I've seen the shell casings here." She picked a brass casing off the ground. "And back at the crash site. One of the other three has a T131 machine gun, while the others have standard Duathic army carbines. One of the girls may have picked up a pistol, but I'm not completely sure." She flicked the shell casing over her shoulder. "I know all that, but where they're headed is anyone's guess."

Can we talk less about us and more about her? I want to know about her and why she's so damn attractive, don't you?

Par ignored his companion and looked ahead toward the mountaintop. "It would appear they're travelling in the same direction their ride was when they were shot down."

"Well, that should make it easy then." Saithe gestured to the airbike that was hovering motionless behind them. "We jump on that thing and race ahead to cut them off."

"I don't think it's going to be that easy. Look."

It was another body lying face down in the middle of a road. Par walked up to the body and turned it over. He was a Duathic man dressed in a simple black uniform with gray hair and dark blue skin and a bullet hole in his head.

"I don't think you're going to get much out of him," Saithe hummed. "I do not know what you need to read a dead man's mind, but I'm afraid there isn't much of a mind left on that one. But if you're willing, it would appear they supplied us with another candidate."

Par looked up to see Saithe pointing at another corpse in an alleyway ahead of them. They stepped over more shell casings at the mouth of the alleyway and they found the second dead man lying in a doorway with a wound in his chest. Another Duathe, this one in an army uniform. Dried blood had stained the concrete all around the man and his face was one of open shock.

Par pressed his hand against the man's chest and released his Shade again. The AI crept out of him, crawling out of his skin and down his arm to the dead man's chest where it swarmed up the corpse's neck and into his mouth. *More corpses. I'm beginning to fear for the safety of our quarry.*

Par did not disagree. They were less than a mile from the crash site and already two of the seven they had begun tracking were dead. Images of the party's flight came to Par's mind as his Shade rummaged through the dead man's memories. The two princesses and their guards had run into someone here. Whether it was the invading Coalition or a band of rebels that mistook them for the former, Par could not tell. What was obvious was that it had cost them two men, one of which had been the leader, the Duathic man with the tattoos. A sniper had killed him, and likely this man as well, killing both with a single shot each. However, the two girls were alive. Par could see that clearly from the dead man's memories. Par silently thanked the Fates that the sniper had claimed only this man's life and not his brain. When the AI had finished, the nano-bots crept back up his arm.

The question of course, is where our little mice are headed. They're scurrying for cover and it seems there's little planning beyond mere survival.

The party was headed in a very general easterly direction, but to what, he could only guess. He turned around to walk back toward the mouth of the alleyway.

He wondered how far behind they were. Hours at most. Though the battle had passed, the bodies were not long dead. Though he could hear the reports and echoes of gunshots not far away, he could still hear the loose gravel crunching beneath his feet. He could hear the crows cawing in the bell tower. The breeze whistling through the ruins. And that's when he heard someone singing. A young boy. The voice was instantly familiar, as what its tune.

Lost like souls, please sleep good fellow,
What devils may visit, what friends may follow;
There we were and there she wasn't,
There he was and wished he wasn't.

He stopped and turned, searching for the voice. Empty doorways and empty windows looked back at him until there, in the alleyway behind him, he saw the shadow of a boy pushing a toy across the ground.

There he was and wished he wasn't...

"Look out!"

Saithe hollered this as she lunged at him, tackling him by the stomach as something snapped against the wall behind him. Par hit the dirt head first and took a face full of gravel. Rolling onto his hands, Par leapt toward a burned-out car as another bullet clanged against its hood. Saithe appeared next to him, her back against the passenger door and a carbine in her hands.

"How did you know?" he started, breathlessly. "And where did you get that?"

"Off the dead man while you were crawling around in his brain." She flipped the carbine's safety off and nodded toward the car's hood. "I saw a shadow in a window. Had the clouds not parted just then, I would not have seen him and one of us would be dead."

Par looked up at the mark on the wall where the bullet had struck, and he knew that the "one of us" would have been him. He spat dust out of his mouth. "Well it would appear he has us pinned down until we can figure out how to get past him. Do you think you can hit him from here?"

She nodded. "It's about a two-hundred-yard shot, but he would have to be looking elsewhere. What are you thinking?"

"Hold tight, I have an idea." He sent his Shade crawling beneath the burned-out car, where it emerged on the other side and dispersed into the air like a cloud of black mites. Racing across the open block, the AI spotted the gunman on the second story of an abandoned shopping center. It entered through the window, sneaking in by twos and threes so the sniper would not see it. The AI then circled the room, studying their foe. It was a Duathic man sitting in a chair and his rifle resting atop a sandbag set on a wooden table, one eye closed with the other pressed against his scope. *I can smell the aggression oozing out of this guy. You're lucky this thing can't punch through that car or you'd be dead. Looks like he's been up here smoking people all day. His leg is hurt, but I can't tell how bad. Might have been left behind, might just have stayed to have fun.*

Par gave his Shade the plan and then looked to Saithe. "Get ready to shoot when I move."

She gave him a nod as she hefted her carbine. *All set,* his Shade reassured him. Par picked himself up and got set into a sprinter's stance. Then he launched himself out from behind the car and dashed across the street. One gunshot rang out across the open lot before he dove into a deep crater, rolling and landing in the dirt with a thud.

"Got him!" Saithe cried out from above.

That she did. He had no idea I had disarmed the primer on his loaded bullet, and she brained him right as he reached to reload. He's got an empty eye socket and his gray matter is all over the back wall.

Par climbed out of the crater as his AI flew back and crawled back inside of him. He found Saithe still behind the burned-out car with her binoculars pressed to her eyes.

The brown-skinned woman lowered her binoculars and pointed to the west. "Look."

An aircraft appeared on the horizon. Shaped like a box with wings, Par could see the Coalition markings on its hull. It landed right next to the crash site they had investigated earlier.

"Sader," Saithe whispered, her voice tinged with fear.

It's a race now. He's going to know we were there the moment he interviews that corpse. And that's if he didn't find the one we tapped back at the camp.

"We've got to move," Par said, "and quickly to keep him behind us."

"But to where?" Saithe replied. "We can only track them so fast."

I'm working on that. We know they're headed east across the city and up the mountain, but we don't know that they're going to make it directly to the launch site, so they're likely seeking some kind of shelter, a place to rest and gather themselves. I'm looking through our files now... I know the King had friends in the city, the trouble is guessing which one... THERE! It's just a guess, but if they're looking for a friend to hide them, I know where they might have gone. But it's only a guess ...

DELEA

The storm drain was damp and stale and stunk of mold, but Delea forced herself to stay still and silent long after she heard the soldiers leave. That the soldiers had failed to look down far enough into the storm drain to see her hiding in the drainage pipe was a stroke of pure luck, a boon she was not likely to waste. But leave they eventually did. At first, they had left two soldiers to guard Motya on the veranda while the rest went inside. A few gunshots had followed—Delea was not sure by whom, the soldiers or Kress or Marental—but soon after, the two guards had taken Motya inside. She had heard the footsteps walking over the stone and then the door closed behind them. She was alone then, she knew, and the only sounds were the birds and the bugs in the mansion's backyard.

And alone she sat, curled up in the stinking mire of the storm drain with nothing but her thoughts and a swarm of gnats to keep her company. Motya's capture was her chief concern. Would they interrogate him? Where would they take him? That he had been captured because he was defending her weighed heavily on her mind, and she found herself crying as she swatted at the tiny bugs that were swarming around her face.

When she finally climbed free of the hole, the sun was no more than a golden sliver against the horizon. Cautiously, she pulled herself up onto the ground and walked to the edge of the veranda wall where she peered around the corner at the mansion's back yard. Seeing no one else moving about, she wiped the tears from her eyes and walked back to the doorway and entered the mansion's kitchen. She was walking past a pair of stone and iron stoves when the door to the hallway opened and Kress and Marental walked in.

"By the Weaver, you are safe!" Marental exclaimed before rushing over and scooping up Delea in a bear hug.

Surprised at the sudden show of affection, Delea could hardly move while her bodyguard's massive arms wrapped around her and lifted her off the ground. When she felt her ribs begin to bend, she let out a grunt of discomfort and Marental set her back down on the floor like a toy.

"I am sorry your Highness," Marental blushed, "but when we saw them marching off with Motya, we feared the worst."

Kress let out a chuckle from the doorway. "Only the Lady herself could have closed their eyes if they saw Motya and not you, your Highness."

Delea let out a sigh. "I'm lucky to be sure, but has anyone seen my sister?"

They found Thayne and Fel in the weeds of the mansion's southern yard. How they had ended up back there, Delea could only guess, for when she questioned Thayne on the matter, he said only that the two of them had gotten split up and little more. Delea wondered, as they walked back inside, if he was trying to cover what he felt was his own mistake or if he was trying to prevent further quarrelling between the two sisters. *Or perhaps it's both?* she thought. *Regardless, I don't have time for Fel's antics now. We're down another man and stuck in the middle of a battle. If she takes to wandering off here, Kress or Marental will just have to tie her up and carry her.*

They returned then to the great dining hall where they had first entered the mansion. There, Delea found an old long table where she began brushing off the dust. "Marental, can you raise Victory again?"

"Of course, your Highness." Marental pulled the radio pack off her back and aimed the antenna toward the dining hall's giant windows. When her first call got no response, she called again and the response was almost immediate.

"Sentinel Four this is Victory One Romeo. Good to hear from you again. What is your status, over?"

Marental keyed the mic. "We are now only five, but I still have both VIPs and we're within only a few miles of your position, over."

"Do you ... wait one Sentinel Four..." Static returned to the line as the operator dropped the mic. Long seconds of silence passed before the response came. "Sentinel Four I have been advised that if your intention is to escape the city before morning, then we need you to come to us …"There was a pause as an explosion came through in the background. "… we can … we have a way out of the city, but it is not by aircraft. Be advised, you may be better off where you are as the enemy is coming to us and not to you. However, should you make it here, we have a …"The voice paused as something else rumbled again in the background. "… there is a possibility we can aid you in reaching the launch site. Over."

All eyes turned to Delea then and she nodded to Marental. "Tell them we'll talk it over and call them back shortly."

Marental did just that.

"Well shit," Thayne said as Marental hung up the mic.

Delea sighed as she pulled out the map she had found in the Duke's abandoned study and unfolded it onto the table. "There are tunnels beneath Sindorum that pre-date my father's rule by some seven hundred years. It was King Orpeum who built them, I think, back before we had ever launched a starship, back during industrial times. When I was little, my father always joked that if anyone led a successful coup against him, that the best way to escape the city would be by foot." She pointed to the mansion's location on the map. "So, we're here, and we need to get across the river to *here*, because if I'm reading this correctly, that is where the catacombs branch out and we can follow this tunnel into the palace."

Then Kress spoke up from behind them. "And what exactly will we be looking for once we arrive at the palace?"

Delea pointed on the map to a black X on the southern side of the palace. "There's an entrance into the catacombs here, which we can reach if we follow the inner wall, and the easiest way to get there is through the temple grounds to the north…"

Thayne leaned over the map and pointed. "But what are them green lines over there?"

"Let me look…" Delea bit her lip as she studied the map's legend. There had not been much time for her to inspect the map before as they were attacked. Now, looking at the lines, she realized how many tunnels were marked. It was a labyrinth. Tunnels marked in green and blue and red spread out in a chaotic spiderweb across the city. However, of all the lines, one stood out to her. Someone with a thick, green marker had started a line at the Royal Palace, the city's center, and drawn it north and east to the Temple of Dusk, where it turned sharply to the southeast and arced around the southern face of Mount Chernon until it came to an end right where the launch site was. Delea traced the line with her finger. "I don't know what they all are, but if this line means what I think it means, we may have found our escape route."

"An interesting development, your Highness, for that *is* the launch site. Though we are left in the same state as before, navigating a war zone to infiltrate the palace."

"Heya, are we even the first to use this thing?" Thayne asked.

"I would guess not," Delea replied. "I can see no other reason why the Duke would have a map marked with the very same route we're looking to use. It appears his party escaped the planet the same way we are hoping to."

Marental and Thayne exchanged knowing glances. Then Thayne pulled out a cigarette and hung it, unlit, in his mouth. "It would seem to me, your Highness, that if other people knew about this route back then, there might be other folk who know about it now."

Realizing he was likely right, Delea frowned at the map. "Do you think we should go another route?"

Marental cut in again. "I don't believe anyone is suggesting that, your Highness, only that we should be prepared, even as we arrive underground."

Thayne grunted his assent as he lit his cigarette. "At least we know where to go if them Victory folk come up short."

"Agreed," Marental hummed in a low voice. "It would appear to be a proper contingency plan, should we need it."

They talked and planned for another ten minutes, quickly going over every detail and every contingency they could think of. All of the bridges were likely guarded or blown up by now, so they would have to find a boat to cross the river and then navigate the water without getting spotted or blown out of the water. Delea studied the map all the while that they talked. They had no assurances that Victory One Romeo or anyone in the palace still had the ability to help them. They had not heard from her father or her mother since their crash, and Delea found herself wondering if either of her parents even knew what had befallen their daughters—or if either was even still alive.

In the past day, they had survived a crash, lived through several gunfights, and covered nearly two dozen miles on foot. To make matters worse, she expected tonight to be no less eventful. A headache was growing in her brain, and as she rubbed her temples, she found herself wondering what it would be like to live the life of a normal girl—at least as 'normal' as any ex-princess could be. She was sixteen. There was plenty of time. She could change her name. She could become someone else. No one had to know she was King Teum's daughter. Perhaps her aunt, this Duchess on Linneaum, already had this all figured out for her. Perhaps they could negotiate with the Republic to exile their mother on Linneaum. Perhaps. Perhaps. Perhaps. Then her thoughts were interrupted when Marental picked up the radio mic again and made her return call.

"Victory One Romeo, this is Sentinel Four. Over."

The response was immediate this time. "Sentinel Four, this is Victory One Romeo. Go ahead."

"Be advised, we are in route to your location now. After viewing our route, our ETA should be no more than ninety minutes. Over."

"Copy that Sentinel Four. Your ETA is noted. Be advised that you will be travelling through contested territory and that, at this time, we can give you no support. Over."

Marental's smile was grim but determined as she keyed her mic in response. "Read you loud and clear, Victory One Romeo. Sentinel Four, out."

TAYLOR

The question was how to get close to their targets. Given their quarry's position, Taylor knew they had no chance of sneaking up unseen—so she and Shale had devised another plan.

Leaving *Unifier*'s fighter bay, Taylor and Shale turned away from their objective and flew around the faces of both moons before swinging around toward asteroid belt in as wide an arc as Taylor dared. It was as subtle and deceptive as she could come up with given the situation. All indications told her that her quarry didn't know it had been detected, and she wanted to keep it that way until the last possible second.

She would have missed them had she not set the benchmark. Her quarry blended in so completely with the asteroid field that the *Wyvern*'s scanners could not differentiate between the floating rocks and her two unidentified objects. Taylor reversed her thrusters and pulled the *Wyvern* to a stop at the very edge of her weapons' range.

She radioed Shale. "Two, swing wide from me and bracket the target."

"Roger that, One," he called back as he swung his Raptor wide and came to a stop eight clicks away. Commander and wingman had conferred before getting in their cockpits. They were keeping their distance. Mission or no mission, if these things made a move, Taylor wanted a reasonable chance that at least she or Shale would get away.

She flipped her sensors to scan mode and carefully ran them over the entire swath of asteroids. No reaction. Taylor breathed a sigh of relief as she watched the readouts come in. Now that she was so much closer, the *Wyvern*'s sensors were able to bring back a much clearer picture of what was sitting in the middle of the asteroid belt. Each of her bogies still looked like three arrowheads welded together, but now she could see the sharpness of their angles, the deliberate lines cut along the edges. That ruled out the off chance of inanimate objects or some galactic anomaly. No, whatever their origin, these were starships.

Looking closer, she could see that what she had mistaken for camouflage before was actually burn markings. The outside of both ships was charred and smoky, as though it had been held inside of some great fire for a long while. Taylor flipped the images every way she could, looking for something that resembled a cockpit, but found nothing.

What in the name of Fate are these things? She switched from her sensors to her fire control system. Every Raptor had a micro-laser they called a stinger that could be used for precision strikes against a target's specific systems. The stinger came with an equally precise camera, but whoever was on the other end would know that she was pointing a gun at them and only them, and that was the challenge.

She warned Shale of her plan as she flipped on the stinger and took aim with its camera. When she zeroed in on the bogey, the arrowhead vessel still did not move, and Taylor breathed another sigh of relief. She zoomed in on the center of the vessel, where the three arrowheads seemed to be fused together around an oval-shaped cage made of rounded bars. However, she could see no paneling, no duraglass, no walls to the structure. She zoomed in once more, to maximum magnification. The cage appeared empty. There was nothing inside. She zoomed back out and ran the stinger's camera all along the vessel's hull, searching for a cockpit. Someone or something had to have brought this thing into the system, but as she searched up and down the sides of each of the arrowheads, she found they were as thin as the *Wyvern's* tail fins. Were they drones? Unless they were dealing with organisms the size of bugs, there was no crew sitting inside the wings. Then she thought she saw something move within the cage and she zoomed back in. The cage, so far as she could tell, contained nothing more than open space, and for a minute more nothing moved. Then, finally, something seemed to ripple like a tiny wave on the water.

Her radio buzzed in her ear. "Um ... One ... don't move."

Shale's voice was quiet like a person trapped in a room with an agitated predator. Taylor looked up. The second vessel was right on top of her, floating above her cockpit like an overcurious animal. For a moment, she froze as the size and the nearness of the thing overwhelmed her. It was three times the size of her *Wyvern*. Taylor found her eyes drawn again to the oval shaped cage at the thing's center. The space between the rounded bars rippled, just like its companion's had, but this time it was followed by a spark and then a flare and suddenly everything was flame.

Taylor would have been blinded if it weren't for the sensors embedded in her cockpit that shaded the duraglass from any light that became too bright. Alarms went off as flames licked the *Wyvern*'s hull. Taylor grabbed her stick and reversed her thrusters, pulling the ship out of the inferno and away from her assailant. The *Wyvern* was a ship's length away from the inferno when a volley of cannon fire from Shale's Raptor ripped through the arrowhead-shaped attacker. However, the damage did little to slow the strange vessel as it barrel-rolled and dove straight down all in one motion, breaking away from them and accelerating with impossible speed. Taylor flipped her sensors back to scan mode just in time to see the arrowhead ship looping behind a massive rock and falling off her sensors.

Shale called to her over the radio. "I've never seen anything move like that. Are you okay, One?"

Taylor flipped through her internal readouts to see how badly her ship was damaged. Other than some minor burn marks on her hull, everything looked normal. She keyed her mic to respond. "I'm fine, but I didn't get a good look. What did you see?"

"I don't … it's hard to explain. It went from reverse to moving forward in one motion without changing its direction of travel. It was more like a fish in water than a starship."

Taylor scanned the asteroid belt again for signs of the mystery ships, but her scanners came back empty. She refocused her sensors on the gigantic asteroid. "Did you see what happened with its partner?"

"No, did you?"

"Negative. But if we're going to keep looking, this is where we should start." She pinged Shale's computer and sent him an image of the asteroid.

There was a pause before Shale responded. "I'm game if you are."

Worries and strategies raced through her mind like panicked mice. *If they can outmaneuver us, can they out-gun us just the same? Was I attacked, or was that just a warning? Or was it something else?*

In the end, she decided there was only one way to find out. She aimed the *Wyvern* toward the asteroid and called Shale to do the same. Her wingman fell in behind her, high and to her left as she left her engines on minimal power and crept toward the massive rock. All the while, Taylor kept her scanner running on active, sweeping over the monstrous asteroid as well as the other rocks around it. Real asteroid fields were rarely like the holo-media, with crowded fields of debris and deadly rock—instead, most belts had asteroids that were spread out with miles of open vacuum between them, just like the span of rocks before her. The only danger would be if Taylor were trying to navigate the field at full speed, and even then, the rocks would be more like well-spaced road cones rather than deadly obstacles. Now, as she slowly made her way toward the massive rock, Taylor's focus was on her scanners and the fact that everything kept coming back empty. Her instruments told her the gargantuan asteroid was nearly as large as a small moon. Twice they circled the massive rock, and twice Taylor's scanners came back with nothing. No movement. No energy signatures. No signs of their foe. Finally, after they had completed the second pass, Shale called her again.

"Well, I hate to say it, One, but this is some spooky stuff…"

She had to agree. Bringing the *Wyvern* to a full stop, Taylor ran a full scan of everything in a thousand-klick radius. Nothing. She flipped her radio over to the command net and asked *Unifier* if they could see anything she couldn't.

The call came back immediately. "Rapier One, this is Unifier Main, we have kept close watch of your every move, and the last we saw of the bogies was when they flew behind that rock you're circling now. Over."

Not the answer I was hoping for, but the same as I expected. She let out a sigh before she keyed the mic again. "Roger that, Unifier Main. I've scanned every inch of this asteroid twice and I can't even find a residue signature. Over."

"Copy that Rapier One, we saw most of what happened. Were you attacked? Or did we misread that? Over."

She paused before she replied. She wanted to say that she didn't know, but the burn marks on her wings and the memory of flame enveloping her cockpit was still fresh in her mind. Finally, she keyed her mic. "Your guess is as good as mine. Over."

"Copy that Rapier," Unifier Main replied. "Wait one." She aimed *Wyvern* back toward the planet, and she could see *Unifier's* thin, black shadow Arc's northern hemisphere. Then, a flash of light shone from behind the Republican mothership, and Taylor could see on her scanner that a medium sized capital ship was speeding toward them.

The radioman aboard *Unifier* called back to her. "Rapier One, we're sending the gunship *Growler* your way now to provide additional coverage and security. They'll be in range momentarily. Our guidance is to give that area one more thorough pass, and if nothing turns up, you are to return to base. Over."

"Copy that," she replied. "Rapier One out."

She watched the gunship speeding across her scanner. The readout told her that the *Growler* would be in range in a matter of minutes. Armed to the teeth with slug-throwers, cutting lasers, and every type of missile imaginable, the *Growler* had enough firepower to level several continents, or even a moon.

Two blips ran across her screen. Two ships were running directly away from both them and *Growler*.

"There they are!" Shale shouted into the radio.

Her bogeys had cleverly put the asteroid between them and everyone else. Taylor spun the *Wyvern* in a tight 180-degree arc and gunned her engines, rocketing around the left side of the asteroid just as Shale peeled off to the right. The *Wyvern* had made it half way around the moon-sized rock when her radio crackled to life.

"Rapier element, this is Growler Two, watch your…"

The rest was lost to static as the asteroid blew apart into a thousand pieces.

Adrenaline flooded into her body as her mind kicked up into another gear. Taylor jabbed her control stick down and to the left, turning her fighter away from the flying rocks. A piece of asteroid twice the size of her ship came spinning at her from the right and she turned sharply to avoid it. Bits of rock spattered the *Wyvern*'s hull like hail as she spun away from a second flying boulder. Then, seeing an opening, Taylor hit her afterburners and was clear.

Looking back, she keyed her mic. "Two, you still with me?"

"Yeah, what the hell?" her wingman replied.

She didn't have time to respond. Keeping her afterburners on, she raced as fast as she could after the two blue dots on her screen. She shivered as tiny nano-bots left their caches within her flight suit and invaded her body, injecting stimulants and stabilizers into her blood stream. Every Raptor pilot's flight suit automatically administered the nano-bots to stabilize their body whenever they sensed an attack or significant g-forces during atmospheric flight. Now her head filled with the sounds of her own labored breathing, and she let out a short curse before her jaw clamped shut from the adrenaline that was rushing through her veins. Her scanners showed that the bogeys were now well beyond the *Growler*'s range, headed fast for the outer limits of the system. However, after nearly a minute of her engines firing on overload, Taylor realized that she was gaining no ground. In fact, the bogeys were pulling away.

Then a call came in over the command net. "Rapier One, this is Unifier Main. Stand down, time now. Over."

Instead of standing down, Taylor toggled her fire controls. She was just in range, but only just. She focused her targeting computer on the nearer of the two arrowheads. They could shrug off .75 caliber cannon shot, but could they shrug off a missile? She had seconds to decide. Her thumb hovered over the arming button, but instead she hesitated. Her targets were fleeing. The danger—for her—was past. Taylor switched off her afterburners and sighed in frustration before she returned the call. "Roger, I read you Unifier Main. Rapier One, standing down."

"If our unidentified interlopers are on their way out, leave them be. We need the two of you re-armed and re-fueled and back on mission. ASAP. Over."

"Roger that, Unifier Main," she replied. "We'll return to base, time now. Over."

Looking down at her readout, Taylor could see that her adventures with her afterburners had emptied the *Wyvern*'s fuel below ten percent.

Just enough for the return trip. The two arrowhead ships were now nearly five hundred klicks away and showed no signs of slowing down. The drug-fueled hyper-alertness still dominated her mind, pushing her hunter's instinct so hard that everything in her mind screamed for her to pursue her prey. However, she knew the hunt was off for today. Instead she set the *Wyvern*'s engines to their most fuel-efficient setting and steered her Raptor back toward home.

ORTHO

Their enemy had finally turned and fought.

Listening to his radio, Ortho knew that Agrippa had anticipated that his assault would turn into a brawl. The Consul Marius and his security detail were only a few miles away from the fight when Ortho had heard Agrippa come over the 88th's net and order his Charlie Company to seize a nearby hotel as a place to treat their wounded. When Ortho told the Consul this, Marius ordered Pansa to make all haste to the hotel so he could be as close as possible to the battle as it unfolded. After an hour of hurried marching, the Consul and his men had arrived at the hotel. Now, Ortho, Mercos and two other soldiers named Horace and Gorbos had gathered on a balcony on the second floor to watch.

The battle for the riverfront had begun.

As dusk had fallen over the city, the shore of the Muirghil River had turned into a blistering light show of tracer rounds, mortars, and rocket fire. It was a wicked gun battle that centered on one building: the Sindorum Royal Theater. Outside, Commander Titus Agrippa and the 88th column had the building surrounded on its north, south, and west sides, leaving the east to the river. Inside, the theater was filled with hundreds of uniformed gunmen, remnants of King Teum's army who had barricaded themselves within the four-story theater like a host of angry hornets defending their nest.

The theater itself was a regal building with sharply rising spires of blue marble and a golden dome for a roof where, at its rounded peak, stood a statue of the Silver Lady, the chief Duathic deity. Brick by brick, the building was now being blown apart. Shattered windows and the pockmarks of bullet holes decorated the theater's walls. Mortar fire exploded at random intervals along its roof and walls and yard as the 88th searched for a way to destroy the enemy within.

Ortho remembered how important the Sindorum Royal Theater was from the Consul's briefing that morning, and now he could see why. The four-story theater building sat right on the Muirghil River where it looked straight across at Duathic Imperial Palace, which was built high atop a crown of artificial rock on the opposite shore.

The guerillas had already repelled the first assault. Alpha Company had tried to rush the theater's north side but the yard had been trip wired, causing mass casualties. Seeing the element of surprise had been lost, Agrippa had quickly called Alpha back. The commander was content to play siege until he could regroup and bring the full power of the 88th to bear.

"Ain't no civilians set that shit up," Mercos said. "Them fuckin' trip wires are vicious man."

"Damn right they are," Gorbos said. He was a tall and muscular grenadier who thought a lot but spoke little. The giant had a face that resembled two pieces of bread dough that had been smashed together, and although Ortho guessed that there were scars mixed in with the ugly, he also knew better than to ask.

"They should just call in another airstrike and then turn the whole place into slag," said Horace, a rat-faced machine gunner with a tall, lanky build and a thin mustache. Facial hair did not come easily to Horace, but that hadn't stopped him from assembling a wispy line of whiskers beneath his nose in an attempt to decorate his face. Ortho had listened to the other soldiers refer to Horace's moustache in terms that involved certain predatory sexual activity, and although Ortho doubted the gunner was capable of such things, Horace did nothing to dissuade the distinction. In fact, the rat faced man rather seemed to enjoy it.

"Naw, man," Mercos said. "We need that building. See how it looks right across the river at the palace? No way we're not taking that building. The Consul and Commander Agrippa are taking that shit whether them Duathe wanna give it to us or not."

Down the street, Alpha Company was making another run at the theater, this time through the parking lot. Half a dozen smoke grenades had been thrown, and the soldiers were sprinting across the pavement. Two Littlehawks swooped in from overhead and launched a volley of rockets that struck the theater's second and third floors. Then the soldiers entered and all anyone could see was fire and smoke and tracer rounds.

"Told ya," Mercos said with a satisfied grin. Beside him, Gorbos grunted and pulled out a smoke.

Horace smiled at Ortho in a way that reminded him of a weasel. "They shoulda just had Intel here call up Rapier One and had her smoke the joint with a couple mark-fives, man. Woulda been so much easier. Then Intel here coulda let us all hear what the hottest chick on the battlefield sounds like."

Ortho shook his head. "If you wanna hear Rapier One talk so badly, I'll let you wear my headset. She checks in on the Coalition main net every thirty minutes." When Horace's face lit up like he'd just been given a present, Ortho checked his watch. "In fact, she's due here in a bit."

"Listen to this guy!" Horace pointed a thumb at Ortho. "Stalkin' chicks on the radio!"

"What? You jealous Horace?" Mercos jabbed. "You wanna stalk chicks on the radio, you creepy bastard?"

"Fuck yeah I do!" Horace snatched the headset from Ortho's outstretched hand. "Gimme that thing. I wanna hear this chick talk."

Ortho raised his hands in mock surrender. "Suit yourself. Just let me know if anyone calls for Eagle One."

The gunner leaned back against the wall and fitted the headset over one ear and promptly demanded a cigarette from Gorbos. Apparently, there was some kind of cigarette debt between the two that Ortho had not yet sorted out.

"Hey Intel," Gorbos said as he put away his lighter. "You seen this Rapier One? They said you were at the command meeting. Was she there? Is she cute or what?"

"Yeah, she was there." Ortho chewed on his cheek, thinking.

"She as hot as everyone says she is?" Mercos laughed.

Ortho looked back toward the theater. Rifle fire was flashing and popping all over the second and third levels now. He wondered, just for a second, how long this fleeting kinship would last, but then something pushed that from his mind and he asked himself: *What does it matter?* He turned back to Gorbos. "I'll tell you about her, but it's gonna cost you a smoke."

Mercos sounded scandalized. "You smoke, Intel?"

"Naw. Never have," Ortho spat over the railing.

"You mean to say…" Mercos said slowly, "…that you're about to have your first cigarette? Here? With us?"

Ortho shrugged.

"Well shit," Gorbos reached back into his shoulder pocket and extended an open pack. Ortho selected a cigarette and carefully placed it into his mouth. It was unfiltered, just a stick of tobacco rolled inside a thin sheet of paper, the kind of cigarette that only a suicidal soldier would dare smoke by the pack. Ortho felt a thrill run up his spine. He could taste the tobacco through the wafer-thin paper as Gorbos readied the lighter.

"Wait. Wait. Wait. Come here, Intel. C'mere, c'mere, c'mere." Waving excitedly and keeping the headset on, Horace hopped over to Ortho, clasped both hands on either side of his face, looked him in the eye, and spoke with the sincerity of a politician. "Listen to me. Do not *not* get addicted. You hear me, Intel? You do this, you're going to smoke for the rest of the war like everyone else, and you're gonna smoke for the rest of your life, and you're going to fuckin' die of cancer like a little good boy. Okay?"

Ortho laughed from the bottom of his gut as Horace extended his palm to Gorbos like a surgeon asking for a scalpel. "Gimme the fuckin' lighter, Gorby. I'm lighting this kid up."

Ortho leaned forward as Horace held the lighter gently to the end of the cigarette. "Breath in just a little, there, that's it, don't inhale yet or you'll kill yourself, you fuck. You just want to get it lit. There, you're lit. Now you're gonna inhale and cough so I can laugh."

Ortho inhaled. Something warm and black grasped his lungs and squeezed the air right out of his chest. Then there was a sharp pain where his heart should have been and he keeled over in a fit of coughing and had to hold the cigarette in his hand for fear it would fall from his mouth. All three of the others laughed at him. When the coughing subsided he laughed as well, and then took another drag.

"Now tell us about Tits McGee up there in that cockpit." Horace cupped his hands in front of his chest. "How big are they?"

"C-cup, at least." Ortho took another puff and inhaled lightly, careful not to cough again. He'd learned his lesson the first time. He felt something tickle his brain, and a rush of blood hit his cerebrum. A dizziness overtook him for a moment and he had to grab the railing to keep from stumbling. Then the vertigo was gone, disappearing like a gust of wind. "She looks great in a uniform, real athletic, you can tell by the way she walks. Every guy at the command meeting was staring at her."

"So is she a fucking real world ten or just a war zone ten?" Mercos asked as he sat down on the balcony floor.

"A war zone ten at least, but I've been deployed too long to say if she's a real ten," Ortho answered.

"Legs?" Gorbos asked as he took a drag from his own smoke.

Ortho whistled between puffs. "It's like she was carved from pure marble. She's like a damn statue."

"Really?" Mercos laughed. "Like thighs and shit? She got that?"

"Yeah man. In spades. She's got the whole thing." He held his hands over his hips to emphasize his point. "You can see it right through the uniform. All them gyms they got for the fleet officers on board *Unifier* and shit. She's gotta work out, like, every day. And she wears the pants tight too, so you can see how skinny her waist is and how round everything is man."

"Fuck," Gorbos spat.

"Shit, you're getting me all turned on now just listening to you talk." Mercos lit his own cigarette. "I been in a god's-damned warzone for too long, some guy just talkin' about a girl I ain't even heard or seen is enough to give me blue balls."

Gorbos grinned. "Mercos, you don't need Intel to give you blue balls, you're so damn horny you do it to yourself."

"Yeah, you're probably right," Mercos said as he scratched his nether regions. "But I think we'll keep Intel around anyway. Don't you think?"

"Yeah, he ain't all bad," Horace quietly agreed.

"That reminds me. Intel…" Gorbos paused as he poked a boney finger into Ortho's chest. "I want to tell you something about Sergeant

Major Contus Sulla. He's a real cunt, but he's good shit, and so don't take anything he gives you too hard. He's always hardest on the new guy."

"Got that right," Horace murmured. "You've already done better than the last two RTOs. If anything, you ain't cried yet, and you ain't dead or dismembered."

All Ortho could do was nod. His voice was caught in his throat so badly that he dared not speak, and for a moment he thought his eyes might tear up. It had been a long time since he had felt any kind of camaraderie from his fellow soldiers, let alone hardened combat men like these. Ortho was fighting his composure while trying to conjure a suitable reply, when the quiet of the moment was interrupted by Mercos who began hopping up and down and waving his arms.

"Wait! Wait! Wait!" Mercos said excitedly. "Here she is! How do I...?"

Ortho reached over to his pack and flipped a switch on the top of the radio. A speaker crackled to life, and then a calm and collected feminine voice came to them through the static.

"We're circling around the south side of Mount Chernon right now. We can be at your position in five-mikes if you need us Reaper One. Over."

"By the Fates," Horace groaned, "she sounds like sex and gun oil."

"She sounds like my future wife," Gerbos grunted.

A male voice replied. "Roger that, Rapier One. I need you to hit a building at coordinates zero-five-niner-two-four, by six-eight-two-three-six. Over."

Mercos smiled like a drunk. "She's even gonna kill stuff for us."

Horace laughed "I'm in love. That's it. I'm in love."

"Roger that, Reaper One," she answered. "We're in route now. I'll give you a buzz when we're in range."

Gorbos pointed at Horace. "Fuck you. She's mine." Horace mockingly raised his hands into a boxer's stance and threw a pair of playful jabs at the broad-shouldered grenadier. Gorbos played for a moment like he did not feel the rabbit-punches of his comrade before his hands shot out, cat-quick, and swallowed Horace in his arms, twisting the smaller man into a headlock.

Horace gasped through the chokehold. "Fuuuuuuuck."

"Say uncle," Gerbos grunted.

Horace wheezed in reply, "Never. I'll … die … for …"

Then the little man snuck a hand around his waist, between Gerbos' legs and the tall man grunted in pain and keeled over, cursing as he let go of the wiry gunner.

"She's mine! Haha!" Horace spun into a mock martial arts stance, holding both his hands before him like blades and chopping at the air in a taunting fashion.

"Andronicus." A deep and commanding voice came from behind them and the shadow of Marius appeared in the doorway.

Ortho sprung around and switched off the radio's speaker. "Yes, my Consul!"

"Pack up. We are away," Marius said and then the shadow walked away.

Like children caught doing something they shouldn't, the laughter and play-fighting between the soldiers stopped immediately. Mercos ripped off the headset and hurriedly handed the radio pack to Ortho, who slung it on his back and hustled to the doorway. Ortho's back yelled at him as he hefted the radio bag and adjusted the straps. He trudged after Marius and silently cursed Major Claudius for the back problems he was sure he'd have later in life. By the time he had caught up, the Consul was jogging down the stairs, and Ortho could hear Captain Pansa shouting for his men to get ready. A squad of soldiers were on his heels by the time he and the Consul reached the bottom of the stairwell.

Ortho counted a dozen wounded soldiers on cots spread out across the hotel lobby. He passed a pair of medics who were leaned over a female soldier with a missing leg and tears in her eyes.

Brennen and Alek raced past as Marius neared the door, and the rest of the squad fell into a formation around the Consul as he started across the street. A howling roar came from the sky and Ortho caught the shadow of a Raptor race overhead. Not a second later he felt the impact followed by the thundering boom of an explosion.

Ortho looked back as they neared the Sindorum Theater. The rest of the Consul's security team was hustling behind them, and he silently noted that this was likely not the first time Marius had unexpectedly gotten ahead of his men.

Marius turned so he was walking backward and facing Ortho. "Andronicus, call Reaper One and get the status of our armored column."

"Right away, my Consul," Ortho said as he switched channels and made the call to Reaper One. Marius continued walking backwards, watching as Ortho received the reply. Ortho kept his eyes downward as he listened, and when he'd heard it all, he looked back to Marius. "They're under attack. Major Ioma says they've been hit hard and taken some casualties, but it's only a few guerillas and they should be on their way again soon. He still expects to meet his timeline, he says."

Marius stopped where he was and turned to look toward the east. The squad stopped with him, each soldier facing out in a different direction with their rifles at the ready. A high-pitched mechanical whine sounded and Ortho spotted another Raptor flash by overhead. Then the tremor of the impact was followed by the distant thunder of an airstrike, and Ortho watched Marius turn his head and look. When Marius looked back at him, Ortho saw something like pain or fear in the great leader's eyes. "Can you ask what part of the armored column has been hit?"

"Yes sir," Ortho nodded, but as he keyed up his mic he saw Marius shake his head.

"Never mind," the Consul said as he waved him off. "Just remind Reaper One to call us if he cannot meet his timeline."

"Yes sir," Ortho said.

The rest of the platoon had caught up to them now and they followed like birds in a flock as the Consul took off again, striding across the street at a brisk pace. The dust and smoke of the battle was heavy in the air as the shadows of dusk were giving way to the darkened fingers of nightfall that were wrapping around the city. One hand on his rifle, Ortho again adjusted the shoulder straps of his radio pack as he looked up at the shadow of the theater that was looming over them.

A helmeted shadow appeared next to him, and Ortho saw Mercos's toothy grin smile at him through the gloom.

"Fun time's over, Intel. We grunts gotta smoke 'em while we got 'em. Ain't no tellin' what's gonna happen next."

"I see that," Ortho replied.

Mercos hit him in the shoulder with a friendly bump of his fist. "One last fight and we can blow this rock. Right?"

Ortho nodded knowingly as he followed Marius through a broken double doorway and into the Sindorum Royal Theater. Just inside the shattered door, the towering form of Titus Agrippa stood waiting.

"My Consul!" the tall man called out when he saw Marius stride through the doorway, and Titus bowed his head as Marius stood before him. "The Sindorum Theater is yours."

The two men clasped hands as Marius broke into a wide grin. "You've done well, old friend. I'll see that your name rings out as the record of the battle is read before the Senate."

"Bagh!" Titus scowled. "Don't waste such tributes on me. The Senate can keep its empty notions of glory. Such things are for younger men, like Ioma. I care not for them."

Marius' smile broadened as if he expected the response. "All the same. We have come far in this war because of you. Now we can finally push to the palace. Teum seems determined to make this as hard as possible. What was the count for taking this building?"

Ortho followed at a polite distance at the front of the security team as Titus led them deeper into the theater. "The last report said we had some fifty wounded, but most can still fight." Ortho detected a subtle and solemn pride from Titus as he spoke. "As for the lost, we've counted twenty-two so far, with one still missing."

Titus led them through the front lobby and up a stairwell where murals of Sindorum's city life adorned the walls. On the second floor, they followed Titus through a doorway and onto a grand balcony that overlooked the theater itself. The shattered remains of a chandelier hung from the domed ceiling high above, and Ortho could see that some weapon had opened a pair of gaping holes in the stage below. "What of our armor?" "Have they made it to the Temple yet?"

"They have been delayed … but only briefly," Marius said. "The irregulars to the western side of the city were thicker than we had expected."

"Hrmph," Titus growled. "How nice we find that out now. Those 'irregulars' cost me plenty as well. I suppose that pup Ioma went charging right into them, didn't he?"

"If he's a pup," Sergeant Major Sulla grinned, "then he's got awfully big paws, my friend."

"But he *is* young and he *is* aggressive," Marius countered. "However, I have every confidence he will be here when we need him."

Something rumbled beneath them. Bits of chandelier fell to the floor, like a shower of broken chimes.

"That was strange," Marius said as he looked at his feet. "That felt like it came from below."

Ortho had felt the same thing, and now he looked down at the tiled floor beneath his boots. He couldn't quite say why, but something about the theater suddenly felt very unstable.

There was another impact then, stronger this time, and Ortho felt the ground shudder again as the glass now fell like a crystalized rain shower.

"I'm afraid you're right, my Consul," Titus said with a hint of fear in his voice.

Marius turned toward the door and shouted. "Everyone get o—"

Then a deafening *BOOM* drowned out the Consul's words and the building shook beneath them. Something above them groaned like a dying machine, and Ortho looked up just as the roof collapsed.

ATTICUS

The column had moved since they had left.

A misting rain had settled in over Sindorum as Atticus led his men past the bombed-out husk of a temple. Major Ioma had pushed the Fifth Armored column into the Essene District, the religious center of the city. Sindorum was not only the capital of the Duathic Kingdom, it was one of its religious centers as well. Cresting a hill, Atticus turned west at a fork, bringing his platoon to a wide road divided by a median filled with trees and flowers and shrubs long left untended and now overgrown. This was the Hunting, the main road of the Essene District. Smaller temples, shops, and hotels—all long abandoned—lined the road here. The sun was now only a faint orange glow shimmering on the horizon, and so Assassin platoon marched into the darkness. Soon, the lights of battle were all that remained. Bombs and mortars flashed in the night, and the faint glow of distant fires and the fireworks of gunfire shattered the shadows around them.

Thrace came jogging up behind him, his boots splashing on the pavement. "Major Ioma says he has pushed ahead of the rest of the column to the White Bridge." Thrace pointed behind them as they walked. "They are actually behind us right now, sir, but we're expected to meet the Major near the bridge."

Atticus stole a glance back toward Vansa, who was walking only a few paces behind Thrace. The medic's eyes were dark and brooding, and her brow furrowed in anger. Atticus found himself remembering the two boys they had left sitting on the curb of the destroyed apartment building.

Then a great, white-hot light lit up the sky, turning night into day for a few seconds. Then the thunderclap of a terrific explosion followed, and the earth shook beneath their feet. The tremor was so strong that everyone stopped where they were as the light faded from the sky.

That was no artillery strike, Atticus thought to himself as he watched the fiery smoke rise into the night. *That was a bomb,* he thought, but he had heard no aircraft fly overhead, nor had he seen any light shine down from orbit. No, this was a bomb that had been placed, planted on the ground for someone to come across. *That wasn't one of ours,* he realized. *That was a trap.*

He looked back toward Thrace who was listening intently to his radio. "I'm not sure what that was sir," the lanky radioman said, "but I'm hearing a lot of traffic right now."

Ahead of them, a fiery plume was rising high into the night sky, a red and yellow flame that raged against the misting rain. Did this have anything to do with why Ioma had called him back? The major had raced ahead of his own column. Perhaps he had anticipated the attack? Atticus pulled out his navigator to see that Ioma's Claymore along with five other tanks were parked just ahead of them, while the rest of the Fifth Armored Column was far behind, the first of which were just now turning on to the Hunting.

Atticus' own platoon was spread out to either side of the great road as they followed the Hunting past a traffic circle and then to the right as the road veered toward the river. There they found Ioma parked on a hill overlooking the water with only a handful of tanks surrounding his own. A bridge stood before them, tall and glowing white in the darkness and below were the black waves of the Muirghil River as it flowed south and west out to the bay. The major was sitting atop his tank, talking into his headset as Atticus approached.

"Over here, Lieutenant," Ioma said, waving from the turret.

The rain picked up as Atticus turned back and signaled his men to spread out and pull security. Then, as Atticus was approaching his commander's tank, Sergeant Jonas fell in beside him, saying nothing. They stopped in the shadow of Ioma's tank as a backdraft hit them from above. Looking up through the rain, Atticus watched a pair of Strykers passing over his head and descending slowly as they landed in the traffic circle behind him.

"We have a situation, Lieutenant." Ioma's expression was sour as he spoke. "The 88th column has been hit with an ambush, perhaps even some kind of planned counterattack. They had reached the Sindorum Theater, which was their rallying point with us. Word is that they've been surrounded and possibly overwhelmed, so I'm changing our immediate plans."

"Are we not headed to the theater, sir?" Atticus asked.

"No, Lieutenant, we're not." Ioma nodded toward a second Stryker as it landed near its brother at the traffic circle. "I'm sending a company of heavy infantry on these Strykers to secure the theater to see if they can break through. As for us…" Ioma turned and nodded toward the White Bridge where a squad of same-faced replicants stood guard. "The Grande Admiral secured this bridge about an hour ago, so I need you to come with me as we scout the way ahead to the palace."

A lone company isn't going to be able to rescue the 88th. He sends a couple hundred men to rescue thousands while he presses forward. Atticus kept his face blank and neutral as he looked up at his commander. "Then our orders have changed, sir?"

Ioma raised an eyebrow. "What do you mean, Lieutenant?"

"Weren't our orders to meet Commander Titus and the 88th at the theater, sir?"

Ioma gave him a long and suspicious look. "Are you questioning me, Lieutenant?"

Atticus felt Jonas stiffen behind him as he shook his head. "No sir, I'm only asking if our orders have changed."

Ioma fixed him with a baleful stare. "The element containing Commander Titus Agrippa and the Consul Marius has been overwhelmed and effectively crippled. Until such time as I have confirmation that either is alive, I must act on the assumption that command of all Republican Forces has fallen to me. I have communicated as such to our remaining forces." Ioma's tone was acidic as he spat over the side of his tank. "I am ordering you across this bridge with me so that we can secure the palace and end this war." Ioma scowled as he looked down on him. "Can I trust you to set your feelings aside and trust me in this matter, Lieutenant?"

Atticus nodded dutifully. "Yes, of course sir."

"And can I trust you to do what needs to be done?"

"Yes, of course, sir," Atticus repeated.

"Without question?"

"Without question, sir."

Ioma spat again as his expression relaxed. "Good. Then you may return to your men and communicate your assignment. Be ready. We will be moving shortly."

"Of course, sir. Right away, sir." Atticus gave a half bow to Ioma as he turned and walked away. Jonas immediately fell in beside him again.

"He wants to keep you close," the sergeant said quietly.

Atticus glanced over his shoulder to see Ioma putting his headset back on, and he waited until he saw the major descend back inside his tank before he responded. "And we don't know why."

Jonas grunted. "But I could gander a few guesses."

Another pair of Strykers were setting down on the far side of the traffic circle. Four of the armored hovercraft now sat humming on the pavement. On the outside of the traffic circle, Atticus could see that the soldiers of his platoon were still dutifully pulling security on the make-shift landing zone. Looking back the way they had come, Atticus could see a crowd of soldiers marching down the Hunting toward them. *The rest of the column will be here soon. I would bet that Ioma won't push forward until he sees the relief forces aboard the Strykers.*

"There's our rescue force, sir," Jonas said as he pulled out his pack of chewing tobacco.

Sure enough, the first of the soldiers walked into the traffic circle and immediately made for the Strykers. Atticus took note of the unit patches on their uniforms. *The 11th Column. Captain Arakin's men. Ioma sends a fraction of his force to aid the Consul while he pushes forward to the palace. Something doesn't make a lot of sense.*

Jonas stuck a wad of tobacco into his lower lip and spat a line of tobacco on the ground as he grunted. "You thinkin' what I'm thinkin', sir?"

"I don't know much, but I think we have conflicting orders," Atticus said as he eyed the back ramp of a Stryker. "What are you thinking?"

"Conflicting orders is putting it mildly, sir." Jonas chuckled. "He'll see you court-martialed for sure. And likely me with you, no matter what lie we come up with." The platoon sergeant let out a snort as he spat again. "But I'm with you, sir. We don't need to tell the kids nothing about what the Major said. We do what we gotta do, and they'll follow. They're ready any way. No matter the fight."

Atticus looked back at his grizzled counterpart and gave him a solemn nod. "Thank you, Jonas."

DELEA

"All clear," Thayne lowered his rifle and nodded back toward Marental, who gave him the signal to move forward.

Quietly, they crept away from their hiding spot along the street corner and hustled one by one into an alleyway. Thayne and Kress went first, bounding across the sidewalk, their weapons at the ready. At the mouth of the alley, Thayne stopped and took a knee behind a burned-out car while Kress set down behind a dumpster, keeping watch with her long rifle. Delea, Fel and Marental came next, running in a crowd.

Delea held her pistol in one hand while she grasped her sister's arm in the other. Something was odd about Fel, something Delea did not understand. Fel had stayed quiet all while the rest of them were discussing their plans to make it to the palace catacombs. What rubbed Delea the wrong way was how Fel was keeping herself so distant from the rest of them. Ever since they'd left the underground shelter, Fel had said nothing, spoke to no one, and had only followed silently as they snuck through the city. There was something going on with her sister, of that Delea was certain—she just didn't have the time to figure out what it was.

The clear and cool night had turned into a warm and heavy rain, and it beat down on them with fat droplets that splattered against the asphalt. It was gathering into rushing streams that hurried down the gutters. Trudging through the rubble and the mud, their tiny party stayed to the darkness and the alleyways as they scurried their way east, toward the river.

Delea wiped the rain from her eyes as she watched a dozen of the Coalition's Strykers fly past overhead, their engines sounding like a flock of violent, gargantuan humming birds. Delea looked back down at her navigator. Kress and Marental had led them to the Essene district, the religious center of the city. They were now travelling down a side road that paralleled the Hunting, the main thoroughfare of the Essene. Nearly seven miles long in its entirety, the Hunting ran north and south through the district until it turned east and used the White Bridge to cross the Muirghil. It was there, across the river, that they would find the Duathic Royal Palace and their underground path across the mountain.

A nearby explosion caused Marental to wave them through a doorway into the shattered lobby of a hotel. Except for a recliner riddled with bullet holes, the lobby furniture was still intact, much to their relief. Delea sat down on a padded sofa and pulled out the navigator to re-check their route. Across the room, Kress set down near a broken window and put the scope of her rifle to her eye to scout the way ahead. A flash of lighting lit the street up like daylight and Kress winced at the sudden brightness. Then, as the flash subsided, Kress lowered her rifle and nodded to the rest of them.

"All clear," she whispered.

At Marental's signal, they filed back through the lobby and then, one by one, left through the same door they had entered. Marental led them back to the rear of the hotel and to the empty street. They could hear nothing but quiet ahead of them now, so Marental signaled for them to slow to a walk.

Delea clung to her pistol and her sister as they marched. She could hear the distant gunfire echoing all around her, and she wondered if she could find it within herself to shoot back like she had before. The firefight at the mansion had been the pure adrenaline of surprise and fear. Now she was so full of nervous energy and anxiety that it was all she could do to keep from shaking as she walked.

Time passed slowly for her as they marched through the Essene District, the minutes draining by in painful fashion. It wasn't just the imminent danger that made Delea uncomfortable, or the possibility that she may have to use her weapon again, it was how everything around her was so empty. She had grown up in Sindorum. The city was her home, and to see it now—with the rubble and the mud and bomb craters—was like walking through a city of ghosts. Marental stopped them at the mouth of an alleyway, and while Kress was looking at the way ahead, Delea watched a pair of wild dogs slinking through the alleyway behind them. Then the flash of an artillery strike lit up the alleyway, and Delea noticed that one of the dogs, a brown and gray mutt, had a ring of blood matted around its mouth. She shuddered and looked away.

The further they travelled down the Hunting, the more the buildings around them grew taller and more ominous. They stopped in a courtyard where a smooth white tower rose above them like the leg bone of a giant. Kress pulled up her rifle again to check the way ahead, while Delea and her sister took cover next to what may have once been a restaurant.

Then a snap and a hiss rushed over their heads and Delea lunged at her sister in an attempt to cradle her against the wall, but Fel slipped from her grasp, pushing her away and shaking her head. Delea couldn't help but give her sister a wounded look, but before either girl could say anything, a rocket exploded against the side of the white tower and Delea shielded her face with her hands as tiny bits of pale rock fell on them like rain. Delea brushed the bits of granite from her clothing, checked to see her sister was okay, and then pulled out her navigator again. She thought she recognized the tower as the Spire of Confession. She kept this assumption as she checked their position on the map. They were close. If she was right, they were only a block from Baggage Loop. Then someone grabbed her by the arm. It was Thayne.

"We have to find cover," he hissed. "They're coming this way!"

Thayne led them across the sidewalk to Kress, who was crouched beneath a broken double doorway. Thayne waved them inside to the first room, which was pitch dark except for the pale light of a single window. Kress quickly circled inside, crouching again near a window, holding her long rifle ready.

"Quickly! Get yourselves down!" Marental whispered as she pushed the door closed behind them.

Everyone hid then, keeping clear of both the hallway and the door. Minutes later, the shadow of a soldier passed by the window. Then another. And another. The pale light of a street lamp cast long shadows through the window as they watched a column of the enemy march by. Huddled in the dark, sitting on the cold floor in her damp clothing, Delea studied their foes through the window. The stature of each man was the same, their posture the same, even their gait was the same. Delea saw no women, smelled no tobacco, and heard none of the light, joking conversation that soldiers so often made while on the move. No, the men passing by their window were like automatons, clockwork soldiers who knew only how to march and fight.

A tank *thrummed* as it took up the entire window. As it passed, Delea looked beyond its hulking shadow where she spotted a road marker, bent and spattered with mud. She squinted, straining to read the letters through the dim light of the street lamp.

Baggage Loop.

The last of the soldiers passed by the window and Delea listened to their footsteps fade into the night. Once she was certain they were well out of earshot, she pulled out her navigator again and slid across the floor to the window. The map on her tiny screen shifted, telling her that the window faced north. If Baggage Loop was to their north, then she knew the White Bridge was no more than a block to their east. She slid back across the floor to Marental and held up the screen of the navigator for her bodyguard to see. Silently, Marental nodded and then signaled that it was time to move.

With Kress in the lead now, they crept out the back of the building where a fenced lawn overlooked the river Muirghil. A misting rain was coming down now, and Delea was wiping the water from her face as she walked across the yard. The White Bridge stood to their left, its pale frame glowing in the misty rain and against the cloudy night sky. Nearing the gate, Kress held up her hand for them to stop. Everyone got down and hid behind the fence and looked to Kress, who was pointing toward the bridge.

"Look," she whispered.

Delea peered over the fence, but she could see nothing except the misting rain that shrouded everything in a dull haze. Then the clouds shifted, revealing both moons once again, and finally she could see the shadows moving across the bridge.

"Shit," Thayne shook his head as he spat.

Marental pointed down the hill. "There is a road beyond the fence that leads down to the shoreline. We should be able to find a boat down there to make our way across the water."

Following Kress out of the gate, they followed the fence until they found a road. It led them down a sloping hill filled with tall and leafy trees that flanked them on either side, shielding them from the misting rain and the wind as it whistled through the branches. Soon they were completely out of view from the soldiers on the bridge.

The cobblestones ended at a shore filled with docks that stood out over the black, rushing waters of the Muirghil. Searching the docks, they found a pair of rowboats tied to a boat landing. Kress and Marental climbed in the first boat while Thayne helped Fel and Delea climb into the other.

Delea had her sister climb into the back of the boat with Thayne while she did the rowing. The lanky bodyguard had put on a brave face, but she could tell his limp was getting worse and she noticed that he grimaced every time he stooped or bent over. Despite this, he had dutifully stayed close to Fel ever since they had left the mansion, always staying within an arm's length of the girl. Fel, for her part, seemed to know the game and was following along with the same sullen expression she'd had since that afternoon.

They were halfway across the river when a spout of spray shot out of the water and splashed their boat. Delea hunched her shoulders from the salty wetness and she heard Thayne utter a muted curse as the boat lilted back and forth in the water.

"A whale!" Fel whispered, leaning over the edge of the boat.

A single gray slopefin whale had surfaced next to their rowboat. It brushed against the side of the hull, rocking the vessel side to side as it sloshed in the water. Another spout of water shot into the air as the whale exhaled through its blowhole and the spray mixed with the rain as it fell about them and inside the boat. Afraid to agitate the animal, Delea held her oars up out of the water. Still leaned over the wall of the rowboat, Fel laughed. Then, reaching toward the animal, she brushed her fingers over the whale's smooth and curved back and then whispered something toward the water.

"What are you doing?" Delea hissed as she fumbled with the oars, turning them inside the boat, but Fel ignored her and instead, leaned closer to the whale, so close that the boat began to lean. Thayne, sitting next to Fel, seemed to stare for a moment as Fel, grinning from ear to ear, whispered something again as she ran her hand across the whale's back. Then the lanky bodyguard sat up and grabbed the girl about the waist and pulled her back inside the boat just as the whale sprayed them again and sank below the surface with a splash. The right side of the boat lolled against the surface. Looking out, Delea saw the river churn where the whale swam away. Delea held the oars inside the boat until she saw the whale surface again, some distance away, before swinging the oars back out and rowing again.

"Fel!" Delea whispered sharply. "Stay inside the boat!"

Fel rolled her eyes as Thanye released her and the girl sat back down on her seat. The bottom of the boat was now sloshing with water that covered the toes of Delea's boots, and she could feel the water seeping into her socks. Paddling the oars, she turned the rowboat back on course, aiming it again for the eastern shore.

This part of the river was less than a half a mile from the bay, and the water here was nearly as salty as the Bay of Sardis, but still Delea wondered what could have possessed the whale to come so far upstream. Perhaps it was because their rowboat was the only vessel on the water now. Or perhaps the slopefin was confused or lost. Either way, the whale had cheered Fel, as Delea could see her little sister was now smiling out at the water with a wistful look in her eyes.

The rest of their journey across the bay went smoothly as Delea followed Kress and Marental's boat to a sandy spot along the shore. Landing on the bank, she and Thayne pulled their boat onto the sand and turned it over. Then the three of them met up with the two giant women who had taken cover in the long grass.

Delea pulled out the navigator again to re-check their route as Thayne and Marental huddled next her to see the glowing green screen. Deeper in the grass, Fel was huddled up next to Kress as the giant woman kept watch on the hillside, her long rifle in hand.

Delea zoomed in the navigator's screen. "We're right here, at the edge of the Muirghil, and right up there is where the Hunting ends at the palace's outer gates." Delea pointed up the hill, as a spatter of rain fell around them. "Just inside that wall is where we'll find the palace's temple, which is where we'll find our entrance to the catacombs."

Since they had left the mansion, a deep darkness had fallen over the city as rain clouds had moved in with the night. The rain had grown heavier as well, waxing and waning as it grew until it was now a shower that swirled about with the wind. Looking up the hillside now, they could see the flashes of explosions and the bright orange and green tracer rounds whipping back and forth in the sky. The Coalition was closing in on the palace.

"Victory One Romeo spoke truly when he said it was a race against time," Marental said gravely. "Our enemies are nearing the palace gates just as we do."

Thanye turned and spat into the grass. "Shit. No sense in waiting."

Delea nodded and turned off the navigator's screen and tucked it back into her pack. Beside her, Marental gave the signal to move, and together their tiny party of five began their trek up the hill. Kress took the lead again, holding her long rifle at the ready as she scanned their surroundings. Thayne came limping behind her, now favoring a leg that hadn't been hurt during the crash. Behind him were Delea and Fel, while Marental brought up the rear. While Fel kept herself close between Delea and Thayne, something about her little sister's demeanor still worried Delea. The way Fel looked about at the buildings and streets around them told Delea that her little sister was looking or waiting for something to happen. Whatever had happened between Thayne and Fel in mansion's garden was still fresh in Delea's mind, and whatever was going on, Delea was not going to allow it to distract them as they entered the final, most treacherous leg of their journey.

Leaving the river's shore behind them, they followed a cobblestone road up the hill and into a residential district filled with three and four-story condominiums. This had been one of the wealthiest parts of the city before the war, but now it was nearly abandoned. The hill and the buildings shielded them from most of the noise from the battle above, making it so quiet around them that the sounds of their bootsteps striking the cobblestones echoed in a way that Delea found eerie and unsettling.

However, as they climbed further up the hill, they began to see signs of life. Cutting down an alleyway, Delea saw two tiny faces, young children, looking down at her from under the curtain of a second story window. Crossing the next street, she saw an old man smoking a pipe on the front stoop of an apartment building. A few blocks later they passed a pair of women sitting next to a fountain that had long since stopped running but was now collecting rainwater from the passing storm. The women were using cups to scoop the water into a bucket that sat between them. Delea could hear the women whispering as they worked, but when Kress stepped out of the shadows, both women fell silent as ghosts as they watched the tiny party pass.

All of these things were quiet, and the people were more like shades than living beings. However, it was not until they neared the top of the hill that Delea felt the quiet grow uneasy in her stomach. Her legs had begun to ache and she was relieved when ground leveled off and Kress finally brought them to a halt behind an abandoned bus on a street corner.

They were a block away from the top of the hill now, and as Delea looked up, she could see the street lights shining along the sidewalks of the Hunting. *Has the battle gone silent, or simply moved further away?* Looking up and down the street, she could see no one moving and no sign of the gunfight they had witnessed from the shore. *Perhaps the battle has moved inside the palace. Perhaps it's overrun.*

After searching with the scope of her rifle, Kress waved them forward again. They crested the hill on a narrow street that ran between two apartment complexes. Kress drew them to a halt again, and they hid in the shadows as they looked out into the dim light of the street lamps. The next street was the Hunting.

It was a wide road, paved with white stones and black mortar in a way that made Delea think of a long and winding gameboard. Street lamps, many of them still lit, flanked the walkways on either side of the road, and as Delea looked across the great street, she was relieved to see the outer wall of the palace grounds. The white wall was just over one-story high with a gleaming silver gate, and beyond that was the domed roof of their goal, the Palace Temple.

Kress leaned around the corner to scan the way ahead. Huddled against the building wall, Delea realized she was trembling. Whether it was from the cold or from the anxiety or from exhaustion, she could not tell. Up above, the clouds had completely enveloped the sky, smothering them in darkness and cold, and the rain was coming down in sheets. Clutching her shoulders, she listened to her teeth chatter. Finally, Kress lowered her rifle.

"All clear."

Delea grabbed her sister by the hand as they sprinted across the rain soaked street, water puddles splattering beneath their boots. Someone had knocked a car-sized hole in the outer gate and they ran straight through it and into the terraced gardens that surrounded the palace temple. A flash of lightning lit up the yard as they sloshed through the muddy grass. Delea's lungs were burning in her chest as she jogged across the temple's courtyard, but she kept Fel's hand in hers all the while. An entire day-and-a-half of running for her life with no sleep and little food was finally catching up with her. Her legs were aching when they reached the temple's columned portico. She dragged herself up its stone steps, pulling Fel alongside her the entire way. When they finally ran through a wooden double door, Delea dropped her pistol on the floor and fell to her hands and knees as she panted, gasping for breath. Behind her, she heard someone slam the door shut, and they were swallowed by the black, hollow darkness of an empty room at night.

Slowly, the burning in her chest subsided and her eyes adjusted to the darkness. Tapestries, pews, and a marbled floor spread out around her and the smell of burning incense tickled her nose. They were in the temple's sanctuary. The room itself was huge, almost like a stadium with a ceiling three stories high, and Delea could hear the soggy footsteps of the others as they walked about the room. She noticed that the windows, which ran floor to ceiling, were covered by overlong curtains, shading them from any light that would leak in from the outside. Walking to the nearest window, Delea peeled back the edge of the curtain to inspect it. They were ornamental tapestries for a royal funeral.

Behind her, she heard Marental's deep voice whispering into her radio. "Victory One Romeo, this is Sentinel Four. We are inside the palace grounds, and we have made it inside the palace temple. Over."

Wild thoughts raced through Delea's mind as she grappled with the implications of the sanctuary's decorations. Did this have anything to do with her father? Was there anyone else still here? Was her father still alive? Was this another game invented by his madness? Her mind was wrestling with these questions when a blinding light came on from outside the temple.

Releasing the curtain, Delea fell to the floor. The floodlight was so bright that it came through the curtains themselves, bathing the temple sanctuary in a reddish glow. Staying low, she crawled on her hands and knees along the wall until she came to the corner where she sat on the floor with her back to the wall. Then someone grabbed her shoulder. It was Marental.

"Your Highness, I am calling Victory, but there is no..." The big woman began, but then Delea heard Marental's radio mic key up.

"Sentinel Four, this is Victory One Romeo. I read your position is at the temple. Can you signal us ... or ... wait one ..." Delea leaned in close to the mic that Marental had pressed to her own ear and they could hear the sounds of gunfire echoing in the background. A stretch of hurried breathing followed as the gunfire faded and he finally came back. "Sentinel Four, I'm afraid we're pinned down at this time and need you to..." The radio cut to a sharp burst of static, and then silence, as though the line had been cut with a knife.

Right then, a chorus of gunfire thundered from outside and the flash of tracer rounds flew past the windows. A sinking feeling took hold of Delea's chest as she began to get the feeling of something gigantic and unstoppable closing in on her. More gunfire followed, and soon the west side of the temple was witness to a full-blown firefight as stray rounds and ricochets began to strike the windows and the walls around them.

"Princess, we gotta get out of here!" Thayne yelled from behind a pew. "Wherever it is that we need to go, we need to go there now, or there ain't gonna be nowhere left to go!"

Delea nodded as she pulled out the map from the mansion. Unfolding it, she strained her eyes to read the markings in the red-tinted light that was streaming through the curtains. *We need to be in the cellar.*

Staying low against the floor, she folded the map back into her pocket as she waved to the others. "Alright. Follow me."

They had to crawl the length of the sanctuary, staying below the level of the windows so to avoid casting shadows. When they reached the far end of the sanctuary, Delea pushed through a wooden door that led them down a stone stairway. The sounds of the battle above began to fade as they jogged down the steps. She passed the door to the first basement and kept going down until the steps ended at an ancient wooden door with iron hinges. Delea tried at the door latch.

"It's locked," she said.

Kress stepped past her and grasped the door's iron handle. The giant woman's muscles bulged as she heaved. When the door did not give way, Kress braced her foot against the wall and threw her back into it. With a creak and a groan, the frame of the door began to bend and then with a loud snap the door flew open.

"Unlocked now." The giant woman laughed as she brushed off her hands.

The cellar was full of wine casks, waist-high and stacked against the walls in rows. Delea found a light switch in the corner and threw it on as everyone stepped into the room. "Okay," she whispered, "according to the map there should be some kind of trap door down here somewhere."

Everyone began searching. The cellar was laid out in a U, with rows of wine casks along every wall. A few empty casks had been left haphazardly strewn about the center of the U, and Delea waded through them as she crossed to the other side of the cellar. She had just reached the other side when a sharp echo came down the stairs. Everyone froze where they were. The doors to the temple sanctuary had just opened.

The sounds of hurried footsteps followed, echoing down the stone stairwell. The Umbreans were here.

Everyone redoubled their search. Delea pressed herself against the wall, straining to look behind the casks. Behind her, she saw Thayne running his hands along the wall, his fingers searching the mortar between the bricks. Kress and Marental began picking the casks up, one by one, and stacking them in the center of the room. The clamor of footsteps coming from upstairs was growing louder and louder as they searched, and Delea wondered what would happen to them when the soldiers came down the stairs and found them all here in the cellar.

Then, a small voice cried out softly in the dim light. "Over here." And when everyone turned and looked, there was Fel standing next to a wooden doorway that she had pulled open from the floor.

Stepping closer, Delea could see the top of the door was disguised to look like same brick and mortar stone that the rest of the floor was made out of. However, when she circled round to the mouth of the door, a set of wooden steps lead down into the darkness.

"Quickly, you two," Marental whispered as she shooed them down the stairs.

Delea reached for her sister, but Fel slipped away down the stairs before Delea could grab her by the hand. Seconds later the trapdoor swung shut above them and darkness swallowed them again. Thayne lit his flashlight, but held his hand over the beam so that only a faint light outlined them like shadows against the black. They were standing in a rounded stone tunnel with a flat bottom. Slowly, they followed Thayne as he walked forward, and after a minute of careful walking, he finally pulled his hand away from the beam and the light lit up the room around them.

A three-way intersection sat before them, with tunnels that lead left, right, and straight ahead. Delea pulled the map from her pocket and Thayne held his flashlight for her as she studied the markings again. They were directly beneath the palace. Not far ahead, Delea could see where all the green lines met up at a box drawn beneath the throne room.

"We need to turn right," Thayne whispered.

They followed the lanky bodyguard to the right as he limped through the darkness, the beam of light held before him. Delea kept her ears aimed behind them, listening for any sounds of pursuit, but none came. They followed Thayne's light through the next tunnel until it opened up into a cavernous room with a tiled roof and a floor covered in tiny rocks. The only sounds for several seconds were their own labored breathing as they looked at the room while Thayne swung his beam of light from one side to the other. The room was so large that the flashlight could barely reach the other walls. To their left and right Delea could see more tunnels. Counting the openings, she added up nearly a dozen tunnels that sprouting from the room. Thayne stepped forward a few feet, his boots swishing in the rocks, until his flashlight lit up the far wall. It was flat but for a pair of openings, tunnels to either end that met with a monorail.

"What was that?" Kress's voice was a whisper.

Something or someone had scraped the floor of the tunnel behind them. Thayne swung his light around, but no one was there. Then the light died as Thayne's flashlight turned off. Darkness swallowed them. For nearly a minute, everything was as black and silent as a tomb. Then something scraped against a wall, this time from the far side of the room.

"Turn it back on," Marental whispered.

"I can't," Thayne said. Delea could hear him striking the flashlight with the flat of his hand. "It died and now I can't turn it back on."

The distant howl of tunneled wind found their ears as Thayne's light suddenly came back on, shuddered, and died again, returning them to darkness. The next thing Delea heard was the distant voice of her little sister.

"Hello. I am here." Fel said.

Then a second voice reached out to them from the black. It was a sweet and soft voice like a woman's or a young boy, but with a lilting and inhuman tone. *"Greetings little sister, I am so glad to see you again."*

Then a wind came rushing at them from the tunnel, carrying the voices away, and Delea heard nothing more.

ORTHO

Ortho came to amidst the dust and crumbling rock. Rolling onto his back, the only thing above him was a wall of granite lying inches from his nose. He tried to recall what had happened, but the only thing he could remember was everything collapsing around him before a big black nothing struck him and consumed him. Now here he was, conscious and breathing and looking around to see why he wasn't dead.

It had all happened so suddenly. He was no longer standing in the grand foyer of the Sindorum Royal Theater, but was lying on his back with his face covered in dust. Turning his head, he saw he was beneath a giant slab of concrete propped up against the stump of a marble pillar. He began wiggling his toes, his legs, his fingers and his arms. Everything seemed to work. Looking up, he saw that the concrete slab above him and the pillar it rested on were the two reasons he still lived, as everything else had fallen around that piece of manufactured rock, forming a kind of cave around him.

His body armor must have saved him somehow, but the memory of whatever had struck him was a missing piece of his mind. He felt the tiled floor beneath him shudder as the ruins shifted and slid against each other. *How long have I been out?* He thought. *How in the Fates am I going to get out of this?*

Something moved above him, stone grinding on stone. Ortho looked up, and he heard boot steps climbing over the ruins. A stream of gravel trickled down through the rubble until it bled out onto the floor next to his hip. Outside the battle was still raging, and for the first time since coming to, Ortho noticed the sounds of gunfire and battle echoing around him. No one would be coming for him anytime soon.

The walls of the rubble seemed to close in on him, and he fought back another cold shiver of panic and fear. He blinked hard twice and let out a series of short breaths as he forced the panic from his mind. He had no right to be alive, yet here he was. Sore but breathing. Startled but conscious. He could not see the sky, but there *was* light, beams of it that crisscrossed his little cave like some haphazard kaleidoscope.

He began to take an inventory of what remained of his gear. His rifle was nowhere to be found. The strap he'd kept attached to its butt-stock was hanging limply from his shoulder like a snapped limb. The radio pack was still strapped to his back, but when he pulled it off, he saw the radio was now a mashed and mangled mess. He pushed it aside and left it. *It must have taken part of the blow that knocked me out. Better it than me.* Searching the rest of his kit, he found he still had his water, a broken hand-mic, and a utility knife. Then, still lying on his back, Ortho began to look for a way out.

The space was perhaps tall enough for him to sit up, but he didn't dare risk it. The base of the concrete slab was resting on the ground next to his feet, so there was clearly no passage that way. To his right a pile of rubble had fallen around the other half of the marble pillar, he would find no way there. It was to his left that held the most promise, as he could see slivers of light pouring down through a maze of crumbling rock and shattered wood. If he was careful and if he took off his gear, he thought he might be able to squeeze through.

He shifted over onto his shoulder and looked toward the front of his cave. And that's when he noticed the body. It was a man, dressed in the same uniform and armor as him.

Ortho rolled over and crawled to him. The man's helmet was cracked in half from a blow to the head and his face was covered in blood and dirt. *He has to be dead.* Ortho thought, but as he reached around to feel the man's neck for a pulse, his gloved fingers found the steady beat of pumping blood. *Now what?*

He cursed silently to himself as he looked over the unconscious body. The man was half buried beneath a pile of shattered debris, and his left arm was pinned beneath a chunk of granite the size of Ortho's leg.

Turning onto his back, Ortho placed his feet against the rock, braced himself against the base of the pillar and pushed with all of his strength. He grunted as the rock began to tilt and when he gave it a heave, the rock finally rolled over, freeing the man's arm.

Ortho blinked hard as the blood rushed into his head, and a dozen black spots ran across his vision. The effort left him dizzy and dazed, and as he lay there, he wondered what kind of injuries his adrenaline was hiding from him. *Internal bruising? Cracked or broken bones? Surely, I have a concussion.* He told himself it didn't matter right now as he spun himself around again to look over the unconscious soldier.

From the elbow up, the man's arm was a mangled and flattened mess, but he was free, mostly. Ortho cleared off the pile of gravel and rock from the man's torso. Then, lying on his back, he stripped off his own body armor and pushed it into the corner beneath the edge of the giant concrete slab. He wouldn't need his armor if he was buried alive. Then he spun back around again to face the unconscious man, grabbed him by the shoulder straps, and pulled him free of the remaining rubble.

Thanking the Fates that he had gotten that far, Ortho looked again toward the light to scout his path. He could see now that it was night outside, but something was shining down with an artificial light, allowing him to see the path ahead. If nothing more collapsed—and if he was careful—he and his unconscious partner would make it. Using his feet and his knees to pull them forward, Ortho slid backward on his belly as he pulled the body behind him. Weaving slowly through the claustrophobic maze of shattered wood and broken stone, Ortho heard another flurry of boot steps pass overhead as bits of gravel fell around him like a summer shower. Something exploded nearby and he felt the rubble shift around him again as he squeezed through a pair of bent metal doors. Pulling the unconscious man with his right arm, he used his left to navigate around a sharp piece of metal. The light around them was getting brighter and warmer the further they went, while the gunfire outside kept getting louder and clearer.

Then the unconscious man got caught on something and Ortho had to stop. Looking down across the body, he could see what had caused the hang up: the man's boot was caught in a twisted web of rebar that stuck out from a broken slab of concrete. Ortho glanced back toward the light. He could see the stars of the night sky hanging over-head and the bright white of a street lamp glaring down at him—and behind it all, the wet smell of rain. They were nearly there. Crawling on his belly, Ortho reached the boot and tried to pull it free, but the foot had twisted itself between the bars so tightly, he dared not force it. Instead, he decided it would be easier to unlace the man's boot. Once he had untied the laces and loosened the boot, he pulled at the foot again, but nothing gave. Grabbing a piece of the rebar, he pulled himself closer. Feeling around the outside of the boot, he could feel that inside, the foot was swollen so tightly that it stretched the leather of the boot. Pulling out his knife, Ortho carefully cut around the foot and the rebar until he was able to carefully pull the foot free of it all. After checking to see that nothing else was caught, Ortho climbed back to the top of the man and, grabbing him again by the top straps of his armor, pulled him up toward the light.

Now sitting atop the rubble, Ortho could see the front half of the theater had collapsed, exposing the guts and bones of the structure al-most as if a giant had taken a trowel and shaved off the front half of the building. Then a loud *SNAP* sounded as a bullet struck a piece of con-crete an inch from his head and buzzed off into the air like a supersonic bee. Several more rounds hissed behind his back as he ducked back into the rubble. Minutes passed as Ortho hid inside the pile of broken con-crete. Finally, he peeked through a hole in a collapsed wall as he tried to determine who had shot at him and if they were still there.

A dozen bodies of his fellow soldiers were strewn about the street like scattered leaves amongst the rubble. Tendrils of smoke were still wafting off the wreckage and a drizzling, misting rain was falling over his helmet and his shoulders, but he could see no one else near him. Then another bullet whipped over him, so close that Ortho ducked his head, and it was then he realized that they were in the middle of an exchange between two forces. He could see by the muzzle flashes from atop the surrounding buildings to his left, and another on the far side of the rubble to his right. The hiss and snap of gunfire was all around, but thankfully no more of it appeared to be aimed at him. Staying close to the rock, he peered out across the street, hoping he would see friendly uniforms and was promptly disappointed. The alleyways and sidewalks were full of Duathic men in plainclothes, running around with rifles and other small arms. He stayed tucked inside the rubble as a crowd of the blue-skinned guerilla dashed across the street and around another building.

Perhaps he could go another way. He climbed atop a pile of rubble and crawled his way upward until he could see the hotel where they had come from. He spotted the flash of gunfire from the windows and a grenade exploded on the first floor, shooting dust and smoke and fire out into the street. *We're surrounded*, he thought as he slid back down. *How many of them are there? Who is left of us? And where are we?*

He turned another way and crawled along the rubble until he could see where the edge of the ruined theater met a slope that ran downward to the river. There he saw soldiers dressed in Coalition uniforms, fighting their way backward down the slope as the guerillas harried them in their wake. That was the only reasonable place to go. He had to move quickly.

Again, he heard the *clomp-clomp-clomp* of bootsteps over stone and he shrunk down as a dozen more Duathic men dressed in plainclothes and armed with rifles ran past. Ortho lay like a dead man until the guerrillas had past. When they had faded, he opened his eyes and looked about without moving. All clear. He scrambled back down the into ruins again and climbed back down to the unconscious man. He felt the other's neck. Still alive. Still breathing.

Ortho realized now how large the man before him was. He had to be near six-and-a-half feet tall, almost a foot taller than Ortho, and built like a powerlifter. The man's face was unrecognizable with the dust and grime and blood that covered it, but when Ortho reached down adjust the man's collar, he got a glimpse of his rank and immediately Ortho knew who he was.

It was Consul Marius.

FEL

4.29.2388 - Arc, catacombs of Sindorum

The last of the light was behind her now. Fel had been crawling for the last several minutes as the blackness of the catacombs swallowed everything around her. She stopped to sit with her back against the rounded wall of the tunnel. It was rough and damp against her shirt, and somewhere nearby she could hear a drain trickling in the dark. Listening, she turned her ears behind her. Delea and the others were calling for her. Her sister's cries were desperate, fearful, and full of anger and grief. Fel knew she could not go back now. Would not. Her sister did not know what was happening and would only try to stop her. If they caught her now, they would keep her so close, watch her so carefully that she would never be able to get away again.

And besides, there wasn't much time left. She could feel it.

Silently, she prayed to the Silver Lady for guidance. Her prayers had been answered before when the water spirit had met her on the river and told her where to go. The water spirit knew the way, for it had travelled these tunnels before as a young raindrop. It had fallen from the sky and then ran down the gutters where it had slipped down a drain. There the water spirit had met with a frog or a salamander (it wasn't sure which), and together they had explored the catacombs below the palace for over a year until the water spirit had grown big enough and strong enough, and it had said farewell to its amphibian friend and ran out into the sea.

When Fel had spoken to the water spirit there on the river, she had told it of her quest and it had happily advised her—it even offered her heartfelt encouragement. "It is an important thing you are doing," the water spirit had said, "perhaps you are even doing the most important thing of all the things that will be done today."

She had to go. Steeling herself, Fel ignored the cries of her sister and her guardians behind her. She rose up off the wall to continue forward. Feeling with her hands, she discovered that she had passed into a larger tunnel and could stand now. Stepping gingerly, heel to toe, heel to toe, she crept forward until she was comfortable enough to move at a walk. She recited the water spirit's directions in her head again. *Third tunnel on the right as you enter the main room, then fifty paces down...* Fel was counting her steps now. *Thirty-one, thirty-two, thirty-three...* At fifty steps, she came to a T in the tunnel.

She held her hand in front of her face and saw nothing. The only sounds her ears could hear now were the trickling of the drain and the distant cries of her sister. Then a fluttering of feathered wings took her and she held very still, for she knew then that the Onier had arrived.

Fel spoke softly to the darkness. "Hello, I am here."

The Onier sighed like a rainstorm as its two, gold, smoke-filled eyes appeared before her. "Greetings little sister. I am so glad to see you again. The others seek you now, but they cannot hear."

"I know, but can't abandon my father," Fel whispered. "Is he still alive?"

"Alive ... is a dangerous word, Little Sister." The Onier laughed. "But yes, your father is right where you left him. His foes are blocked by the very trap they set for him, but perhaps that was the plan all along. I know not what the Powers have in store for him."

"The Powers? Who are they?"

"They are best left alone, is what they are." The Onier chuckled again. "You had best come with me now. So you can finish what he started."

"But I don't want to finish anything!" Fel cried. "I just want to find my father and make him safe!"

The Onier blinked at her. "Ah ... very well then. I suppose we must get you to the gatehouse."

Fel did her best to glare. "Yes."

"To get your father."

"Yes."

The edges of the smoke-filled spirit lit up with a blue flame, outlining her form. The Onier lifted its arm and pointed with a fiery blue finger. "Left. Straight on until you see a light. There should be a hole in the ceiling that will take you up to the base of the wall—but beware, the wall has collapsed. If you can climb that undetected, you should have a clear path across the parapet to the gatehouse's roof. Use the chalk there and you should land right next to your father."

Something like a ratchet sounded to her left and she heard the metallic whine of a door swinging open.

"From there, the door you must seek is the door you first entered, Little Sister. That door is where the secrets are held and secrets revealed. Like thieves we meet and like thieves we shall go. Good luck, Little Sister."

With a wisp of smoke, the Onier disappeared and Fel was left alone in the dark again. Looking left, she could see only darkness and hear only the hollow, empty sound of the tunnel. But left she did go. Step by step, foot by foot, she followed the tunnel. Once, she stumbled over a rock and fell against the wall, but she picked herself up and kept going. On and on the tunnel went and, after many minutes, it angled downward to where she found herself walking in ankle-deep muck. Finally, a sliver of light appeared before her, and when she reached it, she found herself standing beneath a crack in the earth that had punctured the tunnel roof.

A bomb or explosion of some kind had struck here, right where the tunnels formed into another T. The tunnel floor was cracked too, and down below she could see rushing water. Street light and raindrops were leaking through the hole, and she could hear the hum of tank engines and the chatter of soldiers in the street above. Looking up at the hole, she adjusted the pack on her back. It looked big enough for her to make it through.

She propped her legs to either side of the tunnel wall and shimmied up to the hole. The broken concrete formed just enough of a lip for her to grab as she pulled herself up. She was right about the hole—it was just big enough for her and her backpack to squeeze through. The last layer was asphalt, and she raised her head just high enough to look out at the street.

She was about a hundred yards from the gatehouse, where she could see a pair of soldiers standing guard next to a tank. Behind her was the outer wall of the palace. The bomb had struck that too, opening a crumbling hole and spilling rubble out into the street. It was all too easy to climb out of the hole and creep over to the wall.

She climbed up the ruined part of the wall with ease, the rubble forming a set of jagged steps. Hiding atop the parapet, she looked out at the yard. The same-faced soldiers were everywhere. Two stood at every door while squads of them roamed the gardens and yards inside the wall. But she saw none of them atop the wall, at least not yet. Running at a crouch, she jogged across the parapet to where the wall met the gatehouse roof.

Kneeling below the parapet wall, she reached inside her jacket pocket and pulled out a splinter of the red chalk. It was little more than a jagged triangle, but she hoped it would work. She was about to climb up on the roof when a booming voice came up from the gatehouse below.

"HA!" a voice bellowed and another answered. Fel could hear them talking in a language she did not understand. He had an Umbrean accent, but the language he spoke seemed to be Illyari, the language of the Republic.

Pulling the translator from the side pouch of her backpack, guessing that they were speaking in Illyari, Fel placed the translator's earpiece in her ear. The translation was garbled at first, as the computer struggled to catch up, but finally, she could hear and understand the men below her. "Right on time, my young friend, just as you said you would be. Accurate as the cock at dawn!"

The voice that answered was calm and confident and unmistakably Illyari. "Did you expect anything less?"

"Ha! You've never let me down, boy," the Umbrean bellowed. "That's why you're here."

Hiding against the parapet, Fel decided to stay still. She wanted to climb up onto the roof to draw her doorway, and she dared not risk being spotted.

"A better question, Grande Admiral, is where are you keeping the Queen?"

The Umbrean snorted in disgust. "Hrmph, she has slipped our grasp for now. But it is no matter, my cousin will retrieve her soon."

"I had heard her escort had wandered into some mishap. That makes me wonder what game the Queen has been playing."

"I do not concern myself with the games of women. It is her husband who has been our foe."

"And a lucky stroke for that."

"Ha! Teum has never been accused of military genius. Though I had wondered if the madman would chance to bring the place down with him." The Umbrean chuckled to himself. "Come now, my soldiers have secured the palace. Let us gaze upon the fruit of our labors."

She peeked over the top of the parapet wall to see a tall, pale giant striding across the yard and next to him was a dark-haired man in a Illyari Republic uniform. An entourage of the same-faced soldiers followed in their wake.

Tucking the translator back into her pack, Fel waited until they had all disappeared inside before she climbed up on the roof. Sitting on the red tiles, she drew a circle around herself with the chalk. Then the roof opened up and she fell down into the dark.

She could feel herself falling upward again. Not flying but falling up. Like something was pulling her. She tumbled through the darkness until she landed, again bouncing against the mattress-like surface as everything flipped. Landing again, she reached out and caught herself with her hands against the stone floor of the gatehouse.

Something *hisssssssssssed* behind her. Turning around, she saw two of her black-eyed doppelgangers reaching for her through the cage of the window. Crawling away on her back, she felt two hands grab her beneath the shoulders and pick her up. She turned around to face her father and immediately embraced him.

"My little Fel, you've come back!" he cried. "But why? But how?"

"There's no time, Papa. I have to get you out of here."

Holding her father by the hand, she dropped down onto her haunches and drew a circle around both their feet. Then the floor opened up and they both fell through.

They landed in the muck at the bottom of a dark, dank tunnel. She heard her father pick himself up and make a noise of disgust.

"Bleagh. Where are we? And how did you do that?"

"It was a trick someone showed me," Fel said as she reached into her backpack and pulled out her flashlight. "We're in the catacombs, father, not far from the palace."

Fel turned on the flashlight and aimed the beam ahead of them. The white-bearded man that was her father followed the light with his eyes.

"Can you take us back?"

She looked up at him. "Are you sure you want to go back, Father?"

His eyes looked down on her, wide with fear. "Yes."

"But why?" she asked.

He knelt down next to her then and held her by the shoulders. "Because, my daughter, my little girl, it is the only way to drive them out! I cannot leave my people to these monsters. I cannot! I will not!"

"But how will you do that? They're all over the city. They're all over the palace. If we follow the tunnels, we might be able to find Delea and Mary and them and then we'd all leave together. Then we'd all be safe!"

Her father's eyes grew even wider then as he drew back from her. "No one is safe. Not anymore."

"Then why does it matter?" Fel pleaded. "Why don't we just run?"

"Because they are coming," her father said in a voice that was high and nervous. "I have called and they are coming. All we have to do is open the door!"

"Who is coming?" she asked. "The door to what?"

"The door to let them in!"

"*Who* in?"

He grabbed her by the shoulders again. "I cannot tell you, little Fel, for it would not make sense. I can only show you!"

It didn't make sense. Something was wrong, she could tell. The Oni-er had wanted her to leave her father and to do something else. Now her father wanted to open this "door" instead of leaving with her. She was tired. She was scared.

Then she felt her father wrap his arms around her. Softly, he whispered in her ear. "My little daughter, you've been so brave. We have only a little farther to go, and then I can leave. *We* will leave ... together."

Closing her eyes, she let out the breath that she had been holding. Silently, she prayed to the Silver Lady for guidance. Then she opened her eyes and looked up at her father.

"Okay."

"Lead on, my little Fel," her father whispered.

She aimed her flashlight back down the tunnel as he released her. "I think if we turn right, the next tunnel will take us back toward the palace."

And that's the way they went, trudging through the mud and the muck until they met the portcullis that the Onier had opened only minutes ago. The tunnels were dry here, and less foul, and she heard her father breathe a sigh of relief. At the T intersection, they turned right, back the way Fel had come. The tunnel wound and turned like a snake, just as it had on her way there. However, when they reached a four-way intersection, they stopped. Fel couldn't remember which way she had come. Had it been left, right, or straight on. She shined the beam of her flashlight down each tunnel to see if anything triggered her memory, but nothing did. She had not used her flashlight before, afraid that Delea or the other would see her and catch her. Now that she had her father and his mysterious errand with her, she wished that they would.

Then something winked at her—a light that blinked on and off from the tunnel to her right—just as a ghostly whisper reached her ears.

"Little Sister ..."

Taking her father's hand, she led him on into the right tunnel. A dim light shone ahead, and Fel turned off her flashlight when they came to a stairway.

"Ah…" her father whispered. "This leads up into the garden, if I remember. A secret door behind the vines."

And so it did. The light was from a fixture above the doorway. Her father found a numbered panel along the wall and entered a code. They stepped through the doorway and into a canopy made of vines.

The vines opened up into a courtyard, and there stood a metallic orb as tall as a house. As they approached the strange device, Fel saw it was propped up on a circular base while its outer edge was completely smooth like an egg. Carefully, she reached out to touch it and a tether of static electricity met her finger with a *Zap!* and the sphere *thrummmmmmmed.*

"What is this, Papa?"

"Heh." Her father smiled as his eyes looked up to the cloud covered sky. "A signal, to them."

"To whom?"

"To those who would crush our enemies." Her father looked down at her. "To where do we go?"

Fel sighed. "My room. We need to get to my room."

"Then let us go and be done with it," her father said, and she could see that his face was very sad.

They scurried across the courtyard and through a door into a stairwell. Fel recognized where they were now. They were on the southern wing of the palace. Her room was just around the corner.

Booted footsteps coming down the stairs. Her father grabbed her hand and pushed a door into a hallway. At the far end of the hall were soldiers. One of them immediately pointed and shouted something in a strange language.

Fel gripped her father's hand as they dashed down the hallway together. Second door on the left, right next to her parent's room.

Nothing and everything looked familiar. The wooden dressing cabinet sat along the left wall and to the right, two large windows looked out over the river. A bomb or something had hit the room upstairs, opening a hole in the ceiling and throwing debris all over her bed. Most everything else was still in place, except there was no mirror.

Stepping around the dressing cabinet, she saw no doorway, only a bare wall. There was no doorway there, never had been one.

"Where are we going?" her father asked, his voice in a panic.

Reaching into her coat pocket, she pulled out a piece of the red chalk. She bent down to where the wall met the floor and drew a line straight up, then over, then down again. The Onier had said to return to the first door she had entered. She prayed now that she had heard him right.

The boots were now thundering down the hall. The soldiers would be there in seconds. Beside her, Teum was hopping up and down in fear.

"What are you doing? We're trapped! We're trapped!"

Then the wall morphed, changing color from off-white to a ruddy brown. A doorknob appeared right at a perfect height for Fel. She stepped over, turned it, and was rewarded with a *click*. The door opened with the whine of rusted hinges.

"Hurry!" her father cried.

The hallway door burst to splinters behind them. Fel stepped through the magical door and her father ducked in behind her as the bootsteps came rumbling into the room. As Fel closed the door behind them, it melded back into the wall and disappeared.

ORTHO

It was the dark of the night now and though the stars were hidden in a canopy of low rolling clouds, everything around them was alight with tracer rounds and muzzle flashes and the fiery starbursts of flares hanging in the sky. Carrying the unconscious form of the Consul to the mouth of a darkened alley, Ortho could see his fellow soldiers fleeing before him, running and fighting their way down the muddy riverbank. The deadly ambush at the Sindorum Theater had devolved into a running, mud-drenched gunfight as the survivors of the 88th Column fled down toward the Muirghil.

Now away from the scattered streetlights of the theater, Ortho found the night above them was quickly growing black. The clouds that had hung in the sky for the better part of the evening had finally opened up, producing a pouring rain that slicked the riverbank in mud. The fat droplets were battering Ortho's helmet, providing a steady drumbeat behind the random, violent staccato of the battle around him as he looked down at the riverbank. Everyone in a Coalition uniform was fleeing toward the river. Hefting the man on his back, Ortho jogged across an open yard and dropped down on the grass of a muddy embankment. Before him, he could see men and women who were shot, bleeding, dying as they fought their way down toward the river. But he had a long way to catch up with them. No one still on the hillside was wearing a Coalition uniform. Ortho Andronicus had never been so afraid.

He was afraid of the enemy at his back, for they were raining down gunfire from the hillside like hail. He was afraid of his comrades who were retreating before him, lest they shoot him too, for he knew he looked little different than a shadow at their backs. He was afraid of the Strykers circling above him as they dropped flurries of rockets down on the battle below. He was afraid of another bomb like the one that had collapsed the theater. He was afraid of the crossfire. He was afraid of the ricochets and stray grenades. But mostly he was afraid for the man on his back.

With a heave, Ortho pulled the Consul up the embankment. His feet sliding in the mud, he was able to lean down and reach under Marius armpits to hoist him over top of the ridge and together they slid down the wet grass. A gaping crater greeted them at the bottom of the embankment and Ortho pulled the two of them down inside.

A flare rose into the night with a hiss and a flash, hanging over their heads like a gently falling star. When two more flares rose up next to the first, night became day. Their enemy clearly had a lack of night vision, so they were using whatever they could to level the playing field.

He cursed the Fates and his own bad luck. The bullshit assignment from Major Claudius. The march across the city that had worn his body down and pushed him to the brinks of fatigue. The fact that the entire security platoon, nearly everyone he had made the journey with, was likely dead. The fact that if he simply surrendered, the Duathe would probably kill him and keep the Consul as a prisoner and bargaining chip. The fact that he likely wasn't strong enough to carry the Consul to safety. The fact that he couldn't leave the Consul for fear that the guilt would be worse than any painful death. However, as he lay there at the bottom of the crater, all of those thoughts soon melted away, leaving nothing but the primal instinct of survival.

He heard shouting and footsteps coming behind him, and he clutched his knife to his side as he listened to the *flap-flap-flap* of shoes and sandals running on the concrete. *There must be a sidewalk nearby,* he thought as he tried to count the fighters as they ran past. *Nearly a dozen. How many between us and the river? Can we reach the others? Will there be anyone left alive if we do?*

He lay in the dirt as the footsteps faded. When they were gone, he reached down and checked the Consul for a pulse. *Still alive, still breathing.* Rolling from his stomach onto his back, Ortho grunted when a sharp pain shot up his spine as the muscles on his back spasmed. Everything hurt. His knees felt like they were going to break at any moment. His back was full of knots and needles. His feet had gone numb. He vowed to himself that if he lived through this he would lose thirty pounds and get in better shape—or perhaps he would get fat and do nothing for the rest of his life.

Ortho glanced over the top of the crater and was greeted by the snap of a gunshot and a burst of dirt that flew into his eyes and his nose. He fell back into the crater, brushing the debris from his face as a volley of gunfire peppered the earth above him. *I've been spotted,* he realized. They had seen him the exact moment that he had spotted them, a handful of guerillas that were running along a wall. Clods of dirt were now falling down on top of him as his foes continued to fire. He was trapped.

When the gunfire stopped, he raised his head to peer over the crater's edge. A light shown over the top of the ridge before him, and as he looked, the shadows of men with weapons leapt up and came running toward him. In a panic, he slid back down inside the crater. He had no rifle, no gun to fight them, only his utility knife. Frantically, he searched the Consul's unconscious body for anything and found nothing. He could hear the footsteps now, running straight at him. Desperate, he grabbed his knife again and flicked open the blade. They were almost on top of him now. *I'll kill myself!* he thought, as he readied the blade. *No! I'll surrender! Hopefully, they won't shoot me… but what about the Consul?*

Then a single machine gun ripped through the night as a volley of bullets few over his head and a second later came the *pop-pop-pop* of a rifle behind it. Cries of pain and the several mud-slicked thumps came from where his foes were bearing down on him. One of the men landed with a splat atop the crater's edge, and Ortho grabbed the Consul again by the shoulder straps and pulled him up out of the crater toward the machine gun.

Reaching level ground, he slipped in the mud and fell to his knees. The gunfire had stopped. Looking back, he saw a half-dozen bodies lying in the mud, one of which was twitching and writing on the ground as though in a seizure. Then strong hands grasped him by his shoulders and pulled him to his feet.

"I got you brother," a hoarse voice whispered in his ear.

Once Ortho had found his feet, the other man reached down and grabbed the Consul by the arm and together he and Ortho pulled Marius across the open field and behind a wall. Two other men met them there; the first was a taller man who had a machine propped up atop the wall, the barrel still smoking, while the second, shorter man held a rifle. When Ortho finally pulled Marius up behind the wall, the tall machine gunner looked over at him with a surprised look on his face.

"Ortho, is that you?"

Looking up, Ortho immediately recognized both the tall, rangy machine gunner and the stocky grenadier with whom he had shared his first cigarette not a few hours before. "Horace? Mercos?"

"Shit! Intel!" Mercos stepped over and slapped him on the helmet. "You sonofabitch! How the hell did you make it out of there?"

"I crawled... beneath the concrete..." Ortho started but couldn't finish as a wave of shock and emotion washed over him.

"Andronimoose?" the gravelly voice of the man who had helped him out of the crater came from behind him. "You're a lucky bastard, son. Who you got with you here?"

"I... I..." Ortho's voice caught in his throat for a moment as he recognized Sergeant Major Contus Sulla.

The sergeant major looked over Marius' unconscious form. "Well spit it out, son! I can't recognize him with all this gottamned blood and..." Then the recognition washed over Sergeant Major Sulla's face as his voice fell to a deathly whisper. "By the Fates, it's the Consul."

"We... we were trapped beneath the rubble..." Ortho stammered to explain. "...together and ... I didn't know who he was until I had dragged us both out."

The sergeant major's face was grave as he looked down on Marius' unconscious form. "He looks rough. The head wound's the worst of it that I can see. You done good son, but we'll have to be gentle with him from here if he's to live."

"Roger that, Sergeant Major," Ortho nodded eagerly.

Sulla's glance over to Ortho. "You got a weapon, son?"

Ortho shook his head. "Just my knife, sir."

"Then you can help me carry him." Sulla pointed at the other two soldiers. "Mercos, you got the lead. Horace, watch out backs. Let's get to the other end of the wall." Together, Ortho and Sulla picked the Consul up by his waist and his shoulders. "Gently now, by his shoulder, son, so we keep his head above the rest of him." The flares in the sky were slowly dying as they hefted the Consul between them. Then a spark of lightning burst across the sky and threw blue light across their faces as they crept along the wall. Trudging through the weeds and the mud, they followed the wall halfway down to the river. There, at the end of the brick wall, Ortho and the sergeant major set Marius so he sat with his back against the brick as Mercos and Horace kept watch with their weapons at the ready.

They could hear the guerilla fighters on the other side of the wall, yelling and shouting and shooting wildly as they continued to chase what was left of the 88th down to the river. Then a sound like giant hummingbirds filled the air as a pair of Strykers swung low over the rooftops and the rubble. A loud hissing noise came from the belly of each vessel, launching a flurry of rockets that flew in every direction. One rocket struck a stretch of wall behind them and Ortho flung himself over top the Consul's body as hot pieces of brick spiraled in every direction. Then a fiery explosion lit up the sky.

"Someone's gotten lucky as hell," Sulla murmured.

Looking up, Ortho could see that, indeed, someone had. One of the Strykers was smoking from its rear engines and had thrown itself into a spiral. Spinning, the aircraft flew over a hill and toward the Muirghil. Then Ortho heard a metal shriek as the Stryker crashed in the open field between them and the river.

"By the Fates, we're gottamned lucky that bastard landed in the field and not over here," Sulla grunted as he looked out at the burning hunk of metal lying out in the field. Fiery smoke was pouring out of the destroyed vessel and the wind was carrying the smog down toward the river.

Many of the guerillas were still making their way down from the hilltop where the ruins of the theater sat smoldering in the dark. Ortho could see the foremost of the guerillas were just ahead of them; they had set up along a bunch of abandoned vehicles and were shooting down the hill at a pair of buildings that sat along the river's shore.

"This is a damned opportunity if I ever saw one gents," the sergeant major growled as he pointed toward the buildings along the shoreline. "If we make for that wreck, the smoke can cover us while we make a run for the others." Sulla then gestured to Mercos and Horace. "Now listen, we ain't tryin' to shoot our way down this hill. We make it to that smoke without being spotted and we might be okay, so no shootin' unless they've spotted us. Am I clear, gents?"

Both Horace and Mercos nodded in unison. "Roger, Sergeant Major."

"Now let's get, 'cause the longer we sit, the longer they have to spot us. Andronimoose, you help me pick up our leader here again and we'll be on our way."

Ortho bent down to sling the Consul's arm over his shoulder as the sergeant major did the same. Then they ran. The field was bumpy and the snap and hiss of bullets were all around as they followed Mercos across the grass. Ortho looked back over his shoulder. Most of the rifle fire was coming from a road not more than a hundred yards away. *If we're spotted and anyone up there is an experienced rifleman…* Ortho pushed the thought from his mind.

They were no more than fifty feet away when a series of tiny gasps exploded along the hull of the burning Stryker, throwing light across the field. *That's it, they've spotted us, we're done,* Ortho thought as he jogged toward the wreck. A round whipped through the grass behind him and then two more to his front. Forty feet now, then thirty. The gunfire picked up as more the guerillas spotted them and the field around them was filled with the angry hissing of bullets. Twenty feet. Behind them, Horace unslung his machine gun and sent a burst of fire up the hill. Ten feet, and now they were running into the smoke. Ahead of them, Mercos turned into the black cloud, jogging along the edge of the fire and pushing deeper into the smoke that enveloped the wreck. Ortho and Sulla turned as well, carrying Marius between them, and the black air enveloped them. It reached down into Ortho's lungs and he coughed. A few steps in, they had to slow to a walk. The wreck was between them and their enemies now, and Ortho could hear the bullets ricochet and carom off the hull of the downed Stryker. He could see nothing but black smoke, and his only sense of direction was to keep the Consul between him and the sergeant major as they walked. He coughed again. And again. Then he stumbled as his lungs struggled to find air to breath. Staggering forward, he clung to the Consul's arm, more dragging than carrying him. Then suddenly the smoke began to recede and a wall with the shadow of a doorway appeared before him; they steered toward it. Two soldiers appeared in the doorway, rifles raised.

Beside him, the sergeant major raised up his free hand. "Friendlies! We're friendly, gottammit! Coalition! We have a wounded officer. I need a medic!"

One of the soldiers fired a pair of bursts past Ortho's head as the other stepped forward to help them through the doorway. Soldiers seemed to materialize around him as he stumbled and coughed into the room. Hands reached out from nowhere, and as they took the weight from his shoulders, Ortho fell to his knees on the floor. Dizziness began to overtake him as the adrenaline throbbed in his chest. Something inside of him didn't feel right.

Hands reached down to grab him by the shoulders. Someone picked him up and set him down against the wall.

"Shit son, they hit you."

Everything was spinning. Somewhere in the distance Ortho heard chimes ringing in the air.

FEL

Passing through the door, they re-entered her room—as though they had walked through a mirror and arrived on the other side. Fel found herself wondering how that had happened. Was it because she had used the chalk on a wall instead of the floor or a roof? Or was it simply all random? She couldn't be certain.

Her father was fidgety, anxious, even frightened. Ever since she had found him, her father had been possessed by a nervous energy, but now he seemed ready to bubble over. It wasn't normal fear either—half of him was giddy and excited like a little boy picking at a snapping turtle, while the other half was mad. His fear was not a thing he seemed ready to run from. No, he was running toward it. Whatever it was that had made him so afraid was the same thing he was seeking out.

Now he was looking about the room like a panicked animal.

"Ho! … Ho! …" he cried softly as he hopped about the room. He checked the door. Locked. He checked the window. Locked. He drew the blinds closed. He checked the dressing cabinet, which was open, but held nothing inside but for Fel's clothing and jewelry. "Ho! … Ho! Ho!" he said. "We made it!" He turned to her as his voice got loud. "I thought they had us, but we made it!" Then a look of realization washed over his face as his voice got quiet. "Wait! No … SHHHH … shhhhh!" He held his finger over his mouth as he crouched down next to her. "Do you think they heard me?"

They were both silent then as they listened. Nothing moved and nothing stirred; the only sound that came back to them was an empty house. Then a tremor shook the room, rattling the window and the dressing cabinet.

"Hah!" Her father let out a frightened hiss. "What was that? Did you hear it too?"

Fel nodded.

"Another memory stirs and we should go."

"Where are we going, Papa?"

"Out the door. Out the door, my little girl."

He shooed her gently, like she was an animal or a little child. She did her best to ignore him. Perhaps he just wanted her to walk in front—or perhaps her father really had gone mad. Part of her wanted to wonder what that would mean, but she refused to entertain the thought. Her only goal now was to get them both done and out. Whatever that meant.

She cracked open the door and peeked out. The overlong corridor stretched out before her. The red and gold carpet. The beige-colored walls with the white doorways. The lights that flickered on and off.

"Ha!" Her father laughed as he pulled the door open and danced out into the hallway. "We've made it! We've made it! Here we are! Here we are!"

Fel followed him out, looking up and down the hall as she gently shut the door behind her.

"Oh, don't worry about that." Her father waved at the door like it was an annoying bug. "They can't find us here. They never have! We're safe. This is safe. Now all we have to do is find the door!"

He was dancing down the corridor, travelling to her left, when the lights flickered as everything shook again.

"W-Wh-What?" Her father stopped where he was.

Then a woman screamed from somewhere off to her right. It was not a scream of fear or pain. No, the woman was angry, and now she was yelling. The voice sounded familiar, but the words were muffled through the wall.

"Who was that?" Fel asked.

"Your mother," King Teum replied.

Fel remembered the shouting that she had heard the first time she had crossed over to the Other. Back at the camp. With the Onier.

Turning away from her father, she began walking toward the yelling.

The doorway she found looked no different from any of the others, but when she put her ear to the keyhole, another tremor shook corridor. As the rattling subsided, she heard her mother's voice, cold as ice, speaking from the other side of the door.

"That still does not explain why you shot down the Essex."

The voice that answered belonged to her father, though the man in the corridor with Fel never said a word.

"*Me? I* shot her down? No, my Queen. He was under my orders, this is true, but I did not know of what had happened until after."

"You swear it, my King?"

"I swear it, my Queen."

"Then how do you explain *this*?"

Her parents were fighting—she could hear it in their voices. Her mother was angry and accusing in a tone that she only ever directed at her husband. Fel's father was defensive, but she could hear that he was angry too. And there was something else, Fel thought. There was wariness to her mother's voice—and a simmering rage beneath her father's—that told her this argument was also about something they weren't talking about. Something that had happened before.

She kept her ear to the door for several minutes, but nothing more was said. Then she looked back to her father and told him what she had heard. After he had finished listening to her repeat the story, the nervous energy left him for a moment as his face fell and he looked very sad.

"That ... that is an old tale, my little Fel," King Teum sighed. "An old tale best left alone."

Part of her wanted to obey her father, to just leave it alone. However, the other part was tired of all the mystery. Finally, she reached for the doorknob, but as she did, her father reached out and touched her shoulder.

"Wait."

"Why?"

"Because ... because that is a thing long gone, my daughter. A something that happened long ago, before the war. Nothing that happened then can change what is happening now."

She opened the door anyway.

It was her parents' room. The bed sat along the far wall, and her mother's dresser sat next to a grand bay window with the curtains half drawn. Everything was dressed in blue and red and gold, their royal colors. It looked just at it had been before the war. Before anything bad had happened. Back when they had been a family and everything had been whole.

Only one thing was out of place: A jewelry box lay spilled out on the floor. Fel walked over to it and her father did not stop her, but rather waited in the doorway. She sat down on her haunches and inspected the mess of shining objects. Rings, necklaces, and all manner of jewelry were lying on the carpet, but one thing caught her eye. A bracelet. When she picked it up, she heard her father take in a sharp breath.

Holding the bracelet in her hands, she looked back up to her father to see his face was full of fear. "What was mother talking about? The *Essex*? Was that a ship?"

Her father crossed the room and got down on one knee as he held her by the shoulders. "That was a mistake your father made. A mistake that someone made him do. There are some who blame that mistake for the whole war, but truly this was a war that was coming like the rain. Like it or not."

"But why...?" she started again. "Why was mother so angry with you?"

"Because I had been angry with her." Her father tried to smile, but it still looked like he was sad. "Fel, my little girl, I don't... Your mother, she took you away to keep you safe, and I had to stay behind to lead, but... No, there is too much now, but I promise to explain it all to you. Oh I promise, I promise that I will once we are away from here and we are safe. We will find your sister and your mother too, and we will all be together, I promise."

"You promise, Papa?"

"I promise very much."

Fel considered this as she stared at the floor. Then her father hugged her again. "I will explain it all once we are out of here, my little Fel."

Then something rattled in the hallway like a chain and her father's head snapped around.

"What's that?" he said as he ran back out into the hallway.

Fel stayed where she was, turning the bracelet over in her hands. Its edges were polished smooth, even shiny, except for where the figures were carved. Each figure was intricate, as though they had been carved with a needle. There were seven of them. She could see a man with a bow, and another with a knife. There was a man who held a shovel, and another who held a stringed instrument. The next man was bent over a desk, and another who appeared to be looking up at the stars. The final seventh figure was covered in a cloak.

In that moment, she felt so many conflicting emotions that she could not understand them all. She was sad because her father was sad. She was confused and angry because there was something her father wasn't telling her. But most of all, she was scared because she felt something bad had happened between her parents, something that she did not know.

Then a shadow rose up from the floor as the Onier appeared before her. The Otherling drew its black feathered wings around itself like a cloak as its voice reached out to her like a dying breath.

"So close and yet so far, Little Sister. Why is it that you tarry?"

"Something's not right about my father."

"Ahhhhh…" the Onier sighed.

"Was it you that distracted him?"

"Yes. He must not see us together, for like the others, he would not understand."

Fel arched an eyebrow. "But he *can* see you?"

"He has … seen another like me. But we are not certain. That is why we have sent you here to him. To help him on his way, for he cannot do it alone."

"What is it he's trying to do?" Fel asked.

"He is … fixing … no … working … no …. he is … he is opening a door that has been closed and locked for far too long." The Onier smiled in a way that was almost warm. "Though he does it for his own reasons. He rights a wrong, and when he's done, he will get exactly the things he is looking for."

"And what about me?"

The Onier blinked its golden, smoke-filled eyes. "And what about you?"

"What about me? I want everyone back together," she said firmly. "I want our family back to the way it was."

The Onier smiled again. "If everything goes as we have it planned, your mother will be safe with your father and all will be well."

Finally, Fel nodded. She thought she understood, at least as well as she could understand anything that was happening. Ignoring the uneasy feeling in the pit of her stomach, she slipped the bracelet into her coat pocket and left it there.

The Onier disappeared in a wisp of smoke just as her father came rushing back into the room.

"Don't worry, my little Fel," her father said as he stooped down to hug her. "It was only the knocker on the throne room door. But it's all still locked. I checked. No one can get in there but us. Now can you come and open the door for your father?"

She nodded and he released her from his embrace. Reaching into her coat pocket, Fel pulled out the ring of keys that they had retrieved from the gatehouse.

"Where is it?" she asked.

He pointed out into the corridor. "At the very end."

The corridor was longer than a city block, and every step of the way Fel wondered if they would see the ghostly doppelgangers jump out of a doorway to grab them. But none of them did.

It was a double doorway painted royal red with gold and silver inlays. Fel remembered that the door always had a pair of guardsmen. Now, as she fitted the key to the keyhole, there was only the echo of the latch.

As Fel entered the room, the echo of her footsteps mixed with the burning torches. The throne room was packed with people—some were small, but some were giants that loomed over her, throwing their flickering shadows all around them. For a moment, Fel froze in place as her father shut the door behind them, but when the people around her did not move either, she realized that they were not actually people. They were statues.

She had visited the palace throne room a great many times growing up, but she had never seen it quite like this. Tapestries, thickly woven with red and gold dye, hung from every wall. A carpet, also red and gold split the center of the stone floor from the dais of the throne to the giant double doors at the front of the hall. It was like someone was playing dress up and had redecorated the palace as though it were two thousand years ago when everyone was riding around on horses.

And everywhere there were the statues. Next to her was a statue of a woman dressed in rags, and behind her stood a little boy that could have been her son. Beside a pillar stood an old man, carved from marble, dressed in robes and his head adorned with a wreath. Beyond him was an empty suit of armor next to a man kneeling in prayer. Walking further into the room, she passed a gardener or a farmer (she wasn't sure which), and then a woman in a dress and a man holding a sword.

"Ah…" Her father stepped up beside a statue wearing a crown. "We've made it, my little Fel. Tell me, what do you see?"

"The throne room?" she answered, wondering if that's really what it was. "But it's like it's … old. Like we're looking at it from the past, or something."

"Heh, perhaps. Perhaps you are."

"Where did all these statues come from?"

"I don't know," her father answered. "The important thing is that we are here, and we are here because we are meant to be."

Stepping between two stone pillars, Fel followed her father to the carpet at the center of the room.

"And why are we here?" she asked.

"To open something else."

The dais of the throne was flanked by three statues—two to the left and one to the right. First on the left was a creature with the body of a lion but the head and wings of an eagle. Behind that was a statue of an ox made of bronze, but Fel could see that the metal was tarnished and dulled so that there was no shine to it. On the right was a statue of a woman carved from gray stone, dressed in robes, with her arms outstretched and her face looking up toward the heavens.

"Papa, what are these statues for?"

Her father stopped and put a hand on the ox's horns. "I don't know, my little Fel. I don't know."

Jumping two steps at a time, King Teum climbed the dais to the throne and then touched the chair on the arm. As if triggered, two dozen candles appeared behind the throne and lit to life, flames jumping from the wicks as they caught fire. Her father jumped back as the flames receded, simmering down from blue to yellow. Then he laughed like it was all a joke, looking down at Fel and then back up at the silver-bound chair.

"Papa, be careful!" she pleaded.

"Don't worry. We need only to find how to open the doorway and then we can be on our way, my daughter."

Open the doorway… Open the doorway to what? she wondered as she watched her father staring at the flames. Something seemed wrong, like this was a trap, or like they were trespassing, or something—she didn't know what it was, but her father seemed happy … or was he nervous? She couldn't really tell.

Absently, she began looking around the room, searching the faces of the statues for anything that might be a clue. She walked past a man sitting on a chair, holding a fishing pole; another where two children were playing with a ball. The statues did not seem to be arranged in any particular order. They were simply strewn about the room, some in groups of four and five, while others sat alone.

She was walking along the back wall behind the throne when she spotted a man hunched over with his face in his hands as if he were weeping. Something about him seemed out of place. Walking closer, she saw that there was. In his right hand he held a scroll, only the scroll wasn't made of stone. It was made out of paper.

"Papa!" she cried out, pointing to the statue of the weeping man.

"Ha!" her father exclaimed as he leapt off the dais. Walking over to the statue, he plucked the scroll out of the statue's hand and inspected it. The parchment was brownish-gray but thick and bendable, as though it were still new, and holding it closed was a seal of red wax.

"The Scroll of the Weeper," her father said with baited breath.

Something grabbed a hold of her stomach as she watched her father hold the scroll up toward the torchlight, turning it over in his hands, his eyes full of fevered excitement. She felt frozen in place as her father carried the scroll over to the dais of the throne. Something did not feel right, like the room was a puzzle and a piece was now out of place. As she watched her father inspecting the seal, Fel suddenly wanted her mother to be there. And then suddenly she was.

The double doors at the far end of the throne room creaked open, and in stepped her mother. Beside her stood a man made of shadow. Queen Anyse stepped forward on the red and gold carpet, and as she pushed back the hood of her cloak, the torchlight caught the silver of her hair and highlighted the lines on her face.

"Teum... What are you doing, and why is our daughter here?"

Hearing the voice, the King looked up from his parchment to meet his wife's icy gaze. Then he held the scroll up like a scepter. "You're too late, Anyse. I've found it."

"TEUM!" the Queen cried. "NO!"

Beside her, the shadowy man made to cross the room.

"Heh," the King smiled as he broke the seal.

A pit opened up between them as the floor between the dais and the door fell away, trapping the gray man on the far side of the room. Fel watched in shock as the bricks and nearly all of the statues dropped silently down into a starry blackness. In less than a second, the chasm stretched from wall to wall, and suddenly there was no way to cross the room.

The Queen was in shock. "My husband, what have you done?"

Then a great sound rose from the pit. Trumpets blared, a cacophony of noise as each horn—Fel had no idea how many—sounded a different note. She covered her ears, but the noise split through her skull. The chaotic harmony slowly slid together as each trumpet changed its tuning, and soon they were all in unison, sounding the same note before one by one they fell away. For a second, the room was silent.

Then light and smoke and sound and music came pouring out of the pit, blowing the roof off the room and exploding into the sky. A rush of wind followed in its wake, pushing Fel back up against the stone steps of the dais. She could only sit helplessly, shielding her eyes from the smoke and light and exploding fireworks of all colors as the maelstrom poured out of the pit and rose up through the ceiling and into the sky. Her father, who still held the scroll in one hand, stood frozen at the edge of the pit, his free hand held up over his eyes. Then, as suddenly as it had arrived, the maelstrom ended, its tail disappearing into the starry night above just as the wind and the music left with it.

Looking across the room, Fel saw that a dozen of her black-haired doppelgangers had appeared by the door and they were fighting against the man made of shadow. The gray-man now held a black-bladed weapon in his hands as he stabbed one girl in the belly and then slashed at another. He was standing his ground over the body of the Queen, who lay comatose on the floor. He had already beheaded one of the monsters, and the dead girl's gray-black eyes stared back at Fel from across the chasm.

Beside her, Fel could hear her father laughing hysterically.

Then a shadow rose out of the pit and Fel's heart caught in her throat when she saw what it was. Black feathered wings uncurled and the Otherling's gold, smoke-filled eyes looked down on them with glee.

"Ah..." the Onier's voice thundered like an avalanche. "*By the pricking of my thumbs, something wicked this way comes...*"

Fel looked at her father as his body twisted in a spasm, the scroll falling from his hands. She jumped up from the stone and leapt toward him. Everything seemed to happen in slow motion. Her father shook with laughter as the scroll tumbled from his hands. He reached out for him as she ran across the floor, and just as her fingers brushed the edge of his cloak, the claws of the Onier closed around him and pulled him down into the pit. And just like that, her father was gone.

"Father!" she cried as her fingers grasped the empty air.

A shudder shook the room, and the bricks of the wall rattled like coins in a pocket. Fel looked across the room, over the pit, to where a dozen copies of her dead body lay strewn about the floor. There, at the other edge of the pit, her mother lay in the arms of the man made of shadow. She looked like a damsel who had fainted, lying in the arms of the man made of fuzzy nothingness.

"Mother!" she cried as a second quake shook the room again, and then everything began to fall apart.

The walls on the right and left side fell apart first, the bricks crumbling and falling away as though they were blocks of hollow wood, carrying the torches down into the blackness below. Looking across the pit, she saw the shadow man look once back at her before he carried her mother out the double doorway.

Just as the room was falling apart, it was also growing dark. Many of the torches had fallen away with the bricks. Looking up toward the throne, Fel could see the candles behind the dais were winking out one by one, like a ghost was blowing them out. She looked back behind her just in time to see the dais falling apart behind her feet. Scrambling up the steps as they broke apart behind her, she reached the silver throne and climbed atop the seat. Looking out, she could see the towering wooden double doorway breaking apart, board by board, and when her eyes searched for her mother or her shadowy companion, she found only empty darkness.

Her feet on the padded seat of the throne, Fel slumped against its back. Not knowing what else to do, as her mind began to give in to despair, she felt something small and fuzzy climb on to her shoulder.

A Kotling!

When she turned her head, the Kotling leapt off her shoulder and onto the back of the throne and then scurried down behind the chair. Behind her, the bricks of the dais were falling apart one by one. Quickly, she climbed off the chair and slipped around behind the throne to where the Kotling had scurried down to the mouth of a fist-sized hole at the base of the wall. The small, fuzzy Otherling stopped to look back up at her and chirp. Behind her on the dais, the throne itself was being eaten away, disintegrating into a trail of silvery dust floating away into the aether.

The Kotling chirped again, this time toward her arm, and then Fel finally understood. Pulling the bone bracelet from her coat pocket, she slipped her hand through the bone ring and slid it up her arm to where it fit above the elbow. As she pulled her sleeve back down, she noticed the room around her began to bend and warp.

The hole below her was growing larger, and the Kotling with it, swelling up like distorted reflections of themselves before returning to their normal shape. Then she noticed the throne beside her was growing too, and that's when she realized that things weren't growing around her, she was shrinking. Soon she was no bigger than a nail, and she ran towards the hole in the wall, which was now like a door that she could run right through. She leapt over a crevasse between the bricks and then glanced over her shoulder to see the cushioned back of the throne disintegrating and falling away into dust. Reaching the mouth of the hole, which she could see was actually a tunnel, Fel saw the Kotling bend its knees as it lowered its furry head. The Kotling was now, to her, as big as a bear, and she grabbed its furry side and jumped up, throwing her leg over its back and grabbing the fur on the nape of the beast's neck. Behind them, the last of the throne was falling apart, the shards spiraling upward into the darkness. Fel could see the last few bricks of the floor were crumbling away. The Kotling raised its head and, with an excited hop, spun itself around and galloped down into the tunnel.

ATTICUS

They landed so close to the shore that Atticus could hear the water rushing behind him when he ran down the ramp. Scattered gunfire was whipping through the air as the Strykers rose back up into the air. His soldiers had gotten off their Stryker last and as the heavy infantry advanced before him, Atticus counted the shadowy shapes that were his. Twenty-three, twenty-four when he counted himself. He had begun the day with twenty-seven. He wondered how many of them would get through the next hour.

Atticus looked around for his platoon sergeant and found the barrel-chested man near the center of their formation. "Sergeant Jonas! Are we up?"

Jonas raised his thumb into the air. "Ready up, sir!"

Atticus gave the signal to move forward, and Assassin platoon rose to their feet. The snap and hiss of sporadic gunfire sounded all around them as they hurried behind the line of heavy infantry ahead of them. The towering black silhouettes in their dulled black and gray armor were marching through the weeds and the gunfire in a pair of columns so tight that they looked like a moving fence. *We have to get ahead of them if I'm going to find my father.* Something deep inside of him was uneasy. He was uneasy about the callous way that Major Ioma had spoken of this ambush. He was uneasy about how few men were sent to his father's rescue. And he was uneasy about the task before him.

Atticus broke off into a run, waving for his men to follow, and follow they did, racing past the platoon of heavies who kept walking at a march, their power-armor humming and whirring as they moved.

Atticus aimed for a doorway in the nearest of the two buildings, and he lowered his shoulder and burst through it like a battering ram. Loomin's squad came in hot on his heels. As they cleared the first floor, Atticus turned around to shout orders at the rest.

"Mako, set up bases of fire to the north and the east. Raef, clear the second floor. Clarke, clear third and get your long rifles onto the roof." He stayed near the doorway as his soldiers flooded past him, and he could hear their footsteps echoing through the building as they carried out his orders. The last man through the door was Jonas, and his platoon sergeant took a knee next to him with a sigh and a grunt.

"My back hurts, sir."

"I'm sorry to hear that," Atticus said in his most ironic tone. "Are you going to make it?"

"I don't know," Jonas grunted again as he adjusted his body armor. "Can we go home after this?"

"Only if we're surrounded, overwhelmed, and killed."

"Well shit."

Sergeant Mako's voice came to him over the radio to tell him that first squad was set, and Atticus and Jonas both made their way down the hall to the front of the building. The gaunt squad leader met them at the end of the hall and gestured to a window. "It's quite the scene out there, sir."

Atticus stepped forward to look out at the hill before them. Minutes earlier, he had gone against Major Ioma's orders to stay with the 5th Armored Column as it pushed toward the Sindorum Royal Palace. Instead, Atticus had stowed away his platoon aboard a Stryker bound for the riverbank where his father, the Consul, and the 88th Column had been waylaid and overrun by a horde of Duathic guerillas. Looking out the window, he saw an open field, no more than a hundred yards long, before it turned upward and rose up into a wide, flat hillside. A road lined with craters and fires and burned out vehicles wound down toward them; scattered walls and fences and a few ruined houses flanked the street to either side, and above everything was the burning ruin of the theater where the ambush had begun. All down the hillside were the sights and sounds of battle—tracer rounds and explosions and men shouting and screaming and dying.

"Sir? How long until the rest of the column arrives to back us up?" Mako asked.

Atticus exchanged knowing glance with Jonas. He could see Mako's squad was spread out across several rooms, their eyes and their weapons aimed out the windows to the north and the east. No one was shooting—all were still. Atticus sighed and tuned back to Mako. "I'm afraid they're not."

Mako raised an eyebrow. "So, we're being extracted?"

Atticus sighed again. "I'm not sure."

Mako considered this for a moment and then nodded casually. "We'll hold them as long as we can, sir."

Then a hard sound struck the sky and Atticus looked up to see a Stryker spiraling through the air in a chaotic descent until it crashed in the field before them, and the ground shuddered from the impact. Atticus stared at the fiery hulk sitting there, burning in the middle of the field until a rocket came hissing at them through the dark.

"INCOMING!" someone shouted, and Atticus crouched down inside a hallway as the rocket struck the outer wall. A hail of gunfire followed, coming at them from the hillside above, and a mad minute followed as his men fired back. Tracers and muzzle flashes filled the air. Atticus ran up to a doorway and fired several rounds at the house that the rocket had been launched from. He saw a group of shadows run out from behind a wall to his right, but before he could turn to aim, they were immediately cut down by one of Mako's machine gunners. Next, he saw a head poke out from behind a car on the road. Atticus raised his weapon, but then a single rifle shot from the roof sent the head snapping back and then flopping to the earth. As he looked for something else to shoot, the gunfire suddenly died away as quickly as it had begun, and they were all left kneeling on the concrete of the empty building, looking out at the hillside which had suddenly gone dark and still.

Jonas appeared beside him. "They know where we are now, sir. Both sides."

Atticus nodded, never taking his eyes off the hillside. He wondered how many of their foes were up there, and how many of their own. He knew that the commander of this rescue force was Captain Arakin, a man who had borne him nothing but ill will so far. Because he and his men had snuck in on this mission, Atticus had been purposefully avoiding the man so far, hoping his platoon could go unnoticed for as long as possible. However, this also meant that Atticus had no idea if the scar-faced captain planned on holding here or if he would assault his way up the hill in an attempt to search for survivors. He knew that the heavy infantry they had followed from the shore had occupied the building next to them, but wherever Arakin was now, Atticus could only guess.

A door opened behind him.

"Sir! Lieutenant Atticus? Where's the Lieutenant?"

Atticus turned to see Thrace burst into the room, and he raised his hand so the radioman could see him.

"Sir! Your father! The Consul! He's been found! Alive!" Thrace waved for him to follow. "Vansa has him now, sir!"

Following Thrace, he ran to the next room where he found Vansa, his medic, and another soldier hoisting his father's unconscious form onto a stretcher. Atticus took a knee next to the stretcher and looked over to his medic. "How is he?"

"If I had a saw, I'd cut that damn thing right off." The blonde medic ripped open the Consul's right pant leg, exposing an ugly, purple colored thing that was bruised with splotches of blood trapped beneath the skin. She frowned and pointed to the thigh muscle above the knee. "It should really come off right here, sir. Wait much longer and it's going to be worse than that. A lot worse."

Atticus sat down on his haunches and rested his rifle against his knees as he studied his father's unconscious form. Gunfire echoed through the walls behind him as Mako's squad exchanged fire with their enemies on the hillside.

"Do what you can for now, Vansa. Thrace is calling for a medivac now," Atticus answered. "How did he get here?"

Vansa gestured to the next room. "He was carried in. Sexton and Graide are looking to the others right now. The one guy passed out and the other has a leg wound of some kind, but the others appear to be fine."

Atticus looked out the window at the field before them where the burning hulk of the downed Stryker lay smoldering in the grass of the riverbank. The building shuddered again as a rocket struck. A lone rifle on the rooftop sounded twice in response, and Atticus knew that one of Clarke's snipers had struck down another of their assailants.

Atticus looked back over his shoulder. "How far out is our medivac?"

Thrace, his wiry radioman, was huddled in the corner with his eyes closed and his hands pressed against his headset. One eye shot open as he heard Atticus. "I'm listening now, sir. *Unifier* keeps asking about the Queen's transport, which must have crashed or something. Everyone on the ground is trying to make sense of what's happening here on the riverbank. There seems to be some confusion as to where we are, sir."

That's it. The game is up, but at least I found him. "Tell them that's because we aren't where we're supposed to be. Tell them I went against my orders and that we're on the riverbank."

Thrace opened both eyes wide then and he blinked hard as he replied, "Yes sir."

Atticus let out a breath he did not know he had been holding as he looked back down at his father. Arcos Marius had always been an imposing man, but to his son and only child, Marius had seemed a mountain, great and distant. However, the image of his father now, his head bleeding and his arm and leg mangled, was surreal and terrifying. Here on the stretcher, his father's unconscious body seemed unreal, a body double, a fake, a mannequin.

Atticus had disobeyed orders to come here, essentially stowing away his entire platoon on board a Stryker to do so, risking court martial and possibly jail. But his father, Arcos Marius, Consul of the Republic, was alive. And if he could get his father aboard a medivac in the coming hour, Atticus would make peace with whatever punishment came.

He turned again to Vansa. "Is he stable enough to move?"

The blonde-haired medic shook her head as she pulled out a splint from her aid bag. "His leg was crushed by something and his arm might be worse, but I've stabilized the head and the spine…" Her voice trailed off in thought until finally she nodded. "But yes, I think we can move him. Where are we going?"

He gestured to Thrace. "Have the medivac pick us up on the roof."

"Yes sir," the radioman nodded.

He and Vansa lifted his father's stretcher and carried him down the hallway. Passing through the next room, Atticus shouted for his platoon sergeant as they passed. "Jonas! You're in charge until I return."

"Yes sir!" Jonas shouted back.

They entered another hallway, Atticus at the front of the stretcher and Vansa at the rear. Turning right, he pushed through a double doorway and into the main hall of the building. It was an oval shaped room with six pillars that rose up to a high, domed ceiling. At the center of the room stood an impressive stone fountain with a statue of the Duathe's blind goddess.

Both he and Vansa were breathing heavily as they reached the stairs and Atticus decided they would rest for a moment before braving the ascent. Setting the stretcher down, he and Vansa both took a knee and caught their breath. It was then that he saw his father's eyes flutter.

"Huuaaggghhh!" the Consul gasped in fear and surprise as his eyes flew open. Eyes wide in shock, his father looked about the room. "Where? ... The roof! Agrippa!"

Atticus leaned down next to his father. "My Consul ... Father. Agrippa's not here. It's just me and Vansa, my medic."

His father's eyes found his face and his look of confusion deepened. "There ... it was a trap. They knew ... but how?" Then Marius gasped again and closed his eyes as his face tremored in pain. "I ... I have ... you must listen ..." The Consul's eyes opened again and looked straight to Atticus. "Listen, Lieutenant. Listen Atticus ..."

The world shuddered twice as a pair of explosions rocked the outer shell of the building. Simultaneously, the gunfire in the adjacent rooms became a chorus of fire and lightning.

"I have ... I have ..." Marius' voice trailed off as he looked up at Atticus and shook his head. "I have great doubts ... great doubts about you and them and so many other things..."

Atticus lowered his head. "I'm sorry, Father. The medivac is nearly here; we have to get you up to the roof..."

"No!" Marius shouted. "That's not..." He let out a long breath, and his eyelids began to grow heavy, fluttering open and shut. "I have doubts about..."

In that moment, it was hard for Atticus to look his father in the eyes. What was he saying? What was he trying to say? What did he mean by 'doubts'? Atticus could see a wild energy, something close to fear, washing behind his father's eyes as they searched the room. Then a hand snapped out and grabbed Atticus by the collar, pulling him close to his father's face.

"Listen!" Marius gasped. "If they come ... if they come for us, you must be ready. You must be ready to face them. Show no hesitation, no doubt, no weakness, or they will strike you down. Show them strength and they will flee."

Before Atticus could answer, his father's eyes fell as he drifted off into unconsciousness. Beside him, Vansa quickly reached up to the Consul's neck and nose to check his vitals.

"Still breathing, sir. Heartbeat is the same." She looked up at him, her blue eyes like watered glass. "He should make it, sir."

As he and Vansa were picking up the stretcher, the doors behind them burst open as a pack of heavy infantry swarmed into the room. Atticus and Vansa could only stand aside as the soldiers stomped past in their power-armor. An officer stood at the center of the room, shouting orders in a mechanized voice as half of the heavies marched out a back door while the other half branched out to climb the stairs toward the roof. None of them even gave Atticus or Vansa a second glance.

When the room was nearly empty, Atticus grabbed the stretcher's handles. "Let's go," he said softly, "before anyone can stop us." Vansa quickly picked up her end of the stretcher and, with his father between them, they followed the last group of heavies up the stairs.

If they come for us... His father's words echoed in his mind as he climbed the stairs. Who was he talking about? The Duathe, or someone else? Atticus wasn't sure. He glanced behind him to see Vansa holding the handles of the stretcher above her head to keep his father's body level. Behind her was the black shadow of a heavy infantry officer in his mechanized armor, stomping up the stairwell behind him. *I wonder if that's Arakin, or just one of his juniors.*

Gunfire and rain met them on the rooftop. The blood was pounding in Atticus' ears as he and Vansa took cover behind a rusted water tank. They sat there gasping for their breath as they got their bearings. Somewhere up here was Assassin platoon's sniper section, Clarke and Marin and the others. However, everywhere Atticus looked, all he could see were soldiers in black and gray power-armor who occupied every corner of the roof.

Beside him, Vansa was leaned over his father's stretcher to check the man's vitals.

"He still okay?" he asked, and she nodded quickly in response.

A black shadow emerged from the stairwell door. Atticus couldn't see the man's rank, but as the officer removed his helmet, Atticus could see the scar running down the man's face.

"Lieutenant Atticus Marius," Captain Arakin's voice oozed with anger and contempt.

"Yes sir," Atticus stood to face the captain and he could see the scar on the other man's face burning with rage.

"Listen here, you selfish, shit-for-brains *child...*" Arakin's eyes were full of spite and hate as he jammed a gauntleted finger into Atticus' chest. "I have never in my career heard of someone pulling this kind of stunt. You were ordered to stay with the column, and instead you jumped on board one of my birds against orders and without my knowledge. I just got off the radio with Commander Ioma, and you've made me look the fool for the last time, you entitled little punk. Not only is this op no place for a light infantry platoon, but your light-fighters are endangering my men with their very presence. We're surrounded here at least two-to-one, and perhaps even twice that. I want your team off my roof. I want your platoon out of my building. And I order the lot of you to the back of this formation in the safest, darkest place you can find. And that order is effective immediately."

Arakin's face was practically smoldering with anger at this point, and Atticus had made sure to keep his own expression as neutral as possible, lest the man pull a gun on him. When the captain was done, Atticus rubbed his eyes, gave a glance at the cloudy sky, and then turned back to Arakin.

"I'll gladly do all of that, sir, as soon as I get this wounded man on the next bird out of here."

Without looking down at the stretcher, Arakin jammed his gauntleted finger into Atticus' chest. "I don't care who the fuck it is, you're leaving him here with me. No questions asked, or I relieve you of your command and arrest you on the spot, Lieutenant."

Frowning sadly, Atticus shook his head. "I'm afraid I can't do that, sir."

Arakin's face flew into a rage and then tuned back over his shoulder as he shouted out a command. "COMPANYYYYY!"

Together as one, the dark and metallic shapes of the heavy infantry stood and converged on the four of them by the water tank.

Behind him, Vansa's hand went to her rifle. "Sir?"

Atticus put his hand on her arm. "Just wait, Doc."

When Atticus raised his head, a dozen heavy rifles were aimed in their direction. Captain Arakin's face was twisted into a scowl. "You will relinquish your weapon NOW, Lieutenant."

Atticus kept his hand on the pistol grip of his rifle. "I'm afraid I can't do that, sir."

A tremor passed across Arakin's face before he bellowed, "COMPANYYYYY!"

Several of the rifles went from being aimed at his chest to his head. From the corner of his eye, he saw Vansa lean over to shield his father. Atticus stood still and firm, his face a blank slate.

"STAND DOWN, CAPTAIN!"

The voice echoed in the dark and nearly half the soldiers lowered their rifles as Arakin twisted around.

"Who said that?" the captain bellowed.

"I did," the stocky form stepped out of the doorway and onto the roof. "And my name is Sergeant Major Contus Sulla, sir. And in case you haven't heard of me, I'm the mother-fucker who rides alongside the Consul. Be aware, *sir*, that you are standing over the comatose body of your own Consul, Arcos Marius, and so I suggest you measure your next words as carefully as you can." The stocky man waded up to stand toe-to-toe with the taller Arakin. "Now why in the HELL, in the middle of a combat op, do you got your weapons pointed at your fellow soldiers, *sir*?"

Sulla let the last "sir" hang in the air. Arakin scowled as he looked down at the unconscious form of Consul Marius lying on the stretcher.

For a moment, it looked as though Arakin would yield right there. Instead, he turned his scowl back toward the shorter man as he replied in a voice cool and calm. "Lieutenant Atticus Marius disobeyed his commander's direct order and stowed away with my mission, all so that he could kidnap the Consul, for the Fates know what reason. I am arresting him and placing both him and his soldier here under guard."

"You will do no such thing, Captain. Now I might not got rank on you, son, but if you lay one hand on that boy's head, so help me by the graces of Fate, I will see to it so the powers that be bury your career so far down the shitter that you won't be able to find it with a sump pump and a scuba tank. Now get your men back into position, Captain. We got a gottamned fight on our hands here."

Arakin glowered again as he heard this, but Sergeant Major Sulla did not flinch and, in fact, inched closer to the towering man with a pair of stocky steps. Then a pair of rockets struck the outer lip of the roof, spewing fire and smoke and everyone around Sulla and Arakin ducked and covered, but neither man flinched. Shards of concrete flew past as the two men continued to stare each other down. Then, as Atticus picked himself up from shielding his father yet again, he finally saw Arakin bite his lower lip and step away.

"COMPANY STAND DOWN!" Arakin shouted as he pushed past his own men and then aimed his gauntleted hand at the opposing hillside. "The enemy will be upon us soon. Back to your positions, men!"

The crowd of heavies dispersed, their armor whirring and humming as they hustled and jogged back to their positions. Atticus watched as Arakin's dark form stomped away across the rooftop.

Several volleys of enemy gunfire flew at them from the opposing hillside, the tracer rounds burning through the air like fiery ropes. Atticus looked up at Sulla—a man whom he had hardly spoken to—and tried to think of what to say, but his voice caught in this throat. Instead, it was the sergeant major who spoke first.

"I don't know how you got here, son, but I'm glad you did." Sulla looked down at the unconscious Marius. "I'm sure we both are."

Then Vansa spoke up from behind him. "Sir! There's our ride!"

Atticus looked up to see three angular shadows flying over the

Muirghil. As the aircraft reached a bend in the river, Atticus saw them turn and aim straight toward their rooftop. He sighed in relief. *Our Strykers have finally arrived.*

Then an arc of lightning shot down from the sky, and for a moment, the night turned into day as the earth shuddered. A tremor shook them where they stood. Looking up again, Atticus saw that the night sky was full of black, rolling clouds that suddenly were swirling about into a vortex. His jaw dropped as he watched a wave of lightning roll across the twisting eddy in the sky.

And then the earthquake hit.

The building beneath them shook like a tuning rod and everyone was thrown from their feet. Atticus managed to crawl to the stretcher and fasten two safety straps over the top of his father's unconscious form before the shaking became too intense and he had to fling himself over the top Marius and cling to the metal poles beneath the canvas.

A sound like stone breaking echoed through the air, and Atticus looked south to watch the river's shoreline split open like a wound as the Muirghil rushed into the crevasse. Still clinging to his father and the stretcher, he threw out his legs and wrapped them around a pipe of the rusted water tank. He saw Vansa grab hold of the stairway door as the wall of the roof broke apart behind her. Another tremor rumbled across the riverbank, and then there was a mighty crash as Atticus watched the building next to them collapse into pieces. Finally, the quake ebbed and faded away, and then all was stillness and the only sounds were his frantic breathing and the echoes that bounced between the remaining buildings.

No one moved. He looked to the river again but the Strykers were nowhere to be seen. He checked his father again. Still a heartbeat. Still breathing. Slowly, cautiously, the soldiers around him began to move. Vansa pulled herself up to her knees and looked over him. He gave her a thumbs up, and she nodded as she walked over and took cover with him behind the water tank.

Then the palace hill exploded.

They saw the flash before the sound. A white-hot beam of light that rose above where the palace was supposed to be. Then came a deafening impact like a meteor striking the earth and everything around him shook like dry bones in a grave. Finally, a brightness broke out of the earth, a white light without heat, and Atticus had to close his eyes and turn away as something broke from the earth with an inhuman shriek.

TAYLOR

They were flying high above the valley, circling the dark shadow of Mount Chernon and running passive scans on the battle below. Night had crept over Sindorum and Taylor had watched the shadows of Coalition tanks driving over a tall, white bridge that crossed the river and lead into the heart of the city. On her last pass, she'd spotted the tanks' insignia. The 5th Armored Column. Her lover Gaius Ioma's unit. That felt like a day ago now, and so she checked the clock on her dash. Still two hours of patrol left. She sighed in boredom.

A nasty bit of fighting had broken out along the riverbank. She couldn't understand why Ioma would have pushed his armor so far ahead of the fighting along the river, but that was why she was in the air and he was on the ground. The outskirts of the city were quiet. The valley was quiet. She called Shale to tell him they'd be making a wide loop around their area. A wide, *slow* loop.

Unifier called to tell her that their relief was behind schedule. Something about a malfunction with *Unifier's* launch tube. *Just great,* she thought as she looked down at the peaked shadows of the Blackfriars. *By the time they get here, we'll have just enough fuel to get back to orbit, let alone anything else that might come up.*

Passing around the northern end of the valley, Taylor saw a pair of blips cross her sensors. Aerelli and Brannon, her two rookies straight out of the academy on their first cycle of patrols. Perhaps she and Shale could switch zones with them, let the kids at least look at the battle. If anything, Taylor thought, it would give her something different to look at. Half an hour later, they flew clear of the mountain range where the blue-black waters of the Bay of Sardis stretched out below them.

"Hey One? What the hell is that?"

She looked behind them. Mount Chernon was erupting.

Taylor turned the *Wyvern* and gunned her engines back toward Sindorum. Now facing the phenomenon, she could see that it wasn't lava shooting out of the mountainside—it was light and electricity. Racing over the water, Taylor could see that everything from the edge of the valley to the bay was lit up like daylight, as a pillar of pyrotechnics was bursting forth from the center of the city.

And then suddenly it wasn't.

The lightshow died just as they reached the shoreline, and the blanket of night fell over the valley once again. The eruption had lasted all of ten seconds. Flying once around the mountain, they crossed over the city again to see the pyrotechnics had been replaced by a swirling maelstrom of black and grey.

Now it was her turn to call Shale in wonderment. "Two, are you getting this?"

Shale's reply was immediate. "I'm sending a live feed to *Unifier* as we speak. They're probably as stunned as we are."

Taylor slowed the *Wyvern* down to its slowest possible speed as she circled the city. The black swirling mass of clouds were hanging low over the heart of the city. Flipping through her sensor readouts, she tried to make sense of what was causing the phenomena. Infrared told her the clouds were orbiting a single heat source. She flipped to sonar to see a single mass sitting at the storm's center.

She called Shale. "You see this, Two?"

"I sure do. And so does *Unifier*. They've been trying to call it ever since they spotted it."

"Has it answered?"

"No."

Well then what the hell is it? She flipped her radio to *Unifier's* channel and gave them a call. Keep a visual. Monitor and report. She told the ensign to get Admiral Thorus on the line and was rewarded with a more satisfactory response.

"Rapier One, you are free and clear to destroy anything that resembles a threat to either you, our ground forces, or the civilian population. Is that clear? Over."

"Loud and clear," Taylor replied. Flipping channels, she called Shale again. "Let's take another lap, Rapier Two."

She needed to collect her thoughts. They were flying wide around the far side of the valley when she found herself calling her wingman again. "I feel more useless than normal Two. Any ideas?"

The radios were silent as they flew back toward the city. A minute later, Shale finally answered, "Let's call it and ask it what it wants."

"I thought we tried that," she answered.

"Top did," Shale called back. "We haven't."

"Do you speak fireball?" she mused.

"No."

"Then I say that if it gets a safe distance away from the city, we shoot the damn thing and have the eggheads up in Intel send a team to pick up the pieces."

Shale laughed into the mic. "That works too."

They flew around the bay again as Taylor called their secondary patrol and filled Aerelli and Brannon in on the situation. When they neared the shore again, they found the swirling mass of darkness was climbing its way up the side of Mount Chernon. Almost lazily, it crested the mountain and dipped over to its backside as an avalanche of snow fell from the peak and poured harmlessly down toward the bay. When she saw it again, the smoke and mist had fallen away, revealing a black and indigo ball of flame.

She called her wingman. "Here's our chance."

Her targeting computer had no trouble drawing a lock on the thing's heat signature. She flipped the safety off her trigger and launched a pair of Halberd missiles just as Shale did the same. The floating black mass of shadow stopped as if it realized something was coming and it turned, facing the missiles. Then it flew right at them. With blazing speed, the black shadow struck all four missiles consecutively in a chain of four explosions that disappeared into thin air, like a vacuum had sucked them up. The only thing left was the black ball of shadowflame floating in the air, staring at her as she flew by.

And it was staring at her. Of that she was now certain. She could see something akin to a face or an eye, a faint red and blue glow that protruded from the fore of the shadow. It was aiming itself at her.

Unnerved by what she saw, Taylor had to bank sharply to keep from striking the side of the mountain as she passed by it. The thing turned as she passed, the red and blue center watching her the whole while. She felt a chill pass though her and she shivered in her seat. Flying past the mysterious fireball, she kept it focused on her sensors. A single black speck that stood motionless on her array like a stone hanging in the air.

Shale called her again as they flew past. "What did I just see, One? I'm getting that feeling that I'd rather be anywhere but here right now."

Her wingman's voice was tense. She flipped channels to call Aerelli and Brannon. Whatever happened, she wanted as much firepower with her as possible. She checked her readout to see how many missiles she still had left. Six.

When she looked back up, something cold and black passed over her cockpit like a shadow. It was moving twice her speed as it flew past. A blue, gray shadow at its head with a trail of fire blazing in its wake.

She gunned her engines and keyed her mic. "It's running. We have to keep eyes on it Two."

Racing after the creature, she looked at her panel to see that she still had a quarter of her fuel. Raising her altitude to a half-mile above the mountain range, Taylor pushed her Raptor's engines to their max. She could feel the g-forces pull against her as the *Wyvern* accelerated to full speed. She checked her sensor array. She was not gaining. In fact, she was actually falling further behind.

She heard Shale call up to *Unifier*.

"Unifier Main, this is Rapier Two, do you have a read on what we're following? Over."

Precious seconds passed before they answered.

"Negative. We have nothing Rapier Two. Maintain visual. Over."

Shale's response was defeated. "Well shoot."

Taylor hit her afterburners and watched her fuel begin to drop. She had programmed the *Wyvern*'s computer to calculate the distance from her point of origin in relation to her fuel level. By her estimate, she had about seven minutes left.

"You sure it's wise to keep pace at this point, One?"

She sighed in frustration, wondering if he was right. *Unifier* had ordered them only to "maintain visual," but how long could they do that if their target was moving this fast? Finally, she answered. "I just want to see if I can figure out where this thing is headed."

The creature had slowed. Keeping her engines on full burn, Taylor closed the gap. However, when she finally got back into weapons range, it seemed to sense her and speed up. Now she was barely keeping pace with it again, and she could only wonder if that was by the creature's design or if it was actually feeling as taxed as she was.

Shale was close behind her, his own afterburners keeping pace with them as they neared the northern edge of the Blackfriar mountain range. Taylor looked down to see her control panel tell her she had three minutes of fuel remaining before she had to return to orbit.

She looked up just as the thing turned.

It flared hot white as it came at her. The thing was unimaginably nimble, effortlessly reversing direction. A half second was all she had to turn the *Wyvern* into a sharp angled dive as the creature ripped past her. Did it angle toward her? Did it just attack? She felt the violent stab of a migraine pulling at the inside of her skull as she twisted her joystick back to level herself out. But nothing happened. She shook her joystick again, but her controls were dead.

She was freefalling toward the mountains when she heard Shale scream over the radio.

"ONE, ITS GOT…" And then static.

She heard the distant sound of an explosion behind her, but she didn't have the time to worry about her wingman. Something was wrong with her Raptor. It was as if her controls were no longer connected the rest of her ship. She twisted her control stick every which way to no response. Frantically, she pressed the emergency reset on her control panel, but instead of rebooting, the panel simply went black. Then her engines died. Silently saying a prayer in her head, Taylor pulled her ejection lever.

A violent gust of air shot her into the sky.

White. Blue. White. Blue. Darker blue. Grey.

She was tumbling. Then she was bouncing. Then she was floating like a feather caught in a breeze. Looking up, she saw her chute hanging above her like a giant jellyfish. Then she looked down just in time to see the ground coming at her. Fast.

PAR

His Shade had guessed right.

They found the mansion full of dust and ghosts and bullet holes. There had been a struggle here. From what Par and Saithe could tell, a group of soldiers had surrounded the mansion before a brief firefight had occurred. Their quarry had escaped, both princesses in tow but minus one of their guard. That was where the trail got interesting. The soldiers had left first. Why, Par could only guess. His quarry had been scattered about the mansion's grounds by then. Someone, likely one of the girls, had hidden in a storm drain. Several of the guard had fled to the second floor, presumably to make some kind of stand, while two of the others had hidden in a back room. It was there that one of the girls, the smallest, had snuck out to the yard by herself before the others had come and found her. From there the entire party had headed north and east, across the city and up the mountain.

Now Par was standing before a statue of a woman dragging a child and wracking his brain over why one of the girls had snuck off by herself into the garden.

"From what I can tell," Saithe said as she knelt near the base of the statue, "she came and stood here for a long while without moving. Then, the guard came and got her, and they left together down the path."

"There's something going on," Par mused, looking up at the white marble face of the statue.

"All I see is a scared little girl."

He saw more than that. Something else, something elusive. There was an instinct inside of him when he knew he was hunting a person or a thing that was not meant to be prey. Earlier, shortly after he and Saithe had spotted Sader Morgan's ship coming behind them, they had found a shelter hidden beneath a courtyard. There the princesses' party had stopped to plan and regain themselves. While the others had moved around and talked and debated, the smallest of their party, this little girl, had sat quietly in the corner. Now, here in this mansion, she had split off from her protectors in deliberate fashion. Par could see that in the footsteps where she had snuck out through the hole in the wall. This was not someone fleeing for their life. No, this was a seeker, someone searching for a thing she meant to find.

Our enemies are still behind us. And I doubt they'll be stopping to stare at the scenery. By my calculations, if they have left their aircraft behind and settled for a mode of transport similar to ours, then we can likely expect them to catch up in approximately seven to nine-and-a-half minutes. But if you want to look around some more, be my guest. I'll just be contemplating how hard it will be to find a new host.

Par frowned in annoyance. It was hard enough dealing with a smart-aleck AI—it was harder still when the AI was right. They had bought a few minutes advantage by leaving their quarry's trail and guessing, correctly, where they might be headed. Now if he could only get lucky again, then he might be able to snag both of the girls before Sader caught them all.

Par walked past the statue and a few steps down the cobblestone path to where the weeds parted. Here, he could see the city skyline as it travelled up the mountainside. "Wherever they're headed, they'll have to cross the river first. The question is where…"

Saithe stepped up beside him and hummed pleasantly. Ever since she had shot the sniper back in the third ward, she had seemed much more at ease, even happy, causing Par to wonder how much of her replicant programming was "pleasure model" and how much was something else.

"Is your … 'companion' keeping an eye out for our pursuers?" she asked.

All the time.

Par nodded. "He says we should be moving soon or they will be here."

"Well I would agree with him in that. If it is a *him,*" she hummed again as she bit her lower lip. Then she shifted her hips and her eyes fluttered seductively as she looked up at him. "It is unwise to tempt Fate where Sader Morgan is concerned." Hands on hips, Saithe looked back toward the statue and chuckled. "The girl probably came out here to pray. Their father is certainly the fanatic. His daughters are likely of the same mind."

Par looked to her with a raised eyebrow. "Pray?"

Saithe held her hand toward the statue of the woman. "To the Silver Lady. This is the Duathic archangel. She is the earthly instrument of the Father of the Universe. However, in the Imperium we believe in something a little different." The tattooed woman sighed as she looked the marble carved woman up and down. "We believe that our rulers, the Ieses, embody the physical manifestation of heavenly intent, much the same as the Duathe believe in Her."

Par looked back up at the marble face of the woman. Her expression was worried and fearful while her eyes were locked on the boy she held in her left hand. The woman appeared to be pulling the boy somewhere that he did not want to go; he was angry and clawing at her hand as he tried to break free.

Par pointed to the boy. "If she is the Silver Lady, then who is that?"

She shrugged, her eyes playful and flirting as she looked at the boy. "Who knows? Perhaps it is a metaphor. Perhaps he is a sinner she is trying to save. Perhaps it is one of the Children."

"Children?" Par had little time for religious nonsense and had skimmed through most of his research regarding Duathic religious beliefs.

"They are ... a questionable part of the Duathic faith. Many believe they never existed, or that they are only an exaggerated legend." She sighed and rolled her eyes, as if the topic were beneath her. "However, according to their version of the Scripts, there was an angel who fell from grace and she was loose upon the Universe for a time, looking for things to upend the heavenly balance. In her travels, she gave birth to seven children whom she hid before she was captured. It is written in their texts that those children are still loose, searching for that which their mother did not find."

We have company.

An image shot into Par's mind of shadows searching along the mansion's black fenced gate. They were coming from the south. Par grabbed Saithe by the hand. "We have to go."

Wordlessly she followed and together they ran to the airbike that lay waiting along the mansion's northern wall. Par climbed on the back seat as Saithe kicked the bike into motion.

"Where to?" she asked.

Par looked out toward the river where it ran down the mountainside and through the city, wrapping around the palace hill and flowed out into the bay. And it was then he knew.

"The palace. They're headed to the palace."

Saithe kicked the airbike into gear and it purred as it rose up in the air. Then she hit the accelerator and they soared over the black fence that encircled the mansion. Par stole a glance behind him to see if he could spot any of their pursuers, but all he saw behind them were empty windows and towering weeds. Saithe lowered the bike back down to ground level and they flew over the grass and then turned east on the nearest road. At the next intersection, she turned again and headed north, away from the river.

Saithe revved the airbike to full speed and the city blocks flew by in a blur as she turned and called out over her shoulder. "I'm going to deviate a bit before I turn back toward the Muirghil. That way if they're following us, they'll at least have to work a little harder."

Sure enough, after a mile of travelling north, she turned around at a traffic circle to head back south and east toward the river. Soon, Par could see Sindorum's palace hill rising before him in the dying light of the evening. Saithe kept the bike at full speed as they raced down the road toward the river. After they crested a rise, Par could see the dark blue water of the Muirghil River flowing below them.

"Do we dare stop to search the docks?" Saithe called over her shoulder.

"No, they must have crossed by now," Par replied.

Saithe slowed down as she guided the bike off the road and across the grassy bank toward a boat landing. The bike shook as it crossed from the concrete of the landing to the water. Hovering over the river now, Saithe flipped a switch next to her thigh and the bike's anti-grav engines adjusted to the waves. Once the bike stopped shaking, Saithe hit the accelerator again and they sped across the water, leaving a foamy wake behind them.

"Look!" Saithe cried out as she pointed to where a pair of rowboats sat nestled on a sandy bank. The mahogany-skinned woman turned and guided the bike toward the boats and then over the sand. Throttling the bike down, she pulled to a stop between the two boats. Looking inside, Par could see a pair of oars sitting inside the bottom of each vessel.

"There's no dock here," Par said as he searched the shoreline. "That and we're right below the temple and the palace."

Sure enough, as Par looked up on the hill, he could see several levels of apartment and condos that lined the hillside, and above it all, atop the hill was the white gold dome of the temple. To their north, a great white bridge reached across the waters, connecting the hill with the other side of the river, and Par could see columns of tanks and soldiers marching across it.

How nice. We're just in time to see the war end. Last one to the palace gets surrounded and killed.

"Look!" Saithe whispered as she pointed behind them.

Par spun around. A dozen lights were moving around the docks on the opposite shore, not a few yards from where they had crossed.

I can hear the other. He is calling out to us, even though I dare not answer.

Par asked his companion what they were saying.

As an answer, his Shade tuned him in to the transmission. There were no words, only a song, one that Par immediately recognized as the title music from an old tragedy: The Hunter and the Thief.

But who is the hunter and who is the thief?

Par had no intention of waiting to find out. He tapped Saithe on the back and whispered, "Go."

She hit the accelerator and the bike took off up the riverbank. They raced across the grass and up the rise. Crossing a stand of trees, they jumped a curb onto a cobblestone street. Buildings raced by as Saithe sped up the hill. The sounds of battle, once distant, were now all around them. Gunfire sounded from atop the hill, bouncing off the building walls in eerie echoes. Explosions flashed against the hilltop, lighting up sky and casting shadows all around them. A pack of dogs growled at them from an alleyway as they raced past, and someone yelled at them from an open window, but Saithe sped on. Then, nearing the top of the hill, Saithe finally slowed the bike down to the pace of a walk. Par could hear the humming of tank engines on the hilltop above and the whine of aircraft as they soared overhead, all sounds that could mean only one thing: they had found the Coalition Army.

Cresting the hill, they turned down an alleyway. The darkness of night was all around them now with only the flash of gunfire and bombs to guide them.

Par tapped Saithe on the shoulder. "We should stop and leave it here."

The replicant woman nodded and wordlessly pushed the airbike behind a dumpster and turned it off. Par pulled his night vision from his shoulder pack and put it to his eyes. The golden dome of the Duathic royal palace stood before them. Nothing but a wide street and a gated fence stood between them and the palace grounds. This side of the palace showed the royal temple that overlooked the Essene road. With any luck, that was where their quarry would be.

Par could see soldiers swarming about the yard of the temple. Zooming in, Par recognized the soldiers as the same-faced replicant men he had seen at the refugee camp. The replicants were everywhere, marching along the palace's outer walls and all along the street. He saw an entire squad posted near a broken gate that led to the front door of the palace temple. He adjusted the headband on his night vision goggles just as a tank rumbled by on the road between them and the temple. If one thing was clear, they wouldn't just be walking through the front door.

For a moment, he wondered if he had erred. Did the princesses actually make it this far? What did he have—other than hunter's instinct—that proved his quarry had hidden inside the temple? Then, still scanning along the street, he spotted a security camera mounted atop the temple's outer wall. He asked his companion to take a look and the AI sent a dozen microscopic envoys to interview the camera. Seconds later, he was rewarded with an image of the interlopers—three guards and two girls—dashing across the street as the replicant solders converged on the temple. Looking at the camera's clock, he saw that he and Saithe were mere minutes behind their prey now. They had only to figure out how to get inside, and once there, how to get back out again.

Par turned around to see Saithe standing at the other end of the alleyway, keeping watch down the hill. After a moment, she turned and walked back to him. "Sader and his party have reached the shore," she whispered. "If we're going to get inside that temple, we need to do it soon. Are you sure they're in there?"

Par pointed toward the street corner. "A security camera has them crossing the street only moments ago. What's more, there are only five of them left."

An aircraft flew low over their heads, and Par and Saithe sunk back into the shadows as the lights on its underbelly shown down into the alleyway. A glancing beam of light caught Saithe's black eyes and the dark brown skin of her bald head, and Par could see the flirting, laughing expression was gone from her face, leaving only the stone-cold expression he had seen since leaving the mansion.

"Par! Look!" Saithe hissed beneath her breath as she pointed down the hill. A dozen lights were down near the shore, bobbing and weaving through the buildings.

They were fanned out like a search party. It would not be fair from here on. Sader Morgan had seized every advantage. He had more men and more guns. Par was miles away from his ship, while Sader could summon a ride at any time. And with the replicants that were swarming the palace hill, he also had an entire army at his back. For a moment Par considered turning on his foe and facing him. Perhaps their hilltop elevation would be advantage enough. Perhaps he and Saithe could catch Sader's men off guard with a sudden attack. Then he found himself wondering what kind of Taker this Sader was, and his desperation yielded. Not only did his foe have more men, Par had no idea how powerful of a Taker this Sader really was.

And it is him. The transmission of the song is only getting louder. He's got the damned thing on repeat.

"They will be on us any minute now," Saithe whispered, her voice tinged with fear. "It will be better for you when they catch us…"

She doesn't know that.

"You're not one of them," Saithe pleaded. "To them, we replicants are little more than sentient cattle, you know. When they catch one of us who have gone 'rogue', they flay us down to the bone until we're barely alive and then they open our skulls and poke around in our brains until they find out what went wrong with our genetic programming."

Okay, that's terrible. Can we at least hide? I'd rather not find out what they do to an A.I …

Looking across the street, Par could see a tank parked at the broken gate. Its floodlights illuminated both the street and the palace courtyard, leaving hardly a shadow to sneak through. Everywhere else the same-faced soldiers stood guard in twos and threes or marched about in patrols of four and five.

Beside him, Saithe checked the reload on her carbine. "Well, Mr. Riordan, are you formulating a plan, or should I just make a break for it? I would rather be gunned down in the street than the alternative…"

Par looked behind them to see that the lights were now halfway up the hillside. Inside of him, Par's Shade was buzzing with fear. *He knows. He found a husk. One of our nanos got caught in the reeds along the shore and he found it. He knows. He's known since the camp. He knows and he's coming for us now and he's promising how long and slow it will be… You'll die … eventually, at least. From the interrogation. But me! I will live on as a prisoner. A pet for his companion. A slave, more like…*

There had to be another way. Par studied the buildings around them, wondering if any held a place to hide. To fight. Perhaps climb up the dumpster and through a window…

Saithe had returned to end of the alleyway again to look down the hillside. "Par, we can't wait any longer! They're only a few blocks now—I can see their shadows!"

Then when he saw it, their path became clear. They had to go down.

Par ran over to the dumpster, put his shoulder to its side, and pushed. Its corroded wheels creaked and a handle scraped the brick wall of the alley, but if anyone heard it, Par didn't care. There, beneath his feet, was a manhole cover. Par released his companion and his Shade swarmed out of him and fell about the manhole like a thousand angry ants, crawling along its rim and eating away the rust and the corrosion that held its edges before lifting it and turning it aside.

Whispering for Saithe to follow him, Par climbed down inside. He raced down the rungs until finally his feet hit the crusted concrete, and when he looked up, he caught the glimpse of Saithe's shadow coming down behind him before the cover slid shut again and darkness swallowed them.

And we're hidden. Thank the Fates.

"Do you still have your night vision?" Par asked when he heard her feet hit the ground.

"I do." Par's own night vision quickly adjusted and he began to cautiously make his way forward. The pipe itself was nearly half again as tall as he was, allowing him to walk freely. The concrete tunnel was dry, with a layer of sediment crusted over top so that it felt like walking over hard and uneven ground. He had gone only a few steps when he heard Saithe coming behind him.

"It ... smells less terrible than I thought it would," she whispered.

It's likely that, because of the war, this section of the city's sewage system has gone unused for so long that all the truly horrid sediment has either drained or evaporated or dried. Which is really lucky for the two of you as the methane level from an active sewage pipe of this size could actually kill someone, you know.

Par asked his Shade why that had not come up sooner.

Better here than up there. Well ... better for me, mostly. You would be, well, still dead, although I'm assuming that swallowing too much methane is less painful than whatever tortures this Sader character might dream up. Par thanked him for his compassion and then asked him why anyone would build a sewage tunnel so big. *These are formerly the temple catacombs, actually, and were not rebuilt and used for sanitation until about a hundred years ago by Teum's late great-grandfather, who was actually quite the man for public works, it would seem. And so, if we're lucky, there may be some way we can get back up into the grounds or even the temple itself. If you want, I can run a map of the surface parallel to you as we wander around down here in the dark...*

His Shade fed an image of the city map into Par's mind as he walked.

They were moving parallel to the street that ran in front of the palace temple now. When the pipe they were following ended in a T intersection, Par stopped to close his eyes and envision the map again. They needed to go right. Opening his eyes, he made the turn and Saithe followed.

"Do you know where we're going?" she whispered.

"Only somewhat," he answered.

"And your companion is helping, I suppose?" she asked, quietly again.

"A little," Par admitted, though then the tunnel turned away from the palace, curving east instead of west and he cursed beneath his breath. Stepping across the rough tunnel floor, they could see a gloomy light leaking into the tunnel as they rounded the curve. Then, as the tunnel straightened, a hole in the ceiling opened up and the light from the night sky fell down on them.

Par and Saithe both sank back into the shadows as they studied the gaping crater. Something, a bomb or a mortar, had exploded here, blowing a hole through the street above. Par heard the humming engine of a Coalition tank pass by and saw the shadows of soldiers as they marched past. Then Saithe touched him on the arm and silently pointed toward the far side of the hole. There, a crack in the bottom side of the tunnel lay open, and down below, Par could see a rushing stream of water. Staying to the shadows and stepping carefully around the rubble, Par snuck his way over to the rock and looked down inside. It was another pipe of similar size, running crossways beneath them, straight toward the palace. Sliding down onto his backside, Par fit his feet and then his legs through the crack. It was just wide enough, and he lowered himself down until he hung by his hands and finally dropped down into the water below. He landed with a splash, but when he stood, he found that the water came up to his waist. The water here was murky but smelled of chemicals, and Par silently thanked the Fates for sparing their senses again. After he had walked forward a few paces, Saithe landed with another splash behind him.

The soldiers in the street never even looked down. You're lucky. Again. I'll scout ahead.

Wading through the water, Par felt the nano-bots soar through the crack and race ahead of them.

"Are we headed the right way now?" Saithe whispered over the babbling stream.

"We should be," Par answered quietly.

"We're likely behind him now," Saithe replied. "Unless for some reason he stopped to look around."

Par silently agreed. Their detour through the tunnels may have saved their skins, but at the cost of valuable time. He could only hope that whatever advantage he had seeded to Sader would only be temporary. The tunnel stretched on as they waded through the water. Once, as they were walking, everything shook, rippling the water around their waists, and Par had to touch his hand to the wall to keep from slipping.

"Are they fighting inside the temple?" Saithe whispered. "Is that what that is?"

Par could only shake his head. There was so little they knew. So little they could control. They walked on, wading through the water and deeper into the dark. They were descending now as the tunnel here was slanted several degrees downward, and the water was rushing past. Soon, the current became so strong that Par had to lean back against it as he walked.

Watch your step.

Par stopped as the tunnel suddenly ended. It was so dark in front of him that he could barely see the water falling before him in a spray. He felt Saithe's fingers brush his back as she checked the distance between them. Neither of them spoke. Par turned himself sideways, bracing himself against the current as he looked out at the expanse before him. It was a cavernous room, shaped in a square and so dark that, even with his night vision, he could not see the far wall. The mouths of other tunnels lined the walls of the gigantic room, and he could see the floor was covered in tiny rocks. Stepping carefully forward, he peered over the edge to see the water as it fell through a hole in the floor of the great room and down into an impenetrable darkness below.

Par closed his eyes to view the map. They were directly below the palace temple. Now, all they had to do was find the trail again and hope against hope that they were not too late. Behind him, he could hear Saithe's cautious breathing as she waited for him to lead. Looking down, he could see that it wasn't that far to the floor. All he had to do was clear the pit and the waterfall.

Wait.

He stopped, braced against the wall as the water rushed past his legs.

He's here.

The song of the Hunter and the Thief came back into his mind. The horns were travelling through their final chorus as the drums rolled and the strings shivered in rhythm behind it all—but just when the song should have moved into its final stanza, it stopped. Then, from the far dark corner of the great room, a woman screamed.

DELEA

"*Fel!*"

Her cry echoed across the vast, dark room and came back as empty as it had left. Before she could cry out again, someone touched her on the shoulder. It was Thayne.

"I don't ... I don't think she's here your Highness."

"Then where *is* she?" Delea felt desperate and afraid. Afraid that her sister had left and that she would never see her again. Why would she leave? What would possess her to sneak off into the dark when they were so close to escaping this horrible war?

"Wherever she is, your Highness, I do not believe that yelling will help us now," Marental said quietly.

Somewhere in the dark, Kress grunted her assent. Delea tried to calm herself, but her mind was racing. She turned to her bodyguards again. "How long ago did we see her last?"

"She was with us when we came into this room," Marental replied. "We must backtrack the way we came if we hope to find her."

So they turned around and began walking across the tiny rocks that lined the floor of the great room. Kress was the first to pull out her flashlight, swinging it in a wide arc as they walked, but the room was so large that the beam did not even reach the wall on the other side.

Delea could hear an empty wind that was whispering through the tunnels on the far end of the cavernous room, almost as if something unseen was travelling through the air. A cold breeze swept by them, and as the sound of it faded, Delea could hear only the *swish-swish-swish* of the tiny rocks moving beneath their feet. Beside her, Thayne pulled out his flashlight and aimed its beam at the wall to their right.

"I was in the back, but I never heard her walking the other way," Thayne wondered aloud as he limped across the rocks. "If she had, I would have heard her walking across the rocks." Thayne stopped as he aimed his light at one of the tunnel openings. "She had to have crawled into a tunnel or something."

They all stopped there and Delea counted the tunnels between them and where they had entered. There were seven.

"Do you have any idea which one she might have snuck through?" Delea asked.

"Eh…" Thayne mumbled a curse under his breath. "I'm not really sure."

Kress swung her flashlight in a wide arc around them, and again the beam failed to reach the wall on the far side of the room. Delea suddenly felt as though she were a very small thing trapped in a maze of blackness, and somewhere out there was her sister who was running away and she didn't know why.

"We'll have to search each of these tunnels then," Marental said gruffly. "I fail to see another way."

Thayne sighed, his voice still raspy from his wounds. "I'm afraid you're right, ma'am, unless we somehow manage to holler something that makes her come back."

"FEL!" Delea shouted again. "We're not leaving without you! So you better come back or we're all gonna be stuck here because of y—" Her shout died as a massive hand closed over her mouth and Delea froze as she felt a giant set of arms wrap around her.

"Shhhhh, your Highness," Kress whispered in her ear.

"What was that?" Thayne whispered as he swung his flashlight about. Limping forward, his eyes darted about the room.

Delea had heard nothing. Straining her ears, she listened for something, anything of what the others had heard, but the only sounds that came to her was the labored breathing of her companions. Then, behind them, something large and metal groaned as it fought against itself. As everyone spun around, something huge and metal fell from the ceiling and crashed to the floor in a loud, metallic *SMASH*. When their flashlight beams found it, Delea could see it was a gigantic metal pipe, the same size as the one they had walked through before entering the room. It now lay twisted and on its side in the tiny rocks that lined the floor. Aiming her light toward the ceiling, Delea could see where it had broken off, but there was no rust or signs of corrosion. It had sheered itself cleanly, like a giant saw had cut it in two.

"Oh my," Thayne whispered as he looked up at the ceiling.

Then all three of their flashlights died at once and darkness swallowed everything around them. Delea could feel something tingling on her legs and her arms, and when she looked down she saw tiny cobwebs of static lightning rippling its way up her clothing, but then it faded and all was dark again.

"An EMP," Marental whispered. Delea could hear her bodyguard pressing the mic of her radio. "Someone just killed all of our electronics."

Beside her, she heard all three of her remaining bodyguards ready their weapons. Pulling her pistol out from behind her belt loop, Delea checked the safety off and nervously waited. Silently she wondered just how she was going to hit anything in the darkness that surrounded them.

A snap and a hiss came from the corner on the far side of the great room as a tiny fire flickered to life from a pile of trash along the wall. As the flames picked up they cast long, eerie shadows across the expanse. Then Delea's eyes caught a towering, black mass as it raced away from the edge of the light.

"*RUN!*" Marental yelled her command as she grabbed Delea by the cloth of her shirt and dragged her into a run.

Delea scrambled to keep her balance as her giant bodyguard dragged her along. The tiny rocks slipped and slid beneath her boots until she finally got her feet beneath her, and when Marental finally let go of her shoulder, she broke into a dead sprint. Rocks were spraying beneath their feet as they all ran as fast as they could. Something huge was behind them—Delea could hear it, but she dared not look back. The floor was shaking beneath them as they ran, and all Delea could hear was the steady *wham-wham-wham* as the creature gave chase.

Kress was the first to reach the corner where they had entered. She spun around, her back to the wall, as she fired her rifle at the beast behind them. *CRACK-CRACK-CRACK-CRACK.* With every shot, the rifle echoed against the room's cavernous walls. Delea's calves were aching from running against the tiny rocks but as she reached the wall, she managed to leap up into the mouth of the pipe.

"Keep going!" Marental yelled.

"We are!" Thayne cried as he jumped up onto the pipe behind Delea.

Delea hustled down the tunnel, scraping her knees against the rusted metal as she crawled. Then something massive struck the wall behind them and everything shuddered. Bits of dust and dirt fell from the top of the pipe as Delea struggled to crawl forward. The beast behind them let out a bellowing cry, a howl both mechanical and alive that was so loud that her eardrums felt as if they would burst. All she could do was curl up against her arms and cover her ears. When the howl finally died, Delea looked back to see the shadows of her two giant bodyguards fighting with the beast in the flickering light. Kress's shadow loomed and waned as she wrestled with the beast's black limbs, and beyond that was the diminishing shadow of Marental as she crawled across the rocks. Kress screamed in pain and rage as she tore a limb from the beast only to see another grow in its place. Then Marental reached the wall where she picked something up. The sudden blasts of the gunshots flashed four times, throwing bursts of light over everything. Delea finally caught a glimpse of their foe. It was at once black and metal and formless and terrible, and it writhed as Marental shot it four times in the back. On the fourth shot it twisted, spinning around to strike Marental, knocking the weapon from her hand. Then Delea felt Thayne grab her and push her forward, yelling, "Go! Go! Go!" as Marental's screams echoed in the dark.

Delea was scrambling furiously away when the pipe shuddered again as gunshots and a metallic growl echoed against the walls. Then a scream was followed by the sound of flesh being torn from bone. Then nothing. She kept crawling as fast she could. Behind her, Thayne whispered to keep going at all costs, and then the tunnel shuddered again as the beast behind them let out a hot, wet breath that gusted after them. The creature sniffed twice, as though it were trying to follow their scent. Then she heard the beast push away from the wall and let out another long shriek, like glass scraping against a rusty sheet of tin, and Delea had to stop again to cover her ears. Her eardrums ached as needles of pain shot through her skull and rattled her eyes against their sockets. Lying there, holding her hands over her ears, she began to feel numb and nauseous inside as though the fear in her chest had a death-grip on her stomach. They had to get away.

Then someone was screaming again, only this time Delea recognized the voice. It was Marental. She was calling for someone to help her.

Delea tried to spin around in the tunnel but someone kept pushing her back, a pair of hands that kept shoving her, knocking her forward.

"Go!" Thayne whispered harshly. "Go! Keep going and don't turn back!"

Marental screamed again, this time accompanied by the sound of tooth and claw gnashing against one another. Another scream and then a body, wet and bloody, crashed against the pebbles on the floor. Then a low, guttural growl that was half-predator and half-motor echoed against the walls, and she watched a single red eye lower itself down to look through the tunnel mouth.

"GO!" Thayne yelled as he struck her with his palms, shoving her forward.

Her head struck the rusted metal as she rolled against the tunnel floor and back onto her hands. Crawling again, her hands found a metal lip as they reached the other end of the tunnel. Turning carefully around, she lowered herself down feet first. Now standing in a dark room, she listened, turning her attention back the way they had come, but all she could hear was silence.

Her eyes adjusted. There was just enough light to see her surroundings. They had reached a junction—a circular, concrete room where two other tunnels met up with the one they had just left. The first tunnel to their right was huge, half again as tall as she was, while the other on their left was no wider than her shoulders. A ladder hung to one side, leading up to a manhole in the ceiling. Two thin beams of gray moonlight shone down through the manhole's eyelets.

Thayne grabbed her by the arm. "What was that?" he asked.

Hearing nothing, she shook her head. "I don't..."

Then she heard it and her voice caught in her throat. It was like a man bound to a chain, dragging it across the rusted floor as he walked. *Rattle-rattle-step... Rattle-rattle-step...* And it was clearly coming from the tallest tunnel to their right.

She heard Thayne shoulder his rifle as he whispered, "Stay behind me, miss."

Rattle-rattle-step... Rattle-rattle-step...

Thayne fired his rifle, and the flash of the muzzle gave them a glimpse of a shadow, tall and gruesome, shambling down the tunnel toward them. Thanye fired twice more and the shadow darted away. Though it had stood upright like a man, the way it had moved reminded Delea of an animal.

Thanye lowered his rifle an inch, waiting to see if the beast would re-appear. Delea's own pistol had found its way into her hand again, but she was nervous, unsure that if she shot, she might miss and the ricochet would come back at them. Except for the moonlight shining through the manhole, it was completely dark. Slowly, she began to walk backward toward the ladder behind them.

When the back of her leg hit the bottom rung, she turned and climbed up the ladder. At the top, she stopped and reached up to push at the manhole. It didn't budge. Stepping up another rung, she bent her back beneath the manhole and pushed with all her might. Still it did not move.

A man was laughing at them, an amused chuckle that echoed from every tunnel. As it faded, Delea felt all the warmth in her body drain away. A feeling of hopelessness crept over her. They were trapped. They could hardly see. They were alone.

Then Thayne fired twice more down the tallest tunnel—*BLAM! BLAM!*—and a mass fell down against the rusted floor where it lay slumped and unmoving. Delea hopped down from the ladder and pulled the pack off her back. Unzipping it and reaching inside, she pulled out a pair of flares that she had taken from the downed ATC. She pulled the cap off the flare and struck it, dropping it just in front of their feet as its burning red light filled the room. Picking up the flare, Thayne stepped forward and held the burning tip toward the lip of the largest tunnel. Finally, they could see the body of the beast that had come after them. Its hulking form lay mangled on the rusted floor of the tunnel, and its head was twisted backward on its shoulders. Thayne adjusted the light so they could see its face. It was Marental.

The laughter found them again. This time the man was so hysterical that to Delea he sounded mad.

"We have to get out of here," she whispered.

"I know, but to where?" Thayne replied.

Then a gust of wind blasted down the tunnel, throwing rust and dirt into their faces. Delea held her hands up to shield her eyes, and then suddenly the wind was gone. But it wasn't just the wind itself that had left. All of the sound was gone. And so was all the air. They were in a vacuum and she couldn't breathe. The last thing Delea saw before the flare went out was Thayne grasping at his throat, his face twisted in a mask of confusion and terror. Then darkness swallowed everything.

Struggling for air, Delea stumbled toward the nearest tunnel. Reaching the lip of its entrance, she climbed up on her belly. Her lungs were burning in her throat as her knees met the rusted floor, and she began to crawl forward as she gasped for air. Then, with another gust of wind, the air returned and suddenly she could breathe again.

She heard Thayne's rifle clatter to the floor as he struggled for breath. From just above her, she could hear a faint buzzing sound like a cloud of busy insects circling overhead.

"NO!" Thayne cried.

Then Delea heard the soft, wet sound of someone behind stabbed. And again. And again. A body fell to the concrete. Something like a blanket swooped itself around her, picking her up and wrapping itself around her legs and her arms and her mouth. Then all was quiet. All was dark.

ATTICUS

4.29.2388 - Planet Arc, Sindorum (near Muirghil River)

As the palace hill erupted, Atticus lay huddled over his unconscious father. Gathered beside him, his medic Vansa and Sergeant Major Sulla stared with him at the pyrotechnic spectacle. The blinding light poured out of the far hillside with the roar of a howling gale. Then, as suddenly as it had started, the eruption stopped and with a final snap of lighting, the sky was dark again.

Only the maelstrom remained. A thunderhead of black, swirling clouds circled the palace hill, and as Atticus looked up across the river, he could see that it was growing in power and size. What was most unsettling about the storm was not its appearance, but its sound. There was no clap of thunder, no roar of wind. Rather, the swirling vortex sounded as though it were full of broken wind chimes, like shattered glass being blown across hollow metal. The sky now sounded like an ethereal machine giving birth, and the swirling black vortex had mushroomed so large that it stretched from the palace hill to where its outer edge rotated over the ruins of the theater on the far side of the riverbank.

Atticus could only gape in amazement as neither his ears, nor his eyes, nor his mind could grasp or make sense of it. However, there was one thing he was certain of: They had to get *off* the roof.

Grabbing the stretcher by the handles, he saw Vansa get up and grab the other end. Fear and terror were swelling in his belly as they got up from behind the tank and made for the stairs. The heavy infantrymen were now spread out across the roof, fighting with their enemies below, but Atticus could not see where Arakin had gone. Then another wave of lightning passed across the vortex, bathing everything in violent gray-blue light. He saw a bolt of lightning reach down and strike the building next to them, covering the adjacent rooftop in a shower of sparks.

"Hurry up, son," Sergeant Major Sulla appeared before him, holding the door open. "The longer we stay here, the worse this shit's gonna get."

His father's stretcher between them, he and Vansa hustled down the stair with Sulla close behind. Passing the second floor, an aftershock shook everything and Atticus stumbled on the steps, nearly dropping the stretcher.

"Sir, look out!" Vansa cried from behind as a doorway opened.

Out stepped two heavies in full power-armor, guns raised and their barrels trained on the four of them. Atticus froze where he was as Captain Arakin appeared, stepping out from behind his men. The heavies were faceless in their head to toe black armor, but Arakin's helmet was still off and Atticus could see the emotionless expression on the man's face.

"What is the gottamned meaning of this, Captain?" Sergeant Major Sulla pushed his way past both Vansa and Atticus as his face turned red with anger. "Your men better put their gottamned…"

Arakin raised his pistol and fired. Sulla's head snapped back and as his body fell to the floor. Atticus threw himself over his father's body as he saw the muzzle flashes of the heavies' rifles. He heard Vansa cry out behind him. Something punched him in the shoulder and then his leg, and the next thing he knew he was looking up at the wall and the ceiling as a loud ringing filled his ears. He tried to get up, but halfway to his feet, his left leg gave out and he fell back to the floor. When he finally pulled himself up against the wall, he saw the floor in front of him littered with lifeless bodies.

Vansa, her face bloody and bruised, leaned down as she looked him over. "You okay, sir?"

And that's when the pain reached his brain. His shoulder and his left leg suddenly felt like they were on fire and his chest throbbed with pain. When he looked up, he saw Marin and Clarke looking down on them from the third-floor stairwell, the barrels of their sniper rifles still smoking. Then Vansa reached down and grabbed him by the shoulders.

"C'mon sir, we have to keep going," the blonde medic said as she pulled him to his feet.

"What about Sulla?"

"He's dead, sir," she said as they stepped over his body. Atticus could see the stocky man lying in a pool of blood between the lifeless, black armored forms of the heavy infantrymen who had attacked them.

"And Arakin?" He asked.

"Marin got him, sir," Vansa said as she helped him down the stairs. "We need to keep moving. Clarke and Marin have your father sir. Just keep moving, we don't know what the heavies on the roof are going to do. We need to get back to our own."

"We need to find Jonas." His voice did not sound like his own; it was weak and distant, like a ghost that was only half dead.

"I know, sir. That's what we're doing," Vansa answered.

Limping, and with one arm over his medic's shoulder, he made it down the stairs to the ground floor. The pounding in his head began to fade as they reached the hallway that led to the front of the building. He glanced behind him to see Clarke and Marin, their rifles slung across their backs, carrying his father's stretcher between them.

"Don't worry, sir, the Consul is still well, I checked," Vansa said as she pushed them through a doorway.

What's going on? Some kind of mutiny? Why would Arakin try and kill us? The conspiracy theories spun in his mind, but as they neared the end of the hallway, his ears caught the strange sounds that were still coming from outside. Still leaning on Vansa's shoulder, they passed through another doorway and into the front room of the building. Two squads of his men were gathered here, and all of them, to a man, were silent and still as they watched the sky outside. Every gun was silent.

"I'm going to set you down here, sir," Vansa said as she set him down against a wall.

"What's going on outside?" he asked.

Vansa shook her head as she pulled out a syringe and filled it with a clear substance. "I don't know, sir. Hold still," she said as she shot the syringe into his leg. Atticus winced as a cold feeling crept through the lower half of his body, mixing chills with the pain from his wounds. His leg and his shoulder were still burning with pain from the muscles that had been torn apart and as the cold, numbing sensation crept through his lower body, his legs shook in a convulsion and Atticus had to cling to a crack in the concrete to stay seated against the wall. Vansa then pulled the aid bag off her shoulders and began bandaging his wounded shoulder.

When the spasms stopped and his body was finally still again, he looked out the nearest window as his medic worked. Chimes and bells and ringing glass sounded from every corner of the sky. He could see the clouds swirling in the air, black and menacing as lightning raced from one end of the vortex to the next. Then Jonas came to stand in front of him, blocking his view as the barrel-chested man lowered himself to his haunches to look Atticus in the eye.

"What the hell happened, sir?"

Atticus could only cough. Vansa answered for him. "We were ambushed in the stairwell, Sarge. That Captain and two of his men tried to kill us."

"He what?" Jonas drew back in shock.

Atticus cleared his throat but was still only able to manage a whisper. "Arakin. He tried to arrest me on the roof, but …but Sulla stopped him. Then he found us in the stairwell as we were carrying the stretcher. He killed Sulla. Don't know why. Perhaps he was trying to… I… I don't know."

Jonas' face grew dark. "I think we both know what he was trying to do sir."

Atticus shook his head. "It doesn't matter. He's dead now."

Jonas grunted. "Doesn't matter until his company finds his dead body and comes down asking us what happened, sir. Then it's going to matter one hell of a lot."

"How are things outside?" Atticus asked.

Jonas looked to the nearest window where no glass remained and a gaping wound in the wall doubled the size of the opening. "They stopped shooting a few minutes ago. We're not sure why, but its probably got something to do with the electrical storm above us. We've seen a few of them moving out there, but I've told the men to hold their fire. No one's sure of what's happening because of the sky."

Atticus reached an arm toward Jonas. "Help me up."

Wordlessly, Jonas helped him up to the window. Outside, waves of lightening were striking everything along the riverbank. A white bolt shot down from the sky and struck a rusted car on the road and a shower of sparks exploded into the air. Another bolt struck a tree, splitting it in half. Above it all, the swirling, black vortex of clouds still sounded like a freight train filled with glass, and when Atticus looked up, he could see that the swirling mass of clouds was coming lower and lower.

Then it all stopped.

The lightning disappeared first. Then the spinning clouds slowed and came to a stop. Finally, the sound of the howling wind chimes died away as the sky seemed to swallow itself and return to normal.

"What now sir?" Jonas asked.

"I don't know," Atticus replied.

A great wind washed over everything, blowing dirt and debris across the riverbank. The clouds above disintegrated in a matter of moments, opening the sky to the stars.

"Sir!" Mako's voice called out in the dark. "Someone's coming."

Both of Arc's moons now looked down on them, and with the sudden aid of the moonlight, Atticus followed Mako's outstretched arm to see a crowd of shadows walking down the road toward them. Following the road, they reached the base of the hill where they turned, crossing the grass field that lay between them. Atticus could see now that there were three of them walking together, two men and one woman. When the crowd reached the downed Stryker, a single warning shot rang out from the rooftop and a mechanized voice called down for the interlopers to declare themselves.

Raising his hands, one of the men stepped forward. He was a Duathic man with dark blue skin and a plain gray uniform. "Do not shoot us! Our Queen wishes to speak to your commander!"

Beside him, Atticus heard Jonas curse under his breath as they listened to the heavy infantryman on the roof call out for the Duathic party to move forward.

Thrace appeared beside him, his radio mic in hand. "Sir, the guys on the roof say that they want you to speak with her."

From the other room, Atticus heard Mako's voice call out for the crowd of Duathe to move forward with their hands off their weapons.

The three shadows then walked forward, moving brusquely across the grass with their hands raised.

"Let's meet them at the door," Atticus said, his voice so weak he barely recognized it.

Limping with his arm over Jonas' shoulder, Atticus made it to the next room. All eyes from Mako's squad were watching the three approaching shadows. A Duathic soldier met them at the door, his hands up with his palms facing them. He was dark-blue-skinned with scar-like tattoos engraved across his face. His eyes flitted between Atticus and Jonas as he spoke with a heavy Duathic accent.

"The Queen wishes to speak with your commanding officer."

"That'd be me," Atticus said.

The Duathic soldier bowed as he stepped aside. Then a tall and regal Duathic woman dressed in a black hooded robe stepped through the doorway. Her silvery hair was tied atop her head and her skin was white mixed with a hint of metallic blue. There was no mistaking her regal bearing as she stood with her head held high and her eyes affixed to Atticus.

"You are the commander here?" the Queen asked in perfect Illyari.

Atticus swallowed hard. "I am, your Highness."

She looked him up and down like a merchant inspecting a garment. "And what is your name?"

"Lieutenant Atticus Marius."

She raised an eyebrow and the whisper of a smile touched her lips. "The son of the Consul?"

He nodded. "The same."

"How fitting." She glanced around the room at the dozen faces who were now staring at her with a mixture of wonder and amazement. Then she met Atticus' gaze again, her eyes sharp and laughing. "Lieutenant Atticus Marius, I have just come from my husband's dead body to carry out a task that he could not. I, Queen Anyse Corrina Etain, am empowered by the laws of my nation to offer you the full and unconditional surrender of my people."

PAR

The dying moans of the giant woman echoed through the cavernous room as Par and Saithe climbed down from the drain. His Shade's nano-bots had spied the fight for him, and he had seen Sader leave one of the giant women lying along the wall, the flesh ripped from her arms and legs as she bled out, dying. Reaching the ground, Saithe retrieved her rope and winch while Par stole a glance down into the drain, but all he could see was water rushing down into the darkness.

They were on the opposite side of the room from the dying bodyguard, while to their left was the pile of trash that lay burning in the corner. A spark from the wall had lit the flames. Slowly, cautiously, Par and Saithe began creeping across the room. The tiny rocks and pebbles that covered the floor made it hard to stay quiet, but Par hoped the rushing water from the drain and the dying moans of the bodyguard would mask their movement.

There he was and wished he wasn't.

Indeed.

Par was not looking forward to facing Sader Morgan. Not only was the man cruel, but the Umbrean Taker had turned out to be far more powerful than Par had feared. The pale man had not one, but two companions, a rarity among their profession as it marked a Taker as one who had the mental strength and ability to maintain a link between two distinctly different AIs. Watching the battle unfold from the shadows, they had witnessed the terrifying strength and power of Sader's first companion as it had morphed from a swarm of black, beetle sized nano-bots and formed itself into a bear-like beast with a giant, oversized head filled with black, dagger-sized teeth and two glowing red eyes. Staying hidden in the drain, Par and Saithe had watched as the shadowbeast chased the lone remaining princess and her guards across the great room and right into Sader Morgan's trap. Silently, Par had hoped the three guards could stop the beast. They certainly looked formidable enough, the two giant women each stood nearly nine feet tall and looked to be some specialized strain of replicant, while the third man looked like some kind of ex-soldier. Unfortunately, they had been no match. Any hope Par held that Sader Morgan would be lessened had died when the shadowbeast had cornered the two women and beaten them bloody. However, it had been the reanimation trick that had frightened Par the most. It had taken Par years to teach his companion how to commune with a dead corpse. Reanimating a dead body to attack its living friends—well, that was far beyond anything Par had ever dreamed up. Right then Par had decided against challenging Sader Morgan to a fight.

At least not a fair one.

No, nothing needed to be fair.

Guided by the flickering light of the electrical fire, he and Saithe crept along the wall of the cavernous room and Par came to grasp just how big the place was. As long as an arena with a ceiling nearly two stories high, Par wondered what the room had originally been built for. He noticed that the stone of the walls looked older than anything he had seen in the city above, but the room was now a junction for seemingly all the pipes and tunnels that ran below this portion of the city—though only the one Par and Saithe had just crawled through seemed to contain any water.

Creeping along the wall, they crossed the room and reached the corner where the first body lay. Par saw Saithe leaned over the body of the dead woman, so he adjusted his night vision to look down the tunnel before him. He could see where the pipe curved at its midpoint but little else.

He sent the rest of his squad around to cut these guys off, lest they managed to get away from him. He's calling them now and they'll be coming through one of the eastern tunnels. Even if we can steal the girl from this guy, I'm not sure we have a way out that doesn't involve killing a lot of people.

Or them killing us.

That too.

They had a plan. They knew Sader had taken the princess captive in one of the junctions between the pipes, so Par and Saithe were going to come at him from two angles, front and back. Behind him, Saithe touched him on the shoulder. A glimmer of firelight caught her, illuminating the black tattoos that crisscrossed her bald head as she signaled to an adjacent tunnel. He gave her a nod, and she crept away, her rifle in her hands.

Par stepped up onto the lip of the pipe and began creeping his way down the tunnel. Coming from the room ahead, he could hear the echoes of what sounded like a thousand angry flies swarming about. Par had asked his companion to muffle the sounds of his steps as he approached, but he knew his AI couldn't silence the sound in an entire room like Sader's had. It was another thing Par had never seen before. Crouched and sneaking through the giant pipe, he wondered how many tricks this Sader had up his sleeve. The flickering firelight was fading behind him as he reached the bend in the pipe. The tunnel was darker than the room had been, a blackness populated by shadows made of grey. Par adjusted his night vision to its highest setting, but even then, he nearly stepped on the dead body.

Taking a knee, Par saw he had reached the body of the second bodyguard, another giant of a woman with bright blonde hair. Her body was bent and twisted, her head turned backward on her shoulders, her right ankle completely snapped, and her left arm elongated by having been pulled out of joint at both the shoulder and the elbow. Par shivered as he stood. The air around him had gone cold as though all the warmth had been pulled from it like water leaving a drain. Then someone whispered in his ear.

"Shhhhhhhh…"

He couldn't breathe. Not only had something stolen the air from around him, it had stolen the breath from his lungs too. Clasping his throat, he stumbled over the corpse's outstretched leg and fell. His shoulder struck a rivet on the pipe's floor and as the pain shot through him. He tried to cry out, but he could only gasp. The pipe had become a vacuum. Rolling back onto his stomach, Par managed to get his hands beneath him. However, before he could push himself back onto his feet, a foot stepped onto the small of his back and pinned him to the ground. Craning his head over his shoulder, Par saw a pale shadow smiling down at him.

In his hands was a long, thin blade.

A blue flash of electric light washed over the tunnel walls as sound and air flooded into Par's ears and mouth and he gasped for air. Then he heard a sound like a boxer landing a haymaker and suddenly Sader Morgan was rolling on the ground behind him.

Get up! Get up! Get up! Get up!

Par's lungs finally found enough oxygen that he was able to stand and stumble forward. He tripped over the lip of the pipe's mouth and he fell down onto the rocks. Pushing himself back to his feet, he could hear the chittering noise of a thousand beetles scurrying across the walls and the rocks, and he looked up to see the black nano-bots of his enemy's companion crawling, swarming over one another as they formed back into the monster.

Run!

Par took off at a sprint just as the shadowbeast opened its two red eyes and let out a gear-filled growl.

Saithe has the girl and she's making for the east tunnel. The way we came in. Hurry, hurry, hurry!

His companion sent him an image that highlighted the drain along the far wall where they had entered. Looking around the room, the shadowbeast was nowhere to be seen, but Par spotted a single silhouette stepping out from the pipe where he had nearly suffocated. Sader. Turning around again, Par saw Saithe with the princess over her shoulders, jogging around the giant, broken pipe that lay in the center of the room. She was running straight for the drain, and freedom. Par took off after her. Just then, a small yellow ember fell from the ceiling in front of Saithe, who stopped, the rocks skidding beneath her feet. The glowing ember was floating eye-level with Saithe, wavering and flickering like a firefly in the dark, before it exploded in a flash of blinding light. And then the world went mad.

Half-blind from the flash, Par heard a shrill and deafening scream echo from behind him. It was a deafening, high pitched howl that filled the chamber and his head and made his ears feel like they were bleeding and pushed his eyes against his skull. Par threw his hands over his ears as a blur of black and silver flew past him and he heard Saithe scream.

Dropping his hands from his ears, Par called his companion to him and he felt the nano-bots of his Shade swarm over his forearm, covering it from the elbow up as it formed into a black, razor-thin blade.

His eyes were finally adjusting, shedding their blindness, when he heard the shadowbeast open up in a mechanical, rage-filled howl. Spinning to face his foe, Par's blurry eyesight could make out a beast standing before him with a body constructed from a million, chittering, crawling, swarming tiny black robots that had formed into the shape of a bear and the head of a giant piranha. The beast turned its two red eyes toward him as it let out a metallic cry. Par readied his blade.

This is going to hurt.

The beast charged. A great, gaping maw of black dagger-sized teeth opened before him, and Par dodged to his right, planting his left foot as he slashed with his blade, striking the side of the beast's mouth and opening a gash from its jaw to its neck. The shadowbeast jumped back as the crawling nano-bots reformed themselves around the wound; the beast gnashed its teeth and growled. Par steadied himself against the rocks and held his arms together so the blade could reform itself around both of his hands. Then the beast lunged again, leading with its right claw. This time, Par dodged to his left, blocking the claw with his blade. He used the inertia of the blow to whirl around and strike back at the beast's shoulder. When the beast stumbled again, Par stepped forward and thrusted, plunging the black blade of his weapon deep into the beast's side. A blue flash of electricity burst out from his weapon as his Shade shot out an electromagnetic pulse into his foe and Par saw a hole open in the beast's belly as a pile of fried nano-bots fell to the rocks. The beast stumbled. Its red eyes rolled as the beast's nano-bots struggled to reform. Gripping his weapon with both hands, Par took aim at the beast's head.

Lights burst behind his eyes as something struck the back of his skull, and he fell forward, rolling off the side of the thrashing beast. The world spun around him and Par blacked out for a fraction of a second before his face struck the rocks. His mind was a foggy blur of pain as he pressed his hands against the rocks and pushed himself to one knee. Above him, someone was laughing.

Before he could look up, the club came down again, striking him on the crown of his head and then again on his neck. His head was now a buzzing nest of pain. He had only a second to put his hand against the rocks before the club hit him again, this time in the ribs, and then the back, and then his head again. For a moment he couldn't move, and he felt his Shade fall away from his arm as hundreds of the tiny nano-bots fell into the rocks beneath him. Blind and deaf from the pain, Par rolled onto his back, holding his hands and arms in front of his face and his neck to defend from the blows. Looking up, Par caught a glimpse of Sader Morgan, his pale face practically glowing in the darkness and in his hands he held a staff of shining black obsidian. Sader's face twisted into a cruel smile as he jabbed his staff down into Par's groin. Pain shot through Par's waist as he tried to roll away from his enemy, but Sader simply leaned harder on the staff, pinning Par to the rocks.

Then a shocked look crossed Sader's face as he reached up with one hand to grasp at his throat and his mouth opened to let out a tiny gasp. Seizing his opportunity, Par reached up and grabbed the staff with both hands and wrenched it free from Sader's grasp. However, before Par could do anything with the weapon, it dissolved, the nano-bots running from his fingers like white sand. His enemy's companion then flew into the air in a cloud of white that swirled about the pale-faced man who was clutching at his throat.

Par rolled over onto his hands as the voice of his Shade re-entered his head. *Someone doesn't like his own medicine.*

Saithe appeared then, leaping out of the dark and tackling Sader about the waist and driving him into the ground.

Get up. Get up. Get up!

Par rolled up onto his feet, hoping to jump to his partner's aid, but instead he found himself face-to-face again with the black, piranha-headed shadowbeast. Two glowing red eyes looked back at him above a toothy maw of black and silver teeth. The beast let out a low, mechanical growl that opened up into a howl of rage and anger as it charged, teeth barred. Quick-drawing his pistol, Par leapt backward and fired twice into the beast's face before a swiping claw knocked the gun from his hands. Then a second claw raked him from his hip to his ribs. Landing on the rocks, Par ignored the pain as he rolled onto his back and kicked the beast right in the chin. It screeched and stumbled, and Par somersaulted backward and regained his feet. But when Par swung around to face the beast again, he saw that he was too slow—the beast's great maw clenched around his arm and his shoulder. Black teeth the size of daggers pressed into Par's torso as the beast picked him up off the ground and wrung him like a dog whipping a knotted rope. He whipped back and forth four times before the beast flung him against the wall. Lights burst behind Par's eyes as his head struck the wall, and then blackness swallowed him.

He came around to the sound of his companion screaming into his head.

YOU HAVE TO GO. I CAN KEEP HIM BUSY BUT HIS SOLDIERS ARE ALMOST HERE!

A pair of arms grabbed him beneath his shoulders, and he looked up to see Saithe dragging him across the rocks. Her face and head were cut in several places, and the dark red blood mixed with the tattoos on her dark-skinned face. She dragged him to the mouth of the giant, broken pipe that lay in the center of the cavernous room. Dizzy from the concussion, Par tried to stand, but he stumbled and fell out of Saithe's arms and down onto the rocks. She pulled him to his feet again as she gestured to the mouth of the large pipe. There, lying inside was the comatose body of the princess.

"Quickly Par, take her and go!"

"But you…" he started, but Saithe shoved him toward the unconscious girl with one hand as she readied her carbine with the other.

The princess was bound with padded metal bands about her feet and her wrists. Blood was seeping out of his side and his shoulder and his back, but Par could also feel a few spare nano-bots from his companion clotting the blood and sewing up his wounds. Par grunted as he picked the girl up. Throwing her over his shoulder, he carried her like a sack. Glancing back, Par could see shadows running out of a tunnel along the far wall. The soldiers. Beside him, Saithe drew the carbine up to her shoulder and fired a dozen shots at their pursuers.

His mind was too full of dizziness and fog to think. "Where are we going?" he asked.

"To the waterfall," she pointed to the drain of water, rushing from the wall where they had entered.

Moving as fast as he could with the girl on his back, he took aim toward the torrent of falling water. Behind and to his left Par could see Sader, bent over and still clutching his throat as his two companions, now two clouds of white and black, swirled about him. Then the white cloud fell on top of Sader, covering him in an ashen blanket, and then Par heard the voice of his Shade screaming into his mind.

I'M BURNING! MY GODS, IT'S BURNING RIGHT THROUGH ME. I CAN'T... HE HAS...

It left him. There was an emptiness where his Shade had been, and Par's body spasmed, causing him to break from his staggering run and drop to one knee.

Activate End Sequence. Powering down...

For the first time in nearly two hundred years, Par could no longer feel his companion's presence in his mind. The shock of it overwhelmed him as he slid the girl from his shoulders, setting her gently against the rocks. For a moment he sat there on his knees, palms against the rocks, his eyes staring at nothing.

Saithe's shadow appeared beside him, stooping down and picking the girl up. She whispered, "Come on."

Standing, he stumbled after her, glancing back to see the soldiers pushing through the cloud of smoke behind them. Par could hear the rush of the waterfall echoing against the wall and soon, by the flicker of the firelight, he could see the pillar of white foam falling from the pipe before them. He had no idea what the plan was once they fell through the hole, but with the soldiers coming from behind them and Sader Morgan still alive, he could see no other way out. Saithe was nearly there when the shadow fell upon her.

A blanket of black fell from the ceiling, swallowing Saithe and the princess and pinning them to the floor. Par could see the replicant woman wrestling with the chittering black bots, rolling on the ground and ripping them from her body as they swarmed over her torso and her limbs. However, as much as he wanted to, he couldn't help his partner just now.

Stumbling into a jog, Par pulled out his pistol. Readying his weapon in both hands, he walked sideways toward Saithe and the waterfall as he searched for Sader. As Saithe wrestled with the bots, the sounds of struggle mixed with the flickering light of the dying electrical fire. Shadows danced across the room as Par searched for his foe. He could see the corner where Sader had previously been was now empty, as was the fallen pipe at the center of the room. And then he found him. A second too late. A shadow wielding an ivory rod struck him in the face and in the hands. The second blow knocked the pistol from Par's hands and it clattered against the rocks. A third blow struck him in the shoulder, but when he saw Sader's smiling face come at him a fourth time, Par brought his hands up and caught the staff in his hands. Par pulled the staff into him, leaning back with all of his body weight as he tried to either draw Sader into arm's reach or force his foe to drop his weapon. But Sader did neither. In an instant, the end of the staff changed shape, and suddenly Par was holding a narrow, dirk-like blade in his hands.

Sader laughed as he twisted his staff-turned-spear, and the blade bit into Par's palms before Sader thrust it forward, piercing Par's shoulder. Skin and muscle split open as Sader drove him back, pushing him off his feet and pinning him into the wall. Par felt the blade slide past his shoulder blade and out his back. The smiling assassin then leaned on the butt of the pike as he drove the spike deeper into the wall

The shock of the blow wore off as the top half of Par's body was enveloped in pain. He could feel the blood running down his chest and his back. He began to wonder how long it would take him to die. *This is it,* he thought, *I'll go no further. He's won and we'll all be dead soon.* The pain of the pike through his shoulder had drowned out everything, until he heard the cruel laughter coming from the man before him.

"When I took this job, I wasn't counting on competition." The voice was cool and calm as the pale face looked down on him, grinning. "Don't get me wrong, I'm not upset, just surprised."

Blinking through the blinding pain, Par put his foot against the wall and tried to pull the pike free from the concrete. He felt muscle and flesh tear as he strained against the weapon, but the pike head did not move. Sader laughed again.

"Hold still please, I'd like to talk a bit, my friend." Sader gestured with a thumb toward Saithe, who was lying on the ground, a mask of black nano-bots covering her mouth just as they had shackled her legs and her arms. "Her, I get her. Those silly little rebels, the Questors, sent her. Why? I don't know. Perhaps I'll have her a few times before I take her apart to find that out. See if there's any of the 'pleasure model' left in her before I have one of my companions eat her brains. But you… You, I'm not yet sure…"

The soldiers were all around them now—wordlessly forming a semi-circle around Par, Sader, Saithe, and the princess. One of the soldiers lit a flare and threw it toward the center of the room where it landed near the giant, broken pipe. By the burning light of the flare, Par could now see that he was surrounded by the same-faced replicant soldiers that he had seen everywhere about the city. Many of them stood or took a knee sideways, so they could see both out as well as Par and Sader.

"Honestly, I thought you might run," Sader shrugged as he looked back at the princess' comatose form. "I got here well before you did and you're terribly outnumbered. But I have to admit, I'm glad you didn't. I haven't had this much fun in *ages*." Sader casually stretched the muscles of his back before he turned toward Par and leaned in close enough for Par to smell his breath. "Now we can stay down here as long as you like, but I want to know who sent you."

Just as Sader said this, Par noticed a vein of black ink that was creeping down the side of the white staff, and knew that his companion was not gone. Par looked his enemy in the eye.

"You talk too much," he said, smiling.

A deafening screech of pain filled the room as the black nano-bots covering Saithe left her body and flew into the air in an angry cloud. Sader spun around as the black cloud began to spin violently, picking up rocks from the floor as it spun into a cyclone. The miniature tornado travelled in an arc around them, engulfing the replicant soldiers and pelting them with rocks. Sader spun back around to face Par, his face twisted in a mask of rage.

"What are you—" The pale-faced man reached inside his coat pocket for something, but it was too late. The white spear that was also Sader's second companion fell apart and then flew at Sader in a cloud of white. The pale man screamed in horror as he fell to the ground.

His shoulder free of the wall, Par slumped to his knees. The blood was still leaking out of his shoulder when he heard the voice of his Shade come back into his mind.

Get up. Get up. Hurry. Hurry. Hurry. He's on the ground but he's going to get up. You have to kill him because I can't. I can't. I can't.

Par tried to ignore his throbbing head and the splitting pain that had consumed the top half of his body as he crawled across the rocks to where his pistol lay. Picking it up, he dragged himself to his feet and staggered over to Sader just as his enemy rolled over onto his back. Par thumbed off his safety and took aim at the pale man's head.

Sader's eyes went wide as he looked up at Par. "No. Don't …"

Good work. Now hurry.

Someone had lit off a smoke grenade—or multiple smoke grenades, he wasn't sure—but somehow there was smoke everywhere now. Raising his pistol, he shot at two of the soldier-shaped-shadows he saw through the smoke and saw one of them go down. Then something exploded and the other disappeared. The concussion from the blast nearly pushed Par off his feet and he staggered, putting his hand to the ground as he stumbled forward again. His shoulder had somehow stopped bleeding, and when he could feel tiny things crawling around inside of his wound, he knew his companion had returned to him. Or, at least, what was left of his companion. Smoke was everywhere. Par staggered toward where he thought he had last seen Saithe and the princess lying on the ground. Then someone reached out of the smoke and pushed him into the hole.

The light and smoke disappeared above him as he dropped through the drain. Arms flailing, Par fell through the darkness for a full second before he hit the water. The underground river swallowed him and rushed over his wounds, filling them with a cold, numb burn. When

Par's feet hit the bottom, he pushed, launching himself back upward just as he heard someone else crash into the water above him. He looked up to see two shadows descending and he twisted his body as he swam with his legs to avoid them. Breaching the surface, he found the water had a current, but thankfully it wasn't very strong. He guided himself with his good arm as he kicked his way to the edge of the water where he found a concrete walkway there. He was able to reach his good arm up onto the surface to hold himself steady as he looked back for Saithe, who emerged seconds later with the princess awake and swimming beside her. The girl's eyes were wide with fear as she swam toward the concrete. Not strong enough to pull himself up, Par had to wait for the two women to climb up out of the water before Saithe came over to help him. With one hand, she easily pulled him up out of the water.

Standing, Par found himself standing face to face with the princess. The security lights along the walkway had turned on, bathing them in a warm, golden glow that allowed Par to see the young woman before him. She had light blue skin and dark blue hair that was almost black. She looked him up and down with large, white eyes. Her face was a mixture of fear and shock as her stare travelled from his wounds to his face and back to his wounds.

Saithe was apologetic. "Had no choice but to wake her. It was the only way to get her through the fall and the water."

"What are you...?" the princess stammered as her gaze travelled from Par to Saithe and back to Par. "who are you...? What are...?"

Lie to her fucking face! There's no time!

Par put his hand on her shoulder and looked the princess in the eye. "Your Highness, your father knew you were in danger and so he sent us to find you and see you to safety."

Her eyes turned up toward the waterfall. "But what about Kress and Marental and..."

Par tightened his grasp on her shoulder and shook her. "There's no time! We have to run!"

And so they ran. As the rushing water fell away behind them, a nano-bot lit up like a firefly and they followed it as they jogged down the walkway.

"What's that?" the princess asked.

"Our guide," Par said.

Your guide and your savior, you mean. I'm blocking all of the pain in your body that I can, and I stopped most of the bleeding or you'd have died in the water, you know. That map we photographed back in the mansion has done nothing but help us. You're lucky our foes don't seem to have seen it. By the way, you can also thank me that none of the soldiers saw you three drop down the waterfall. I used their own smoke grenades against them.

The left side of Par's body was now almost completely numb, though he could still feel the cuts the shadowbeast's teeth had left in his chest and his shoulder. Despite it all, he was still able to stumble forward into a jog. The tunnel curved, angling slightly downward as they ran along the water's edge, following the glowing nano-bot all that way.

Beside him, Saithe whispered to him as they jogged, "Where are we headed?"

To the bay. I've summoned the Nameless. *This drain runs down into another drainage pipe that ends in a culvert along the Muirghil and the right out into the bay. So we should be able to make it to the bay from there. Your ship should be able to meet us somewhere along the shore.*

Par relayed this to Saithe and she seemed satisfied, though the princess beside her was just as scared as before. Par wondered how frightened the girl would be if she truly knew whom she was with. Thankfully, there wasn't much time for either of them to think about it, because they soon found the tunnel mouth. Saithe, who still had her carbine, jumped down first and helped the princess down. Par gingerly sat down on the tunnel lip and hopped down onto the sand. Up above, the night sky was filled with wispy clouds and twinkling stars. In contrast to the war zone they had left only an hour earlier, the city itself seemed almost asleep now as Par could hear only a few scattered gun shots in the distance.

They slowed to a walk and Saithe took the lead. Their glowing nano-bot had disappeared at the mouth of the tunnel. The river to their left, the city to their right, they found a cobblestone walkway that stayed to the river's edge. Once, Par was sure the walkway had been a scenic spot, but it was now nearly overgrown with brambles, vines, and trees that hung over the concrete. The branches formed a canopy so low they had to stoop to walk in spots. Saithe said nothing as she guided them along the path, her carbine resting in her hands as she kept an eye out. Having lost his pistol in his fall through the drain, Par had no weapons left save for what remained of his companion. Once, the princess tried to ask again where they were going, and Par told her that he had a ship waiting for them near the bay. And soon that's where they were.

They followed Saithe through one last tangle of branches that parted to reveal the gray-blue waves of the Bay of Sardis. A concrete stair led them down to the beach where the dull black shadow of the *Nameless* was waiting along the shoreline. When the princess reached the bottom of the stair, she looked up at Par with her eyes watering from a mixture of, what Par could only guess, was joy and grief and fear.

"Are you from the Duchess? Are you taking me to Linneaum?"

Par solemnly looked her in the eyes as he reached into his coat pocket for his injector. Thankfully it was still there, tucked away where he had left it, seemingly ages ago, in a zippered pocket.

The princess looked to Saithe. "Are there others? Have they found my sister? Do you…"

As she looked back toward Par, he stuck the injector into her neck and squeezed. A look of surprise and fear washed over her face and the beginning of a cry left her lips before Saithe stepped up behind her and covered her mouth. A moment later, the girl was unconscious again.

They put her in one of the Nameless' two sleeper cells that Par had modified for prisoners. When Saithe settled into the co-pilot's chair, he asked her if there was anything else she needed before they left. She only smiled and shook her head. Par said no more as he turned his ship back to manual control. Minutes later, they were flying low over the ocean with the stars overhead when Par finally felt the remainder of his companion climb back into his head.

It's a lovely night, don't you think?

TAYLOR

4.29.2388 – Arc, Blackfriar Mountain Range

Taylor Caelynn was cold.

Every pilot was allowed to pack any extra necessities into the survival bag that attached to the bottom of their ejection seat. Many pilots took great care in packing theirs, as it was often the only thing they would have available after an emergency ejection in combat. Taylor was *not* one of those pilots. This was not out of superstition or some abstract concept of optimism or confidence—she just had never seriously considered getting shot down and living to talk about it. Then again, she had never planned on chasing an unidentified flying ball of purple fire through a mountain range on the very last day of the war. Either way, she was in the mountains now without a parka and with very little food and she had no one to blame but herself. This had not done wonders for her already wounded pride or her disposition. All in all, as Taylor looked out at the night sky over the mountains, she found she was beginning to develop a very foul mood that likely promised to last either until her rescue or until she froze to death on some cliff.

She had grabbed both her meager survival bag and her Raptor's black box off the back of her seat. Then she had folded her chute up into the survival bag, which she hoped to use as a blanket, and then set off for higher ground. Leaving everything else behind, she began hiking her way up through the rocks and the trees. It would have been a lovely walk had it not been for how pissed she was.

An hour later she was walking on the hard-packed snow that came with the freezing-thawing-freezing cycle that happened in the mountains during the spring. She was marching through a vale of pine trees when she came clear of the woods and found herself in full view of two rising pillars of smoke, one from the mountain across from her and the other several miles south down the range. For a second she let herself wonder if Shale could possibly have survived, but then she remembered watching his Raptor disintegrate before her eyes. She pushed the memory of her wingman aside. She had little time for grief right now. She had to get to higher ground.

Several hours later, she decided that she had gone far enough. The air had gotten thinner, and she was tired of stopping to catch her breath. It was also well into the night and the wind had found its bite. Her temper had dropped with the temperature, and when she found an outcropping where the rock wrapped itself into a semi-circle, the only thing she felt was grateful for the shelter. Pulling the parachute out from her pack, Taylor wrapped herself inside its layered fabric and set the black box in front of her. A red light at the top of the box blinked off and on, off and on, as its transponder sent out its signal. Then she shivered and tried to convince herself that she wasn't as cold as she felt.

She had been on the mountainside for a little less than two hours when the search-and-rescue team found her. Before she boarded the shuttle, Taylor spent one last look in the direction of the downed Raptors. A separate team had likely already been dispatched to recover Shale's remains and demolish both of their vessels. As she stood on the ridgeline, she felt a pang of loss over both, then guilt, then anger, and then everything mixed together. Finally, she hefted the survival bag over her shoulder and walked up the ramp.

Back aboard *Unifier*, her debriefing with Admiral Thorus dragged on for nearly two hours as the Admiral and her staff asked her every question they could think of in relation to both the strange vessels she had encountered in the asteroid belt and what they called "the anomaly" that she and Shale had squared off with above Sindorum. Where they related? Had she noticed any similarities between them? Had she seen a pilot in either? Weaponry? Defenses? Communication? Taylor had sipped her coffee while doing her best to answer each in turn. She did not resent the debriefing or its length—she knew it was better to get the story straight while it was still fresh in her mind, but in the end her answer to most of the questions was the same: She didn't know. Nobody did.

When it was finally over and the Admiral released her, Taylor trudged back to her quarters like a zombie. The after-effects of the drugs had left her feeling hung over as if she had been on a three-day bender.

She turned on the shower and let the hot water rush over her. She could feel the stress leaving her body as the water ran through her hair and down her back and her legs and down to her heels. She knew the days ahead would see her filing report after report to various offices and agencies in an attempt to explain what had happened. Fortunately, the *Wyvern's* transponder had stayed intact, carrying with it images from the chase and dogfight that had taken place over Sindorum and then into the Blackfriar Mountains. But all of that could come later. When she finally turned off the water, she dried herself, pulled on her nightgown and rolled into bed. The last thought in her mind as she drifted off to sleep was the smoke from Shale's Raptor rising into the night.

She woke to a loud buzzing. Lifting her head, her skull felt as though it were filled with liquid cement. The buzzer sounded again and she winced from the noise. It was the door. Her neck and her shoulders ached as she rolled out of bed and adjusted her robe. She wondered who had come for her. Was it Admiral Thorus summoning her back for another meeting? Had the Consul arrived and wanted to speak with her? Could it be something about Shale?

She checked her hair in the mirror, checked her robe again and opened the door. As the metal panel slid away, his eyes met hers and Gaius Ioma gave her a rakish smile as he leaned against the doorway with his arm.

"Hey," he said.

She grabbed him and pulled him into the room.

Nothing more was said, and they made love twice before she fell asleep again. Some hours later, she awoke to Gaius lying face down on his pillow and snoring loudly. She contemplated waking him up for another round, but instead she carefully slipped out of bed and picked her robe up off the floor. She saw him roll over as his eyelids floated up and down, and up and down again before he drifted off. Taylor pulled on her robe, walked over to her kitchenette and made tea. Ioma did not wake. Cup in hand, she pulled a chair over to her cabin's one window, propped her feet against the sill, and looked out at the stars.

FEL

Time Unknown – Downside of the Here

The Kotling galloped down the tunnel and soon the sounds of destruction and crumbling brick disappeared behind them. Fel kept her hands clenched tightly about the Kotling's mane as the animal bounded down into the darkness. Leaving the throne room behind them, the torchlight soon vanished. However, as it got dark, Fel noticed the fur of the Kotling began to glow blue, lighting their way. Whoever or whatever had created the tunnel, it looked to be burrowed and dug from the stone of the castle, though soon the brick and mortar gave way to earth and stone. When the Kotling scurried around a root nearly as thick as Fel's waist, the tunnel began to spiral downward, turning left as it descended deep into the earth. Here the Kotling slowed to a trot and so Fel sat up, bouncing on the Otherling's shoulders as it hopped across the packed earth.

She leaned down to whisper into the Kotling's ear. "Where are we going?"

But the Kotling did not answer, nor even look up at her. Fel wondered where their descent would take them. Where did this tunnel lead? Were they still in the dream-world where she had met her father? The 'Downside of the Here' as the Onier had described it? Was the Kotling taking her somewhere, or was it simply running away in fear? She was wondering all of these things as the tunnel straightened out and leveled off, ending its descent. Then the blue glow of the Kotling's fur faded as a warm, silvery light appeared before them and the tunnel ended.

Trotting out the hole and onto a dusty wooden floor, the Kotling stopped as it leaned back on its rear legs and sniffed the air. Fel hopped off her furry steed and looked up at a row of giant books. They were back in the library, the same place where she had caught up to her father, only now the bookshelves towered like skyscrapers above her and the ceiling looked as distant as the sky.

Looking down, Fel saw that she was standing in a giant footprint in the dust. Suddenly she remembered the hurried conference that she and her father had here less than an hour ago. Then her mind returned to the pit in the throne room and the storm of smoke and fire and music. Her mind replayed the Onier pulling her father down into the pit of black nothingness. What had the Onier done to him? Was he still down here somewhere, waiting to be found? Was he trapped? What had she done? Somehow, she felt it was all her fault, and a wave of regret and grief washed over her.

She looked over at the Kotling, whose nose was still twitching in the air.

"I don't suppose you know what's happening, do you?"

The Kotling chirped into the air and then turned toward her as it bowed its head again. Fel sighed at the Otherling, but made no move to mount it, and instead stayed standing where she was.

"Where are we going to go?" She shrugged. "Where is there *to* go?"

Then a quake rumbled from behind them and the books rattled and knocked against each other on the shelves. The Kotling looked up again briefly, twitching its nose at the stale air and then bowed its head again.

Something had fallen against the pit of her stomach, a knot of fear and regret that sagged against her guts. Hanging her head, she sighed again and climbed back atop the Kotling's shoulders.

No sooner had Fel's hands closed around the Otherling's fur than the beast leapt forward and took off at a run, galloping across the dusty floor. The Kotling was sprinting now, and Fel clenched her knees against the beast's shoulders and leaned forward against its neck as her steed raced across the library floor. Books and shelves flew past them until they passed under a high, wooden table where the Kotling turned, galloping between the table legs and then under a chair and then under a desk. Nearing the wall, the Kotling hopped through a crack in the wood to land in the hollow space between the boards.

The Kotling slowed to a trot as it ran between the wooden panels. They had to stoop, and Fel pressed herself flat against the Otherling's back as they passed between another wall that may have been a boundary between two rooms, but Fel wasn't sure. Twice, the walls shook and the floor trembled as a quake rumbled through the endless building. Fel was certain now that she was still in the dreamworld, the Downside of the Here as the Onier had called it, and though part of her wanted to jump off the Kotling and try to find her father, she knew in her mind that she had no idea where anything was, just as she had no idea what had happened to her father.

Then, after many minutes of trotting through the walls, the Kotling turned and hopped through a crack in the wood and out into the open air.

The smell of morning dew on the grass met them as the Kotling trotted to a stop on the cobblestones. They were on a walkway next to a wall made of stone and mortar and past that ... a gate. Fel looked up. A red-tiled roof and the parapet of a wall looked down on her. They were standing outside the gatehouse, and before them was the garden. The Kotling let out a chirp as it hopped and skipped from the walkway into the grass, and soon Fel's pants were wet up to the knees. They cut across the yard, running through the freshly cut grass and the flower beds that marked the gardens at the front of the palace.

Once, Fel thought she spotted the ghoulish shadows of the doppel-gangers that had, not hours ago, chased her and her father through the mansion. However, they did not see her. Or, rather, they did not think to notice a Kotling and its tiny rider as they dashed across the palace yard.

They scurried through a door left ajar and the next thing she knew, they were trotting down a long corridor toward her room. Second door on the left. They found it still ajar and the Kotling squeezed itself through.

She hopped off the Kotling as they entered. This version of her room was as still as she had left it, not hours ago, when she'd come through with her father. Two windows along one wall and the wooden dresser along the other. The narrow door was no longer there, however, having disappeared after she and her father had stepped through. Fel reached into her coat pocket but found all the chalk had turned into red dust. Not a solid piece of it remained. Walking up to the wall next to the dresser, she tried smudging the chalk on her fingers to draw on the wall, but all she made were marks on the wall. No doors or portals appeared.

The Kotling chirped behind her and she turned around to watch it climbing up the blanket on her bed. Its tiny claws clung to the fabric as it pulled itself to the top of the mattress. Fel shrugged and walked over.

In her shrunken form, the bed was nearly as tall as a one-story house. However, as she reached up on her tiptoes, her hands found the edge of the blanket and she began climbing up. Bits of thread were loose, allowing her for footholds along the way and she soon managed to pull herself up next to the Kotling, who sat watching her climb the whole way.

Now atop the mattress, the Kotling chirped again as it led her over to the windowsill. The window was open just a crack, and Fel could feel the breeze blowing through.

As they had in her real room, these windows looked out over the city to the ocean. However, the Bay of Sardis here had no water, but was a salt-covered basin. Looking out over the white-crusted flats, Fel spotted four shadows approaching the city. She reached into her pack and pulled out her binoculars. They were horses. All four of them were walking in a line, shoulder to shoulder. From the left, the first horse was a stallion, white as snow. Next to him was a red horse with a ruddy mane. The third was a black that strode like a shadow over the salted earth. The fourth horse was pale and spotted and it held its head low as it walked a step behind the other three.

Then a finger of lightning struck the sky and Fel saw a shadow, large as a mountain, rising up from the horizon. Beside her, the Kotling chirped and lowered its head, asking her to mount, but for a moment Fel was frozen in fear as she watched the titanic shadow rise. It was winged, that much she could see, with three heads like snakes and when it spread its wings, they swallowed the horizon.

When the Kotling chirped again, she snapped out of it. Hopping back atop the furry beast, it bounded down from the windowsill to the bed and then from the bed to the floor. Landing with a hop, the Kotling spun around on the floor and scurried back under the bed. When they neared the headboard, a crack opened up in the floorboards and the Kotling hopped through just as the walls and the windows began to shake and rattle.

And down they fell into the darkness.

They landed with a *whump* and Fel was covered in cold softness.

Rolling off the Kotling's back, Fel found she was standing waist deep in powdery snow. Looking over, she saw the Kotling shrinking below her, becoming smaller and smaller until she realized that no, the Kotling was not shrinking—she was *growing*. In a matter of seconds, she was standing back up at normal height and the Kotling below her was no larger than her boot. Fel looked around as she adjusted the straps of her backpack. She was standing on a platform in the middle of a staircase, and the walls were made of leaves and vines. Curious, Fel reached both arms into the snow-covered leaves and pushed them apart, but when she looked inside, all she saw were more branches and leaves and vines. Stepping back from the wall of leaves, she looked up between the stairs to see what they led to. But all she could see were more stairs.

Below her, the Kotling chirped as it began hopping up the first set of stairs. Fel sighed and followed the Kotling. Each step sunk her boots ankle deep in the snow and she could feel the flakes catching on the top of her boots as they formed an icy ring around her calves and shins.

Wondering again how much further she and her furry guide had to go, she tried to look up and down the middle of the stairwell again to see if she could spot a top or a bottom, but all she could see were more stairs. Fortunately, they did not have far to go.

A dozen flights of stairs later, the Kotling stopped on another platform and stood on its hind legs to wait for her. Behind the Kotling, Fel could see where the vines and leaves parted to reveal a wooden doorway with a rusted brass knob. All around the base of the doorway, the snow had melted to reveal the cracked stone of the stairwell. Fel stepped over the Kotling and opened the door.

Her boots met with matted grass and as the doorway closed behind her, Fel found herself standing in a dimly lit tent. An empty cot sat to her right and she could see two rows of cots on either side of the long, canopy tent, some empty, some occupied. Looking behind her, she saw only the back of the tent and the warm glow of a campfire burning nearby.

Then a tiny desperate voice called out in the dark.

"Heya! Wake up!"

Fel could see a boy hopping up and down on the other end of the tent. Someone turned over on their cot as the tiny voice became insistent.

"Dad. Dad, I wake up, I gotta pee!"

Fel could hear the boy's father mumble something inaudible. Then two shadows stood up on the far end of the tent and wandered toward the door. Was she back at the refugee camp? Stepping carefully down the center of the cots, she followed the boy and his father out the door.

The friendly smoke of crackling flames met her as she stepped out into the open air. The morning cookfires. Fel was standing on a hilltop near the center of the refugee camp, where rows of white tents stood among the ancient ruins of Aelia's Palace. Above her was the leafy canopy of an Ulvus tree, and behind the branches, she could see Arc's twin moons fading into the eastern sky. To her left were the boy and his father, walking hand in hand toward the outhouses. Looking down, Fel could see a pair of women at the bottom of the hill, chuckling over gossip and the morning laundry. To the west, she could see the sun was coming up. Then a breeze blew through the Ulvus tree, rustling its leaves like a song and somewhere out behind her, she could hear the hungry cries of a newborn babe.

THE END

Acknowledgements:

First and foremost, I'd like to thank my wife, Kate, and my two sons, Thomas & Clayton, for putting up with me throughout this long project. Without your patience and support, this never would have happened. Next, my parents, Ed & Jill, for giving me the tools to do this. I learned more work ethic and life skills working on my dad's farm than I have anywhere else, and it's not even close. I get my love of books from my mother who read *The Hobbit* to her children back when they were just a little older than my children are now. My brother Tim was my first beta reader (along with my wife). His feedback was key to several plotlines in this book. My sister Beth has been with me on several unfulfilled projects and has always been a source of encouragement and inspiration.

Next, I'd like to thank a few of the friends I've known in my life. I've been blessed to know so many great people. To everyone I ever knew in the US Army, whether 2nd Stryker Cavalry Regiment or the 82nd Airborne Division, you may recognize pieces of yourselves in these pages. You may even see your name. Ya'll can sue me later.

My longest running group of friends are my gaming friends. Many of my story telling techniques were developed playing Dungeons & Dragons and Star Wars. I've stolen some of your names too, just like I always said that I would.

Finally, I'd like to thank some of the professionals I've worked with to put this thing together. My amazing cover artist, Sebastian Luca. My cover & interior designer, Sarah Beaudin. And my copy-editor, Keith Gordon. All of your help was invaluable to putting this project together.

Thank you, Lord.

Matthew E. Nesheim

I'd like to thank you for reading. We are hard at work on Book 2.

For information about future projects,
I can be found on Twitter @THE_ST0MP.

Made in the USA
Middletown, DE
19 December 2018